CITY ON FIRE

Also by Don Winslow

CITY

ON

FIRE

A Novel

Don Winslow

WM

WILLIAM MORROW
An Imprint of HarperCollins*Publishers*

HarperCollins books may be purchased for educational, business, or sales promotional use. For information, please email the Special Markets Department at SPsales@harpercollins.com.

FIRST EDITION

Designed by Kyle O'Brien

Art by Michelle / Adobe Stock, yuplex / Adobe Stock, Vinoverde / Adobe Stock, Beppe Castro / Shutterstock, Inc.

Library of Congress Cataloging-in-Publication Data

Names: Winslow, Don, 1953– author.
Title: City on fire : a novel / Don Winslow.
Description: First edition. | New York, NY : William Morrow, [2021] | Identifiers: LCCN 2021011578 (print) | LCCN 2021011579 (ebook) | ISBN 9780062851192 (hardcover) | ISBN 9780062851178 (trade paperback) | ISBN 9780062851208 (paperback) | ISBN 9780062851215 | ISBN 9780062851185 (epub)
Classification: LCC PS3573.I5326 C58 2021 (print) | LCC PS3573.I5326 (ebook) | DDC 813/.54—dc23
LC record available at https://lccn.loc.gov/2021011578
LC ebook record available at https://lccn.loc.gov/2021011579

ISBN 978-0-06-285119-2 (hardcover)
ISBN 978-0-06-320544-4 (international edition)

22 23 24 25 26   LSC   10 9 8 7 6 5 4 3 2 1

To the deceased of the pandemic.
Requiescat in pace.

Then at last
I saw it all, all Ilium settling into her embers . . .

Virgil
The Aeneid
Book II

CITY ON FIRE

PART ONE

Pasco Ferri's Clambake

Goshen Beach, Rhode Island
August 1986

'Take your meal, now; we prepare for combat.

Homer
The Iliad
Book II

ONE

DANNY RYAN WATCHES THE WOMAN come out of the water like a vision emerging from his dreams of the sea.

Except she's real and she's going to be trouble.

Women that beautiful usually are.

Danny knows that; what he doesn't know is just how much trouble she's really going to be. If he knew that, knew everything that was going to happen, he might have walked into the water and held her head under until she stopped moving.

But he doesn't know that.

So, the bright sun striking his face, Danny sits on the sand out in front of Pasco's beach house and checks her out from behind the cover of his sunglasses. Blond hair, deep blue eyes, and a body that the black bikini does more to accentuate than conceal. Her stomach is taut and flat, her legs muscled and sleek. You don't see her fifteen years from now with wide hips and a big ass from the potatoes and the Sunday gravy.

The woman comes out of the water, her skin glistening with sunshine and salt.

Terri Ryan digs an elbow into her husband's ribs.

"What?" Danny asks, all mock-innocent.

"I see you checking her out," Terri says.

They're all checking her out—him, Pat and Jimmy, and the wives, too—Sheila, Angie, and Terri.

"Can't say I blame you," Terri says. "That rack."

"Nice talk," Danny says.

"Yeah, with what *you're* thinking?" Terri asks.

"I ain't thinking nothing."

"I got your nothing for you right here," Terri says, moving her right hand up and down. She sits up on her towel to get a better view of the woman. "If I had boobs like that, I'd wear a bikini, too."

Terri's wearing a one-piece black number. Danny thinks she looks good in it.

"I like *your* boobs," Danny says.

"Good answer."

Danny watches the beautiful woman as she picks up a towel and dries herself off. She must put in a lot of time at the gym, he thinks. Takes care of herself. He bets she works in sales. Something pricey— luxury cars, or maybe real estate, or investments. What guy is going to say no to her, try to bargain her down, look cheap in front of her? Isn't going to happen.

Danny watches her walk away.

Like a dream you wake up from and you don't want to wake up, it's such a good dream.

Not that he got much sleep last night, and now he's tired. They hit a truckload of Armani suits, him and Pat and Jimmy MacNeese, way the hell up in western Mass. Piece of cake, an inside job Peter Moretti set them up with. The driver was clued in, everyone did the dance so no one got hurt, but still it was a long drive and they got back to the shore just as the sun was coming up.

"That's okay," Terri says, lying back on her towel. "You let her get you all hot and bothered for me."

Terri knows her husband loves her, and anyway, Danny Ryan is faithful like a dog. He don't have it in him to cheat. She don't mind he looks at other women as long as he brings it home to her. A lot of married guys, they need some strange every once in a while, but Danny don't.

Even if he did, he'd feel too guilty.

They've even joked about it. "You'd confess to the priest," Terri said, "you'd confess to me, you'd probably take an ad out in the paper to confess."

She's right, Danny thinks as he reaches over and strokes Terri's thigh with the back of his index finger, signaling that she's right about something else, that he *is* hot and bothered, that it's time to go back to the cottage. Terri brushes his hand away, but not too hard. She's horny, too, feeling the sun, the warm sand on her skin, and the sexual energy brought by the new woman.

It's in the air, they both feel it.

Something else, too.

Restlessness? Danny wonders. Discontent?

Like this sexy woman comes out of the sea and suddenly they're not quite satisfied with their lives.

I'm not, Danny thinks.

Every August they come down from Dogtown to Goshen Beach because that's what their fathers did and they don't know to do anything else. Danny and Terri, Jimmy and Angie Mac, Pat and Sheila Murphy, Liam Murphy with his girl of the moment. They rent the little cottages across the road from the beach, so close to each other you can hear your neighbor sneeze, or lean out the window to borrow something for the kitchen. But that's what makes it fun, the closeness.

None of them would know what to do with solitude. They grew

up in the same Providence neighborhood their parents did, went to school there, are still there, see each other almost every day and go down to Goshen on vacation together.

"Dogtown by the Sea," they call it.

Danny always thinks the ocean should be to the east, but knows that the beach actually faces south and runs in a gentle arc west about a mile to Mashanuck Point, where some larger houses perch precariously on a low bluff above the rocks. To the south, fourteen miles out in the open ocean, sits Block Island, visible on most clear days. During the summer season, ferries run all day and into the night from the docks at Gilead, the fishing village just across the channel.

Danny, he used to go out to Block Island all the time, not on the ferry, but back before he was married when he was working the fishing boats. Sometimes, if Dick Sousa was in a good mood, they'd pull into New Harbor and grab a beer before making the run home.

Those were good days, going after the swordfish with Dick, and Danny misses them. Misses the little cottage he rented behind Aunt Betty's Clam Shack, even though it was drafty and colder than shit in the winter. Misses walking down to the bar at the Harbor Inn to have a drink with the fishermen and listen to their stories, learn their wisdom. Misses the physical work that made him feel strong and clean. He was nineteen and strong and clean and now he ain't none of those things; a layer of fat has grown around his middle and he ain't sure he could throw a harpoon or haul in a net.

You look at Danny now, in his late twenties, his broad shoulders make him appear a little shorter than his six feet, and his thick brown hair, tinged with red, gives him a low forehead that makes him look a little less smart than he really is.

Danny sits on the sand and looks at the water with a yearning. The most he does now is go in and have a swim or bodysurf if there are any waves, which is unusual in August unless there's a hurricane brewing.

Danny misses the ocean when he's not here.

It gets in your blood, like you got salt water running through you. The fishermen Danny knows love the sea and hate it, say it's like a cruel woman who hurts you over and over again but you keep going back to her anyway.

Sometimes he thinks maybe he should go back to fishing, but there's no money in it. Not anymore, with all the government regulations and the Japanese and Russian factory ships sitting thirteen miles off the coast and taking up all the cod and the tuna and the flounder and the government don't do shit about them, just keeps its thumb on the local guy.

Because it can.

So now Danny just comes down from Providence in August with the rest of the gang.

Mornings they get up late, eat breakfast in their cottages, then cross the road and spend the day gathered on the beach in front of Pasco's place, one of about a dozen clapboard houses set on concrete pylons near the breakwater on the east end of Goshen Beach.

They set up beach chairs, or just lie on towels, and the women sip wine coolers and read magazines and chat while the men drink beer or throw in a fishing line. There's always a nice little crowd there, Pasco and his wife and kids and grandkids, and the whole Moretti crew—Peter and Paul Moretti, Sal Antonucci, Tony Romano, Chris Palumbo and wives and kids.

Always a lot of people dropping by, coming in and out, having a good time.

Rainy days they sit in the cottages and do jigsaw puzzles, play cards, take naps, shoot the shit, listen to the Sox broadcasters jaw their way through the rain delay. Or maybe drive into the main town two miles inland and see a movie or get an ice cream or pick up some groceries.

Nights, they barbecue on the strips of lawn between the cottages, usually pooling their resources, grill hamburgs and hot dogs. Or maybe during the day one of the guys walks over to the docks to see what's fresh and that night they grill tuna or bluefish or boil some lobsters.

Other nights they walk down to Dave's Dock, sit at a table out on the big deck that overlooks Gilead, across the narrow bay. Dave's doesn't have a liquor license, so they bring their own bottles of wine and beer, and Danny loves sitting out there watching the fishing boats, the lobstermen, or the Block Island Ferry come in as he eats chowder and fish-and-chips and greasy clam cakes. It's pretty and peaceful out there as the sun softens and the water glows in the dusk.

Some nights they just walk home after dinner, gather in each other's cottages for more cards and conversations; other times maybe they drive over to Mashanuck Point, where there's a bar, the Spindrift. Sit and have a few drinks and listen to some local bar band, maybe dance a little, maybe not. But usually the whole gang ends up there and it's always a lot of laughs until closing time.

If they feel more ambitious, they pile into cars and drive over to Gilead—fifty yards by water but fourteen miles by road—where there are some larger bars that almost pass for clubs and where the Morettis don't expect and never receive a drink bill. Then they go home to their cottages and Danny and Terri either pass out or mess around and *then* pass out, and wake up late and do it all over again.

"I need some more losh," Terri says now, handing him the tube.

Danny sits up, squeezes a glob of the suntan lotion onto his hands, and starts to work it onto her freckled shoulders. Terri burns easy with that Irish skin. Black hair, violet eyes, and skin like a porcelain teacup.

The Ryans are darker-skinned, and Danny's old man, Marty, says that's because they got Spanish blood in them. "From when that armada sank back there. Some of them Spanish sailors made it to shore and did the deed."

They're all black Irish, anyway, northerners like most of the micks who landed in Providence. Hard men from the stony soil and constant defeat of Donegal. Except, Danny thinks, the Murphys are doing pretty good for themselves now. Then he feels guilty thinking that, because Pat Murphy's been his best friend since they were in diapers, not to mention now they're brothers-in-law.

Sheila Murphy lifts her arms, yawns and says, "I'm going to go back, take a shower, do my nails, girly stuff." She gets up from her blanket and brushes the sand off her legs. Angie gets up, too. Like Pat is the leader of the men, Sheila is the boss of the wives. They take their cues from her.

She looks down at Pat and asks, "You coming?"

Danny looks at Pat and they both smile—the couples are all going back to have sex and no one's even being subtle about it. The cottages are going to be busy places this afternoon.

Danny's sad that summer is coming to an end. He always is. The end of summer means the end of the long slow days, the lingering sunsets, the rented beach cottages, the beers, the fun, the laughs, the clambakes.

It's back to Providence, back to the docks, back to work.

Home to their little apartment on the top floor of a gabled three-decker in the city, one of the thousands of old tenement buildings that went up all over New England in the height of the mill and factory days, when they were needed to provide cheap housing for the Italian, Jewish, and Irish workers. The mills and factories are mostly gone, but the three-story houses survive and still have a little of the lower-class reputation about them.

Danny and Terri have a small living room, a kitchen, a bathroom, and a bedroom with a small porch out the back and windows on every side, which is nice. It ain't much—Danny hopes to buy them a real house someday—but it's enough for now and it ain't so bad. Mrs. Costigan on the floor below is a quiet old lady and the owner, Mr. Riley, lives on the ground floor, so he keeps everything pretty shipshape.

Still and all, Danny thinks about getting out of there, maybe out of Providence altogether.

"Maybe we should move someplace where it's summer all the time," he said to Terri just the night before.

"Like where?" she asked.

"California, maybe."

She laughed at him. "California? We got no family in California."

"I got a second cousin or something in San Diego."

"That's not really family," Terri says.

Yeah, maybe that's the point, Danny thinks now. Maybe it would be good to go somewhere they don't have all those obligations—the birthday parties, the first communions, the mandatory Sunday dinners. But he knows it won't happen—Terri is too attached to her large family, and his old man needs him.

Nobody ever leaves Dogtown.

Or if they do, they come back.

Danny did.

Now he wants to go back to the cottage.

He wants to get laid and then he wants a nap.

Danny could use a little sleep, feel fresh for Pasco Ferri's clambake.

TWO

TERRI'S IN NO MOOD FOR preliminaries.

She walks into the little bedroom, closes the drapes and pulls the bedspread down. Then she peels off her bathing suit and lets it drop on the floor. Usually she showers when she gets back from the beach so she don't get sand and salt in the bed. Usually makes Danny do the same—but now she don't care. She digs her thumbs into the waistband of his swimming trunks, smiles and says, "Yeah, you're worked up from that bitch on the beach."

"You too."

"Maybe I'm bi," she teases. "Oh, feel you when I said *that*."

"Feel *you*."

"I want you in me."

Terri comes quickly—she usually does. She used to be embarrassed by it, thought it made her a whore, but later, when she talked to Sheila and Angie, they told her how lucky she was. Now she jacks her hips, works hard to make him come, and says, "Don't think about *her*."

"I'm not. I won't."

"Tell me when you're going to."

It's a ritual—every time since they first did it she wants to know when he's about to come, and now when he feels it building he tells her and she asks, as she always does, "Is it good? Is it good?"

"So good."

She holds him tight until his thrusting stops, then leaves her hands on his back, and Danny feels when her body gets sleepy and heavy, and he rolls off. He sleeps for just a few minutes and then wakes up and lies beside her.

He loves her like life.

And not, like some people think, because she's John Murphy's daughter.

John Murphy is an Irish king, like the O'Neills in the old country. Holds court in the back room of the Glocca Morra pub like it's Tara. He's been the boss of Dogtown since Danny's dad, Marty, fell into the bottom of the bottle and the Murphy family took over from the Ryans.

Yeah, Danny thinks, I could have been Pat or Liam, except I'm not.

Instead of being a prince, Danny is some kind of minor duke or something. He always gets picked in the shape-ups without having to pay off the dock bosses, and Pat sees that other kind of work comes his way from time to time.

Longshoremen borrow from the Murphys to pay off the bosses and can't catch up, or they put the paycheck on a basketball game that goes the wrong way. Then Danny, who's "a strapping lad," in the words of John Murphy, pays them a visit. He tries to do it at the bar or on the street so as not to embarrass them in front of their families, upset their wives, scare their kids, but there are times when he has to go to their homes, and Danny hates that.

Usually a word to the wise is enough, and they work out some kind of payment plan, but some of them are just plain deadbeats and boozehounds who drink up the payments and the rent, and then Danny has to rough them up a little. He isn't a leg-breaker, though. That stuff rarely happens anyway—a man with a broken stick can't work and a man who can't work can't make any kind of payment at all, not on the vig, never mind the principal. So Danny might hurt them, but he doesn't hurt them bad.

So he picks up some extra coin that way, and then there's the cargo he helps walk off the dock, and the trucks that he and Pat and Jimmy Mac sometimes take on the dark road from Boston to Providence.

They work with the Morettis on those jobs, getting the word and the nod from the brothers and then taking the trucks down, the tax-free cigarettes going into the Moretti vending machines, the booze going to Moretti-protected clubs or the Gloc or other bars in Dogtown. Suits like they took last night get sold out the trunks of cars in Dogtown, and the Morettis get their cut. Everybody wins except the insurance companies, and fuck them, they charge you up the ass anyway and then raise your rates if you have an accident.

So Danny makes a living, but nothing like the Murphys, who get points from the dock bosses, the no-show wharf jobs, the loan-shark ops, the gambling, and the kickbacks that come from the Tenth Ward, which includes Dogtown. Danny gets some crumbs from all that, but he don't sit at the big table in the back room with the Murphys.

It's embarrassing.

Even Peter Moretti said something to him about it.

They were walking down the beach together the other day when Peter said, "No offense, Danny, but, as your friend, I can't help but wonder."

"Wonder what, Peter?"

"With you marrying the daughter and all," Peter said, "we all figured you'd get a little boost up, you know what I mean."

Danny felt the heat rise to his cheeks. Thinking about the Moretti crew sitting around the vending machine office on Federal Hill, playing cards, sipping espressos, shooting the shit. Danny didn't like it his name came up, especially not about this.

He didn't know what to say to Peter. Truth was, he'd figured he'd get a boost, too, but it hadn't happened. He expected his father-in-law to have taken him into the back room of the Gloc for a "chat," put his arm around him and given him a piece of the street action, a card game, a seat at the table—something.

"I don't like to push," Danny finally said.

Peter nodded and looked past Danny out at the horizon, where Block Island seemed to float like a low cloud. "Don't get me wrong, I love Pat like a brother, but . . . I don't know, sometimes I think the Murphys . . . Well, you know, because it used to be the Ryans, didn't it? Maybe they're afraid to move you up, you might have thoughts of restoring the old dynasty. And if you and Terri have a boy . . . a Murphy *and* a Ryan? I mean, come on."

"I just want to make a living."

"Don't we all?" Peter laughed, and he let it drop.

Danny knew that Peter was making onions. He liked Peter, considered him a friend, but Peter was going to be Peter. And Danny had to admit there was some truth to what Peter said. He'd thought it, too—that Old Man Murphy was shutting him out because he was afraid of the Ryan name.

Danny don't mind it so much with Pat, a good guy and a hard worker who runs the docks well and doesn't lord it over anyone. Pat's a natural leader, and Danny, well, if he's being honest with himself, is a natural follower. He don't want to lead the family, take his father's place. He loves Pat and would follow him to hell with a squirt gun.

Kids from Dogtown, they've been together forever—him and Pat and Jimmy. St. Brendan's Elementary, then St. Brendan's High

School. They played hockey together, got slaughtered by the French-Canadian kids from Mount St. Charles. They played basketball together, got slaughtered by the Black kids at Southie. Didn't matter they got slaughtered—they played tough and didn't back down from nobody. They ate most suppers together, sometimes at Jimmy's, mostly at Pat's.

Pat's mom, Catherine, would call them to the table like they were one person, "*Patdannyjimmyyyyyyyy!*" Down the street, across the little backyards. *Patdannyjimmyyyyyyyy! Suppaaaaaah!* When there was no food at home because Marty was too drunk to get it together, Danny would sit at the big Murphy table and have pot roast and boiled potatoes, spaghetti and meatballs, always fish-and-chips on Friday, even after the Pope said it was okay to eat meat.

With no real family of his own—Danny was that anomaly, an Irish only child—he loved the sprawling Murphy household. There was Pat and Liam, Cassie, and, of course, Terri, and they took Danny in like he was family.

He wasn't exactly an orphan, Danny, but a near thing, what with his mother running off when he was just a baby and his father pretty much ignoring him because all he could see in him was her.

As Martin Ryan fell deeper into the bitterness and the bottle, he was hardly a fit father for the boy, who more and more took refuge on the streets with Pat and Jimmy and at the Murphy house, where there was laughter and smiles and rarely any yelling except when the sisters fought for the bathroom.

Danny was a lonely boy, Catherine Murphy always thought, a lonely, sad boy, and who could blame him? So if he was at the house a bit more than was normal, she was happy to give him a smile and a mother's hug, some cookies and a peanut butter sandwich, and as he grew up and his interest in Terri became obvious—well, Danny Ryan was a nice boy from the neighborhood and Terri could do worse.

John Murphy wasn't so sure. "He's got that blood."

"What blood?" his wife asked, although she knew.

"That Ryan blood," Murphy answered. "It's cursed."

"Stop being foolish," Catherine said. "When Marty was well . . ."

She didn't finish the thought, because when Marty was well, he, not John, had run Dogtown, and her husband didn't like the thought that he owed his rise to Martin Ryan's fall.

So John wasn't all that unhappy when Danny graduated high school and moved down to South County to be a fisherman, of all the goddamn things. But if that's what the kid wanted to do, that's what he wanted to do, even though he didn't understand that jobs on the boats were hard to get and he only got his place on the swordfish boat because its owner thought the Celtics were a lock at home against the Lakers and they weren't. So if the owner wanted to keep his boat, young Danny Ryan was going to be on board.

No reason for Danny to know that, though. Why ruin it for the kid?

Pat, he didn't understand Danny's move, either.

"What are you doing this for?" he asked.

"I dunno," Danny said. "I want to try something different. Work outdoors."

"The docks aren't outdoors?"

Yeah, they are, Danny thought, but they weren't the ocean and he meant what he said—he wanted something different from Dogtown. He knew the life he was looking at: Get his union card, work on the docks, pick up some spare change as muscle for the Murphys. Friday nights at the P-Bruins hockey games, Saturday nights at the Gloc, Sunday dinner at John's table. He wanted something more—different, anyway—wanted to make his own way in the world. Do clean, hard work, have his own money, his own place, not owe nobody nothing. Sure, he'd miss Pat and Jimmy, but Gilead was what, half an hour, forty-minute drive and they'd be coming down in August anyway.

So he got himself a job on the swordfish boat.

Total fucking doofus at first, no clue what he was doing, and Dick, he must have yelled himself hoarse trying to teach Danny what to do, what not to do, called Danny every name in the book, and for a good year Danny thought his first name was "Dammit."

But he learned.

Became a decent hand and overcame the prejudice most of the old guys had that no one who didn't come from at least three generations of fishermen could work a boat. And he freakin' loved it. Got his drafty little cottage, learned to cook—well anyway, bacon and eggs, clam chowder, chili—earned his salary, drank with the men.

Summers he worked on the swordfish charter, winters he caught on with the boats that went out for the groundfish—the cod, the haddock, the flounder—whatever they could net, whatever the Russians or the Japs didn't get and the government would still let them have.

Summers were fun, winters a bitch.

The sky gray, the ocean black, and the only word that could describe Gilead in the winter was "bleak." The wind would come through his cottage like it had an invitation, and nights he'd wear a heavy hooded sweatshirt to bed. When the boats could get out in the winter, the ocean would make every effort to kill you, and when you couldn't get out the sheer tedium would take its shot. Nothing to do but drink, watch your belly grow and your wallet shrink. Look out your window at the fog, like you was living inside an aspirin bottle. Maybe watch some TV, go back to bed, or put on your toque, jam your hands inside your peacoat, and walk down to the docks to look at your boat sitting there as miserable as you were. Go to the bar, sit around and bitch with the other guys, Sundays you had the Patriots anyway, you weren't unhappy enough already.

But those days they could go out, Jesus Christ it was cold, colder than a witch's tit, even with so many layers of clothes on you looked like the freakin' Michelin Man. Thermal long johns and long-sleeve shirt, thick wool socks, a wool sweater, a sweatshirt and a down jacket, thick gloves and he was still cold. Out at the dock by four in the morning, chopping ice off the moorings and the gears while Dick or Chip Whaley or Ben Browning or whoever he was working for tried to get the engine to turn over.

Then it was through the channel and out through the Harbor of Refuge, the whitecaps splashing on the icy rocks of the breakwater, then out through the West Gap or the East Gap, depending on where the fish were. Sometimes they'd be out three or four days at a time, sometimes a week if they hit it good, and like the rest of them Danny would catch two- or three-hour naps between watches or putting the nets out and hauling them back in, dumping the catch into the holds. Going below to clutch a steaming-hot cup of bitter coffee in his shivering hands or bolt down a bowl of chili or chowder. In the morning it was always bacon and eggs and toast, as much as he could eat because the captains never stinted on the food; a man working that hard has to eat.

On the trips when they were lucky enough to hit their quota, whoever was captain would say they were headed in, and that was a glorious feeling, that you'd done your job and been rewarded and there'd be a fat check with your share of the full hold reflected in it, and the men would go back to their wives and girlfriends proud that they could put food on the table, go out to a movie and dinner.

Other times, the bad times, the nets would come up light or even empty and it seemed like there wasn't a fish in the whole dark Atlantic Ocean and the boat would skulk back into port with a feeling of shame pervading the whole crew as if they'd done something wrong, as if they weren't good enough, and the wives and the girlfriends knew to step lightly because their men would be angry and ashamed and feel not quite like men and the mortgages and rents might not get paid and the repairs the car needed would have to wait.

And that happened more and more.

Summers, though.

Summers were wonderful.

Summers, Danny was on the swordfish boat, light and fast, on blue seas under blue skies chasing the game fish, and Danny's post was right on the bow because he was a good harpooner. And Dick, he could find swordfish like he was one of them. A freakin' legend out of that port. Sometimes they'd take clients out to sport-fish—rich guys who could afford to charter a boat and a crew, and they'd go after the swords and the tuna with poles and lines, and then it was mostly Danny's job to cut bait and make sure the clients had cold beers, and they had some pretty famous people on that boat but Danny will never forget the time that Ted Williams—Ted freakin' Williams—came on and was a good guy and tipped Danny a hundred when they were done.

Other times they went out to catch the swords to sell at the fish markets and then it was all business, Danny standing on the bow with his harpoon and when they hit a bunch of swords Danny would throw the spear, which was attached to a heavy buoy that would wear the sword down, and sometimes they'd have five or six swords tied up before they went back to fight the tired fish onto the boat and those were goddamn wonderful days because they'd come in by dusk and celebrate and drink and party and then Danny would fall face-first into bed, happily exhausted, and get up to do it again the next day.

Good times.

It was one of those summers, one of those Augusts, when the Dogtown crew was down at the beach and Danny joined them for drinks and hot dogs and burgers and saw that Terri was something more than Pat's little sister.

Her hair was black like a winter sea and her eyes weren't blue, Danny swore they were violet, and her little body had slimmed in some places but filled out in others. Back then she didn't have money for perfume and her mother wouldn't have let her buy it anyway, so she'd dab vanilla extract behind her ears and now Danny jokes he can still get hard from a sugar cookie.

He remembers the first time they'd felt each other, clasped each other behind some sand dunes. Hot, wet kisses, her tongue a busy surprise flicking in and out of his mouth. He was so happy when she let him undo two buttons on her white blouse, slip his hand inside, cop a feel.

A few weeks later, one of those hot, humid August nights, parked in his car at the beach, he unsnapped her jeans and she surprised him again by lifting her hips to let his hand inside and he felt her underneath her plain white cotton panties and her tongue quickened on his and she held him tighter and said, "Do that, yes, do that." Another night he was rubbing her and she stiffened and whimpered and he realized that she had come. He was so hard it hurt and then he felt her small hand unzip his jeans and she dug around inside, unsure and inept, but then she grabbed him and stroked him and he came inside his shorts and had to pull his shirt over his jeans to hide the dark spot before they went back to join the gang sitting around outside the cottage.

Danny was in love.

But Terri, she didn't want to be no fisherman's girlfriend, no fisherman's wife.

"I can't live all the way down here," she said.

"It's a half hour," Danny said.

"Forty-five minutes," Terri said. She was so attached to her family, her friends, her hairdresser, her church, her block, her neighborhood. Terri was a Dogtown girl and always would be, and Goshen was okay for a few weeks in the summer but she could never live there, especially with Danny gone for nights at a time and her worried whether he was coming back. And it was true, Danny knew, that boyfriends and husbands died out there, slipped off the deck into the icy water, got their brains beat out when a net boom swung wildly in the wind. Or drank themselves to death when the fishing was bad.

And there was no money in it.

Not for a deckhand, anyway.

If you owned a boat, maybe you strung a couple of good seasons together, but even most of the boat owners were hurting now with the fish playing out.

Terri grew up comfortable in the Murphy house and didn't see herself being a poor "fishwife," as she called it.

"Daddy can get you a union card," she said, "and a job at the port."

The Port of Providence, that is, not Gilead.

The docks, swinging a hook.

Good money, good union job, and then who knew? A move up with the Murphys. Maybe a desk job as a union official, something like that. And a taste of Murphy's other businesses. What he would have had anyway, if his father hadn't drunk it away, his old man getting so sloshed so often that he became a liability and the guys worked him out of the top job and then out altogether. For old times' sake kicked him enough to live on and that was about it.

There was a day, when Danny was just a little kid, that the name Marty Ryan struck fear. Now it just provoked pity.

Danny didn't want it anyway, didn't want nothing to do with the rackets, the loan-sharking, the gambling, the hijacks, the union. Problem was, he did want Terri—she was funny and smart and listened to him without taking any of his bullshit, but she wouldn't give it up without them being at least engaged, and his take from the boats wasn't enough for a diamond, never mind a marriage.

So Danny took the card and went back to Dogtown.

First person he told about wanting to propose to Terri was Pat.

"You going to give her a ring?" Pat asked.

"When I get enough money for something decent."

"Go see Solly Weiss."

Weiss had a jewelry store in downtown Providence.

"I was thinking Zales," Danny said.

"And pay bust-out retail?" Pat said. "You go see Solly, tell him you're with us, who it's for, he'll make you a price."

Not for nothing was the unofficial state motto "I know a guy."

"I don't want to give Terri a diamond fell off a truck," Danny said.

Pat laughed. "They're not stolen. Jesus, what kind of brother you think I am? We look after Solly. You ever heard of him getting robbed?"

"No."

"Why do you think that is?" Pat asked. "Look, if you're shy, I'll go in with you."

So they went in and saw Solly and he sold Danny a full-carat princess-cut diamond at cost with layaway payments, no interest.

"What did I tell you?" Pat asked as they left the store.

"This is how it works, huh?"

"This is how it works," Pat said. "Now you have to go to the old man, though, and I'm not going in with you."

Danny found John Murphy at the Gloc—where else—and asked for a minute of his time. John took him into the back, sat down at his booth, and just looked at him; he wasn't going to make it easy.

"I came to ask for your daughter's hand in marriage," Danny said, feeling like a dork and also scared shitless.

John wanted Danny Ryan for a son-in-law like he wanted flaming hemorrhoids, but Catherine had already warned him that this was likely to happen and that if he wanted a happy household he had better give his permission.

"I'll find her somebody else," John had said.

"She doesn't want somebody else," Catherine said, "and let's get this done before she walks down the aisle in a muumuu."

"Did he knock her up?"

"Not yet," Catherine said. "They're not even sleeping together, if you believe Terri, but . . ."

So John went through the dance with Danny. "How do you intend to support my daughter?"

How the hell do you think? Danny thought. You got me my card, my job at the docks, some stuff on the side.

"I'm a hard worker," Danny said. "And I love your daughter."

John gave him the whole "love isn't enough" speech but eventually gave his blessing, and that night Danny took Terri out to a nice dinner at George's and she pretended to be surprised when he got down on one knee and popped the question, even though she had told her brother to make sure that Danny was clued in as to getting a good ring without going into debt.

The wedding was elaborate, as befitted a daughter of John Murphy.

Not Italian elaborate, they didn't go as far as all that, but all the Italians were there and came with envelopes—Pasco Ferri and his wife, the Moretti brothers, Sal Antonucci, his wife, and Chris Palumbo. All the important Irish of Dogtown were there, even Marty showed up for the full wedding mass at St. Mary's and the reception later at the Biltmore. John sprang for all that, but not for the honeymoon, so Danny and Terri went all the way across the Blackstone Bridge to Newport for a three-day weekend.

No one was happier than Pat when Danny and Terri got married.

"We've always been brothers," Pat said at the rehearsal dinner. "Now it's official."

Yeah, it was official, so Terri finally gave it up.

Enthusiastically, energetically—Danny had had nothing to complain about. Still doesn't. Five years into their marriage and the sex is

still good. Only problem is, she hasn't gotten pregnant yet and everybody feels it's perfectly okay to constantly ask her about it and he knows
it hurts her.

Danny, he's in no hurry to have a kid, doesn't know if he wants
one at all.

"That's because you were raised by wolves," Terri said to him
once.

Which isn't true, Danny thinks.

Wolves stay.

Now he looks at the little alarm clock on top of the old dresser and
sees it's time for the meeting at the Spindrift before Pasco's clambake.

The Saturday night of every Labor Day weekend, Pasco Ferri
throws a party and invites everybody. You could be just walking past
Pasco on the beach in front of his house, notice the hole he's digging,
and he'll invite you, he doesn't care. He'll spend all day digging that
hole and laying the coals, and then he'll go get the clams and quahogs
fresh out the water.

Sometimes Danny goes with him, stands ankle-deep in the warm
mud of the tidal ponds and digs with the long-handled clam rake.
It's slow work, pulling that rake out of the bottom, digging through
the mud in the tongs with your fingers to find the shellfish, and then
dumping them into the bucket floating in the inner tube that Pasco
ties to his belt with a frayed length of old laundry line. Pasco works
steady like a machine—stripped down to the waist, his Mediterra-
nean skin tanned a deep brown, sixty-something years old and his
muscles still hard and ropy, his pectorals just starting to sag. The man
runs all of southern New England, but he's happy as hell standing
under the sun in the mud, working like an old *paisan*.

Yeah, but how many guys has this old *paisan* had clipped, Danny
wonders sometimes, watching him work so peaceful and content. Or
done himself? Local lore has it that Pasco personally did Joey Bon-

ham, Remy LaChance, the McMahon brothers from Boston. Late-night whiskey talk with Peter and Paul whispered that Pasco was no gunman but did his work with a wire or a knife, so close he could smell the sweat.

Some days Pasco and Danny would go to Almacs, buy some chicken thighs, then drive over to Narrow River, where Pasco would tie a long piece of string onto the chicken, toss it out into the water, and then pull it back real slow. What would happen was a blue crab would fasten its claws onto the meat and not let go until Pasco pulled it right into the net that Danny held for him.

"Lesson for you," Pasco said once as they watched the crab thrash in the bucket, trying to get out. Then he tied another piece of chicken and repeated the process until they had a bucketful of crabs to boil that night.

Lesson: Don't hold on to something's going to pull you into a trap. If you're going to let go, let go early.

Better yet, don't take the bait at all.

THREE

DANNY AND LIAM HOP INTO Pat's Camry and drive five minutes over to Mashanuck Point.

"So *what* are we meeting about?" Pat asks his brother.

"The Morettis are taxing the Spindrift," Liam says, reminding him.

"It's their territory," Pat says.

"Not the Drift," Liam answers. "It's grandfathered."

This is true, Danny thinks as he looks out the window. The rest of the places on the shore kick to the Italians, but the Spindrift has been Irish since his father's time. He knows the place well, used to get drunk there when he worked the boats, sometimes went in to listen to the local blues bands they'd book on weekends in the summer.

The owner, Tim Carroll, is a friend.

They drive past cornfields, and Danny's always amazed that this land hasn't been developed. The same family has owned it for three hundred years and they're stubborn, those Swamp Yankees, would rather grow sweet corn than sell the land and retire rich. But Danny's grateful for it. It's nice there, farms right up to the ocean.

"So, what?" Pat asks Liam. "Tim came to you?"

It's a violation of protocol. If Tim has a beef, he should go to John, or at least Pat. Not the younger brother, not Liam.

"He didn't *come* to me," Liam says, a little defensive. "I was having a beer, we got talking . . ."

There's so many little peninsulas and tidal marshes along the shore, Danny thinks, you got to drive inland, then along the coast, then back toward the sea to get to any particular place. Quicker if they drained the marshes and built some roads, but that's Connecticut, not Rhode Island.

Rhode Island likes things difficult, hard to find.

The other unofficial state motto—"If you were supposed to know, you'd know."

So it takes a few minutes to drive to the Spindrift, when they could have just walked up the beach. But they go by road, past the cornfields and then the little grocery store, the hot dog stand, the laundromat, the ice cream stand. As they make the curve that takes them back along the ocean, there's a trailer park on their left, and then the bar.

They park out in front.

You walk through the door, you know this ain't no money machine. It's an old clapboard joint, pounded by salt air and winter winds for sixty-some-odd years, and it's a wonder it's still standing. One good blow, Danny thinks, could knock it down, and hurricane season is coming up.

Tim Carroll is standing behind the bar, jerking a brew for a tourist.

Skinny Tim Carroll, Danny thinks, a pound wouldn't stick to him with glue. Tim's, what, thirty-three now, and he already looks like the responsibility of running the place since his old man died is aging him. He wipes his hands on his apron and comes out from behind the bar. "Peter and Paul are already here," he says, jerking his chin out toward the deck. "Chris Palumbo's with them."

"So what's the problem, Tim?" Pat asks.

"They come in tugging their cuffs," Tim says. "They're here about every afternoon, drinking pitchers they don't pay for, ordering sandwiches, burgers . . . You seen the price of beef lately? Buns?"

"Yeah, okay."

"Now they want an envelope, too?" Tim says. "I got basically ten, eleven weeks of summer to make money, the rest of the year I'm fucked. A few locals and fishermen nursing their beers for two hours at a time. No offense, Danny."

Danny shakes his head, like *Forget it.*

They walk through an open slider out onto a deck precariously cantilevered above some rocks the state put in to try to prevent the whole building from sliding into the ocean. From out there Danny can see the whole southern shoreline, from the lighthouse at Gilead down to Watch Hill.

It's beautiful.

The Moretti brothers sit at a white plastic table next to the railing that Chris Palumbo's got his feet up on.

Peter Moretti looks like your classic wiseguy—thick, slicked-back black hair, black shirt rolled up at the sleeves to show off the Rolex, designer jeans over loafers.

Paulie Moretti is a skinny guinea, maybe five-seven, with caramel skin, his light brown hair highlighted and permed into tight curls. *Permed*, Danny thinks, which is the style now but nothing Danny can get down with. Danny thinks Paulie's always looked a little Puerto Rican, although he ain't gonna say it.

Chris Palumbo's something else. Red hair like he came from freakin' Galway, but otherwise he's as Italian as Sunday gravy. Danny remembers what old Bernie Hughes said about him—"Never trust a redheaded wop. They're the worst of the breed."

Yeah, Peter is smart, but as smart as he is, Chris is smarter. Peter don't make a move without him, and if Peter does make the big step up, Chris will be his consigliere, no question.

The Irish guys pull up chairs as a waitress brings two pitchers and sets them on the table. The men pour their beers, then Peter turns to Tim. "You went running to the Murphys?"

"I didn't 'run,'" Tim says. "I just was telling Liam—"

"We're all friends here," Pat says, not wanting to get into the protocol of who told what to whom.

"We're all friends here," Peter says, "but business is business."

Liam says, "This place doesn't pay tax. Never has, never will. Tim's father and my father—"

"His father is gone," Peter says, then looks at Tim. "May he rest, no disrespect. But the arrangement passed with him."

"It's grandfathered," Pat says.

Peter says, "They're tax-exempt forever because thirty years ago some bogtrotter boiled a potato in here?"

"Pete, come on . . ." Pat says.

Chris kicks in, "Who do you think got the Works Department to put this rock in, the place doesn't turn into a raft, you're Huckleberry fucking Finn? That's thirty, forty grand of material, never mind the labor."

Pat laughs. "What, *you* paid it?"

"We *arranged* it," Chris says. "I didn't hear Tim crying then."

Tim says, "I already use your food supplier. What they charge me for meat? I could do a lot better someplace else."

It's true, Danny thinks. The Morettis are already making money out of this place, what with the vending machines and kickbacks from the wholesalers. Never mind the freebies.

"And the last time you had a health inspector really go through your kitchen," Chris says, "will be the first time."

"Then don't eat my fucking food, all right?"

Peter leans across the table toward Pat. "All we're saying is that we've had expenses related to the place lately and we think Tim should contribute a little. Are we being that unreasonable?"

"I can't give you what I don't have," Tim whines. "I don't have the money, Peter."

Peter shrugs. "Maybe we can work something out."

Here it comes, Danny thinks. The demand for a tax was just a come-along. The Morettis know that Tim don't have it. That was just to open the door for what they really want.

"What do you have in mind?" Pat asks.

"One of our people," Peter says, "went to do a little transaction in the men's room here last week, and Tim here got heavy with him."

"He was dealing coke," Tim says.

"You laid hands on him," Paulie says. "You physically threw him out."

"Yeah, and I will again, Paulie," Tim says. "If my old man knew that was going on in this place—"

Danny remembers an argument that Pat and Liam had, about Liam's trips to Miami. He goes down there on what he calls "fornications." Danny has his suspicions about Liam's Miami runs.

So does Pat.

Danny was there when Pat cornered Liam and said, "Hand to God, Liam, if you're bringing back anything from Florida besides herpes . . ."

Liam laughed. "What, you mean coke?"

"Yeah, I mean coke."

"Lot of money in blow, bro."

"Lot of jail time, too," Pat said. "Lot of freakin' heat from the feds and locals. We don't need that."

"Yes, Godfather," Liam said. He went into his Brando imitation. "We'll lose our judges, our politicians . . ."

"I'm not kiddin' here, baby brother."

"Don't get your panties in a wad," Liam said. "I'm not moving any coke, for Chrissakes."

"See that you don't."

"Jesus. Enough."

Now Danny remembers that conversation and has to wonder what the fuck they're really talking about here.

"Look," Peter jumps in, "maybe we can cut a little slack on the payments if Tim would be a little flexible on this other thing."

"Why this place?" Pat asks. "In the winter it's nothing but fishermen."

"Fishermen don't do coke?" Paulie asks. "Don't kid yourself. The worse the fishing is, the more they need. The better the fishing is, the more they want."

Danny don't like the remark. Hard to make a living, support your family—guys take a little consolation where they can find it. Used to be booze, now it's blow. Well, it's still booze, but now it's blow, too.

"I'm just saying there are other places you could do that business," Pat insists.

It's true, Danny thinks. He knows at least five joints up the coast where you can score coke.

"You can't shake your dick at the urinal those places you don't hit a narc," Peter says. "I thought we were all friends here. A friend denies a friend a favor?"

"It's a big goddamn ask," Tim says. "I could lose my liquor license. Shit, they could confiscate the place."

Pat puts his hand out to silence him. Danny recognizes the gesture. Seen it a hundred times from Old Man Murphy. Must be genetic.

"Who do you have selling down here?" Pat asks.

"You know Rocco Giannetti."

Danny knows him—slick twenty-something, drives a freakin' BMW. Now Danny knows how he makes the payments, the insurance.

"Rocco is showy," Pat says. "Loud. He attracts attention."

"What, you're human resources now?" Paulie asks.

Peter asks, "You'd prefer someone else?"

"I'd prefer a *grown-up*," Pat says.

"We can do that," Peter answers. "How about Chris here?"

There it is, Danny thinks—that was the play all along, to set Chris Palumbo up to sell coke in here. And it wasn't the Morettis' idea, it was Chris's; the red-haired guinea probably got the Morettis all jacked up about the tax, then suggested the coke deal as a compromise. He'll make on the blow, then kick up to Peter and Paul.

Pat makes his ruling. "Twice a week, during the off-season. Nothing during the summer. Chris can meet his buyer inside, but he goes out to his car to move the dope. Nothing bigger than an ounce, ever."

"We can't do business in the summer?" Paulie complains. "What is that?"

"We don't have to give you *anything*," Liam says.

"The fuck you—"

"Okay," Peter says, shutting his little brother up.

"Tim, you good with this?" Pat asks.

"I guess."

He's reluctant and Danny don't blame him. But what are you gonna do? It's the way of the world. Their world, anyway. Pat didn't give away nothing that the Morettis couldn't just take. It just makes good sense to be gracious about something you can't prevent.

Besides, Pat is looking to the future. Pasco has been talking about retiring—Mashanuck in the summer, Florida in the winter. Someone is going to step up to take the number one job and Peter Moretti might be the guy. He's young but already a captain and big earner, and if Moretti Senior wasn't doing twenty in the Adult Correctional Institutions, *he'd* be the man, so Peter feels it's his due. Pat Murphy knows down the line he's going to be doing business with Peter and wants to keep a good relationship.

"You'll square this with Pasco?" Pat asks Peter.

"We don't need to burden him with this," Peter answers.

A beat of silence and then they all burst out laughing. What the hell, they're feeling their oats and their strength and their youth, knowing they're taking over the world. Can do things without the old guys knowing, without their okay. Not that it isn't serious fucking business, dealing dope in Pasco's backyard without him knowing; it was just funny the way Peter said it is all, and for a few moments there they're all friends, all boys having a laugh, putting one over.

"And Peter," Pat says, "lay off the burgers a little, huh?"

"You worried about my waistline?"

"Pay for a sandwich, you cheap prick."

That starts them laughing again.

It's good, Danny thinks, being young in the sweet days of summer.

But, driving back, Danny can't shake the feeling that Liam just set himself up to deal coke with the Moretti brothers.

FOUR

DANNY GETS BACK, TERRI SENDS him right out again.

"Take the groceries to your father's," she says.

She went to Stop & Shop in the morning, got groceries for them and Marty, too. Picked up Marty's bacon, eggs, coffee, milk, bread, his Luckies, his Bushmills, his Sam Adams, his Hormel corned beef hash, his lotto tickets. Now she has it all sitting out in two plastic bags for Danny to deliver.

It's only fair, Danny thinks—she did the shopping. Stood in line Labor Day weekend, everyone buying stuff for their cookouts.

Danny picks up the bags and heads over to Marty's, just up the gravel street, a cottage the old man insists on renting year-round. He knocks on the screen door, doesn't wait for an answer, and nudges it open with his foot. "It's me!"

Marty's sitting in his chair, where he always is, sucking down a Lucky and a beer, listening to the Sox on the radio. Ned Egan sits on the couch by the window. You usually don't have to look too far from Marty to find Ned.

"You bring my Hormel?" Marty asks.

"When does Terri forget your Hormel?" Danny asks, setting the bags down on the kitchen counter. "Hi, Ned."

"Danny."

"I thought maybe *you* shopped," Marty says.

Ned gets up and starts to unpack the groceries, put them away on the shelves, in the refrigerator. Ned's in his forties, has a body like a fire hydrant. Still lifts weights every other day. When he reaches up to put the cans away, the .38 in his shoulder holster shows.

You want to get to Marty, you gotta get through Ned, and no one is going to get through Ned. Marty Ryan's not important enough anymore that anyone wants to kill him, but Ned ain't taking chances. Anyway, Danny's glad his old man has company, someone to heat up his hash for him, bitch about the Sox with.

"You get my scratchers?" Marty asks.

Marty plays the lotto like he has an in with Saint Jude. Usually he just wins a little beer money, but once he won a hundred dollars and that keeps him at it. He's sure he's going to hit the lottery or something and Danny wonders what Marty would do with a few million dollars if he did.

Skinny, bitter old man sitting in that chair in the same red plaid shirt that Terri gave him, what, three Christmases ago? Buttoned up to the neck, with a slice of the white T-shirt showing? Baggy, dirty old khaki trousers that Terri can talk him out of maybe once a month to wash? White socks, sandals?

Marty Ryan.

Martin Ryan.

A goddamn legend.

When Big Bill Donovan came up from New York and told the Providence boys they were joining the New York branch of the ILA, it was Marty Ryan, just a kid then, who sent him packing. Marty and John Murphy, back in the day. They stared New York down and it was New York that blinked, so we have our own union and our own docks, Danny knows. A few years later, Albert Anastasia himself came up, tried to pull the same shit, Marty told him, "We got our own guineas here."

It was true—young Pasquale Ferri was standing right beside them. They worked it out, Marty and John and the Italians. The Irish kept the docks, the Italians took the trucking, and both unions were run from Providence. Marty and John told the outsiders that "local" meant just that—local. We didn't leave Ireland to be a colony of anybody's anymore. So, for years, nothing came into Providence it didn't come through Marty Ryan, John Murphy, or Pasco Ferri. By truck or boat, didn't matter. They had their joke about the bite they took, called it "the Paul Revere"—one if by land, two if by sea.

The stuff that walked off those boats and trucks fed Dogtown for decades. Not just the dockworkers or drivers, either. Guys who worked in the factories, making costume jewelry, tools, and just enough to cover the rent, they knew they could buy their kids a new pair of sneakers from the back door of the Glocca Morra. They could get canned goods, booze, cigarettes without paying retail to make the rich Yankees richer. Later, when the factories moved south and the buckle on the Rust Belt got tighter, guys couldn't cover the rent and those back-door sales were a matter of survival. Men who would have put a bullet in their heads before they took food stamps would go to Marty to find out what had come off the trucks and the boats that week. Cans of soup, cans of tuna, cans of stew grew legs and walked off the docks onto family tables.

That was Marty back when his neck was thick from swinging his longshoreman's hook and his fists. Back when he had his pride.

"You're going to the clambake, right?" Danny asks him now.

"I don't know."

"You should come," Danny says. "Get out, it will do you good."

Friday nights Terri usually manages to drag Marty down to Dave's for fish-and-chips. Marty's had fish-and-chips every Friday night since Danny can remember, a break in his otherwise steady diet of bacon and eggs, corned beef hash, and booze.

"I don't know," Marty says.

Ned don't say anything. Ned rarely does.

One hard case, Ned Egan. When he was a kid at St. Michael's, the priests and nuns beat him half to death trying to straighten him out. The sister would make Ned stretch his hand out on the desk, then slam the edge of a ruler down on his fingers, and he'd just look at her and smile. He'd get home, his old man would see the welt on his hand and figure that Ned had done something to piss off the sister, so he'd lay Ned down on the bed and bring a razor strap down on the backs of his legs until Ned cried.

Problem was, Ned *wouldn't* cry and his old man wouldn't give up. Those days, no one had heard of Child Protective Services, it wasn't even a concept, so Ned took some ferocious beatings. He'd go to school the next morning with blood leaking through the backs of his pants legs, which would stick to the seat of his chair whenever he went to get up. The teachers learned not to call him to the blackboard those days so as not to embarrass the boy.

When Ned was fourteen, his old man picked up the strap and told him to lie down but Ned swung on him instead, put him on the floor, then ran out and tried to join the merchant marine. They laughed at him and told him to come back in four years. So Ned lived on the streets for a while, until Marty Ryan had a cot put in the storage closet at the Gloc, let the lad sweep up the place for a bowl of lamb stew or shepherd's pie or whatever was left over at night.

One afternoon, Ned's old man came into the pub with a ball bat in his hand and announced he was going to teach his no-good son a lesson he'd never forget. Marty was sitting in his booth and quietly said, "Billy Egan, unless that lesson is how to hit a curveball, I'd suggest you turn around and walk back through that door. I'm a bit short of cash now to have a mass said for you." Ned's old man turned milk white and walked back through the door. He knew just what Ryan was telling him, and he never stepped into the Gloc again.

The day he was sixteen, Ned quit school, went down to the docks, where Mr. Ryan got him his union card. Ned started swinging the hook, made a decent wage, got himself a little apartment on Smith Street and bought his own groceries. His father would see him in the neighborhood, he'd cross the street. His mother wrote him a letter when the old man died.

Ned didn't write back. Far as he was concerned, Marty Ryan was his father.

Now Danny says to his dad, "I'll drive you over there."

"Ned can bring me."

"I'll drive you," Danny repeats.

Marty's in his midsixties but he acts more like he's in his eighties. What the cigs and booze and bitterness will do to you, Danny figures.

To Marty, anyway.

Danny remembers him lashing out, screaming, *You're just like your mother! You got that bitch's blood!* In that quiet clarity before passing out, Marty muttered, *I didn't even know I had you. I went to Vegas, had a fling with a broad I met at a bar—a year later she shows up with a kid.* You. *Tells me, "Here, here's your son. I'm not cut out to be a mother." Only truth ever came out of her lying mouth.*

Truth also that Marty loved her. Kept her picture under his bed. Danny found it there one time, looking for *Playboy* magazines—tall, statuesque showgirl with red hair, green eyes, long legs, big tits. It was only later, during one of Marty's drunken diatribes—this time show-and-tell—Danny realized it was his mother.

It was hard to believe, though, that his old man had ever nailed a woman like that. You looked at Marty Ryan, you didn't see a ladies' man. Old Pasco set Danny straight on that score, though. They were out digging clams and Pasco said, "Your father, back in his day, was one good-looking kid. Marty came to the party, hide your women."

Danny knows his father still has the picture.

FIVE

WHEN THEY GET TO PASCO'S, there's already a houseful. People everywhere, the women moving around the kitchen like a well-practiced drill team, Mary Ferri presiding over the whole thing. Danny gets Marty into a chair and then goes back and finds Terri helping out in the kitchen.

"Where'd you go this afternoon anyway?" she asks. "I woke up, you weren't there."

"Business."

Terri says, "Over beers?"

"A couple pitchers is all."

She looks at her brother. "How much did Liam have?"

"He's okay."

"He looks a little *too* okay," Terri says. "Keep an eye on him, all right?"

Danny says he will, but he resents it a little. Everyone always has to keep an eye on Liam. Pat's been doing it his whole life. Even on the ice it was well known that if you took a run at Liam, Pat was going to drop the gloves.

This goes all the way back even before Liam was born, Danny figures. One drunken night Pat told him the story of how Catherine's pregnancy with Liam was supposed to be difficult, maybe even life-threatening for her, and John, devout Catholic that he is, wanted her to abort the baby. But Catherine wouldn't do it and the baby, Liam, was born a couple of months premature, less than three pounds, wasn't expected to live and was declared dead twice.

So pampering Liam, looking out for Liam, bailing Liam out from the consequences of whatever shitty thing he did is a Murphy family habit.

Danny looks over where Liam is charming Mary Ferri, and sees that he has that flush high on his cheeks, and that amused-at-everything, too-cool-for-school smile on his face.

"Jimmy and Angie here?" Danny asks.

"Outside," Terri answers.

"You want a drink?"

"I'd take a beer."

Danny goes to a big steel bucket on the floor, full of ice, and pulls out two cold beers. Then he sees Cassandra. Tall, wavy red hair, those startling dark brown eyes. She smiles at Danny and he feels awkward, the two beers in his hand.

"Hi, Danny."

"Cassie, hi," Danny says. "I didn't know you were home from . . ."

"Treatment?" she says. "You can say it, Danny."

It was like her, what, second or even third time in rehab or the psych ward? Cassie is the unlikely black sheep of the Murphy family, and John barely bothers to hide his shame of her. She was the angel once, daddy's little girl—Terri once admitted to Danny that she was jealous of her big sister—a fine singer of the old folk music, a dancer who won awards at *céilís*, but then she started drinking, and then it was grass, and then it was all kinds of dope. She was on the street for a while after the Murphys went the "tough love" route and kicked her out of the house, and then Danny heard she'd agreed to go back to this place in Connecticut.

Danbury, someplace like that.

She looks good now, though.

Clear eyes, her skin glowing.

"One of those beers for *me*, Danny?" she asks.

"Jesus, Cassie, don't even joke."

He and Cassie were always close—maybe it was because each of them was something of an outsider in their family and so they were natural allies.

"No, I can *joke*," she says, "I just can't *drink*."

"Probably a good idea, huh?"

"At least that's what they say at the meetings," Cassie says.

"Yeah, you go to the meetings?"

"Ninety in ninety."

Anyone who lives in an Irish neighborhood knows what that means—ninety AA meetings in ninety days.

"Good for you, Cassie," Danny says.

"Yeah, good for me," she says. She always liked Danny. There was something soft in him, something hurt. Small wonder, him being Marty's kid. "You'd better get back to Terri before her beer gets warm."

"Right."

Danny takes the beer back to Terri and says, "Cassie is here."

"Yeah?"

"I mean, should she be?" Danny asks. "With all the drinking and everything?"

"She has to learn to deal with real life *some*time," Terri says, taking the beer from him. "Besides, no one here is going to let her drink."

Mary Ferri is teasing Liam about not having a date for the party.

"This is a first," she's saying. "Usually it's some model from New York, or an actress, always the prettiest girl . . ."

"I decided to play the field tonight," Liam says.

"It's a small field," Terri kicks in. Almost everyone is married now, starting in on families. The clambakes—even among the younger generation—have taken on a decidedly domestic flavor. A little boring for Liam.

"I'll just have to do my best," Liam says.

"You should get married," Mary tells him. "Forget all these models and actresses. You want me to find you a nice Italian girl?"

"You'd do that to a nice Italian girl?" Terri asks.

"My sister," Liam says. "Thanks."

"Liam's a sweetie," Mary says. "He just needs the right woman."

"He *had* the right woman," Terri says, "and he blew it."

Danny knows she's referring to Liam's ex-girlfriend Karen. A trauma nurse at Rhode Island Hospital, she had it all—beauty, brains, and a good heart. They all really liked her. And she really loved Liam, but he had to fuck it up by fucking around.

Liam is Kennedy handsome—curly black hair, striking brown eyes—he's cut a sexual swath through Rhode Island, not so easy to do in a mostly Catholic state where most girls have older brothers.

"The right woman?" Liam asks. "But you're already taken, Mary."

The joke is that Liam didn't kiss the Blarney Stone—it kissed *him*.

Kissed him? Danny thinks. It fucking *blew* him.

"Listen to him . . ." Mary says, pleased. She looks at Terri and suggests, "Maybe Tina Bacco."

"Maybe," Terri says, and glances at Danny. They both know that

Liam took Tina down to Atlantic City for a weekend and boffed her eighteen ways to Sunday. At least that's what Tina told Terri. Liam was great in bed, a few laughs, but as a husband? Forget it.

"You're the prettiest woman here," Liam says to Mary. "You should leave Pasco, run away with me."

"Make yourself useful," Mary says, "and go ask my husband if the food is ready yet."

"I'll go with you," Danny says.

They walk out onto the beach, where Pat's helping Pasco dig the clams out from the pit, and Peter and Paulie and their crew are standing there watching them.

Sal Antonucci's there.

Danny don't like him.

Sal has his own crew now, doing some serious work for the Morettis. One of his guys, Tony Romano, is standing with him, grinning at Danny like an ape. Sal and Tony did time together in the joint and they're like brothers. Spent literally years passing weights back and forth and now they're muscle-bound guidos.

Thing of it is, Sal is a stone killer.

He's moved up with the Morettis because he does their wet work for them. Tall, heavy-muscled, broad face like a slab of marble, blue eyes cold as a January morning, Sal smiles at Danny and asks, "How's it hanging?"

"Down to my ankles, Sally," Danny says, because he knows Antonucci don't like being called Sally and for some reason Danny likes to annoy him, or maybe has to show he's not afraid of him.

Danny looks over at Romano. "Tony."

Tony nods.

Pretty much what Tony does, because he's dumber than a rock. What Tony's got going for him are his friendship with Sal, his muscles, and his looks. Thick, curly black hair, sculpted face, lithe body, he could be one of those male models hawking cologne or Calvin Klein underwear or whatever in the magazines.

"I'd do him," Cassie told Danny once, "if he'd just bang me silly and keep his mouth shut."

Cassie talks a big game, Danny thinks, but to his knowledge she's never been with anyone.

Danny nods back at Tony—this is what passes as conversation with Romano—and moves on to say hello to Jimmy and Angie but then he doesn't.

Because he sees, walking up the beach . . .

. . . that woman.

The goddess who came out of the sea.

SIX

S HE'S WITH PAULIE MORETTI.

"I'd like you to meet my girlfriend, Pam," Paulie says.

Who knew, Danny thinks.

Who knew that Paulie could pull a girl like this? Every guinea's dream of a white woman. And it would have to be a freakin' Pam. Not a Sheila, a Mary, a Theresa. A Pam.

"Nice to meet you all," Pam says.

She's friendly but a little reserved. Who wouldn't be, Danny thinks, meeting this group for the first time. And not at all stuck-up, like Danny thought she'd be when he saw her coming out of the water. But she has a voice like sex, low and a little gravelly—they all feel it, even the women, and it triggers a little tremor through the group.

"How do you all know Paul?" Pam asks, making conversation.

She's smart, Danny thinks—including them all but connecting it around to Paulie, as if she's trying to say, *I'm not after your men. I'm not a threat to you. I'm one of you, really.* Beautiful women have their burdens, too, he realizes—other women's jealousy is one of them.

"Our families have known each other since Noah's ark," Danny says, feeling a little shy. She has a man's white shirt on over her jeans. Danny wonders if it's Paulie's, if she put it on after they made love because it was handy or because she just thought she looked good in it, which she does.

Paulie puts his arm around her shoulder.

This is mine. She's mine.

"How did you meet Paulie?" Liam asks in this tone like he can't believe it could happen in the first place.

"At a bar," she says with a self-deprecating smile. And she pronounces it "bar," with an *r*, not "bah" like the locals, and even that is sexy. "I was out with some coworkers, and there was Paul."

"Paul," Danny hears. Not "Paulie," "Paul." He hasn't heard Paulie called Paul since, well, ever.

"Where did you move here from?" Terri asks Pam.

She's starting to get the lowdown, Danny thinks. The wives will pounce on Pam like fresh meat and get her whole life's story, it's so rare a guy other than Liam brings anyone new. They've all known each other forever and never even dated outside their own high school. They know each other's stories too well, and they're the same freakin' story anyway.

"Connecticut," Pam said. "I do real estate, and Rhode Island seemed to offer more opportunities."

Another first, Danny thought—someone using "opportunities" and "Rhode Island" in the same sentence.

"Pasco," Danny remembers to say, "Mary's asking about the food."

"Tell her she can start serving the pasta," Pasco says without looking up from what he's doing.

"Nice to meet you, Pam," Liam says.

On the way back to the house, Danny says, "No."

"What?" Liam asks.

He knows.

"Just no."

"First woman Paulie's ever dated who didn't have a mustache," Liam says.

"Don't go busting balls," Pat tells his little brother.

"Since when do I bust balls?"

"Since always," Pat says.

It's true, Danny thinks. Liam likes his jokes and always gets away with them. He especially likes getting under Paulie's skin, probably because it's so easy to do. And Danny feels like he did when he first saw her come out of the water.

She's going to be trouble.

Women that beautiful usually are.

SEVEN

CHRIST, THE FOOD, DANNY THINKS.

The clams, the quahogs, the crabs. The huge pots of spaghetti and gravy, stuffed peppers, and sweet Italian *sausiche*. The joke is that the Irish are never, *ever* allowed to cook, but one time Martin wrapped a potato in tinfoil and had Danny secretly bury it in the coals and when Pasco dug the clams out he found that spud and yelled, "Marty, you old mick!"

God, how they eat. The food never stops. After the shellfish and the pasta, the *sausiche* and the peppers, the women bring out big boxes of the sweet little Italian cookies from Cantanella's bakery in Knightsville. Only Cantanella's cookies will do; someone was always designated to stop in Cranston on the way down from the city and pick up those cookies.

First time Danny made the Cantanella's run, the boxes of cookies were on the counter waiting for him but when Danny reached for his wallet the girl looked at him like he was pulling a gun. Lou Cantanella came out from the back waving his arms like a football referee signaling an incomplete pass.

Danny felt a little bad about it when he was loading the boxes into his trunk, but then again, he knew that Lou never had to worry about the store being robbed, deliveries not arriving on time, health inspectors jamming him up on some bullshit violation, or the city deciding it needed to put parking meters on the street outside his stores. And whenever one of the Italians got married, Lou Cantanella always provided the cake, and the father of the bride paid bust-out retail, because that was a daughter's wedding and it was a matter of honor to pay.

How sweet those cookies are against the strong, bitter espresso, and how good the hot coffee feels going down as the fog comes in and the night gets colder. Mary always keeps extra sweatshirts in the house, big thick sweatshirts worn pale by use and sun, and Danny goes in to get one for Terri, and decides he might as well take a piss while he's at it.

Opens the bathroom door and there's Paulie, Pam, and freakin' Liam in there bending over lines of coke on the counter. They look at him like guilty kids and Liam says, "Oops."

"We forgot to lock the door," Paulie explains unnecessarily.

And Danny's like, *What, are you out of your freaking minds, doing blow in Pasco Ferri's house?* Apparently so, because Liam finishes snorting a line and holds the rolled-up dollar bill to Danny.

"I'm good," Danny says. "Wipe your noses off before you come back outside, for Chrissakes."

He forgets about taking a whiz, finds a sweatshirt for Terri and goes back outside and helps her get into it.

"Thanks, baby," she says, and leans back against him. Someone has brought a mandolin out and is playing while Pasco sings a sweet, sad ballad in Italian. His voice comes out of the fog like it drifted

across the Atlantic from Napoli—an old song from an old country
that washes up on this New World shore like driftwood.

> *Vide'o mare quant'è bello,*
> *spira tantu sentimento,*
> *Comme tu a chi tiene mente,*
> *Ca scetato 'o faie sunnà.*

> *Guarda gua' chistu ciardino;*
> *Siente, sie' sti sciure arance:*
> *Nu profumo accussi fino*
> *Dinto 'o core se ne va . . .*

Pasco finishes the song and it's very quiet.

He says, "Your turn, Marty."

"Nah," Marty says.

It's a ritual. Marty demurs, Pasco insists, then Marty lets himself
be persuaded into singing. While this goes on, the three come back
from the bathroom—Pam in a sweatshirt now, still looking sexy as
hell. She and Paulie sit down together; Liam comes to the opposite
side of the fire and plops down next to Danny and Terri.

Then Marty sings "The Parting Glass" in his quavering voice.

> *Of all the money e'er I had,*
> *I spent it in good company.*
> *And all the harm I've ever done,*
> *Alas! It was to none but me.*

> *And all I've done for want of wit*
> *To mem'ry now I can't recall,*

So fill to me the parting glass
Good night and joy be with you all.

How they had fought each other, these two immigrant tribes, for a place to put their feet. The Irish in Dogtown, the Italians on Federal Hill, toeholds carved out of grudging New England granite. The old Yankees hated the slick micks and greasy guineas, the bogtrotters and dagos who came to ruin their pristine Protestant city with their Catholic saints and their candles, bleeding effigies and incense-swinging priests. Their smelly food and smellier bodies, their incontinent breeding.

First it was the Irish, back around the Civil War, who filled the tenements outside the slaughter yards that teemed with packs of feral mutts prowling for offal and giving the neighborhood its name, Dogtown. The men worked the slaughterhouses, the quarries, the tool factories, making fortunes for the old Yankee families, then marched off to die in the war, and those who came back came back determined to claim a piece of the city. They came out of Dogtown and took the firehouses and the police precincts, then they organized the wards and voted themselves into political, if not economic, power, satisfied to run the city if they couldn't own it.

Around the turn of the century the Italians came, from Naples or somewhere in Mezzogiorno, and fought the Irish. Two sets of slaves battling each other for the crumbs off the master's plate until they finally figured out that together they had the numbers to take the whole table. They carved the city up like a roast beef, but were smart enough to leave the old Yankees sufficient slices to keep them fat and happy.

Oh, all the comrades e'er I had,
They're sorry for my going away,
And all the sweethearts e'er I had,
They'd wish me one more day to stay.

But since it falls unto my lot
That I should rise and you should not,
I gently rise and softly call,
Good night and joy be with you all.

One night at the clambake, Danny saw Pasco Ferri reach out and touch Marty's hand, and they both started laughing. Sitting there, full of food and wine, wrapped in the warmth of their friends and families, their children and grandchildren, they just laughed. And Danny wondered about the things they had seen, the things they had done to share that clambake on the beach.

Pasco seemed to see the question in Danny's eyes, and, unbidden, said, "We didn't outfight the *old Yankees . . .*" He paused to make sure that the children were in bed and the women were in the house and then continued, "We out*loved* them. We took our women to bed and made babies."

It was true; what had made them poor—small houses crowded with hungry mouths—had made them rich. What had ostensibly made them weak had made them powerful.

Looking at him now, it makes Danny sad. Liam interrupts his reverie. "What's she doing with that little greaseball?"

Danny doesn't have to ask who he's talking about. He's looking across the fire at Pam, who's leaning against Paulie. Even with the hood of a sweatshirt covering most of her hair, she looks beautiful in the firelight.

"Leave it alone."

"I'll leave it alone," Liam says.

Marty finishes his song.

If I had money enough to spend
And leisure time to sit awhile,

There is a fair maid in this town
That sorely has my heart beguiled.

Her rosy cheeks and ruby lips,
I own she has my heart in thrall,
Then fill to me the parting glass,
Good night and joy be with you all.

It gets quiet then. Mary and some of the women start picking things up and bringing them back into the house and other people just sit and look into the fire or start drifting off.

Danny nudges Terri. "Let's go down the beach."

Trying to look inconspicuous but feeling self-conscious, Danny gets up and he and Terri sneak down the beach until the fog hides them. He pulls her down and unsnaps her jeans.

"Twice in one day?" Terri asks. "Some kind of record."

"The baby ain't gonna make itself."

He doesn't last long, and what with all the sun all day and the sex and the booze, they fall asleep.

SHE WAS FOURTEEN years old.

Cassie was in bed reading a book, having fled from her parents' party downstairs, when "Uncle Pasco" opened the door and slipped into her room.

"I came upstairs to use the bathroom," he said, "and I saw your light on."

"I was tired of the party."

"I don't blame you," Pasco said. "A bunch of old farts. Nothing to interest a pretty girl like you. You are a pretty girl, you know that, don't you?"

"I don't know," she said, suddenly feeling sick to her stomach.

"Yes, you do," Pasco said. "You know you're pretty and you know how to use it. I've watched you."

He shut the door behind him.

Cassie can still smell him. Fifteen years later, sitting on the beach by the embers of the fire, her arms wrapped around herself, she can still smell Pasco's cologne, the cigar smoke on his clothes, the red wine on his breath as he moved toward her on the bed, leaned over, took her chin in his hand, tilted her face up and kissed her. She can still feel his tongue swirl in her mouth, the spit from his mouth seep into hers.

"Don't," she said. "Please."

He answered by running his hand up the inside of her blouse.

"Nice," he said.

"No," she said. "I don't want this."

"Yes, you do. You just don't know you do."

"Please, Uncle Pasco."

His hands reached under her jeans.

"I'll tell," she said.

"No one will believe you," Pasco said. "And if they did, what will they do? Do you know who I am? Do you know what would happen to your father, your brothers, if they came after me? You know what would happen, because you're a smart girl."

She knew.

Fourteen years old, she was wise to the ways of their world. She knew who her father was, who Pasco Ferri was, what would happen. So when he pulled her jeans down and then climbed on top of her she stayed silent.

Stays silent still.

It wasn't long after that she started to steal sips from the bottles her parents kept in the bar. Or found guys to buy for her. Then it was grass, then it was heroin, because heroin gave her distance from that night, made it seem like just a bad dream.

When her mother asked her why, and her father screamed at her and called her a junkie and a disgrace, she held her tongue and never told because she was afraid that they wouldn't believe her and more afraid that they would.

She never wanted to be touched by a man again.

And never has.

DANNY'S OUT COLD when he hears the shouting down the beach.

Pam's voice, not so deep but still throaty.

"He grabbed me!"

Danny looks up and sees her, pretty drunk, staggering in the deep sand, coming toward him, walking back toward the fire that's dim now. He zips his fly, gets up and, still groggy, asks, "What's the matter? What's going on?!"

It's like a weird, bad dream.

"He grabbed me! That son of a bitch grabbed my boob!"

Now Danny sees Liam walking up behind her, this stupid grin on his face, his hands spread in mock innocence. "It was an accident. A misunderstanding."

"Shit, Liam." Terri's on her feet now. She wraps Pam in her arms and Pam starts crying. "It's all right. It's all right."

Terri looks at Danny, like *Aren't you going to do something?* Then Danny hears people running toward them and then Paulie and Peter, Pat and Sal Antonucci, and Tony come running out of the fog.

Danny grabs Liam by the elbow. "Come on. Get out of here."

Liam jerks his arm away. "It's no big deal. I just brushed against her tit is all. Misunderstanding."

"We need to get you out of here."

"Where were you?" Paulie asks Pam. "I been looking all over!"

"I went for a walk," she says. "To clear my head. That son of a bitch must have followed me!"

She points at Liam.

"Did he hurt you?" Paulie asks.

"He grabbed my breast."

"The fuck, Liam!" Peter yells.

Sal starts to move in. That's Sal, Danny thinks, he takes care of things for the Morettis. Pat steps between them. "Take it easy."

"A mistake." Liam smirks. "I was trying to find my way in the fog, I reached out and . . . tit. *Oops.*"

"Shut your stupid mouth," Pat snaps.

Danny grabs Liam, holds him tight this time and pulls him away because Paulie is going apeshit.

"I'll kick your fucking ass!" Paulie yells. "I'll fucking kill you, you motherfucker!"

Liam yells, "You'll *try*, asshole!"

Danny cuffs him on the side of the head. "Shut up."

Liam breaks away and runs down the beach away from them. Danny starts to chase him, but Jimmy Mac is there now, grabs hold of Danny and says, "Let him go."

Jimmy looks as Irish as corned beef. Curly red hair, pale skin with freckles, a face as open as a book. He's stocky leaning toward chubby, and Danny knows sometimes his softness makes people think he's weak.

It's a big mistake.

Jimmy's a gearhead, maybe the best wheelman in New England. What he can't do with a car can't be done. He'll get you in and he'll get you out. But he's more than that—you get into a beef, you want

Jimmy with you. He'll go with his hands, with a knife, or with a gun, that's what it takes. Angie bosses him around like he's a cocker spaniel, but that's because he loves her and he lets her.

Jimmy Mac has balls.

So Danny doesn't fight him, he watches Liam disappear into the fog.

Pat walks up to Paulie and Pam. "I'm sorry. I apologize for my brother."

"He's an asshole," Paulie says.

"I can't disagree."

"What he did is *not* acceptable," Peter says.

"He's drunk."

"No excuse."

"No, it's not," Pat says. "I'll talk with him. We'll deal with it."

"Can we get her in out of the cold?" Terri asks. "The poor girl is shaking."

"He didn't do anything more to you, did he?" Paulie asks her.

"No, he just touched my breast."

They take Pam back to their cottage because they don't want to wake up Pasco and Mary with this. Terri gets her settled down, even laughing a little bit, and then Paulie takes her back to his place.

"Your fucking brother," Danny says when they've all left. "I swear."

Terri, she looks sad. "I can't help feeling bad for him."

"What for?"

"It's his way of getting attention," Terri says. "It's not easy being Pat's younger brother. Pat the hockey star, Pat the basketball star, Pat the star student . . . the star son. His whole life, Liam's been in Pat's shadow. Now Dad relies more and more on Pat in the business . . . *that* will be Pat's. Liam just wants something that's *his*, you know."

But Pam isn't his, Danny thinks. That's the problem. "There's going to be hell to pay for this."

"What'll they want?"

"Money," Danny says.

At the end of the day, the Morettis always want the money.

LIAM MURPHY STUMBLES around in the fog feeling gloriously sorry for himself. Everybody's mad at him, and they shouldn't be. Okay, he thinks, I had a little too much to drink and I felt her tit. It's not like I raped her or anything, for Chrissakes.

He plops down in the sand, drains the last of his beer, and throws the empty can into the water.

I'm going to catch it tomorrow, he thinks. I'll get it from Pat, from my old man, from all the wives. Not to mention Pasco and Mary Ferri. And the Moretti brothers. I'm going to spend the next two days going around apologizing to everybody—including, of course, Pam—and will have to eat a healthy ration of shit. Maybe I should just go down to Florida until this blows over.

Anyway, it's tomorrow's problem.

He pushes himself up off the sand to go back to his cottage. Sleep this off, deal with the hangover, and then figure it out. He walks up the beach and is almost to the road when he sees four figures in the fog.

Peter, Paulie, Sal, and Tony.

"Hello, motherfucker," Paulie says.

He raises the baseball bat.

Liam smiles and says, "I guess the coke deal's off, huh?"

Paulie swings the bat.

DANNY'S BEEN ASLEEP maybe an hour, hour and a half when he hears the screen door bang.

What the hell, he thinks. Danny rolls out of bed and gets his jeans and a shirt on and goes to the door.

Liam lies on the stoop, one hand stretched up toward the door handle. There's blood all over him.

"Jesus Christ," Danny says. Then he yells, "Pat! Jimmy! Come here quick!"

THEY GET LIAM into the back seat and Jimmy Mac drives like a bat out of hell up Goshen Beach Road and onto Route 1 to South County Hospital. It takes a long ten minutes and they aren't sure Liam is going to make it. He goes into convulsions, his body jerking and racking while Pat struggles to hold him still.

The doctor isn't sure Liam is going to live, either. His skull is fractured, there's swelling on the brain. He has two broken ribs and maybe internal injuries, something about a ruptured spleen.

"What the hell happened to him?" the doc asks. He's young, a junior guy on staff to pull this shift, and he's shook up. Nobody tells him anything even though they know goddamn well what happened: Paulie, Peter, Sal, and Tony went looking for Liam, found him on the beach, and beat the wicked piss out of him.

They got carried away. Liam had *something* coming to him, no question. They should have slapped him around a little, but not this.

The nurses roll Liam into the operating room.

Long goddamn night in that hospital. Pacing around the waiting room, drinking coffee, waiting for word.

"I swear, if he dies . . ." Pat says.

"Don't think like that," Danny says. They go through the usual bullshit—he's a fighter, he's young, he's strong.

Terri gets there with her parents. John Murphy has seen a lot in his life, but he hasn't seen a son die. "What the hell happened?" he asks Pat, like it's his fault, like he should have been looking after his brother and didn't.

Pat tells him.

"You shouldn't let him drink," Pat's mother says to him. "You know that."

The waiting room is crowded—the Murphys, Danny and Terri, Jimmy and Angie, Pat and Sheila, Cassie. It's Sheila does most of the talking with the doctors, comes back with the reports that there's nothing to report. Except that it's touch-and-go.

Down at the coffee machine, Cassie says to Danny, "Don't go all Irish on this. If you go after the Morettis, there'll be a war, and then someone will get killed."

Danny don't say anything.

First things first. They have to see what happens—but if Liam dies, there's going to be no restraining Pat.

He'll drop the gloves.

PASCO FERRI KNOWS that, too.

Peter Moretti is smart enough to go over first thing in the morning and tell him what happened, because the old man doesn't like surprises and Peter doesn't want him to get the story from the Murphys first.

Pasco ain't happy.

Takes in the story, thinks about it for a long minute, then looks over his coffee cup and says, "*Now* you come for permission? No—you come for permission *before* you do something. If you had, I wouldn't have given it."

Paulie starts to say, "What Liam Murphy did—"

"You wanted to be a man," Pasco says, "you should have gone after him one-on-one with your fists, not with three other guys and a bat. Now you just look weak."

"Weak? I bashed his fucking head in."

"One of my *guests*!" Pasco yells. "At *my* party! In front of *my* house*! I should put you in the bed next to him!"

Peter says, "You're right, Pasco. Of course. We should have waited."

"Now we have to make this right," Pasco says.

"Make it right how?" Peter asks.

"You're going to pay half the medical bills."

"Bull*shit*!" Paulie yells.

"Do you want to repeat that, young Paulie?" Pasco leans slightly over the table and looks at him.

Paulie drops his eyes. He knows the next word out of his mouth could put him in a landfill.

Pasco is furious. Everything we spent years putting together, keeping together, is going to fall apart over a piece of ass?! If this horny Irish fuck taps out, I'll have to give John something, maybe even Paulie Moretti, or go to war with him. And if I do that, I might lose a whole wing of the family, hard to know how Paulie's old man will react from inside the ACI. Hard to know which way the Antonuccis and Palumbos of the world would go. I don't know, maybe John would settle for one of them. If I go to war against John, I'll win. But at what cost, in blood and money?

Fuck these hotheads.

"Be grateful it's *half*," Pasco says. "And then you go to church, light a candle, and pray this kid don't die."

THEY PUT LIAM in an ambulance and haul him up to Rhode Island Hospital in Providence because South County can't do the surgery needed to relieve the pressure on his brain. He's still unconscious and the doctors won't say if he's going to make it or not.

Liam's ex-girlfriend Karen comes out into the waiting room and hugs Cassie. "I'm sorry . . . I can't work on him. I'm too close."

"I understand," Cassie says.

"They have good people in there, though," Karen says. "The best. I'll keep you informed. I promise."

She looks shook, sad, Danny thinks. Christ, she still loves him.

"Thank you." The wives close rank. Sheila, Terri, and Angie look after Catherine Murphy, go for coffees, bring back trays of food, make the phone calls that need to be made.

Jimmy Mac takes Danny aside. "I say we hit them now."

Danny says, "We have to wait. If Liam makes it, we're looking at one scenario; if he doesn't, we're looking at another."

"We at least owe them a beating," Jimmy says.

"Let's wait to see what we owe them."

He stops talking because two men walk in and Danny lamps them as cops—detectives—right away. They walk up to Danny and one says, "Detective Carey, South Kingstown Police. Are you Daniel Ryan?"

"Yeah."

"You found the victim?"

"He came to my door."

"Did he tell you who did this to him?" Carey asks.

"No," Danny says. "He passed out. He's been unconscious since."

"Do you have any idea who might have done this to him?"

"No," Danny says.

"You all come down from Providence, right?" Carey asks. "Rent places in Goshen?"

"That's right."

"You're friends with Pasco Ferri."

So this cop knows exactly who we are, Danny thinks. He knows the score—that no one is going to tell him shit, and we'll handle this internally. "I know Pasco, yeah."

"We're going to go talk to him, too," Carey says.

"I doubt he knows anything."

Carey smirks. "Me too."

Pasco has a good relationship with the local cops.

Carey hands Danny his card. "If you think of anything you may have forgotten, give me a call. I'll keep a good thought about your friend."

"Thanks," Danny says. "Hey? Don't bother the family. They don't know anything, either."

Carey walks away and Danny steps over to a trash can and tosses the card. That's when he sees Chris Palumbo get off the elevator.

"Shit," Danny says.

He and Jimmy walk over to head him off.

"Maybe not the best time, Chris," Danny says, wondering who sent him, whether it was Peter Moretti or Pasco. Or maybe Chris came on his own boot, to see if there's any information he can use for himself.

"Jesus, Danny," Chris says. "This is terrible. A terrible thing."

"Yeah."

"How did this get so out of hand?" Chris says.

"Ask your buddies," Jimmy says.

Chris holds up his hands. "I had nothing to fuckin' do with this. They had asked me first, I would have told them, go through channels."

"Too bad they didn't ask you, then," Danny says.

"Look," Chris says, "I know everyone's pretty raw right now—"

"You think?" Danny asks.

"—but we all need to keep cool heads," Chris says. "Let's get Liam out of the woods, then we can—"

"Get out of here, Chris," Danny says. "Nothing personal, but no one wants to see anyone from the Moretti family right now. Jesus, Pat sees you here . . ."

"I get it," Chris says. "I'm gone. Do me a favor, though? If the right moment comes up? Give my respect?"

"Yeah, okay. Goodbye, Chris. See you."

Palumbo gets back in the elevator.

"The balls on that guy," Jimmy says.

"He's covering his ass," Danny says. "He's probably on his way over to Federal Hill now to tell the Morettis they did the right thing."

And to tell them Liam's still alive.

LIAM MAKES IT through surgery, which Karen tells them is a big deal. But he's not out of the woods yet. It's two more long days before they're ready to say that Liam is going to make it.

Loses his spleen and needs plastic surgery to repair the broken orbital bone under his eye. But his brain is okay.

Well, as okay as Liam's brain can be, Danny thinks.

He and Pat go to talk to Pasco.

They find him on the beach in front of his house, two poles in the water, baited for stripers.

"What Liam did wasn't right," Pasco says before Pat can get a word out.

Pat says, "But he didn't deserve *that*."

"They beat him half to death," Danny says. "He almost died."

"He touched a made guy's woman," Pasco says, adjusting the tension on one of the lines. "If that girl and Paulie were married, Paulie would have been within his rights to *kill* your brother."

"Liam was drunk," Pat said. "We all were."

Pasco shrugs. Drunk or sober, Liam had disrespected Paulie Moretti in a very personal way. The beating got out of hand, no question, but the Murphy kid had taken his chances.

"I came here out of respect," Pat says. "I came here to ask your permission."

"To do what?" Pasco asks. "Give Paulie a beating? Peter and Sal and Tony, too? You think—even if I give the nod—you can take all four of them?"

"I think *we* can," Pat says.

Pasco smiles. "*Patdannyjimmy.*"

"Just fists, I swear," Pat says.

"Where do you think you are, high school?" Pasco asks. "Let it go. Your brother is alive, God bless, I made Paulie cover the bills, let it pass. What does your father say?"

"I haven't talked to him about it."

"When you do," Pasco says, "he'll tell you what I'm telling you and what I told Peter and Paulie: We worked too hard to put this thing together. I'm not going to let it fall apart because your brother got drunk and felt some *tette.*"

Young men are stupid and their balls are too full. Pasco remembers when it was that way with him, and the old bulls had to teach him what was what. Now he has to be the teacher. He turns and looks at these two young Irish bucks, all on fire with indignation and the hunger for revenge. They have to learn—vengeance is an expensive luxury, too expensive in this case. Too rich for *their* blood, anyway. He says, "Take your brother home—be glad you're not at his wake."

Danny knows that if they hit back at the Moretti brothers or Sal, it will be a personal affront to Pasco Ferri. Then Pasco would approve a hit on *them.*

"They're going to get away with it," Pat says as they drive away and head back up to Providence.

"Looks like it," Danny says.

It sucks, but there it is.

End of story.

EIGHT

EXCEPT IT ISN'T.

It might all have died down and blown over like a summer squall, but a week later Danny goes to visit Liam in the hospital, and when he gets up to the room, she's there.

Pam.

Smiling, looking gorgeous in a white summer dress, holding Liam's hand, and he's smiling back, weakly but bravely.

Danny, he don't know what to say, but Liam says, "Danny, I think you know Pam."

You think I know Pam, you dumb fuck? You think I know *Pam?*

"Sure. Yeah. Hi."

"Hi, Danny."

Like this is just another day at the freakin' beach. She yaps on about some real estate shit or something, but Danny ain't hearing none of it. His head is whirling. Finally, he hears her say, "Well, I'd better be on my way."

"Thanks for coming by," Liam says.

Pam leans down and kisses him on the cheek.

Danny follows her out into the corridor.

"No disrespect," he says, "but, Pam, what the hell?"

"He apologized to me," Pam says. "He was very sweet. And what Paulie did to him was wrong."

"The hell you think Paulie would do to him *now*," Danny asks, his temper rising, "he saw you here with him, holding his hand?"

"I'm not with Paulie anymore," Pam says. "He's an animal."

Fucking A, he's an animal, Danny thinks. And "animal" don't begin to describe it, what he's gonna do when he hears about this. "Does Paulie know?"

"Does he know what?" she answers, really cool, like Danny has no business asking her questions.

"That you're dumping him."

"He calls," she says. "I don't call back."

"Jesus, Pam."

"It's my life," she says.

Yeah, it is and it isn't, Danny thinks. It's your life, but it's all our lives you're fucking with, and you have to get that, you're not stupid.

Pam says, "Anyway, I feel a little guilty, like maybe some of it was my fault, what happened. I was kind of drunk, maybe I led him on . . . and he didn't really hurt me. Maybe I was just being, you know, a drama queen."

Yeah, *now* you think this, Pam?

She shrugs one pretty bare shoulder and walks away. Right past Pat, coming down the hall with a coffee cabinet for Liam. Pat takes one look at her, walks into Liam's room, hands him the milkshake and says, "You dumb shit."

Liam's smile is phony. "She just came to apologize for what happened."

"Yeah, well you tell her you forgive her," Pat says, "and that's that."

"Big brother," Liam says, "you don't tell me what's what."

"You've already caused enough trouble."

"And what have you done about it?" Liam asks. "Nothing."

"It's not that simple."

"Whatever you say."

"Fuck you, Liam," Pat says.

"Yeah, fuck me."

"You stay away from that girl."

YEAH, EXCEPT A week later, when Liam is taking the wheelchair ride out of the hospital, it's Pam pushing the chair, Pam who drives him home, Pam who moves in with him.

Okay, Danny thinks, maybe Liam is really in love with her, but maybe it's a giant fuck-you to Paulie Moretti. Like, look who really won the fight. You may have beat me up, but look whose bed she's in now. Look who's tapping your girl. It's freaking genius, really. Liam can't physically hit back at Paulie, so he gets back at him in the worst way—slicing his balls clean off, turning him into a *cornuto*.

Every bar, every club he goes in, Paulie hears about it. His goombahs walk right up to the edge with him—"Hey, whatever happened to that Pam chick? Did I see your old squeeze out the other night? Who did I see her with? Can't remember." Dangerous shit, but irresistible. I mean, you have to bust balls, right?

Who the fuck knew that Paulie really loved her? That she wasn't just arm candy, a walking status symbol? Who knew that, as he confessed to his brother in the small hours of a dark morning, Pamela ripped his heart out?

Now the slow burn is on up Federal Hill. The Morettis fume, the embers of their resentment stoked by the whispered jokes, the sly, snide looks, the sight of Pam out with Liam Murphy. Providence is a small town in a small state. You can't go anywhere without seeing someone you know, someone who knows you, somebody who knows somebody.

It's going to happen, Danny knows.

It just needs a spark.

Dumbass Brendan Handrigan touches it off.

Handrigan is a minor player—like Danny, a collector for the Murphy loan-shark operations. Early October, he and Danny are sitting in a bar after doing a job, tossing a few back, and Brendan says, "Liam's cock is like the Starship *Enterprise*, boldly going where no man has gone before. A good two inches past Paulie, anyway, what I hear."

"Jesus, Brendan," Danny says.

Because Frankie Vecchio hears it. Frankie's a soldier in the Moretti crew; he's sitting at the next table with a couple of his guys, hears it and looks over. "You'll keep your fucking mouth shut if you know what's good for you."

Yeah, well, Brendan Handrigan never knew what was good for him—if he had, he might have graduated high school, or gone into the navy or something. Now he makes some lame response about it being a free country, but finishes his drink and leaves the bar.

"You should tell your friend there to button his lip," Frankie V tells Danny.

"He don't mean no harm," Danny says. It was a stupid joke, the kind guys make to each other a dozen times a day. Back in the good times, before the clambake, they'd laugh about it. But that was before, and now feelings are raw, and Liam has stolen Paulie's woman, and it isn't funny.

Frankie V can't freakin' *wait* to find Paulie and tell him—he goes hustling over to the American Vending Machine office, an old two-story white building on Atwells Avenue that doubles as the Moretti family base and a social club, and tattles like a girl.

Paulie goes predictably apeshit.

"We gotta do something about this," he says to his brother. Liam Murphy groping his girl at a party is one thing. Taking her away is another—and now the whole town is clowning him? A dipshit like Brendan Handrigan thinks it's okay to run his mouth? "I mean, where's it going to end, Peter?"

Peter gets it. People start to disrespect you in one area of your life, it leaks into others. Pretty soon they don't want to make payments, they don't think they need to do what they're told, they think maybe they can step into your spot. With the move up Peter wants to make, he can't let his little brother look like a douchebag. He has other reasons, too. Peter is a little bit of a philosopher—he believes that no problem comes without an opportunity. "What do you want to do?"

"You know what I want to do."

But Pasco Ferri tells them no.

Standing in the little kitchen area, he stirs the chowder that's been simmering on the stove since early morning. Real Rhode Island chowder, with clear broth, not that milky baby puke they throw at you up in Boston. He turns and looks deliberately at Paulie Moretti. "If you hit John Murphy's son we'll be in a war that won't end until we kill every mick in Rhode Island."

"Okay with me," Paulie says.

"Is that right?" Pasco asks. "It's okay with you some of our own people get killed in the process? Our businesses are disrupted? Okay with you we lose cops and politicians when we start littering the state with bodies? This *stronza* is worth all that? Some joke about your little *pesce* is worth all that?"

It isn't, Pasco thinks as he turns his eyes to Peter. But the Murphy-controlled docks are, aren't they, Peter?

To you, though. Not to me.

I've fought my wars.

Paulie says, "If my father was in charge—"

"But he isn't," Pasco says. "If you want to go to the ACI and ask him what you should do, be my guest—he's going to tell you the same thing: you can't clip Liam Murphy over this."

"They disrespected us," Peter says. "We can't just do nothing."

"Did I say do nothing?" Pasco asks.

He sips the chowder, then adds a little pepper. The doctor has told him no pepper, but what do doctors really know?

NINE

DANNY FINISHES HIS CHOP SUEY and wipes up the gravy with bread. The old Chinese joints, they still serve slices of white bread with the chop suey because their mostly *gweilo* customers don't want to waste good gravy.

Brendan is doing the same thing.

The two of them came to get the three-dollar lunch special before going to visit this deadbeat over on Hope Street. The irony isn't lost on Danny that a degenerate gambler lives on Hope Street.

Where the hell else would he live?

"Let's go do this," Brendan says.

Danny nods. Ain't neither of them too happy about it. It's never fun, going to break a guy down. He wipes his lips on the paper napkin, gets up, pushes back his chair and follows Brendan onto Eddy Street. At first he thinks it's tomato sauce on his shirt, but he remembers he had Chinese, not Italian, then he sees Brendan crumple to the sidewalk.

"Big-mouth motherfucker," Paulie says, and he shoots Brendan two more times in the stomach. Then he steps back into a car and Frankie V drives him away.

Danny can't fucking believe it's happening—he's never seen anyone shot before. Brendan is crying, trying to hold himself inside himself.

"God, Danny, help me. Jesus."

He bleeds out, right there in front of Danny, right there on Eddy Street in the clichéd broad daylight. Everybody sees everything and nobody sees nothing.

That's what John Murphy tells Danny that night in the back room of the Glocca Morra pub in Dogtown.

It's your classic Irish American joint, done in dark wood with a few tables and deep booths. The tricolor flag on the wall, Irish music in the jukebox, faded photos of Republican martyrs on the wall. Posters reminding you not to forget the men behind the wire. You go in there to be Irish, Danny thinks, as if you're not already, as if you can get away from it anywhere anyway.

Saturday nights they have live music—some musicians from Ireland or some Americans who just *think* they are—fiddles and tin whistles and banjos and guitars and it's a little too "come all ye" for Danny's taste. The kitchen serves up lamb stew and shepherd's pie, fish-and-chips and a decent burger, and you often have three generations in the place at the same time.

Nostalgic, Danny thinks, for a life we never led.

But the Gloc has been the headquarters of the Irish mob since the turn of the century, and it isn't going to change, even though Dogtown is dying. Fewer of the Irish, the Jews, the Chinese; more Blacks, Puerto Ricans, Dominicans. In a way it's a good thing, because more of the Irish have moved to the better parts of the city, or the suburbs. They left the docks and the factories to become doctors and lawyers and businessmen.

The old men, they hold on because the neighborhood is like an old chair they've grown used to. They're sitting in the back room now, the inner sanctum where John Murphy holds court, him and his cronies, sipping their whiskey and plotting. Conspiracies that go nowhere, Danny thinks, dreams that are stillborn.

John Murphy is the king of an empire that died a long time ago.

The light of a long-dead star.

The old men crouch around that booth like leprechauns and advise that they have no choice now, there is no gray area now, this time they have to hit back.

Pat agrees.

His dad doesn't.

"That's what Moretti *wants* us to do," John says. He taps the tips of his fingers against the side of his head. "Use your brains. Do you really think that Peter gives a damn about your brother stealing Paulie's girlfriend? All he cares about is money—he'd sell his sisters to a Chinese cathouse if he thought there was a dollar in it. Your idiot brother just gave him an excuse, is all, for a provocation."

"What do you mean?" Pat asks his father.

"As long as Pasco is the boss," John says, "we'll have peace. Unless you do something stupid, that is. But Pasco is moving on soon, and the Morettis are just looking for an excuse to start a war. You want to hand that to them, wrapped up in a pretty bow, do you?"

"They want the docks," Bernie Hughes pipes up.

Tall, skinny, saturnine—hair as white and wispy as the cotton in an aspirin bottle—Bernie is an accountant, John's money man, Marty's before that. He sees nothing but the bottom line. "Peter wants to move up into Pasco's empty chair, but to do that he needs to show he can be a big earner, make everybody a lot of money. But he's maxed out on his own businesses—the vending machines, the protection, the gambling, the drugs—and needs a fresh source of income. That would be *our* source of income, Pat."

"That Peter is smart," John says. "And Chris Palumbo is smarter. If we give them a war, they'll take the docks. We can't stop them. They have too many men and too much money. They'd have done it already—it's only Pasco holding them back. If we answer for Handrigan, Pasco will have no choice but to bring his entire family against us. He'll bring in Boston, if he has to, and Hartford. Maybe even New York."

"So we have to just take this?" Pat says.

Bernie Hughes says what John doesn't want to. "Look, we all know it should have been Liam who got shot. Pasco Ferri stayed Paulie's hand from that, but had to give him something, so they let him do Handrigan. It can end there."

"Fuck that," Danny says. "I'm telling the cops what I saw."

Brendan's blood is still spattered on his shirt.

"That's not our way," John says.

"Fuck that *omerta* bullshit," Danny says. "I don't owe those wops nothing."

"What do you owe us?" John asks.

The question hangs there.

Finally Pat says, "You're family, Danny."

"Am I?" Danny asks.

"How many times have you broken bread at my table?" John asks. "How many times did I put food in your mouth when your own father—"

"Enough, Dad," Pat says.

"I gave you my daughter, for Chrissakes!" John thunders. "My daughter!"

And this is the first time, Danny thinks, the first time you've brought me into the back room to sit with the men, with the family.

But he don't say that.

•   •   •

THAT NIGHT, TWO Providence homicide detectives bring Danny into the interrogation room. It stinks of cigarette smoke and fear. They sit him down at the table and start in.

"You were with Handrigan when he got shot," O'Neill says. He's your classic veteran Irish cop—broad face, nose splintered with red veins, cheeks going to fat, dead eyes.

"Yeah."

"Who shot him?"

"Didn't see."

"Shit," Viola says. "You got his blood all over you, I heard."

Viola's the younger partner—thinner, darker, black hair slicked straight back, a nose like a ferret.

"Didn't see anything," Danny says.

Danny knows they're just going through the motions, and the last thing in the world they want is for him to speak the name Paulie Moretti.

The fix is in.

They do the dance for an hour and then kick him out.

Danny goes home, Terri is waiting.

"What did you tell them?" she asks.

He looks at her like she's a total fucking idiot. She's John Murphy's daughter, she knows what he told them.

TEN

JOHN MURPHY DRIVES DOWN TO the shore and meets Pasco in the parking lot of Stop & Shop. He gets out of his own car and slides into Pasco's.

"It breaks my heart," Pasco says, "that this started at my party."

"The young are hotheaded."

"They think with their dicks," Pasco says. "Hey, were we any different?"

Murphy laughs. "No."

"I'm sorry about Liam," Pasco says. "If they had come to me first . . ."

Pasco is fed up with all this. What he wants to do in his old age is sit on the beach, dig quahogs, catch crabs, take siestas, play with his grandkids. He's made his money, made his bones, now he wants life in the sunshine. Spend summers at his beach house, a few weeks in January and February down in Pompano.

"You won't respond to this last thing?" Pasco asks.

"It's over as far as we're concerned," John says. A good deal for him—poor, dumb, insignificant Brendan Handrigan takes the bullet in place of his son. "But what about the Moretti brothers? Are they ready to let this go?"

Pasco says, "It would help if Liam would stop seeing that woman."

"I'll talk to him."

DANNY IS THERE for the talk. After Sunday roast beef at the Murphys'. They're out on the lawn, him and Pat and Liam and the old man, having a couple beers while the women clean up, and Murphy says, "This girl, she's out of your life."

"Says who?" Liam asks. "The Morettis?"

"Among other people."

"Who?" Liam asks, an edge coming into his voice. "Pasco Ferri? What the fuck."

"Watch your mouth."

"They tell us who we can love now?" Liam asks. "Who we can't? Tell you what, Dad, why don't we just pull down our pants and let them fuck us in the ass?"

"In your mother's house, on a Sunday."

"There are thousands of women out there," Pat argues. "Why her?"

"I love her."

"More than your own family?" Pat asks.

"Love someone else," Murphy says. "She's not for you."

"I *love* her, Dad."

Pat grabs him by the collar and shoves him against the old oak tree. "You selfish prick. We're going to put Brendan Handrigan in the ground and all you think about is yourself."

"Let him go, Pat," Murphy orders.

Pat releases his grip.

"She's out of your life, Liam," Murphy says. "End of story."

Looking at Liam's face, Danny wonders.

THE FUNERAL IS wicked sad.

Brendan didn't have a lot of friends, no wife, no girl. His father died when Brendan was, what, twelve, so there's just two sisters and the mother. The whole Murphy clan and associates show up, though. Murphy didn't have to tell them, either.

Respect is respect.

But Liam isn't there.

"Where the hell is my brother?" Terri whispers to Danny as they walk down the aisle, slide into the pew to kneel.

"He'll come," Danny says. But he isn't so sure. Liam's probably ashamed to show his face, knows that this is partly his fault. And maybe it's best he don't, maybe better for Brendan's family.

The mother, she comes up to Danny on the church steps after the mass, her red face twisted with grief.

"You didn't see nothin', Danny Ryan?" she asks. "You didn't see *nothin'*?"

Danny don't know what to say.

She turns away from him, and her daughters lead her to the car for the ride out to the cemetery.

"It's okay," Terri says.

"No, it's not," Danny answers.

They drive out to Swan Point for the burial.

Stand around the graveside in their black suits and dresses—like crows, Danny thinks—listening to the priest drone on.

Then the bagpipe starts in.

•   •   •

THEY WAKE BRENDAN at the Glocca Morra.

Brendan's mother is resentful as hell at the Murphys, but not so resentful she don't let them lay out the spread. What's she going to do? She don't have any money, and it's the least the Murphys could do, after her son took a bullet for theirs.

So there's a spread laid out, open bar, of course, and people stand around trying to think of good things to say about Brendan until the liquor kicks in, and the food, and it winds down into just another party.

Then Liam walks in.

With Pam.

Classic in-your-face, fuck-the-world, I-do-what-I-want Liam Murphy.

"You believe this?" Jimmy Mac asks.

"He's a pisser," Danny says.

Cassie, she's wryly amused. Watches this scene unfold and says, "Oh, this is going to be good."

The whole place gets quiet as Liam leads Pam to a table, holds out a chair for her and then sits down. He looks like he's getting off on the drama, but Pam doesn't—she looks damned uncomfortable. As well she should, Danny thinks, with Brendan Handrigan just laid into the ground.

Up at the bar, Sheila Murphy's jaw gapes like it's broken, then she swivels on her stool and turns her back.

Pam visibly flinches. Leans over and whispers something to Liam, who shakes his head, then gets up and walks over to the bar to order. Stands right next to Pat and Sheila.

"Pat, Sheila," he says. But his eyes are like, *You got anything to say?* He orders a Walker Black for himself and a glass of white wine for Pam, waits while Bobby the bartender pours the drinks and then he walks back to his table with this fuck-you smile on his face. He sets the glass of wine in front of Pam, sits back down, and then looks around the room to see if anyone wants to challenge him.

No one does.

Which, Danny knows, isn't going to work for Liam.

So Liam stands up, taps on his glass for attention, and announces, "I just want everyone here to know that Pam and I went to Las Vegas and got married. So, everyone—raise a glass to Mr. and Mrs. Liam Murphy."

"Jesus," Danny murmurs.

"Amazing," says Cassie.

Terri shakes her head.

Bobby walks out from behind the bar and scoots into the back room.

"Now the shit's going to hit," Jimmy Mac observes.

"Truly."

The door to the back room opens and John Murphy comes out, Pat right behind him.

"Showtime," Cassie says.

Danny's waiting for Murphy to ask his son to step into the back for a private word, and then for Liam to come back and take Pam out of there, but that's not what happens. What happens is Murphy leans over, kisses Pam on the cheek, and says, "Welcome to the family."

"Jesus shit," Cassie says.

Pat comes over and sits next to Danny.

"Pat, what the hell?" Danny asks.

Pat shrugs.

Old Man Murphy reaches over and takes Pam's hand.

"This is going to end badly," Cassie says.

Danny thinks it's one of her cynical jokes but then turns and sees that her eyes aren't laughing, they're serious.

Serious and sad.

Like she sees something the rest of them don't.

ELEVEN

PAM MURPHY (NÉE DAVIES) NEVER thought she'd honeymoon in a run-down house in the country. Then again, she never thought she'd marry an Irish guy from Providence, Rhode Island.

Greenwich, Connecticut, is only 150 miles from Providence, but it might as well be on the other side of the world. A leafy, old-money, high-WASP bedroom community of New York, Greenwich couldn't be more different from blue-collar, Irish-Italian Providence, and Pam couldn't have had an upbringing more different from her husband Liam Murphy's.

Her father was a stockbroker, not a gangster. He took the train into the city every weekday morning, was home for 6:30 cocktails and 7:15 dinner every night. Her mother was a Connecticut matron, a genuine beauty often described by admiring friends as "swanlike" who spent her days on charitable committees, gardening clubs, Daughters of the American Revolution activities, and vodka tonics.

Pam's big brothers, Bradley and Patton, lettered in lacrosse and hockey at their private boarding schools, carefully made gentlemen's

B's and nothing higher, sailed Long Island Sound, and were protective of their little sister.

Not that she required much protection, not from boys, anyway.

She wasn't an especially pretty child. Going into middle school, the kindest description of her was "plain." If her mother was, indeed, a swan, Pam was the ugly duckling, and she felt her mother's poorly hidden disappointment keenly.

Pam resisted all efforts to pretty her up—the makeup, the dresses, the dance lessons to improve her grace and posture—preferring to stay in her room and read. After Montessori elementary school, she was shipped off to Miss Porter's School in Farmington, whose alumnae included—in addition to her mother—Barbara Hutton, Gloria Vanderbilt, and Jackie Kennedy Onassis.

She certainly wasn't the richest girl there, nor the poorest, but somewhere in the lower middle. The cruelty of that age gifted her with acne and the inevitable comparisons to a pizza. The sadism of schoolgirls knows no bounds—they attacked her for her complexion, her awkwardness, her lack of interest in boys. Word was joyfully passed that she was a lesbian, that she harbored secret crushes on several of the prettier girls, who had, of course, summarily spurned her.

"If I was going to the Y," one of her alleged targets said, sticking her tongue between her index and middle fingers, "I'd go to a much prettier Y."

Her freshman year, she fled home almost every weekend, holed up in her room, variously crying, reading her books, and dreading Sunday nights, when her parents would drive her back to Farmington, lecturing all the while on the importance of making friends and participating in the social life of the school.

Pam didn't tell them about the taunts.

She was too ashamed.

Pam thought about running away from school, running away from home, killing herself.

Something happened between Pam's sophomore and junior years. She blossomed.

The family had a summer home in Watch Hill, Rhode Island, twenty-five minutes but still a world away from Goshen, and Pam got up one morning ready for another day of hiding beneath a sun bonnet at the beach club.

It would be an exaggeration to say that it happened overnight, but it seemed to have happened overnight. Looking into the mirror to scrub her face, she saw skin that was almost clear, as if some compassionate goddess had come during the night and stripped her of her shame.

The summer seemed to do the rest. Over the next few weeks, the sun turned her skin a clear tan, baked her body into fine marble, bleached her "mousy" hair to a golden blond, her eyes an oceanic blue.

One rainy morning that wasn't a beach day, Pam asked her mother if they could go shopping.

Not for books—for clothes.

Janet Davies was ecstatic—she finally had a daughter.

They went shopping, first in Watch Hill, then over in Newport, later on Fifth Avenue. Davies complained about the credit card bills but was secretly pleased, happy for both his wife and daughter.

It would be easier now.

It wasn't.

What had been a mother's pity became a mother's jealousy.

As Pam transformed into a young woman of exceptional loveliness, friends, family, even people sitting at tables next to theirs in restaurants started to remark on Pam's beauty and charm. The swan began to see the wrinkles in her own elegant neck and compare them unfavorably to her cygnet's alabaster skin.

The mother withdrew.

Not physically, Janet was always there *physically*, but she removed herself emotionally. Had she been asked, she would have denied it indignantly. She probably didn't realize it herself—mirrors reveal so little—but she left her daughter to undergo and try to comprehend the unanticipated metamorphosis.

Pam learned the wrong lesson: that if she was suddenly, for the first time in her life, valued for her beauty, her beauty was her only value.

So when the best-looking boy at Hotchkiss spotted her at a mixer and moved in fast, Pam was as defenseless as an orphaned fawn and found herself in a Farmington motel room looking over his shoulder at a cheap painting of a sailboat.

The funny thing was, Trey Sherburne actually fell in love with her.

What eighteen-year-old man-boy wouldn't have?

Robert Spencer Sherburne III wasn't as much a predator as he was a romantic, and in the morning he wanted to drive to New Hampshire, where for some reason he thought he could marry a sixteen-year-old girl he didn't yet know was pregnant.

Pam was ready to go, she was in love.

They didn't make it to New Hampshire; they didn't even make it to the parking lot. Pam's two brothers, acting on tips from friends, tracked them to the motel in the morning, beat the shit out of Trey, and hauled their sister back to Greenwich to face the collective family shame.

At first Dad wanted to prosecute Trey for statutory rape, but Mom wanted to spare her daughter the public disgrace ("our names in the newspapers, darling"). The Davieses and the Sherburnes worked it out as their families had been doing since the freaking *Mayflower*—quietly and discreetly. The Davieses didn't press rape charges against Trey, the Sherburnes didn't have the brothers charged with aggravated assault, Trey did a gap year on a service project in Tanzania, and Pam went off to New Mexico for a discreet abortion.

Pam came back to finish Miss Porter's, then went to Trinity College, where she majored in business administration with a minor in classics and sorority parties. If she ever thought of Trey or their unborn child, it was neither deeply nor for long; she had learned from her mother the fine art of burying a warm heart under a glacial field of ice.

After college, she got a job with a high-end real estate firm in Westport and did very well, spending weekends at the family house in Watch Hill.

Watch Hill is either New England money so old it needs a walker to circulate, or "new" New York money, meaning the families have owned homes there for less than two hundred years. Westerly is a granite quarry town settled by Italian immigrant stonemasons who made beautiful churches and big Sunday dinners.

In Watch Hill, money works for people, and in Westerly, people work for money. If people in Watch Hill go to Westerly, it's usually for pizza, but Pam went slumming there one night at a local bar, where Paulie Moretti started flirting with her because why not take a shot?

Pam flirted back because, well . . .

. . . other than an actual Black guy or a Puerto Rican, who could she date that would piss her parents off more than an Italian? Even a Jewish guy would have been preferable, and sleeping with Paulie Moretti was Pam's revolt against her utter WASPishness.

Not that she ever brought him home to meet Mom and Dad— that would have been a total disaster. Her revolt was secret, satisfying only to herself, a fling, an adventure before settling down with Donald or Roger or Tad or whoever.

So when Paulie invited her to a clambake not in Watch Hill but in the more blue-collar reaches of Goshen, she was glad to go, because by this time she had figured out that he was actually in the Mafia, which added a frisson of danger.

Then Liam Murphy grabbed her breast, then Paulie showed what a Mafia guy is really like, then she went to the hospital to apologize and . . .

. . . there was the Irish version of Trey.

The best-looking boy in the mob.

Charming.

Hurt.

Vulnerable.

She felt the ice melting.

Next thing she knew, she was in a Las Vegas wedding chapel marrying Liam Murphy, without the least idea of the ramifications.

Now, tucked away in a crappy "safe house" ten miles from anything, with a husband who a lot of people want to kill and who responds to it by drinking half the day and all night, she's starting to learn.

TWELVE

THE PRISON SITS OFF ROUTE 95, Rhode Island's central thorough-
fare, like a constant reminder of what can happen to you if you
slip on the banana peel. You can't go from Warwick to Cranston to
Providence without seeing it, and maybe that's the idea.

It's old, built in 1878—the central section is gray stone with a tin
cupola, the newer side buildings are red brick, a high fence topped
with coils of barbed wire surrounds the complex.

When Danny was in elementary school, they used to take the kids
on field trips to the ACI to scare the shit out of them, but it usually
backfired because a lot of the kids in Danny's school used the occasion
to visit relatives.

Now the Moretti brothers sit across a table from their father in the
visiting room at the ACI. Jacky Moretti's hair is still thick but it's gone
white in the joint. He's still a strong man, though, neck like a bull's,
big sloping shoulders. No one is going to mess with him in here, even
if he wasn't connected.

Most people in there could tell you Jacky Moretti stories.

How he was all of nineteen when he first got wet, on a two-bit booster who didn't want to pay his street tax. How he did his first stretch on a grand theft auto and didn't give up no one—not his partners, not the chop shop, not nobody. How he got made by taking out two guys from New Haven who thought eastern Connecticut should belong to them and not Pasco Ferri.

Or how about the degenerate gambler who thought Jacky was an asshole he didn't have to pay, and Jacky ripped him out of the lobby of the jai alai fronton in Newport, took him out into the parking lot, opened his car door, and asked him which hand he used to take out his wallet.

"What?" the terrified guy asked.

"When you go to buy a jai alai ticket, which hand do you use to take out your wallet?"

"My right."

Jacky made him stick his right hand into the car door and then kicked it shut. Then, with the guy's hand still in the door, he drove the car around the parking lot.

After that, Jacky was an up-and-comer, a meat-eater, an earner who got his own crew, put more money on the street, did bank jobs and truck hijackings.

But mostly they tell the story about Jacky and Rocky Ferraro.

Pasco had put out a ban on selling or using heroin because it brought down so much heat from the feds. Rocky Ferraro, one of Jacky's crew, ignored it on both counts, first selling to the moolies in South Providence and then starting to use his own product.

It was a problem, and Jacky said he'd take care of it.

He and one of his guys picked Rocky up one night to go to a Reds hockey game, except they never made it there. Jacky pulled over, then pulled his gun, stuck it in Rocky's mouth, and pulled the trigger several times.

What made the story extraordinary was that Rocky was Jacky's half brother.

Which made the next Thanksgiving dinner, well, *awkward*.

And also apparently really offended both the judge and the jury when—*six years* later—Jacky's guy flipped and put him in the jackpot for the murder.

"He embarrassed the family," Jacky said at his sentencing hearing.

"So you killed your own brother," the judge said.

"*Half* brother," Jacky said. "What, maybe I should have only half killed him?"

The judge maxed him out.

Even then Jacky had a chance to save himself. The feds offered him the complete package—immunity, the program, the whole nine yards—to go rat on Pasco Ferri, but Jacky told them they could line up and suck his dick. So now a series of punks perform that service for him as he resides in the North Wing of the old stone house, plays cards, and cooks pasta for the guys on Sundays.

Now the guard stands far off and keeps his back turned. Ain't supposed to, but there's no CO in Rhode Island dumb enough to crowd the Morettis on visiting day. The guards have to live in the state, they have brothers and cousins out there, and a very nice contribution gets made every year into the widows and orphans fund.

Jacky sucks on his cigarette. He's got emphysema, but he knows he ain't ever coming out of this place anyway, so what the fuck. He looks at Paulie. "You ain't the only guy ever got dumped. Sack up, get a new girl, move on."

"They're rubbing it in our faces," Peter says. "It's deliberate disrespect."

"What does Pasco say?" Jacky asks.

"Fuck Pasco," Paulie says.

"You'll have a hard time repeating that with dirt in your mouth," says Jacky. There are things you don't say. There are things you don't even *think*.

They sit quiet for a few seconds.

"It should be you," Peter says. "On top."

Jacky smiles. "I'm in here, Pasco is out there, that's the way it breaks sometimes. What, you want me to talk to him?"

"Yes," Paulie says.

"No," Jacky answers. "He's the boss, he's made his ruling, that's it."

"He wants us to sit down with the Irish," Paulie says.

"Then sit down," Jacky says. "You're on the goal line, don't cough the ball up. Pasco retires to Florida, then you do what you want. String the Murphys up by their skinny Irish dicks; Pasco's more concerned about his pinochle hand, bocce ball, whatever. But you go against him *now*, he has you clipped, and I give my blessing."

"On your own sons," Peter says, apparently forgetting his father's history.

"You have love for your family," Jacky says, "and you have love for this thing. They're two different loves. But, yes, your love for this thing comes first."

Old-school, their old man, Peter thinks.

Old freaking school.

They agree to the sit-down.

THIRTEEN

PASCO SETS THE LOCATION AT the last minute.

Then changes it.

Danny understands that it's SOP to prevent either side from setting up an ambush, but the reality is, at the end of the day, Pasco Ferri
is Italian. If he decides he has to yield to the Morettis and let them do
something, the Dogtown Irish are walking into it.

They're just trusting Pasco.

"Can we?" Pat asks.

Danny shrugs. A lot of clambakes together. Drinks and laughs.
His old man says they can.

"Pasco Ferri is a man of his word," Marty says. "If he says we're
safe, we're safe."

Marty has been invited to the meeting at Pasco's insistence. A
reminder, Danny guesses, that it was Pasco and Marty who put together the Irish-Italian peace that has lasted for a generation, and that
breaking the alliance is an affront to both of them.

Marty dresses carefully for the meeting, fussing with Danny

about getting his tie straight, a real pain in the ass. The old man's last glory day, Danny thinks. He's important again.

They set the meeting for the Harbor Inn, a hotel and restaurant down in Gilead, just across the channel from Dave's Dock. The restaurant has been closed to the public at four o'clock for the "private party."

Danny and Ned Egan walk Marty to the front of the restaurant. Jimmy Mac slides out from the driver's seat and stands there looking nervous, his pistol bulging under his sport coat.

The Murphys pull up behind them. Pat's driving, his dad next to him, Liam slumped in the back seat, like he'd rather be anywhere else in the world. Can't blame him for that, Danny thinks.

Pasco comes out, flanked by two of his guys. Vito Salerno, his longtime consigliere, and Tito Cruz, a half-Sicilian, half–Puerto Rican who has done a lot of wet work for the family over the years. Serious people, a clear signal that Pasco isn't going to put up with any bullshit here.

A good thing, Danny thinks.

Pasco walks over to him. "All hardware stays in the cars, Danny."

Danny sees the flicker of alarm in Ned Egan's eyes. Pasco sees it, too, and adds, "Same with the Morettis."

Danny walks back to the car and puts his gun in the console. Jimmy Mac does the same, looking almost relieved. It takes Ned a few seconds to adjust to the idea, but then he steps over and lays his .45 on the front passenger seat.

"I'll stay with the car," Jimmy says.

THE BACK ROOM of the restaurant has a fishing theme: buoys and nets across the wall, a pretty bad painting of the harbor, some photographs of fishing boats. A long table has been set up in the center of the room with some plastic coffee carafes, pitchers of water, cups and glasses. Danny understands that Pasco is saying this is business, and business that he's annoyed with, so there's no expensive dinner and wine. Just work it out, get it over with.

Fine with Danny. If this goes well, he's going to take the old man over to the other side to Dave's for some good fish-and-chips. If it goes bad, well, nobody's going to have an appetite.

Peter and Paul Moretti sit on one side with Sal Antonucci and Chris Palumbo beside them. None of them look up as the Murphy party comes into the room and sits down across the table; they just stare into the water pitchers like there's some pretty tropical fish in them or something.

Old Man Murphy takes the chair nearest the head of the table, with Pat beside him. Then Liam, then Danny, then Marty. Ned Egan stands right inside the door. Pasco comes in, sits down at the other head. Vito and Cruz close the door and then take chairs in the corner.

Pasco pours himself a glass of water, takes a drink, and begins. "There's been a tear in the fabric of our association. I've called this meeting to mend that tear. Who would like to speak first?"

Danny's surprised when Marty lifts his hand. Proud of the old man when he says, "First things first. One of our people has been killed. There needs to be recompense."

Pasco looks at Peter.

"He had no family, right, this Handrigan kid?" Peter asks. "No wife, kids?"

"A mother," Marty says.

Peter turns from the table and leans over as Chris whispers in his ear. Then he turns back and says, "She has a candy store? Magazines, papers, that sort of thing? We have machines in it?"

"That's right," Marty says.

"She keeps the full take from our machines," Peter says. "We'll give up our cut. Okay. We done with that?"

"We're done," Marty answers.

Just like that, Danny thinks. An item of business. A few more quarters from some vending machines, and Brendan is forgotten.

"Good," Pasco says. "Next?"

"My brother has been insulted," Peter says, looking at Liam. "Our family has been insulted."

Liam smirks like a kid and says, like it's rehearsed, "I had too much to drink. My behavior was unacceptable. I apologize."

"You still drunk now?" Paulie asks.

"Why, you want her back?" Liam grins at him.

"No, you can keep your sloppy seconds."

The grin comes off Liam's face and he gets to his feet. "That's my wife you're talking about."

"Sit down," Pat says.

"He—"

"Sit down."

Liam sits down.

"You've had an apology," Pasco says to the Morettis, prompting them.

"We're not apologizing for the beating," Peter answers. "He had it coming. Also, *we* need recompense for the insult."

"I think beating him half to death was sufficient 'recompense,'" John Murphy says.

"I don't," Peter answers.

"What do you want?" Pasco asks.

"Three jobs on the docks," Peter says.

Murphy looks to Pasco. "Times are hard. I don't have three no-shows on the docks right now."

"You have city jobs in the Tenth Ward," Chris says.

"Those are Irish," says Pat.

Chris looks at John. "Should I be talking to *him* now?"

"Should I be talking to *you*?" John answers.

Pasco asks, "Is this something you think you could do, John?"

Murphy shakes his head, then lays his chin on his chest, looks down and thinks a little. "I could do one job in the Tenth. Not three."

Peter smiles. "Split the difference—two."

"I don't have two," Murphy says. "I have the Blacks now, you know, to take care of. It keeps them quiet."

Peter and Chris huddle again. What the hell, Danny thinks, Pete can't take a piss unless Chris holds his dick for him? It's a sign of weakness, something to be noted for the future. If you want to get into Peter's ear, you talk to Chris.

Peter comes back and says, "One city job, one dock job."

Murphy looks at Liam, like *See what your dick costs us?* Then he says, "If that will keep the peace, fine. Yes."

"Peter?" Pasco asks.

"We're satisfied."

Over, Danny thinks. Done. Peace in our time and all that happy bullshit. Until Paulie has to open his stupid trap.

"I got one question," Paulie says. "Liam, does she still like it up the ass?"

Liam gets back on his feet. Vito grabs Paul as Tito comes around the table and stands behind Liam, ready to grab him.

"That was way over the line!" Pat says.

"He was out of line," Peter agrees.

But Paulie yells at Liam, "What are you going to do about it?! Huh, pussy, what are you going to do?!"

"You're a brave motherfucker when you got guys with you," Liam says. "Let's see you run your mouth when you're by yourself."

"You got it."

"Outside. Right now."

"Let's go."

Pat says, "Liam, you're in no condition to—"

"Fuck that," Liam says.

"This is stupid," Danny appeals to Pasco.

But Paulie and Liam are already heading for the door, and the rest follow. Danny's way in back, he has his old man's elbow, and by the time he gets outside Liam and Paulie are in the parking lot, fists up, and then Danny hears the shot and Paulie drops. He rolls on the gravel, holding his leg, blood leaking out from between his fingers.

Tito has his gun out, looking toward the boats docked across the channel, because that's where the shot came from.

Peter kneels beside his brother. Liam heads to his car, Pat striding behind him in confusion. Danny grabs his father tighter by the elbow and with Ned's help hustles him toward their car. Jimmy's already pulling it up to them.

"Hit it," Danny says to Jimmy. "Get the fuck out of here."

Thinking, Please, God, don't let Paulie die.

FOURTEEN

WHAT DID YOU DO?!" Pat screams at his brother. He grabs him by the front of the shirt and shakes him. *"What the hell did you do?!"*

The bedroom door is open and Danny can see Pam sitting on the bed, watching the scene in the living room. He starts to get up and shut the door, then thinks, Fuck it—let her see the man she chose.

"Who was the shooter?" Pat asks.

Liam shakes his head. Pat slaps him hard across the face. Danny sees Pam flinch as she watches.

But she watches.

Liam says, "Mickey Shields."

"Who?"

Danny don't recognize the name, either.

"He's from the other side," Liam says.

"Fuck."

Danny blows a sigh. Liam is always messing around with this

Irish shit, now he brought someone over to do a job?! Jesus Christ, Liam. You knew you couldn't get anyone in New England to do this, so you went to the hard men in the North?

"What did you pay him?" Pat asks.

"I told them maybe we could help them out with some guns or something."

Danny feels like his head is going to blow off. On top of all the shit that's going to come down on us now, Liam makes promises to the freakin' IRA?! About *guns*? Which will bring heat from the FBI? So if the Italians don't kill us, we spend the rest of our lives in a federal lockup?

"Do you know what you've done?" Pat asks his brother. "Liam, do you know what you've done to us?"

Danny glances through the open door at Pam.

She knows.

TWO HOURS LATER, Danny and Jimmy sit in the basement of Jimmy's mom's house down on Friendship Street. She's out at her bingo night.

They're freaked.

Freaked fucking out.

The only good thing, the *only* good thing, is that Paulie Moretti is going to pull through. The bullet didn't strike the femoral artery or bone, but the peace is kaput, and Pasco Ferri has no choice now but to let the dogs loose. He's been personally insulted, shown up, and blood has been spilled. Now they're all in the shit, big time.

Danny does the odds in his head. They have ten, maybe fifteen guys who can be counted on in a fight; the Morettis have at least twice that number. The Irish have no resources outside Dogtown to call on; the Morettis can bring in shooters from other Mafia families. The Irish have a few councilmen from the Tenth and some of the police; the Morettis have the mayor, a handful of state legislators, and a bunch of cops, including two detectives from Homicide O'Neill and Viola.

The money battle is lopsided: the Irish have the longshoremen's union, the docks, and some small gambling and loan-sharking; the Morettis have the Teamsters, the construction unions, the vending machines, cigarettes and alcohol, major gambling, major money on the street, strip clubs and prostitution.

That's the problem with a war: you have the challenge of trying to stay alive and at the same time make a living. Hard, when you're being hunted, to go out and make your collections, or make a score, or even get back and forth from work. You need a bankroll, a war chest, to last you while you bunker up and fight it out, and not many of the Dogtown Irish—Danny included—have a lot in the savings account.

Jimmy stares at Danny.

"What do you want me to do?" Danny asks.

"Liam's a worthless little prick," Jimmy says. "You know it and I know it."

"He's my wife's *brother*, for Chrissakes," Danny says. "I've known him since he was a kid. I made him fucking peanut butter and banana sandwiches."

"Danny . . ."

"What."

"Do you know where he is?" Jimmy asks.

Danny nods.

"I'll come with you," Jimmy says.

Danny shakes his head. "No. I'll take care of it myself."

•   •   •

THEY HAVE LIAM stored all the way up in Lincoln, some old house out in the country, down the end of a dirt road.

Danny stops for some White Castles on the way up there.

He drives up to the house. Gets out of the car and knocks on the door. "Liam, it's me, Danny. I brought you some food."

He hears movement inside, then the door opens a crack. The safety chain is on, and Liam peeks through the opening, slides the chain off and lets him in.

The place is a dump. Old carpet, musty smell. Not what Liam's used to, Danny thinks, probably not what Pam expected when she married the prince. Liam sits back on an old sofa, watching TV. Danny hands him the white paper bag of burgers.

"Hey, thanks," Liam says.

"They're cold, but—"

"They're still good," Liam says. "You want one?"

"Wouldn't mind." Danny sits down on the couch. "What's on?"

"Some horror movie," Liam says. "Take your coat off and stay awhile."

"Where's Pam?" Danny asks.

"Zonked out in the bedroom," Liam says. "Valium."

Can he see it in my eyes? Danny wonders. Hear my heart pounding? Know I won't take my jacket off because a .38 is in the pocket? Probably not, Liam's too self-absorbed to notice anyone else's shit.

"You don't have, like, a Coke or something?" Danny asks. "Ginger ale?"

"Go in the kitchen and look," Liam says.

Danny gets up and goes into the kitchen, finds a Coke in the fridge, comes back into the living room and stands behind Liam, who seems absorbed with the horror movie.

This is the time, Danny thinks. Right now.

He grabs the gun inside his right jacket pocket and takes it out. Eases the hammer back, hopes that Liam don't hear the click.

He don't. He's devouring the fucking hamburger, laughing at the cheesy monster that's crossing the screen toward the little fake Japanese city. Not a care in the world, Liam. It's his fucking universe and the rest of us are just renting space.

Danny holds the gun low, behind the back of the couch where Liam can't see it if he turns around. "Hey, Liam?"

"Yeah?"

"You remember catechism?"

"How could I fucking forget?"

"Yeah, well, I was trying to remember the Act of Contrition. Jimmy and I had a bet and I couldn't remember it."

"Child's play," Liam says, his eyes not leaving the screen. "Oh my God, I am heartily sorry for having offended Thee—"

Do it now. To hell with his immortal soul, do it now.

"And I do detest all my sins—"

Danny lifts the pistol.

"Not because I fear hell, but because—"

Then he hears the toilet flush, the old plumbing whine.

Pam's awake.

Danny hears water running. She's washing her hands.

Jamming the gun back in his pocket, Danny says, "Hey, Liam, I better go."

"You just got here."

Pam comes in the room.

"I'm going to give you guys a little privacy," Danny says.

"Privacy is what we've got," Pam answers. "We got plenty of privacy, don't we, Liam?"

Danny goes back to his car.

He don't think he could have done it anyway.

DANNY DRIVES BACK to Dogtown, can only find a parking spot three blocks from the house, and has the heebie-jeebies as he walks.

This is what it's going to be like, he thinks, for the rest of my short fucking life. Looking over my shoulder, hearing sounds that ain't there, scared of what's around every corner.

He hears a car coming slowly up behind him and forces himself not to run. Jams his hands inside his jacket pocket and feels for the .38. Grips it hard, then lets himself have a glance over his shoulder.

It's a cop car.

Not a black-and-white, but an unmarked Crown Vic that the plainclothes guys use. It pulls up beside him and the front passenger window rolls down. Danny half expects a blast of bullets—his heart is in his freakin' throat and he feels like he might piss his pants, but O'Neill says, "Take it easy. While you're at it, take your hands out of your pockets for me, okay?"

Danny can see past him to where Viola sits behind the wheel.

"It's okay," O'Neill says. "Someone just wants a word with you."

Danny carefully takes his hands from his pockets. O'Neill gets out, pats him down and takes the piece from him. "I'll give it back after you have your conversation."

He opens the rear door and Danny gets in.

Peter Moretti sits there.

Danny tries to get out but the door is locked. The two cops stand out on the sidewalk and grab a smoke.

"I just finished visiting my brother in the hospital," Peter says.

"How's he doing?"

"He got a fucking bullet hole through his leg," Peter says, his temper flaring. He takes a breath and says, "But he's going to be okay."

"That's good."

"Fucking A, that's good," Peter says. "Listen, Danny, I wanted to have a word with you, tell you that we got no beef with the Ryans. We already know you had nothing to do with the disgraceful action that occurred this afternoon."

"Peter, the Murphys didn't—"

Peter holds up his hand. "Don't even bother. That train has left the station. There is no possibility of a peace with the Murphys, even if they dangle that little piece of shit motherfucker from the flagpole at the statehouse. What I came to tell you is the Ryan faction can sit this one out. The Murphys put you in a very difficult position; you have every right, on the basis of that, to opt out of this war."

Pasco made him come, Danny thinks, on his friendship with my old man. But it's also a smart move. Peter knows that if the "Ryan faction" sits on its hands, he's deprived the Murphys of me, Jimmy Mac, Ned Egan, and maybe a couple of other potential shooters. And Bernie Hughes, who was one of Marty's guys before the fall. He'll stick with the Ryans, and Peter knows that.

"What have the Murphys ever done for you?" Peter asks. "Hell, they took your old man's part of the business and they throw you some scraps from the table. Treat you like the redheaded stepchild."

That's all true, Danny thinks.

"I'm not asking you to go against them," Peter says. "I know you wouldn't do that and I respect you for it. But if you just sit this out, when it's over . . . and you know how it's going to end, you're not a stupid person . . . we'd be prepared to restore to you what is rightfully yours. Your father would get the respect he deserves; you would be the boss."

"Has Pasco—"

"He signed off on this, of course," Peter answers. "But you need to know that he's going down to Florida, he's really going to retire this time. I'm the new boss of the family. Paul will be my under-boss."

So Dogtown's done anyway, Danny thinks. With Pasco out of the way, the Morettis will take what they want and use this whole Liam mess as their excuse. The ship's going down, it's just a question if I want to go down with it.

Peter Moretti is tossing me a big life preserver.

"Don't give me your answer now," Peter says. "Think about it, get back to me. You can approach O'Neill or Viola there."

"Okay."

"But don't take too much time," Peter says. He nods to the cops outside and O'Neill opens the door. Danny starts to get out. Peter reaches over, touches his hand and says, "Danny, I want you to know that we have nothing but respect and affection for you and your father. Please give him my personal regards."

"Sure."

"Good night, Danny. I look forward to hearing from you."

"Good night."

Danny walks home, gets out of his clothes and slips into bed beside his wife.

She's warm under the blankets.

"I'm late," Terri murmurs.

Danny thinks she's half-asleep. "You mean *I'm* late."

"No," Terri says. "I'm late."

Must have been that night on the beach, she tells him, after Pasco Ferri's clambake.

PART TWO

City on Fire

Providence, Rhode Island
October 1986

Thus on the beachhead the Achaeans
armed . . . avid again for war,
And Trojans faced them on the rise of plain.

Homer
The Iliad
Book XX

FIFTEEN

THE PHONE WAKES HIM EARLY in the morning.

Danny rolls over and answers it.

"Hello?"

"Thank God." It's Pat. "Danny, get the hell out of there."

"What are you talking about?"

The Morettis hit and hit hard.

Three guys dead.

"Who?" Danny asks, his brain still a little cloudy.

"I'll run it down when you get here," Pat says. "Just get the fuck out."

"Jimmy?"

"He's my next call."

"I'll call him." Danny sits up, punches in Jimmy Mac's number.

"What is it?" Terri asks, waking, irritable.

"It's not good," Danny says. Feels like he can't breathe, like there's this heart-attack band around his chest as he listens to Jimmy's phone ring. Pick up the fucking phone, pick up the fucking phone, Jimmy . . .

"Danny? The fuck."

Danny tells him the news.

"Jesus Christ."

"Come heavy." Danny hangs up and punches in his father's number. Marty answers it on the first ring, says, "I'm still breathing, that's what you're wondering."

"Pat call you?"

"John."

"Ned with you?"

"Yeah."

"I'll call you when I know more."

Danny pulls on his jeans, a T-shirt, then straps on a shoulder holster with the .38 and puts a denim work shirt on over it. He goes downstairs, Terri's already in the kitchen. She's got the coffee going and has bacon in the pan for his eggs. Danny likes it crispy, almost burned. Doing the little things, keeping the routine, Danny knows it's her way of dealing with it.

"Just tell me," she says, not looking up from the stove. "Is it Liam?"

"I don't think so."

"Dad?" Her voice quavers.

"Pat would have said."

"Then who—"

"I don't know, Terri. I just know it's bad."

Wants to tell her that he's safe for the time being, that he has the choice of just opting out of this thing. But he hasn't decided what he's going to do yet, and don't know how to tell her anyway. "Go to your parents', take care of your mom."

The bacon starts to smoke. Terri takes it off and lays it on a folded paper towel on a plate, then cracks two eggs in the pan and fries them in the hot grease. Then she takes two slices of Wonder bread out of the bag and pops them into the toaster.

"What are we going to do?" she asks.

"About what?"

"We're gonna have a *baby*, Danny."

She has tears in her eyes. Unusual for Terri; she don't cry about a lot. Danny wraps his arms around her and she lays her head on his shoulder and cries.

"It's going to be all right, Terri," he says. "It's going to be all right."

"How, Danny?" she asks, straightening up and looking him in the eyes. "How's it going to be all right?"

"Let's just go," Danny says. "You, me, and the baby."

"Where?"

"California."

"California again," Terri says. "What is it with you and that place?"

"It's supposed to be nice."

"You don't just pick up and move," Terri says. "It takes money to relocate. You don't have a job there . . . and we need your health insurance."

She breaks away from him, goes back to the stove, flips the eggs and uses the spatula to break the yolks. Danny likes his eggs over hard with the yolk spread out.

"I'll get a job," he says. "With benefits."

"How?"

"Terri, quit *nagging* me, all right?!"

"Don't yell at me!"

"Well, don't yell at *me*!"

"Make your own fucking eggs. Jerk."

She walks out.

Danny turns the heat off on the stove. Decides he doesn't have time for bacon and eggs, so he pours himself a cup of coffee, milk and sugar, and takes it with him.

"Go to your parents'!" he yells.

He heads out the door.

Walks down to the Gloc.

Head on a swivel just in case the Morettis think they didn't get their answer quick enough.

Two unmarked police cars are parked out by the Gloc as Danny walks up. Good thing to know, he thinks, we still have a few cops left. The Morettis aren't going to hit the Gloc in daylight, not after last night, but it doesn't hurt to be cautious. He nods at the cops and goes in.

Bobby Bangs is behind the bar, making fresh pots of coffee. Jimmy Mac is already there, watching the door. He takes Danny by the elbow and says, "They want you in back."

"Yeah?"

"What they said."

Danny opens the door to the back room. They're gathered at the usual booth—John, Pat, and Bernie.

He don't see Liam.

"Thanks for coming, Danny," Pat says. He walks over, puts his arm around Danny and walks him to the booth.

Now, Danny thinks, I get a seat at the table.

Now.

John nods to him. A gesture of respect, acknowledgment. Danny thinks he looks suddenly old, and maybe he is, because it's clearly Pat who's running the meeting.

"You want something to fortify that cup?" Pat asks Danny.

"No, I'm okay."

"All right," Pat says. "Here it is and it's not good . . ."

Brian Young, Howie Moran, Kenny Meagher, all dead. Young and Moran shot from long range—single bullets to the head or heart. Meagher gunned down at close range coming out of an after-hours club.

No wonder John looks like an old man now.

Danny ain't feeling so young himself. Brian and Kenny—both friends, guys he went to school with or knew from the neighborhood. Parties, pickup hockey games, weddings.

Now it will be wakes and funerals.

"They must have been planning this for a long time," Pat is saying. "They knew habits, cars . . ."

Pat says, "It was Sal Antonucci."

"For the close stuff, maybe," Danny says. "The others? Long range? That ain't anyone on Sal's crew, even Peter and Paul's. They brought someone in."

"You thinking what I'm thinking?" Pat asks.

"Steve Giordo?"

Steve "the Sniper" Giordo supposedly got his nickname because he'd been a marksman in the army, but Danny thinks it was more from the fact that a sniper rifle is his weapon of choice.

Giordo is out of Hartford and takes jobs for both Boston and New York. Bad news on a couple of fronts—Giordo is very good, and Boston and New York would have to have given their nods for him to do a job in Providence.

It's a grim situation—Boston and New York backing the Morettis, Sal Antonucci and Steve Giordo out in front, and three of the guys who might have matched up against them are already dead.

It was well planned, Danny thinks.

So was Peter's move to try to take the Ryan faction out of the lineup. Even while he was talking to me, his soldiers were out killing people. Planned, timed, and coordinated—nothing he could have done in the space of time since the "peace" meeting. The Morettis were going to move anyway, use the peace to lull us to sleep, and then hit us.

Liam just jumped first.

And gave them the excuse.

Now Peter gets what he always wanted and he gets to be the aggrieved party, the injured innocent.

"Okay," Pat says. "We're down but we're not out. If we can get to Sal and Giordo, we're still in this thing."

Like it's a hockey game, Danny thinks.

Bernie Hughes speaks up. Blows on his cup of tea and says, "Sal is one thing, sooner or later he'll pop his head up and we can take it off. Giordo's another. The man never surfaces except to kill, and that, briefly. He's a world-class professional and we don't have anyone to match him."

"How about Ned Egan?" John asks Danny. "Would your dad give us the loan of him?"

"Ned likes close-in work," Danny says. "Ned is your man for walking up to someone and popping him in the chest, but he's no sniper."

They all know he's right.

"I'll do it," Pat says.

Danny sees John flinch.

"You're out of your weight class," Bernie says quickly.

Which Danny knows is code for *John isn't risking one of his own kids but can't say it himself.*

Pat ain't having it, though. Pat is a freaking hero, a stand-up guy, plus he feels guilty it's his brother caused all this and is hiding out while other people bleed for what he did.

Pat thinks he has to redeem the family honor.

And he'll die doing it.

So Danny says, "Let me take a crack at it."

Awkward silence, which Pat finally breaks by throwing his arm around Danny's shoulder and saying, "Danny, I'm grateful, believe me. But you're no killer."

Danny Ryan is good with his hands, but he's never done the job on anyone, never mind a stone killer like Steve Giordo.

"I'll get in close," Danny says.

"You won't *get* close," Pat answers. "None of us will."

"I know how," Danny says.

Everyone in the room just looks at him.

"I know how," Danny repeats.

SIXTEEN

IT'S FREEZING ON THE BEACH.

Freakin' October and already cold. Wind blowing out of the north, the whitecaps look like the beards of sad old men.

Even in his heavy peacoat, Danny shivers and stamps his feet, waiting for Peter Moretti to show up. Finally, a car pulls into the parking lot and Danny sees O'Neill and Viola get out, check to make sure that Danny is alone.

They must be satisfied, because Peter gets out of the car and walks onto the beach.

Camel-hair coat, but bareheaded because he's always been vain about his hair and won't mess it up with a hat. Danny, he has a wool toque on, because fuck vanity. It's good to see that Peter feels the cold, though. Good to see him shiver.

"We couldn't have done this at the North Pole?" Peter asks.

"If anyone saw me with you . . ."

"I was beginning to wonder," Peter says. "It's been what, almost two weeks?"

"I've been busy," Danny says, glaring at him. "Funerals and wakes."

Peter shrugs. "War is war. The fuck did you think I was going to do?"

"You wanted this war," Danny says. "You want the docks, the rest of the Murphy operation."

"Let's talk in the car," Peter says. "Good heater in that thing."

"I like it out here," Danny says. "And Cagney and Lacey over there take one step toward us, I'll shoot you in the gut."

"So why did you want to meet me, Danny?"

"Because you're going to win," Danny says.

Peter nods graciously. Smug fucking smile on his face. "See? This is what I mean. The Murphys always underestimated you. You're smarter than any of them."

"Here's what I want," Danny says. "One: the Ryan part of the business comes back to my father and me, like you said, with me in the corner office. Two: nobody touches my father, not now, not ever."

"Is there a three?"

"Pat Murphy gets a pass."

"No fucking way," Peter says.

"Go enjoy your heater."

"Be reasonable," Peter says. "Even if I was to give Pat a pass, he wouldn't take it. You know him—he won't stop coming. I admire it, frankly. But give him a pass? After what the Murphys did to my brother? Forget it."

"You haven't heard what I have to offer."

"You can't offer what—"

"Liam."

Peter actually looks stunned. He asks, "You'd do that?"

"I have a kid on the way," Danny says. "My own family to look out for. But you have to give me Pat."

Peter looks out at the ocean like there's an answer on Block Island. Then he says, "You deliver Liam, I won't make a move against Pat unless he comes for me or mine."

"Okay," Danny says. "So Liam has a piece on the side."

"You're fucking kidding me," Peter says. "He's tapping *that*, and he's going out for strange?"

Danny shrugs. "He sees her Thursday nights. Fifty-eight Weybosset Street."

"Who is this chick?" Peter asks, suspicious. "A working girl?"

"She's a pro-am," Danny answers. "Slings drinks at the Wonder Bar. Cathy Madigan. Check her out, you want. Liam goes over around nine, bangs her, leaves by ten or eleven, tells Pam he was out on business."

He knows they'll check it out. And they'll find a Cathy Madigan working at the Wonder Bar. They'll confirm her address. They might even see her bring a john home. The rest of the story, about Liam, is bullshit. But he also knows that they won't approach the girl, won't question her, for fear of scaring Liam off. Even if they do, Cathy Madigan's gambling problem has her underwater for over five grand plus the vig, she's scared to freaking death and will say what she's told to say.

"If this pans out," Peter says, "you're gold."

"Don't fuck it up," Danny says.

He walks back to his car.

Turns the floor blower on high.

Good to get his feet warm.

SEVENTEEN

JIMMY MAC LIKES THE DODGE Charger because it has a V8 engine and good, heavy doors, some muscle and some metal, to get you out of trouble fast or at least give you a little protection. He flips a toggle switch rigged below the steering wheel and says to Danny, "This kills the interior lights. And check this out—"

He points to a different toggle switch. "I put in another oil pan and connected it to the tailpipe. Flip this switch and it leaves a cloud of black smoke behind. Real James Bond shit, huh?"

"Does it have an ejection seat?"

"You want to give me a couple days," Jimmy says. "I step on the gas, this thing is going to *go*, son. We do the thing, you jump in, we're in Vermont before your balls come back down from your throat."

Jimmy's trying to reassure himself because this thing is *risky*. Danny's basically going out as bait, trolling for Steve Giordo, and Jimmy don't like it. He thinks Liam should go himself, but Old Man Murphy ain't havin' it.

Actually it was Danny talked them into it being him.

"I'm about Liam's height," he said. "I'll wear a hoodie, get out of his car in front of Madigan's building, it's dark, they won't know the difference."

"I can't let you do this," Pat said.

"Just make sure the shooter is good," Danny said.

Thursday night they drive up to Pawtucket to pick up the shooter.

The Murphys have him stored in a second-floor efficiency in the back of a building. They went out and bought him some tea and cans of condensed milk that he wanted, and some eggs, sausages, and bread so he could do a "proper fry-up."

The shooter is from a Provisional IRA brigade in Armagh.

Danny isn't a believer in the Cause. Thinks the maudlin "patriotism" for a country they've never seen is bullshit. Couldn't care less if the Six Counties stay British or become part of Ireland or Iceland, for that matter.

The Murphys are big into it. Think they have responsibilities as Irish who have survived and thrived. What did Pat call it? The Irish diaspora? Whatever the hell that was. They'd get all weepy on the anniversary of the Easter Rebellion, hold a little ceremony, pass the hat for the "men who still fight." It was after the Sands thing they started singing the Irish national anthem at closing time. In Gaelic, no less, as if anyone understood it.

Danny puts it down to guilt. That they hadn't died in the old country with grass in their mouths, or been blasted to pieces by a Brit firing squad. The truth was, though, that a lot of the Providence Irish had come from the north counties, from Donegal in particular, and still have family ties back there. And connections to the hard men who need guns and are willing to trade personnel for weaponry.

"It stinks in here," Jimmy says as they stand in the hallway outside the door. "The fucker must fry everything. Jesus, his arteries."

The door opens.

Danny doesn't know what he expected a Provo man to look like, but it isn't this. He's short, in his midtwenties, has a thin, small face, jet-black hair, and a three-day growth of beard.

"I'm Mickey," he says. "You'd be Ryan?"

"I'm the guy you *don't* shoot," Danny says. "This is Jimmy. You ready?"

"Born ready." He slips the AR–15 rifle into a plastic case and slings it over his shoulder. "I've killed a few Brits with this, I can tell you."

Great, Danny thinks. Some poor kids from some shitty British slum have no other choice than enlisting in the army, get their asses sent to Northern Irish ghettos little different from their own neighborhoods, and get killed by a long-range bullet shot by a guy they never see.

For what? A change of flags? Meet the new boss, same as the old boss.

THEY GO BACK outside.

Jimmy and Mick get into the work car.

Danny gets behind the wheel of Liam's black BMW.

THEY KNOW HOW Giordo will do it.

He'll be in his own work car—maybe with a driver, maybe by himself—parked somewhere across the street from Cathy Madigan's building. He'll watch for Liam's car, roll down his window, wait for Liam to get out, do the job and take off.

That's the most likely scenario and the one they're planning on. The other is that the Morettis got access to a second-floor apartment across the street, the old Al Capone shit. Or Giordo will be up on a roof. If it's either of those, Danny is pretty much fucked.

But he doubts it.

Getting into an apartment means witnesses, and roof shots are tricky, even for the Sniper. The Morettis know this could be their one shot at Liam, and they're not going to take chances. And Giordo likes to get in and get out fast.

So it's most likely a car.

Still, Danny's nervous—Be honest, he thinks, *shit scared*—as he drives over. He's not even sure why he's doing this—maybe it's the three murdered friends, or that Peter fucked him, or that he feels guilty that he considered his offer. Probably it's more he still has this loyalty thing with the Murphys, this connection he can't seem to break. Like he's always trying to prove something to them.

He's not sure what.

But if they can take Giordo off the ice, it leaves Sal as the Morettis' main guy. Maybe Peter gets cold feet and asks for negotiations.

Danny heads toward Weybosset Street.

Probably the only time in my life, he thinks, I'll drive a BMW.

IN THE WORK car, Mick says, "I have some rules. When we get close, no unnecessary talking. I don't want a lot of nervous chatter. You lower the window when I tell you to, not a moment before, not a moment after. And don't get rabbit feet on the pedal—you keep the car stock-still until I tell you to go. Then you go. Got it, champ?"

"I have a rule of my own," Jimmy says. "That's my friend out there. You fuck up and he gets hurt—I take this pistol in my pocket and blow your brains out. Got it, champ?"

DANNY TURNS ONTO Weybosset.

The street is full of parked cars, shoved up against the dirty, sooty snow. Hard to know which one is Giordo's—the silver Audi, the black Lincoln, the old van. He finds a spot and starts to parallel park, which he sucks at. Normally, Danny would drive a half mile before he'd parallel park, and now his hands are shaking. He hears the back tire scrape against curb, figures he's close enough, and shuts off the engine.

He's wearing an old gray Providence College sweatshirt under his peacoat. He checks that the .38 revolver is still in the jacket pocket, buttons it up, pulls the hood over his head and gets out.

Danny's pissed that his legs are shaking and he's having a hard time breathing. The feet in his work boots feel like lead as he steps out onto the sidewalk. Takes a deep breath, jams his hands into his pockets, and starts walking the thirty or so feet to Madigan's building.

If the shot's going to come, it's going to come now.

Then he sees Jimmy in the work car coming up the street.

The passenger window rolls down, Mick sticks the rifle out the window and lets a full clip go into the silver Audi.

Danny ducks into Madigan's doorway as muzzle flashes come out from the Audi. The bullets hit Mick full in the mouth, cleave off his tongue and shatter his jawbone. The Irishman slumps onto the door handle. It opens, and he topples into the street.

Jimmy guns the car and flies down the street.

GIORDO, A PATCH of blood on his shoulder, gets out of the car, looks to see where "Liam" went, and then spots Danny in the doorway.

Danny will never know what happened, but something takes over in him and he pulls the pistol from his pocket, pulls the trigger over and over again, screaming in rage and fear as he charges across the street at Giordo.

Every shot misses.

Giordo backs away, though, as he fires.

Danny feels a punch hit his hip. The blow spins him around and he can't stay on his feet or hang on to the pistol as the world seems to pull him down to his knees. He props himself up on one hand and sees Giordo aiming the rifle at him.

Oh my God, I am heartily sorry for having offended Thee
And I do detest all my sins

Jimmy roars backward down the street, putting the car between Danny and Giordo. Leaning down, he opens the passenger door, grabs Danny's wrist, and pulls him into the car.

Giordo's bullets smack the car like hail.

With Danny still hanging half out of the car, Jimmy hits the gas and flips the toggle switch.

The cloud of smoke shields them from Giordo's aim.

Danny blacks out.

HE WAKES UP in a hospital bed.

Crisp, clean sheets and distant pain.

A woman sits in a chair beside the bed. Beautiful woman with long red hair. At first Danny thinks she's a nurse, but she doesn't have a nurse's uniform on. She's expensively dressed and her perfume is enchanting.

He gets scared for a second because he thinks maybe he's dead and this is heaven. He flashes on the shooting, the searing pain as the bullet struck his hip bone.

Maybe I died out there, he thinks, maybe I'm dead.

"Who are you?" he asks groggily.

"You don't recognize me?"

Now he looks at this woman and remembers a photograph in his father's dresser drawer.

It's her.

His mother.

Madeleine.

"Get out," Danny says.

I didn't need you then, I don't need you now.

"Danny," she says. Beautiful green eyes wet with tears. "My baby."

"Out," he repeats. Like talking through cotton, a cool silver mist. Just let me go back to sleep. When I wake up, you'll be gone, like you were always gone.

"You're going to be all right, baby," Madeleine says. "I got you the best doctors."

"Go to hell."

"I don't blame you, Danny," she says. "When you're older, maybe you'll understand."

When you hurt, I hurt.

EIGHTEEN

IT STARTED YOUNG.

Madeleine McKay's own mother opined that the girl was born "already fourteen years old," because she seemed sexually aware, even as a toddler. And what a beautiful little girl she was, with a perfectly symmetrical face, high cheekbones that seemed carved from Calacatta marble, sparkling emerald eyes, vibrant red hair.

Young Darlene (she wasn't Madeleine yet) was aware of her beauty, precociously sensual, seductive in a way that made adult women passively hostile and grown men actively uncomfortable. She knew it, she used it with a glorious absence of shame. She discovered her body early, its potential for pleasure; she played with it as a marvelously joyful toy, a gift from God.

In truth, few other gifts had been given to her.

Darlene's family was poor, even by the modest standards of Barstow, California. Her father, Alvin, never met a job he couldn't lose, but at the same time insisted that "no wife of mine is going to work." Outside the home, anyway—Alvin had ample spare time to knock Dorothy up and fill the revolving-door rental homes and trailers with five kids, Darlene being the oldest.

She had no childhood—she was too busy being a mother to two brothers and two sisters, because after baby number three, Dorothy checked out. Call it postpartum, call it plain depression, call it fatigue, the steady erosion of poverty, the unrelenting assault of landlords seeking past-due rent, but she pretty much gave up. Spent most of her nights on the sofa, washing down cheap pills with cheaper booze, her days in bed with the covers pulled over her head.

Alvin, that paragon of Puritan work ethic, once described her to Darlene as "useless as tits on a bull."

So it was Darlene, from about age eight, who got the kids up for school, made their lunches, washed their clothes, who showed up (ludicrously but earnestly) at parent-teacher conferences, gave them baths, dried their tears.

Darlene shed few of her own, comforted herself instead with the consolation of her body. Her best companion was her image in the mirror, her imagination of what she would become.

She wanted to be Marilyn Monroe.

She carefully cut photos from Dorothy's magazines and kept a scrapbook under her bed. She tried to fix her hair like Marilyn's, followed her changes of style, her manner of dress. There was no money, of course, for new clothes, but Darlene had a flair, a knack for making the frumpiest frock look fresh with just a ribbon, a used belt, an unconventional slice of the scissors.

In adolescence her body developed differently from her idol's. She had MM's bust, but her legs grew long and lean. Her face took on a sculpted sharpness, as opposed to MM's softness; her lips were thinner, her mouth wider.

She wasn't disappointed. Darlene marked the looks she got from boys at school, men on the street, the envious glances from women; she knew she was attractive, that she could have any boy she wanted.

Darlene didn't want any of them.

Not in Barstow.

Darlene wanted Hollywood.

What she didn't want was to get knocked up. Darlene didn't want to sleep with some boy in Barstow, get pregnant, become her mother. She maintained an iron discipline with the few boys she dated. She would go parking, but only in the front seat. She'd allow them to touch her breasts, but only over her sweater, and never anything below the waist. She would French kiss, once rubbed a boy's crotch over his jeans, but no matter how they begged, how they whined about "blue balls," she wouldn't jerk them off, never mind give them blow jobs.

It was as frustrating for her as for them, and after a night of frantic fumbling and rigid resistance, she would go home, get into bed and satisfy herself.

Of course, her reputation for promiscuity rose in direct inverse ratio to the reality of her chastity. In revenge for her refusals, the boys bragged about what they did to her, what she did for them; they called her "Darleasy" and "Whorelene."

She had no friends—the other girls were either jealous or judgmental. The boys either tried to screw her or stayed away because they knew they couldn't. Her siblings were more her children.

Darlene was lonely, but in a personality as strong as hers, loneliness becomes self-sufficiency. She was enough for herself, saw herself as alone in the world, that the only person she could rely on was the girl in the mirror, and was okay with it.

The girl in the mirror wasn't Darleasy or Whorelene.

She was Madeleine McKay.

Rich and independent.

Glamour girl.

Movie star.

She went the other way with it.

Literally.

In those days, the chief reason for the existence of Barstow was as a halfway point between Los Angeles and Las Vegas. The former lay to the west, the latter to the east, on Highway 15.

When she was seventeen, Darlene looked into the mirror and took stock, a cold-blooded objective inventory. She was five feet, ten inches tall—too tall to be a movie star. That this was unfair occurred to her only briefly—she dismissed the sexism as reality and decided that the road to her future was to the east.

In Las Vegas, the longer the legs, the taller the girl, the better.

If she couldn't become an actress, she would be a showgirl.

It wasn't her dream, but it was better than being a waitress, a mother, or a housewife.

So one night, Darlene dutifully bathed her brothers and sisters and put them to bed. She arranged their clothes, fixed their lunches for morning and put them in the refrigerator. Then she packed her few things in a small bag, walked out the door to a truck stop just off Route 15 and stuck out her thumb.

She was picked up immediately.

In some of the first good luck of her life, the driver only wanted a little company, even bought her a burger when they made a stop in Baker, and delivered her on the Las Vegas Strip unmolested.

His name was Glen and she never forgot him.

In Las Vegas, pretty girls were like flecks of metal and magnets were everywhere. High rollers, low rollers, pimps, gangsters, managers, agents, talent scouts, and combination plates of all of them.

Darlene was lucky again.

Stuffing herself at the buffet in a cheap casino hotel, she was spotted by a relatively honest, relatively nonpredatory agent-manager by the name of Shelly Stone, who approached her with his card in his hand. "Are you looking for work, young lady?"

"Yes."

"What's your name?" Shelly asked.

"Madeleine McKay."

She picked the name because it sounded like Marilyn and besides, it was French and classy.

"Nice name." He pretended to believe her. "How old are you?"

"Twenty-one."

He pretended to believe that, too. She certainly looked twenty-one, like an adult, anyway. "Can you dance?"

"Yes."

This he didn't even pretend to believe. But for the starter jobs he had in mind for her, she didn't really have to dance, all she had to do was walk and hold her head up. Which wasn't as easy as it sounded, but the girl had a confidence about her that he liked.

"If I get you a job, I get ten percent of everything you make," Shelly said. "I pick up your paycheck, I give you your money."

"No," Madeleine said. "*I* pick up my paycheck, I give *you* your money."

Shelly laughed.

This girl was going to make it.

He got her a decent motel room and told her it was an advance against her first paycheck. The next morning he took her to an audition at one of the lesser shows in town, where the director, whom Shelly had known since Christ was a road guard, looked her over like a piece of meat and liked what he saw. "You're a gazelle with boobs. What experience do you have?"

"None."

"Good," he said. "I won't have to unteach. You come every night, you watch the show, first girl who gets sick or noticeably knocked up, you fill in."

Richard Hardesty taught her a lot.

"Do you know why I am such a good director?" he asked her one night as she watched the show. "Because I have no interest at all in what's between your legs. I only care that they move in perfect coordination."

Another night he asked, "Do you know the difference between a stripper and a showgirl? And it has nothing to do with the relative amount of clothing or lack thereof. A stripper sells a visceral fantasy, a showgirl sells an ethereal dream."

One night he asked her, "Do you know why men bring dates to these shows, often their wives? Because it titillates both of them. When they get back to the room, Mrs. Iowa becomes you."

Two weeks into this Socratic tutorial, Madeleine got her chance, thanks to some bad shrimp at the buffet. She put on her costume—a sequined two-piece, a tall feathered headdress, and high heels—and appeared in *Venus in Vegas.*

A week after that, she got a regular slot and a raise when Richard fired a girl for gaining three pounds.

Madeleine worked steadily after that. She shared an apartment with two other girls from the show. When it closed, Shelly moved her to a bigger show at a better hotel and she was on her way.

While it's an exaggeration to say that every guy in Vegas tried to fuck her, it wasn't *much* of an exaggeration. She was a sensation, the beauty among beauties who really stood out, a fresh look, and just about every single guy—and a lot of married ones—who saw her made a move on her.

She was impervious.

Literally impenetrable.

Got a reputation as an ice queen.

Just about drove a high-stakes poker player out of his mind one night in his comped suite when she wouldn't give it up.

"I don't want to get pregnant," Madeleine said.

"Jesus," he said, "haven't you ever heard of rubbers?"

"They're only ninety percent effective."

"I'll stop before ninety times, how about that?" he asked.

"If you think that's how odds work," she said, "you should find another profession."

"Okay, how about a blow job?"

She went down on him. It was okay, it was fine. He thought it was better than fine, and told her so, but Madeleine said, "I'm glad. Now you do me."

"What?"

"Fair is fair," she said. "I'm your lover, not your hooker."

He was okay, not great. She didn't stay with him for long. Being a gambler's girlfriend was not in her plan. Neither was being a showgirl the rest of her life, or until she gained a few pounds or wrinkles and they kicked her to the curb.

There was no future in it.

What she wanted was security.

Which boiled down to money.

But how does a girl with no high school diploma make serious money, security money, the kind of money that makes her safe in this world? The answer was plain—if a woman can't make money, she has to make a man who makes money.

This is how the most beautiful woman on the Strip married the ugliest man in Las Vegas.

Manny Maniscalco was the Undergarment King of the World. His factory outside of Las Vegas made heavily structured wired brassieres, girdles, corsets, and belts designed to make busts stand out and waists suck in. His was a unique kind of engineering genius, and his company expanded to make lingerie that could never be accused of being overly subtle.

His creations were a Las Vegas staple for all the big shows, his undergarments could be seen—at least discerned—in Hollywood films, his lingerie was particularly ubiquitous all over the third world.

Manny spent his life creating his own vulgar version of beauty, which made sense because he himself was ugly as they come and knew it. How could he not, with his club left foot that dragged behind him as if he wore a ball and chain, shoulders that stooped over his six-foot-four frame, and a heavy head that some likened to a Saint Bernard's, only . . . ugly.

He had a big head and a big heart—when Manny loved, it was with the intensity of an angel, and he loved Madeleine McKay.

A denizen of the shows—ostensibly to check on his creations but in reality to bask in beauty—he was well known to every chorus girl as a regular at the front-row tables. "Manny's out there" became a standard line in the wings. Some of the girls were amused, others dismissive; none would meet his gaze, even with his reputed fortune.

But one night he spotted Madeleine, and that was it.

He sent flowers backstage, baskets of fruit (no man in the know would ever send a showgirl candy), bottles of perfume, samplings of his products in what he accurately surmised were her sizes. The accompanying notes were never pushy, always signed simply *From your admirer, Manny Maniscalco.*

The other girls filled her in on Manny and his millions, laughed about the gifts that were piling up, sympathized with her. The man came to the show *every night* and sat there staring only at Madeleine. It was creepy, they said, embarrassing for her.

Madeleine wasn't embarrassed.

One night Manny arrived at his regular table to find a very nice bottle of red wine waiting, with the note *From your admiree, Madeleine McKay.*

He sent back a note: *Could we share the wine over dinner?*

If a note could have stammered, it would have.

They had dinner after the show the next Saturday night and married two months later.

Somewhat to her surprise, Madeleine found Manny to be intelligent, thoughtful, charming in his own hesitant way, and the possessor of a deep strength that can only come from perfect self-awareness.

"The only reason," he said without a trace of rancor at that dinner, "that a young woman as beautiful as you would date a man twenty years her senior, as ugly as me, is my money. Am I wrong?"

"It certainly was the reason I came," she said. "It would only be part of the reason I would stay."

"But a major part."

"Of course."

They came to an equally frank understanding. If money was the main currency, as it were, of their relationship, she would only be a purchase, not a rental. If he wanted to take her off the stage, he had to set her at the altar. He would marry her, give her a luxurious life, settle an independent fortune on her. In return, she would give him her beauty, her wit, her companionship.

She couldn't promise her heart.

He accepted that.

The gossip columns called the match, inevitably, "Beauty and the Beast," reveled in printing photos of the statuesque bride and the hunched-over groom. The bridesmaids composed a virtual chorus line, giving the ceremony an erotic charge; his groomsmen were mostly his cousins. Shelly walked the bride down the aisle.

"You don't get ten percent of this," Madeleine joked.

"But I should," Shelly said. "I'm losing a lot of income here. Are you sure you want to do this, kid? It's not too late to run."

"I'm sure."

Out of respect for Manny—and there was immense respect for him among the smartest and most powerful Las Vegas operators—every important person in town attended the ceremony and came to the lavish reception.

Madeleine and Manny spent their wedding night in the bridal suite of the Flamingo.

Madeleine took a long time in the bathroom, making sure her hair was coiffed in a stylish updo, that her makeup was perfect. She slipped into one of Manny's less cheesy negligees, filmy black silk, over one of his red corsets lined with black lace, black mesh stockings and garters.

Nothing she would have chosen for herself, but she knew it would please him.

She came out and struck a pose in the bathroom doorway, one long leg bent and extended, one arm raised, her hand along the doorframe.

He lay on the bed in a set of blue silk pajamas, an effort that did nothing to improve him nor mask his erection.

"What do you think?" she asked, shifting her hips.

"So lovely."

Madeleine walked over to the bed and stood in front of him. "You know, you're my first."

"No, I didn't."

"Am I yours?"

"No."

"Good," she said, lying down next to him. "You'll know what to do to me."

He didn't, not really.

His prior experience had been entirely with hookers, simple commercial exchanges to satisfy a physical need. So he climbed on top of her, pushed up the hem of the negligee, fumbled with the rubber, and put himself between her legs.

"I don't want to hurt you," he said.

"You won't." Although Madeleine wasn't so sure. She wasn't wet, not even a little turned on, and he was big. Putting her arms around him, under his pajama shirt, she felt his back. It was hairy, like an animal's, and sweaty. In her best breathy Marilyn Monroe voice, she said, "Take me, darling. Make me yours."

It did hurt.

It got a little better, not painful, even slightly pleasurable as he thrust into her mechanically, like one of the machines in his factory, proceeding with rhythmic precision to produce a set result.

For him.

Out of affection for him she moaned, wriggled and whined, whispered naughty nothings into his ear, shut her eyes to block out his ugliness and feigned orgasm moments before he came.

A few moments later he said, "It will get better."

"It was wonderful."

"Don't lie to me," Manny said. "It's beneath you."

They honeymooned in Paris. Stayed in the best hotel, ate in the finest restaurants, shopped in the most exclusive boutiques, and he looked painfully out of place in all of them.

Madeleine gave him everything she had in bed—dressed provocatively, screwed him in every position she could imagine, sucked him off, let him go down on her. That was part of the deal, and, an honorable woman, she honored it. She gave him immense pleasure; her own was mild at best.

Toward the end of the two weeks in France, Madeleine told him,

"This has been wonderful, and I'm truly appreciative, but Manny, I don't need all this. What I want is a nice home, a steady, quiet life."

They went home to his mansion outside of town, a one-level neo-Spanish colonial on acreage. A large swimming pool outside a slider from the living room, a garden of citrus trees. A circular driveway wrapped around a fountain.

Manny put fifty thousand dollars in her bank account.

She was nineteen.

Being married to Manny was . . . pleasant.

She got up early in the morning with him, their cook made them breakfast, he went to the office and she did calisthenics to keep her showgirl figure. She spent most mornings growing her portfolio. Manny introduced her to stockbrokers and financial advisers, and she studied the market assiduously, making conservative but incisive investments. One of the companies she bought shares in was Maniscalco Manufacturing.

In the afternoons, Madeleine might play tennis with the hired coach, or swim in the pool, or go into town to have lunch with old show friends or shop. She was most often home before Manny, would sit on the terrace and read.

They would have dinner together, watch a little television, and go to bed early, making love once or twice a week.

Madeleine came to have genuine affection for Manny. He was kind and considerate, had a quiet but sharp sense of humor, never chased other women, was totally devoted to her. He would patiently answer all her questions about business and finance, and when he didn't know the answer would refer her to someone who did.

And he didn't mind that she wanted to keep her own last name, for professional purposes.

They didn't go out much—when they did it was for business-social functions or fundraisers, although he did take Madeleine to see any of the big performers she wanted, so she saw Sinatra and Dean Martin and the rest of them on opening nights, and the Maniscalcos were always invited to the after-parties.

She stayed faithful for almost two years. Might have been longer if Manny hadn't been a fan of boxing. He had ringside seats at all the big fights and finally persuaded Madeleine to come with him.

Jack Di Bello was a brutal middleweight out of Jersey City with a body forged from iron and a heart made in hell. He used to say that he hated early knockouts because he wanted to bust the guy up first. That he never minded getting hit because it was nothing compared to what his old man used to give him.

He spotted Madeleine during the introductions.

She spotted him back.

First round he worked his opponent—a talented Venezuelan contender—into the ropes in front of Madeleine and pounded the hell out of him. Blood and sweat flecked on her dress. As he spun away, Jack took a second to glance at her.

Knew that she dug it.

The fight went seven rounds, a bloody affair, before Jack got tired of slicing up the Venezuelan, went low for a paralyzing liver shot and then upstairs to the jaw for the knockout.

His man dropped face-first like a felled tree.

Jack raised his arms and looked straight at Madeleine.

She didn't look away.

"You probably don't want to go to the postfight party," Manny said as the crowd started to leave.

"No," Madeleine said. "I'd like to."

Di Bello was run by the Chicago Outfit with an investment from the New England mob, so the party in the suite at the Sands was full of wiseguys. They all knew Manny, they all respected him. Most of their *gumars* wore his creations, gratis. He was welcome at the party, especially as he brought with him a woman as stunning as his wife.

No one was happier to see them than Jack.

His face was flushed and puffy, his left eye black, and his swollen jaw didn't diminish a crooked grin. He alternated holding a cold beer bottle against his cheek and drinking from it while looking across the room at Madeleine.

Now she avoided his eye; it was getting too obvious.

And she was feeling too much.

Jack waited until she went to the bathroom and stopped her on the way out. He got right to it. "What are you doing with that mutt?"

"Excuse me?"

"What a waste."

"Get out of my way."

"Come see me tomorrow." He told her his room number.

His manager tried to warn him. "Stay away from that trim. Her husband's connected."

"He's not made, though."

"No, but he's *connected*, Jack."

"The wiseguys wouldn't lay a hand on me," Jack said. "I make them money."

"You make them tens of thousands of dollars," his manager said. "Manny Maniscalco makes them millions. So if he asks them to break your hands, or splash acid on your face, or cut off your guinea dick, they would do the math. Do you understand what I'm trying to tell you?"

"I know, but look at her," Jack said. "She'd be worth it."

The next afternoon Madeleine said she was going to have lunch with some of her old show friends and do some shopping. Her feet took her straight to Jack's room.

He might have had the decency to act surprised, she thought when he opened the door. Instead he grinned and let her in.

Jack didn't make love to her, he fucked her.

She fucked him back.

Dug her fingers into his thick, curly black hair, ran her fingernails across his broad back, bucked against him like she was trying to bounce him off. He stayed with her, plunged into her like he was punching her, going for the knockout.

Madeleine got the first orgasm of her life that she didn't give herself.

And the second and the third.

She didn't even like the guy—arrogant, rough to the point of brutality, crude and foul-mouthed—but she was crazy about him. He felt the same way—Jack had never fucked such a beautiful woman.

Then again, few men had.

"Don't give me bruises," Madeleine said one day. "Manny might notice."

"You still fucking him?"

"He's my husband," she said.

"The old bastard's so grateful," Jack said, "he wouldn't notice my jizz on his dick."

"You're disgusting."

"Then why do you keep coming back?"

"I come back to get off."

She kept going back. They started to take precautions, didn't meet at his hotel but rented rooms away from the Strip.

Two or three days a week for the next three months.

Madeleine came home one evening—she really had been out shopping with friends—and Manny was sitting on the living room couch, a glass of scotch in his hand.

"I want you to look at something," he said, patting the cushion beside him for her to sit down.

He opened a folder on the glass coffee table and Madeleine saw black-and-white photos—some taken from a closet, others from out-side a window—of her and Jack in bed. They were graphic: Jack kneeling between her legs, Madeleine with his dick in her mouth, her on all fours with him behind her.

"These were taken by a gossip rag," Manny said. "Fortunately, we have a friend there who offered them to me first. I paid twenty thousand dollars to see my wife with another man. Do you love him?"

"No."

"But he does for you what I can't," Manny said. He was calm, didn't seem angry, not even hurt.

Madeleine nodded. "Yes."

"I knew you could never love me," Manny said, "not in that way. You were very honest about that. I know I don't meet your needs—"

"Manny—"

"Be quiet now," he said. "I just want you on my arm when I go out, I want to see you when I get up in the morning and when I go to bed at night. You have needs, they should be met, I accept that. What I will not accept is a scandal. I will not be embarrassed.

"This thing with Di Bello stops now. No more famous men, no celebrities, no long-term affairs. They're too risky. I expect you to be discreet in the men you choose and careful in the way you conduct yourself. Do we have an understanding?"

"Yes. I'm sorry, Manny."

"Sorry is for children," he said.

Later, lying in bed, Madeleine heard him drag his heavy foot into the room. A while later she felt his weight on the mattress. Then she felt him crying.

Madeleine heard the next day that Jack Di Bello had moved to New York.

She and Manny limped through the paces after that, polite but distant. He was still kind and considerate, they slept in the same bed, but he never touched her and she never made the first move.

Manny was right, though, she had needs.

Madeleine found her lovers in restaurants and bars, at blackjack tables and roulette wheels, on tennis courts and golf greens. They were never Las Vegas locals, always tourists or traveling businessmen. She met them once and only once, summarily dismissed them, and then went home to shower them off her.

It went on for two years.

The last one of these men was Marty Ryan.

The son is so much like the father, she thinks now, looking at Danny lying in the hospital bed. The same reddish-brown hair, the same eyes, the same delicate pride, the same wounded dignity.

She met Marty in the bar at the Flamingo and knew before the ice had melted in the first drink that she was going to do him.

He was so handsome, with that boyish, mischievous smile and that looking-for-trouble glint in his eyes. And he had the worst, corniest pickup line, so bad it was charming. "It's a shame for someone so beautiful to be drinking alone."

"Maybe I'm waiting for someone," she said.

"No, I was talking about myself."

She laughed out loud and didn't object when he sat down next to her and signaled the bartender for another round.

"I'm Marty Ryan."

"Madeleine McKay."

He saw her wedding ring and the big rock Manny gave her when he proposed. Didn't seem to faze him at all.

"Where are you from?" Madeleine asked.

"Providence. That's in Rhode Island."

"What brings you to town?"

"Taking care of some business," Marty said. "I'll just be here a couple of days."

"Do you like it here?"

"I do *now*."

"Marty . . ."

"Madeleine . . ."

"Do you like to fuck?"

"No," he said. "I *love* to fuck."

He really did. She gave him the name of an out-of-the-way motel and they spent the afternoon making love. And that's what it was—making love. She felt something with Marty that she hadn't felt with Jack or Manny.

Madeleine broke her rules—saw him every day for a week. The last day, when she got up to put her clothes on, he asked, "When can I see you again?"

"That's not going to happen."

He looked stunned, angry, hurt. "The hell you mean?"

"Marty, it was wonderful," she said. "Truly. But there can't be anything more between us. Ever."

"I'm in love with you."

"Don't be ridiculous."

"No, I am," Marty said. "I'll move here if you want."

"I don't," she said. "I'm married, Marty."

"You didn't seem so married a few minutes ago."

"It's complicated."

"It's simple," he said. "I love you."

"Well, that's too bad." She kissed him lightly on the lips. "Goodbye, Marty."

And that was it, as far as she was concerned.

Except it wasn't.

Her next period was late, then it didn't show up at all.

A doctor confirmed she was pregnant.

"Get rid of it," Manny said. "I know a doctor. He's discreet."

"I'm not going to do that," she said.

"Don't expect me to raise someone else's bastard," Manny said. "Everyone will know it's not mine. Get the abortion or . . ."

"Or what?"

"We had an agreement," Manny said. "You weren't going to be careless, you weren't going to embarrass me. You've done both, so the agreement is void."

"So I'm just a bad business deal?"

"That was your choice, Madeleine, not mine."

The man is absolutely right, she thought. I made this business, so why shouldn't he? "I'll go away and have the baby. No one will know. I won't contest the divorce, and I don't want anything beyond what you've already given me."

She left in the morning and flew to New York. Had the baby at St. Elizabeth's and listed Martin Ryan as the father.

MADELEINE TRIED TO be a mother, she really did.

She did the diapers, the feedings, the sleepless nights. It was hard being a single mother in those days, it was a scandal even in the bohemian Village, and the neighbors in her building on Seventh Avenue pretended to believe her story about her husband being a longshoreman who was out at sea. Madeleine had cared for children before, when she was herself a child—it wasn't that, it wasn't the difficult present that caused her to abandon her son, Danny.

It was the future.

Madeleine couldn't picture it.

What was she supposed to do, saddled with an infant, then a toddler, then a little boy? She had some of her money from Manny, had invested it wisely, but it wouldn't last—she would have to go to work.

Doing what, though?

And who would look after Danny?

She knew one thing: She wasn't going back to Barstow. To throw herself on the mercy of her parents, to face the humiliation of being a single mother, to see the sneers of the men she had rejected and hear the snickers of jealous girls.

Madeleine took stock of her assets, decided that she had two— beauty and brains. But she couldn't use either with a kid in tow.

So one day she got up, wrapped Danny in a blanket and caught the train for Providence. It wasn't hard to find Martin Ryan, everyone knew him. She walked into some dingy Irish bar, handed him the bundle and said, "Here, here's your son. I'm not cut out to be a mother."

Then she walked out.

Went to Los Angeles.

Madeleine knew her assets and used them to her best advantage. Men loved to look at her, loved to be seen with her on their arms, loved to fuck her. It's not that she was a hooker, it wasn't a cash-on-the-barrelhead proposition, but she let it be known that she was a girl who required gifts. And not flowers and candy, either. Clothes, furs, jewelry, vacations, cars, apartments, houses. Stock tips, stock options, inclusion in real estate development deals.

Her looks wouldn't last forever.

She started going to parties with headline comedians, singers, and then movie stars. Through the movie stars she met politicians, through the pols she met the Wall Street types.

Madeleine never fucked down. When she went with studio heads, she quit the actors. When she started banging billionaires, she left the studio heads. It was her simple rule. All the men understood, they didn't resent her for it. Men like that know the pecking order.

The only guy she ever felt bad about was the son she left behind. But she couldn't have done it, couldn't have lived in Dogtown as the wife of an Irish dock boss, even if he was connected. Didn't see herself doing laundry, cranking out kids, going to confession on Saturday afternoon, the dreary pub Saturday night, mass on Sunday morning.

It was death.

But her only regret was her baby, her boy.

Left behind with an angry drunk while she fucked her way from Hollywood to Washington to New York. Now she was back in Vegas again, with a real estate and stock portfolio, no need to worry about being in her fifties and losing her looks. Even if she was still stunning, still good in bed, still a charming companion, she knew that her sell-by date was fast approaching and it didn't worry her.

She had money.

In this world, money keeps a woman safe.

Money and influence.

She used it when she heard about Danny. An old friend in the Justice Department made the connection and called her. Your son is hurt and in trouble. Another friend provided a private jet and she was in Providence the next day. She made calls on the flight—got the story and pulled on some cords of memory.

Nobody from the Strip to Sunset to Pennsylvania Avenue wanted Madeleine McKay writing her memoirs.

A protective net was thrown around Danny Ryan.

Her son, who hates her.

NINETEEN

DANNY'S LEFT HIP IS DESTROYED.

The ball joint is shattered, the tendons torn away.

Without the best doctors, Danny will have a severe limp the rest of his life, maybe be on crutches, certainly headed for an early wheelchair.

This is what Dr. Rosen tells Danny when he's well enough to listen.

"Lucky for you," Rosen says, "you have me."

Turns out he's the head of orthopedics. Has done surgeries on a few of the Patriots and the Bruins. Guy is the best. Now he tells Danny, "I'm going to take you through three procedures. You have an infection going on in there. I have to go back in—"

"*Back* in?"

"When you first came in, the trauma guys took out the bullet and the bone fragments," Rosen explains. "Lucky for you, they're good and didn't fuck you up permanently. But you have an infection going on—that's why you're feverish—that I have to clean up. When that looks good, I'm going to go in and give you a new ball joint. A couple of weeks after that, I go back in and repair the tendons. You'll never be a threat for Olympic gold, but if you work hard in rehab, you'll walk just fine."

"I can't pay for all that," Danny says.

"Your mother is picking up the bill," Rosen says.

"The hell she is."

"*You* tell her that, chief," Rosen says. "I don't want to end up as my own patient."

THE FIRST DAY or so, Danny goes in and out of consciousness. Madeleine is there by his bedside. Her or Terri or both. If Danny has a resentment against Madeleine, Terri doesn't. She likes her, is grateful for what she's done for her husband.

Danny doesn't much care one way or the other that first day or so. He just goes in and out. Out is better, because his hip hurts like a motherfucker. The juice of the poppy is sweetness itself, sweet relief, sweet dreams. Floating in liquid warmth.

Yeah, but he comes out of it, sees her face, and it pisses him off. *Now* she wants to be part of my life, *now* she loves me? Now she cares? Where was she when . . . when . . . when . . .

So the first few days are a blur. He only wishes the next few were—they're in all-too-sharp relief. The doctors don't want him getting hooked, so they step down his morphine, let him feel pain that sets his teeth on edge. Then infection comes back, and fevers, and they have to leave the wound open to drain it and every minute in that bed feels like an hour. Nothing to do but lie there and worry: Am I going to fucking die? Am I going to be a cripple?

What he doesn't have to worry about is the cops.

No detectives come in to smirk and harass him, get drug-induced statements that would take him from the hospital to the cell.

Danny Ryan was an innocent bystander in a drive-by shooting, end of story.

The Murphys didn't arrange that.

His mother did.

WHEN THE INFECTION subsides, Rosen goes in for the surgery to reconstruct the hip. The operation goes well, but Danny's immobilized for long days and nights.

Jimmy Mac comes to see him.

"Thanks," Danny says.

"For what?" Jimmy asks.

Danny lowers his voice. "Saving my fucking life."

Jimmy blushes. He's a little embarrassed because he panicked at first when Mick's face got blown off, and he hit the gas to get out of there—like anyone would, Danny thinks—but he came back. He could have got away safe but he came back for Danny, right into Steve Giordo's gunsights.

"You'd have done the same for me," Jimmy says.

Danny nods.

It's true.

"Your father come around?" Jimmy asks.

Danny shakes his head. "He won't come. Says he won't be in the same building as, you know . . ."

Jimmy grins. "Jesus, Danny, I saw her in the lobby. She's a looker, your mom."

"Work it out with Angie, it's okay with me."

"Hey, I didn't mean—"

"I know."

The next day Pat comes to visit.

"You took one for the team," he says.

"Sorry it didn't work out like we'd planned."

"Giordo's on the sidelines for a while," Pat says.

"Well, that's good."

"Yeah, that's good."

It's awkward between them, like it never has been before. Pat doesn't know quite what to say and Danny doesn't know how to deal with his silence. They do the usual bullshit—the families, the kids—and they're both relieved when the nurse comes in and kicks Pat's ass out of there so Danny can get his rest.

He wakes up when he hears Terri saying, "—the hell are *you* doing here?"

Peter Moretti is standing there with flowers in his hand. Smile smooth as his silk tie. Terri glaring at him, Madeleine fixing him with a calm, hard look.

"I came to see my friend Danny," Peter says.

Terri spits, "Get out."

"It's all right," Danny says.

Peter comes over to the bed, sets the flowers down on the side table, leans in and, still smiling, whispers, "You're dead, Danny. Soon as you get out, you're a dead man."

They all know that a hospital is off-limits. Last thing in the world you want to do in a war is piss off doctors and nurses, because you might be seeing them in a trauma ward, and they let you bleed out because you've exposed them to gunfire at their place of work. Ditto with priests, who might be giving you last rites. You don't want them to be nervous and fuck up the words that stand between you and hell.

Peter straightens up and turns to Terri. "Anything I can do, anything you need, please let me know."

"Get out."

"I don't know why you're being this way," Peter says. "I had nothing to do with what happened. You want to know what your husband was doing down there that night, ask him."

"I don't need you to tell me what to say to my husband."

"Of course not," Peter says. "I overstepped. I'll leave you alone. I'm sure Danny needs his rest."

Madeleine follows him out of the room. "Mr. Moretti. Do you know who I am?"

Peter's smile edges toward a smirk. "I heard."

"Then you've also heard what I'm capable of," Madeleine says. "If you hurt my son, or even *try* to hurt my son, I'll put you where your father is."

"You were right to leave Providence," Peter says. "You should have stayed away. And you should stay out of this."

"Perhaps your father would be more comfortable in Pelican Bay," Madeleine says. "Twenty-three hours a day in solitary and no pretty little Puerto Rican *maricóns* satisfying his baser desires. If I make one call to a certain federal judge . . ."

"You know," Peter says, "whether a whore blows a guy for a dime bag or a million dollars, she's still a whore."

"But she's a whore with a million dollars," Madeleine says. "I happen to have a lot more. Take me on, Mr. Moretti, I'll string your balls on a necklace and wear it around town."

A FEW MORNINGS later Danny gets into a fight with Terri when he finds out that Madeleine paid their month's rent and bought groceries.

"What am I supposed to do, Danny?" Terri asks, in tears because he yelled at her and she was so stressed out about his shooting anyway. "You're not working and the bills still come."

Even though he's run out of sick days, they're still punching him in down on the docks. But money is tight. Regardless, the thought of his mother putting food on his table makes him furious. "You do not take her fucking money, Terri."

Terri throws up her hands and looks at him, mouth agape, like *Who the hell do you think is paying for this room?* Danny doesn't have an answer—he's aware of his hypocrisy.

All the more so when Rosen says that the best thing for Danny is six weeks at a special rehab facility up in Massachusetts. Which costs about what it sounds like. Danny's insurance with the union is pretty good, but it ain't private-out-of-state-facility good, it's local-outpatient-clinic good.

"Is there that big a difference?" Danny asks him.

"The difference is a cane," Rosen says. "The local place gets you the next thirty years on a cane, the private place gets you the next thirty without one."

Madeleine insists on springing for the private clinic.

"Money is not my problem in life," she tells Danny.

"No? What is your problem in life?"

"Right now, you are. You're my son acting like my *child*."

Terri tells him pretty much the same thing.

"Think about me," she says. "Maybe I'd rather have a husband who doesn't need to set down his cane to pick up his baby? Maybe I'd still like to get laid every once in a while—"

"Terri—"

"They're *nurses*, Danny," she says, "they've heard 'laid.' How about I'd like to take long walks on the beach with you, maybe get on a bicycle, ride around Block Island or something? Maybe I'd like to dance with you again. You don't let your mother do this for you—for us—I'm done with you. My hand to God, pregnant and all, I'll leave you. You can be a bitter, lonely old man like your father."

Danny goes up to Massachusetts.

TWENTY

PETER MORETTI ISN'T HAPPY.

The deal he thought he had with Danny Ryan turned out to be a double-cross, so the hit on Liam Murphy ended up as a hit on Danny, which wouldn't have been so bad considering the circumstances except that Ryan survived it and his *puttana* mother won't let Peter go at him again.

Danny's jacked up, off the board for the foreseeable future, but so is Steve Giordo, who departed with the sentiment that he ain't gonna walk into another ambush because the Moretti brothers can't tell one mick from another.

He has a point, Peter thinks. Worse is that New York and Hartford are less likely to lend out any of their people anymore because they don't want to waste an asset on some outfit that gets suckered by a cheap leg-breaker like Danny Ryan.

So now Peter really isn't happy when he's just trying to eat breakfast at the Central Diner and Solly Weiss walks in, plops his ancient ass down across the table and starts in before Peter can even have a look at the sports page. "Peter, my store was robbed."

Peter don't need the newspaper to know this. It isn't news. Two of his guys, Gino Conti and Renny Bouchard, hit Solly's jewelry store last night and took at least a hundred thousand in diamonds and some other pieces. "That's too bad, Solly."

"Haven't I always made you a deal?" Solly asks. "That necklace for your *gumar* . . ."

"I didn't rob your store, Solly." Which, Peter thinks, is technically true.

"Peter, please," Solly says. "Do not treat me like a child. I was in business before you knew what business was."

Solly has a few strands of white hair that remind Peter he needs to stop at Rite Aid for dental floss. He says, "You're insured, right? You're going to make a profit off this thing."

"These particular pieces weren't insured."

"If you brought them in from overseas and you didn't declare them, that's not my problem," Peter says. Then he gets to the point. "Anyway, I thought you were under the Murphys' protection. If you was with us, this wouldn't have happened."

"I want my rocks back."

"I want a twelve-inch dick," Peter says. "I got shorted by an inch, what can I tell you."

Solly goes into this whole song and dance—he has to put his sister in a nursing home, his wife has a condition, the roof needs repairing—

"*Basta,*" Peter snaps. "With all due respect—"

"I'm glad to hear you say 'respect,' young Peter Moretti," Solly says, "because that's what this is all about. I showed respect to your father, I showed respect to Pasco, they showed respect to me, they showed respect for my business." His voice is shaking.

"My father is in the joint," Peter says, "Pasco is in Florida, and I'm in charge now."

"I didn't come empty-handed," Solly says. "If these pieces are returned, I'll establish the same relationship with you that I had with John."

"Which was what?"

Solly lowers his voice. "An envelope first Thursday of every month. Thirty percent discount—off wholesale—during the holidays. And of course, if you ever have a special need . . ."

It's one of those *if* moments.

If Peter were in a better mood, if Peter'd had a second cup of coffee, if Peter had got a chance to look at the sports page, if Chris Palumbo had got his ass out of bed in time to have breakfast with Peter, if Solly's hair didn't for some reason annoy the shit out of Peter this morning, then maybe Peter accepts his offer and none of the horrible shit that follows happens.

A lot of *if*s people will look back on.

None of them matter, because Peter says, "I have a special need *now*."

Solly smiles. He's going to get his rocks back. "Tell me."

"I have a special need for you to get the fuck out of here," Peter says. "You want to see your rocks, I'll let you watch them bounce up and down on my *gumar*'s tits while I'm fucking her. Look, just don't piss me off, okay, Solly? It's safer for you that way."

Peter's already given one of the pieces to his *gumar* and he's not about to go in there and tell her she has to take it off her neck.

Solly looks at him sadly, shakes his head, gets up and totters out the door.

Old Jew, Peter thinks, going back to his paper, lives up John Murphy's ass for thirty years, now he wants to swap me a hundred K for thirty percent at Christmas?

Fuck that.

End of story.

NOT FOR SOLLY it isn't.

He goes home, gets right on the horn to Pasco Ferri down in Florida and plays "remember when."

Remember when you proposed to Mary and you had no money for a decent ring? Remember when your son was in the same position with his fiancée? Remember when you needed a contribution for the rides on Saint Rocco's Day? Remember when you were running that legislator and needed to wash some money? Remember when . . .

"I don't have the Alzheimer's, thank God," Pasco says. "What's going on, Solly?"

Solly tells him about the robbery, tells him about how he was treated by young Peter Moretti. "He told me to come watch him fuck his girlfriend."

"That was out of line," Pasco agrees. He's getting a little tired of the Moretti brothers causing him agita. First it's a war over a damn titty, now it's this. Maybe it's time the Morettis got taken down a peg or two.

"I have friends," Solly is saying. "Friends in the mayor's office, friends at the precinct houses . . ."

"I know you do, Solly."

"I made him a respectful offer, Pasco," Solly says. "Reflecting the new situation, and he treats me like some *schwarze* he caught with a hand in the till? I won't have it."

"Solly, do me a favor?" Pasco asks. "Let me take care of it."

PETER'S AT AMERICAN Vending when he gets the call from Pasco. "Peter, what the hell? Solly Weiss?"

Peter gets defensive. "Technically, he wasn't under our protection so he was fair game."

There's a long silence, then Pasco says, like he's real tired, "You ever think about making friends instead of enemies?"

"I have a right to earn."

Pasco sighs. "The ring on my wife's finger—"

"Pasco, with all due respect," Peter cuts him off, "you're retired, God bless . . ."

Don't stick your nose in.

When Peter hangs up he turns to Paulie and says, "That old kike went crying to Pasco, do you believe that? Shit, I should rob him again."

Chris Palumbo looks at him.

"What?" Peter asks.

"Maybe you should return the old guy's shit," Chris says. "Solly goes way back with Pasco and all those guys. He's given prices to every cop in town. You might want to show him the respect, Peter."

Paulie says, "I agree."

"You agree?" Peter says. "You want to pay him out of *your* pocket?"

"No."

"Then shut the fuck up," Peter says. "Anyone remember we're in a war here? It costs money."

Chris tries again. "You really want to piss on Pasco's shoes?"

"Pasco has to be retired," Peter says, "or not be retired. I can't run this thing if everyone thinks they can go over my head every time they disagree with one of my rulings."

"Upstairs to the booth," Paulie says.

"What?"

"You know, like in football," Paulie says. "Instant replay . . . up in the booth."

"Yeah, okay, whatever."

Yeah, okay, whatever, Chris thinks, but it worries him.

•   •   •

THE BODIES OF Gino Conti and Renny Bouchard are never found.

Those two guys are just gone, and everyone knows they aren't coming back and everyone knows why not.

It's not just Conti and Bouchard—which is bad enough—but in the nine days since Peter told Solly Weiss to take a walk, two of his card games have been busted, three bookies have been popped, and every girl has been chased off the streets—all shit the cops would usually have left alone.

Solly Weiss has friends, all right.

But Peter gets his feet dug in even deeper. "Over my dead body."

"That's not outside the realm of possibility," Chris answers.

"Come on."

"Ask Gino and Renny," Chris says. "Oh, that's right, you can't."

"That was the Murphys."

"Bullshit."

It's classic Pasco Ferri, Chris thinks. Peter disrespected him and he doesn't whack Peter, he whacks a couple of underlings to teach him a lesson.

A lesson Peter better learn.

Before we all get clipped.

"Peter—"

"I don't want to hear any fucking more about it, Chris," Peter says, and walks away from him.

So now Chris goes to Sal Antonucci, finds him down in Narragansett looking at a house by the shore, just two blocks from the beach.

"It's more than we can really afford," Sal says, "but I can put a big down payment on it."

No shit he can put a big down payment. Word is that Sal and his crew did an armored car thing up in Manchester, New Hampshire, and scored big.

Chris says, "It's a buyer's market."

"I figure I can knock them twenty, thirty off the ask," Sal says. He stands back and looks at the house. "Never thought we'd be able to do something like this, but . . . Anyway, Judy and I thought it would be nice for the kids. Looking down the road, grandkids. Someplace for the family to gather, you know?"

"Otherwise they scatter," Chris says.

"What I mean," Sal says. "What brings you down here?"

Because Chris don't do nothing for nothing. He never comes just to shoot the shit, there's always an agenda.

"This Solly Weiss thing . . ." he says.

Sal frowns. "You're Peter's consigliere. Did you talk with him?"

"Until I'm blue in the face," Chris answers. "He doesn't want to listen. I'm afraid if I bring it up again . . ."

Chris leaves it out there—Sal should go make Peter see the light on this one. Peter will listen to him, because Sal's been doing most of the heavy lifting in the thing with the Murphys, and Peter needs Sal to keep doing what he's doing.

Especially with Giordo gone.

Sal takes the bait, like Chris knew he would.

"I'm not afraid of Peter," Sal says. "I'll talk to him. What do you think about the house? I don't know, it's a lot of money."

"Interest rates being what they are," Chris says, "I don't see how you can afford not to."

SAL GOES TO see Peter. "Give the rocks back before we all end up in a landfill."

"What, you giving me orders now?" Peter asks. "I'm the boss of this family."

"Good—we can put that on your fucking headstone," Sal says. "I'm not giving you orders, but shit."

"Shit, what?"

"Forget it."

"No, Sal," Peter says, pushing it, "you got something on your chest, get it the fuck off."

"Okay, fine," Sal says. "You and Paulie sit in here in your office drinking coffee, eating doughnuts, while it's me and my crew doing all the work, and now we got two guys dead because you don't want to give back something you shouldn't have in the first place!"

"You do not tell me what I should, shouldn't have!"

"Guys, come on," Chris says.

"Yeah?" Sal asks, standing up from the table. "What would you have, Peter, if my crew and me weren't out there getting it for you? You'd have *ugatz*."

Paulie says, "You are talking to the boss—"

"—of this family," Sal interrupts. "Yeah, I heard. So maybe he should start *acting* like the boss of this family and do what's *best* for this family and not just the Moretti brothers!"

"Cocksucker!" Paulie says.

"Come on, bring it!" Sal says.

"Guys!" Chris steps in between them. Even Frankie V gets up from his chair and steps in to calm things down.

"You want me to give the jewelry back?" Peter says. "Fine, I'll give it back."

"Good," Sal says, settling down a little.

"But you're going to kick to me on that Manchester job," Peter says.

"What?!"

"You think I didn't know about that?" Peter asks. "You think I wouldn't find out?!"

"That's my fucking money."

"What," Peter asks, "I'm supposed to walk away empty-handed? Everyone eats but Peter Moretti? Fuck that. You should have been kicking to me from moment one. Fifty percent. I was going to let it slide, but if we're going to play by the rules now, we're *all* going to play by the rules. I want it all now—not fifty, a hundred. A tax for not doing the right thing in the first place."

Sal turns to Chris. "You believe this fucking guy?"

Chris shakes his head. "He's the boss, Sal. He's within his rights here."

Sal's hands flex, like he's ready to go.

Frankie V reaches inside his jacket for his piece, just in case.

But Sal just slowly nods, then looks at Peter and says, "Fine. You got it. You want the money, you got it, you greedy fuck. But take a good look at this face, Peter, because it's the last time you'll see it."

"What do you mean?"

"I'm out of your war," Sal says. "Me and my crew. I don't even know why I got in it in the first place—the Murphys never did anything to me, I never had a beef with them. I got in out of loyalty to you, but loyalty is a two-way street. Like respect. You want it, you have to give it."

"You took an oath," Peter says. "It's for you to show respect and loyalty to me."

"*I have!*" Sal yells. "I'm going to hell for the shit I've done for you. I'm going to hell, Peter. What more do you fucking want?"

"Go ahead," Peter says. "Run away, you're scared. You're waiting for me to beg you to stay, don't hold your breath. Who needs you?"

We do, Chris thinks, but he doesn't say it.

Sal, he smiles at Peter, nods, and walks out.

"Make sure you get that money," Peter says to Chris.

THANKS FOR TAKING my back," Sal says to Chris when the consigliere comes for the money.

"Sal—"

"You're a two-faced son of a bitch, you know that?"

"Sal, you can't just walk away."

"No?" Sal asks. "Who's going to come after me? You, Chris?"

Chris doesn't say anything.

"What I thought."

Tony comes out of the back room with a duffel bag and hands it to Chris.

"That was my house," Sal says. "The house I showed you. For my grandkids."

"I'm sorry, Sal."

"Between you and me?" Sal says. "One of these days, I'm going to put that motherfucker in the dirt."

Chris doesn't have to ask which motherfucker he means.

TWENTY-ONE

DANNY LETS GO OF THE metal bar and steps forward.

Hurts like a son of a bitch, but it's a good hurt because if he can put any weight on the left leg it means his hip is healing. He's still a little afraid, though, that he's going to hear some awful snap and the hip joint is going to come popping out of his skin.

By the time he makes it all the way down the length of the bar without grabbing it to balance, he's tired and sweating hard.

Ten whole feet, he thinks, reminding himself that it's progress. Also reminds himself that he's an outpatient now—after three grueling weeks they let him leave the clinic and move to the nearby Residence Inn with Terri.

With Madeleine staying in a room down the hall.

His wife and his mother have become as thick as thieves. They have long days on their hands while he's doing his rehab and they go shopping, go to lunch, go to the movies.

Danny don't like it.

"What do you want me to do?" Terri asked when he brought it up. "Sit in the room all day, watch TV?"

"No."

"Well?"

Danny didn't have an answer.

"She's nice," Terri said. "We have fun."

"Good." He means it, sort of. It's good for her to have company and also to be away from her family and Dogtown, with everything that's happening.

Danny follows the war in the papers and on TV.

The media loves it. They haven't had a full-out gang war to cover in years and it makes for great headlines and photos. Film at eleven. Readers and viewers following it like they'd follow baseball—get up in the morning to read the box scores.

Dante Delmonte, one of Paulie's crew, shot in his car after making a collection in South Providence. And two more of Moretti's guys, Gino Conti and Renny Bouchard, are gone—although it's Pasco who's reputed to have given the order.

Which is very interesting, Danny thinks. Maybe Pasco's decided it was a mistake to give Peter the top job. Maybe he's looking around. If that's the case, there might be a possibility of making a favorable peace.

What he doesn't get in the papers Jimmy Mac fills him in on. Jimmy comes up about once a week, brings him all the inside news. Now he watches Danny take his first tentative steps.

He hands Danny his cane and they go down to the little cafeteria.

"Sal Antonucci and Peter are at odds," Jimmy says, then tells him about the shit that followed the Solly Weiss job. "Sal says he's going to sit this one out."

Shit, Danny thinks, that's big fucking news. Maybe they can do better than Sal just taking a knee, maybe get Sal in the game on their side. The offer would be simple—Hey, Sal, if you decide to go up against the Morettis, we'll back you.

Danny thinks a few moves ahead: Sal's nowhere near as smart as Peter Moretti, never mind Chris Palumbo. If Sal took the throne from the Morettis, he'd be easy to manipulate. Especially if we're the ones who helped him take the big chair.

"Where does Chris come down on it, I wonder?" Danny muses.

"Chris will go with the winner," Jimmy says. "But the word we're getting is that Sal's wicked pissed with Chris for taking Peter's side on this thing."

"Pissed enough to do something about it?"

"What are you thinking?"

What Danny's thinking is that Chris is Peter's brains. Without him, it would be just a matter of time before the Morettis do something fatally stupid.

Danny says, "Get word to Sal that if he decides to go for the corner office, we'll back him. If he takes the crown on Monday, we make peace on Tuesday."

"He killed three of our friends, Danny."

"I know," Danny says, but he also knows that at the end of the day you don't make peace with your friends, you make peace with your enemies.

Let the dead bury the dead.

"Shouldn't we run this past John or Pat first?" Jimmy asks.

Yeah, probably, Danny thinks. But he also thinks he wants to be the one to make a difference, maybe get taken seriously. "Let's wait and see how it goes first, then we'll bring them in."

Jimmy asks, "How do we get to Sal?"

"Tony Romano," Danny says. Him and Sal are joined at the fucking hip. If Sal is interested, great; if not, no real harm done—neither the Murphys nor Sal would lose face.

"And if Sal says no?" Jimmy asks.

Danny's ahead of it. "We work it the other way. We make the approach to Chris. Maybe's he's tired of cleaning up the Morettis' messes. Maybe he wants to be the number one guy."

Jimmy grins.

"What?" Danny asks.

"When did you start thinking like a boss?"

"I got no ambitions," Danny says, "except we all survive this thing."

SAL ANTONUCCI PULLS his pants up, zips his fly and buckles his belt. Sits back down on the bed to put his shoes on.

Tony's still naked. Just lies there on top of the bed, his body stretched out, no shame or nothing.

He's a beautiful fucking man, Sal thinks.

"By the way," Tony says. "Jimmy Mac came to see me."

"'By the way'?" Sal says. "That's kind of big for 'by the way.' Why didn't you tell me this right off?"

Tony grins. "I had other things on my mind. Bigger things."

"What did he want?"

"You," Tony says.

Sal smiles down at him. "I'm taken."

"I know," Tony says, clasping his hand and then letting go. "He wanted me to sound you out."

"About what?"

"Hitching your cart to the Murphys."

Sal bends down to tie his laces. "No shit? What did he say?"

"Just that Danny Ryan would be open to talking."

Sal runs it through. Ryan speaks for the Murphys. It doesn't take a fucking genius to figure out their move—I join in alliance against the Morettis, we put Peter and Paul at the bottom of the Narragansett Bay, I take over, and it's back to business the way it used to be.

But holy fuck—whacking the Morettis?

You'd have to get the nod from Boston and New York.

Never mind the old man down in Florida. Christ, would Pasco give his okay? Peter really jerked his chain on the Solly Weiss thing, but Conti and Bouchard picked up the tab for that. Still . . .

"What do *you* think?" he asks Tony.

Tony says, "I think it's worth checking out."

So do I, Sal thinks. He finishes lacing his shoes and sits back up. Lot of spade work to be done, though, a lot of pipe to be laid. And even that's dangerous—someone will have to approach Pasco, sound him out, and even just doing that could get them all killed, Pasco don't like what he's hearing.

But if he does, Pasco takes care of Boston and New York.

"You're the balance of power now," Tony says. "The Murphys are coming to you, Peter will have to come back to you, sooner or later. It's really a matter of taking the best offer."

But Peter won't offer me what the Murphys are, Sal thinks.

His position.

The safe move would be to go back with Peter, finish off the Irish, and then deal with Peter later. The gutsier move would be to join the Murphys, get rid of the Morettis, and then put the Irish back in their place.

"The worst thing," Tony says, "would be if the Murphys won without you. Then you're fucked."

Out in the cold, Sal thinks.

"Can they win?" he asks. Outmanned, outgunned, Danny Ryan on the sidelines . . .

"With us on their side, maybe," Tony says.

"The balance of power."

"The balance of power." Tony smiles.

"I can't take a chance being seen with Pat," Sal says. "Not until all the ducks are in a row. If we have a meet, it will be you. You good with that?"

"Of course."

"Go back to Jimmy," Sal says. "Tell him I might be interested in sitting down, but not before certain roads are opened in Florida. This works out, you're my consigliere."

He looks down at Tony, who's still lying there, the lazy fuck that he is. The lazy, beautiful fuck.

"Jesus," Sal says.

"What?"

"If my wife, my kids . . ."

"You don't think Judy already knows?" Tony asks.

"Hey, I give it to her good."

"She knows," Tony says. "She just doesn't want to say."

"Other guys have their *gumars*."

Tony bristles. "I'm not your fucking *gumar*."

"I know. I didn't mean . . ."

Sal gets up, puts on his coat, goes out the door.

TWENTY-TWO

HER PERFUME PRECEDES HER INTO the room—Danny, resting after his rehab session, smells her before he sees her. Madeleine sweeps into the clinic, looking all cool and lovely, and it just pisses him off.

"I want you to talk to somebody," she says.

"Who?"

"He's out in the parking lot," she says. "Danny, please, for your family's sake, just hear him out."

He follows her out to where a car is parked. Madeleine opens the passenger door for him and says, "Just keep an open mind, Danny. Please."

Then she's gone.

The guy in the car says, "Danny, I'm Phillip Jardine. FBI."

No shit, Danny thinks. Jardine looks like FBI, because the feds have a look. Short hair, dull ties, bland WASP faces. This fucking Jardine fits the bill—razor-cut blond hair, clear blue eyes, a real Eagle Scout.

Except Danny knows the fed Eagle Scouts get badges in throat-cutting.

But he gets into the car. Because if someone he knows pulls up and sees him talking to someone they *don't* know, they want to know who and why. "Make it quick."

"I want to help you."

Yeah, right, Danny thinks. Famous first words. I want to help you fuck your friends, become a rat, go into the Witness Protection Program and sell chicken feed in East Bumfuck somewhere. What feds mean by "I want to help you" is "I want to help you help me."

Danny knows the federal pitch: *Friendship? Fuck friendship. I know you were boys together and all that happy crap, but now it's time for you to grow the fuck up. You have kids, you want them to know their father? Or you want to see them once a month over a metal table, you're not allowed to touch them? How about the wife? No offense, but is she going to wait? How long is she going to toss and turn in an empty bed before she finds a new man she teaches your kids to call "Uncle"?*

"Help me do what?" Danny asks.

"Have a life," Jardine answers.

"I have one."

"For how much longer?" Jardine asks. "You're losing the war. You know it, I know it, everyone on the street knows it's just a matter of time. You have a wife, and a kid on the way. A family that loves you."

Danny feels a flash of anger. "What do you know about my family?"

Jardine shrugged. "If you love them, and you have a chance to give them a life, you'll take it."

"What, you're offering me that chance?"

"That's right," Jardine says. "You finish your therapy up here and you go. You and Terri and the baby she's carrying."

"Into the program."

Jardine nods.

"But I'd have to testify against my friends," Danny says.

"Your friends?" Jardine asks. "Which ones? The Morettis? They want you dead. The Murphys? You think you're one of them? One of the family? You're not. They may let you eat at their table, but they'll never give you your own chair."

"Fuck that. No." No way, no fucking way in hell he's testifying against his friends. Against Pat, or even John.

Jardine smiles. "I told your mother that's what you'd say."

"She should have listened to you," Danny says, fumbling with his cane, reaching for the door handle.

"There's a middle way," Jardine says. "You give me a little information now and then. If a hit's planned, maybe you tip me off. Just trying to keep the body count down here, Danny."

"And you do what for me?"

"Things go south," Jardine says, "the Bureau steps up, goes to bat for you. In court, in judge's chambers, in the DA's office. We take care of our own. If we were to hear about a threat to you, we'd give you the word, you're not there when the event is supposed to go off."

That's what you really want, Danny thinks. You want a snitch in play on the streets. You made the program offer to keep my mother's fuckbuddies happy, but you'd really rather have me out there as long as I'm useful. Soon as I'm not, fuck me. The FBI uses snitches like Kleenex. Jerks off on them, tosses them away. If a snitch gets whacked, it's like *Oops, next*.

"Don't answer now," Jardine says. "Think about it."

"Think about go fucking yourself."

"That's not the answer to your problems, Danny."

The fuck you know, Danny thinks, about my problems?

Madeleine's waiting for him in the lobby. "You have a family to think about."

"You should talk."

"I'm here now."

"Yeah, *now*." Twenty-seven years too late. "Where will you be tomorrow?"

"That isn't the question, Danny," she says. "The question is where will *you* be tomorrow? Where will Terri be? Where will your child be?"

"They'll be with me."

She tries a different tack. "You could have a life somewhere."

"I have a life here."

"What life?" she asks. "You're a shift boss on the docks and a collector for the Murphys, and you would be a murderer except that you screwed it up. If we're being honest here, that's what you are."

"At least I'm not a whore," Danny says. He sees the hurt in her eyes, sees that he hit his target, but can't help adding, "If we're being, you know, honest here."

"I've done the best I could with the cards I was dealt," Madeleine says.

It sounds practiced to him, like a line she's told herself a thousand times, waking up beside men she didn't love. And I could say the same thing, Danny thinks. I've done the best I could with the cards you handed me.

"So this is what you want?" she asks incredulously. "You want to stay in Dogtown?"

"It's where you left me."

Where you *left* me.

"If you want me to go away, I'll go away." She walks past him to the door, then turns around. "But don't hurt your family because you hate me."

•   •   •

HE'S BACK AT Residence Inn, half-asleep a couple of hours later when he hears Terri come in, set some bags on the counter, and walk into the bedroom.

"How was rehab?" she asked.

"Good. I walked."

"Really?"

"Yeah," Danny says. "Your husband's a two-year-old."

She looks down at him and says, "I don't think a two-year-old has *that*."

"I must have been dreaming."

"It better have been about me," she says, unzipping his fly.

"Oh yeah, it was."

"Yeah?" she asks. "Was I doing *this* to you?"

"Jesus, Terri."

"Or this?"

Her mouth is warm and wet, her tongue flicks, he knows he ain't gonna last long. Sensing this, she stops and starts to straddle him.

"Can you do this?" he asks. "I don't want to hurt you or the baby."

"It would feel good," she says. "But will it hurt *you*?"

"You're not that heavy."

"Are you kidding? I'm a whale."

"I don't know if I can—"

"I'll do the work."

Terri moves on him with surprising grace, rocks back and forth, closes her eyes and takes her pleasure. It's been a long time; he struggles to hold back, but when he hears her come, feels her grip him, he lets go.

She rolls off him carefully, lies on her back and falls asleep.

Danny don't. Usually he does but he has too much on his mind—a potential deal with Sal—or maybe Chris—and an end to the war. Then there's Jardine's offer—or offers, plural. Become a rat, go into the program, or become a snitch, an informant.

He listens to Terri breathe and for the first time really considers it.

Maybe I do owe that to her, to the baby in her belly.

A fresh start somewhere, a legit job.

She'd be torn, because it would mean turning on her family, but on the other hand she'd be relieved to be safe.

But could I do it?

I could flip on John, but on Pat?

He chews on it, and somehow it all gets mixed in with his mother's abandonment of him and his dad; it becomes all about Dogtown and loyalty and all that shit and it just goes sideways, like a boat drifting into the rocks.

TWENTY-THREE

PETER MORETTI HAS TO EAT serious rations of shit.

He knows he's starting to lose the war and has to make moves to turn things around.

Painful, humiliating moves.

First he had to give Solly Weiss his stones back, and the old prick was so sanctimonious about it Peter would have liked to shoot him in the face. But he had to go, hat in hand, apologize, and hand over the stones. Not before he had to take that necklace off his *gumar*'s neck, which didn't exactly make her horny for him.

That was bad enough, but then he had to extend a hand to Sal Antonucci, because without Sal and his crew, the war with the Murphys was swirling the toilet. Truth was he needed Sal, he needed Tony. But Peter couldn't go himself, he just couldn't make himself do it, so he sent Chris.

Chris argued against sending *anyone* to see Sal. "It's a mistake. He's an egotistical motherfucker in the first place, and now we go begging him? It will only make his head swell up more. Anyway, believe me, he can't help himself, he'll get back in the fight."

"Yeah, but on which side?" Peter asked.

THEY SIT DOWN across a table at Fiori's, Chris and Frankie V on the one side, Sal and Tony on the other.

Technically Sal is the host, even though Chris asked for the meeting, because this is his turf and the restaurant is under his protection. So Sal orders a good bottle of wine, sips it for approval, and pours a glass for Chris.

Chris gets right down to it. "Peter is prepared to give you back the tax he took from the Manchester thing."

"Why?" Sal asks. "Why is that?"

"C'mon, Sal, you going to make me suck your dick?"

"I promise I won't come in your mouth."

"Peter knows he was wrong," Chris says. "He knows that and he's sorry and he wants to make amends."

"Then why isn't he here?" Sal asks.

"I advised him not to," Chris answers. "If he comes in person and you spurn his overture, he loses enormous face, you know that. If we can come to some kind of arrangement here tonight, if I can take that back to Peter, I know he'll be eager to come over himself. I could hardly hold him back tonight."

"But you managed," Tony says.

Chris looks at Sal. "He talk for you now?"

"He's free to speak his mind," Sal says. "And let's be honest— Peter didn't have no 'change of heart,' he didn't wake up one morning and it hit him, 'I was a dick to Sal.' You're losing the war, you need me and my crew."

Chris doesn't answer, but he dips his head in a way that says this is the case.

Always the fucking diplomat, Sal thinks.

"You could take this money, buy your house," Chris says, and then sees from the look on Sal's face that this was a mistake.

"The house got sold," Sal says, his voice low and angry.

"There are other houses," Chris says, trying to recover.

"Not like that one," Sal says.

"I wasn't finished," Chris says. "You come back, after this thing is over, you get the longshoremen's union."

It's big—far more than the Manchester job was worth. A big chunk of the Murphy business, a big piece of Moretti's potential income. It's a real sacrifice by Peter—a real offer.

"I don't want it," Sal says.

"What?" Frankie V asks.

He sure as shit wants it.

"I've been thinking," Sal says, "about this thing of ours. It's changed, not like the old days. There used to be rules. Now? Peter can come in and jerk my money from me just like that? What says he couldn't do it again? He 'gives' me the union? Fuck that, I *took* the union for him. He 'gives' me shit. And then he can just pull it away with the other hand when he feels like it?"

He lets that sit in the air for a second, then says, "Nah. I have businesses—the restaurant, the parking lot, the linen—my family eats. Maybe I just sit back now, be content with that. Because I'll tell you? Looking around the last few years? Everyone ends up dead or in the joint. I'm thinking of dying at home."

Frankie V goes old-school. "That's not how it works. You took an oath. Until you die."

"Who's going to enforce that, Frankie?" Sal asks. "You?"

Frankie turns to Chris. "The fuck we wasting our breath for? He doesn't give a shit his friends are getting killed. His family eats, right? Fuck this. I'm out of here."

Chris looks across the table at Sal. "So what shall I tell Peter?"

"Finish your drink," Sal says. "Then take Peter's money, his union, and his 'sorries,' and tell him he can stick them up his ass."

"What happens when the Murphys come for you, Sal?"

"Why should they come for me?"

"*I* wouldn't leave you on the board."

Well, thanks for telling me that, thinks Sal. If I don't come back into the fold, you're going to take me out. But he says, "They come after me I'll deal with them. Until then, I got nothin' against the two of you."

Buy a little time, maybe get them debating if they really want to go up against him.

When they go out the door, Sal says, "The next time they come, they're coming heavy. Chris will ask for a sit-down just between me and him; Frankie V will be there to take me out. Then you'll be next."

Tony asks, "So what do you want to do?"

"Make the meeting with Murphy," Sal says. "Tell him I'll take the deal. Go now."

Because it's urgent. Soon as Peter gets his "no" answer, he's going to answer back, and it ain't gonna be with words.

"I don't have my car," Tony says.

"Take mine."

JIMMY MAC DRIVES Danny over to the Gloc.

When Danny walks back in, he isn't using the cane at all. He limps a little, but otherwise you wouldn't know that Steve Giordo shot the shit out of him. Everyone in the neighborhood knows it, though.

Everyone knows that Danny Ryan was the bait in the botched hit on Liam. That the mother had swept in and pulled him out of the shit, that this sent his father on a bender of epic proportions, Marty Ryan hitting the bottle like a speed bag.

"I'll wait out here," Jimmy says.

The Gloc is decorated for Christmas. Well, as much as it ever is. A scraggly fake tree with a few bulbs and tinsel that looks like it's left over from World War II. The sound system squeaks some Irish band doing "Santa Claus Is Coming to Town," which Danny thinks is a really bad idea.

John and Pat are in the back room.

Pat comes up and wraps his arms around Danny. "I'm sorry I didn't come up and see you more."

Danny says, "Pat, we need to talk."

They go off to a booth, Danny tells him about the potential deal with Sal.

"You did that on your own boot?" Pat asked. "I wish you'd checked with me first."

"I gotta check with you, Pat?" Danny asks. He knew he should have, and the old him would have. But there's something about getting shot that makes him want to be his own man.

"With something like that, yeah."

"It's a chance to end this thing, put it to bed," Danny says. "If Sal and his crew come over to us, Peter's going to ask for peace, especially if Pasco isn't backing him anymore."

"He patched up that beef with Pasco."

"He hasn't patched it up with Sal," Danny says. *"We can end this war, Pat."*

Stop the bloodshed.

Pat shakes his head. "Italians are Italians. End of the day, they believe in blood. End of the day, they're always going to side with each other. Anyway, it's too late—you don't have to worry about Sal Antonucci anymore."

"What are you talking about?"

"Nothing you need to know."

"Nothing I need to know?" Danny asks. Shit, pal, I took a bullet for you. Now I'm Johnny Jerkoff? Because, what, my last name isn't Murphy?

"I'm just protecting you, Danny," Pat says. "You can't testify about what you don't know, open yourself up to charges."

"You don't trust me."

"I trust you," Pat says. "You're my brother. But this thing with Sal, I wish you hadn't done that. Things are already in motion."

"I sent a message to the man, Pat."

"And you shouldn't have," Pat says. "You look tired, Danny. You shouldn't push it. Go home, get some rest."

Dismissed, Danny thinks.

Out of the back room.

"Come on," Danny says.

Jimmy sets his beer down. "You okay?"

"Yeah, I'm good."

They go out on the street.

The car comes at them fast.

Roars up the street and Danny doesn't hesitate. Doesn't stop to think, or try to see who's behind the wheel, he just pulls his gun and empties it into the windshield. The car goes out of control and slams into the back of a delivery truck parked along the sidewalk.

Danny and Jimmy get the hell out of there.

Smash Danny's gun up and leave parts of it in the river, in a dumpster, in a ditch.

•   •   •

SAL LOOKS OUT the window, watches Tony walk to the car.

He's a beautiful creature, Sal thinks.

A beautiful fucking creature. Like a noble racehorse, sleek, muscled, and proud of his strength.

Tony opens the door and gets into the front seat. He looks out the window, sees Sal looking, smiles, pleased to be watched, his teeth white as new snow, and turns the key.

The car erupts in flame.

Sal sees Tony open the door and lurch screaming out into the street. He's on fire, arms in front of him like a blind man. He takes two steps, then twirls, then falls.

THE IRONY IS that Tony had always said he wanted to be cremated when his time came, and the joke (although no one repeats it to Sal) is that he sure as shit was. Anyway, they put what's left of him in an urn and they have a mass and a memorial service and a reception that Sal springs for, but Sal, he's inconsolable.

Peter, he's just happy that Pat Murphy accomplished what he couldn't—bringing Sal back into the Moretti fold.

It doesn't happen right away.

Sal goes into a deep depression, just closes the door to his den and won't come out.

Peter Moretti comes over personally with a suitcase of cash—the "tax" from the Manchester job—but Sal won't even see him. Peter leaves the money with Sal's wife and takes off.

CAR BOMBS?!" DANNY yells in the back room of the Gloc. "That's who we are now? Jesus, Pat, what if his wife and kids were in the car?"

"They weren't," Pat says, but he knows that he's taken things to a place they shouldn't have gone.

Danny's furious. They had Sal out of the war, maybe even ready to come over to their side, and now it's a dead solid lock he'll come back in with the Morettis. Fuckin' Irish, always looking forward to our next defeat. We can't get out of our own way.

That old saying, "If it was raining soup, the Irish would run outside with forks."

Pretty much what happens now.

Danny would think about it in years to come. The "what if" of it. What if Tony had his own car with him. What if Danny could have persuaded Pat to sit down with Sal.

But none of that happened.

God's way of fucking with you.

THE PROVIDENCE COPS pick Danny up.

Put him in the back seat of their unmarked car. Viola slides in beside him and asks, "What do you know about the car bombing?"

"Nothing."

"Same old Danny Ryan," O'Neill says from the driver's seat. "He never knows nothing. I suppose you don't know nothing about those two guys gunned down in their car the other day, either. The De Salvo brothers?"

I only know they tried to kill me first, Danny thinks. He doesn't answer.

"Tony Romano burned to death," Viola says to Danny. He's angry. "You fucking donkeys did that."

"I don't know anything about it."

"You burn to death in the chair, too," Viola says. "Did you know that? I'd like to put you there. I'd flip the fucking switch myself."

"We done here?"

"For now," Viola says.

Danny opens the door and gets out.

PASCO CALLS.

Danny is surprised when the phone rings and he hears the old man's voice. "Jesus Christ, Danny, what the hell is going on up there?"

"I dunno, Pasco."

"We can't be having this shit," Pasco says. "Cars blowing up? You know what kind of heat this is going to bring down? There's nothing I can do to stop it."

Danny knows.

Someone getting whacked is one thing—the public almost expects it. But car bombs? Where innocent people could get hurt? That's another story—that's Northern Irish shit and the public isn't going to put up with it.

"I don't want to know who did it," Pasco says.

Everyone knows who did it, Danny thinks.

"You know how Sal is going to react to this?" Pasco asks. "He's going to go crazy, and we can't have that. We have to keep this thing contained."

Yeah, how's that gonna happen? Danny wonders.

Pasco tells him.

"What I want you to do," Pasco says, "is I want you to go to Sal and tell him that you and the Murphys had nothing to do with it."

"He ain't gonna believe that."

"Lie through your ass," Pasco says. "Make him believe you."

"He's more likely to shoot me."

"Are you afraid, Danny?" Pasco asks.

Goddamn right I am, Danny thinks. You know Sal. When he gets in a killing frame of mind, whoever is in front of him gets killed. I don't want that to be me.

"You're the only one on your side of this thing that can make the approach," Pasco says. "Sal respects you."

"He hates me."

"But he *respects* you," Pasco says. "I'm expecting Marty Ryan's son to do this."

So that's that—what Pasco Ferri expects, Pasco Ferri gets. So Danny drives down to Narragansett, parks down the block and across the street from Sal's house and waits. Word is that Sal's been holed up grieving, but he has to emerge sooner or later.

The fog comes in first.

When a heavy mist blows in off the ocean here it can arrive in a hurry. One second, it's a clear dusk; the next, it's a silver blanket thrown over everything. The temperature drops as suddenly, so it's cold and thick when Danny sees Sal come out of the house, carrying something under his arm.

Danny gives him some space, then gets out of the car and follows him three blocks down to the ocean.

A seawall runs above Narragansett Beach for most of its length. A sidewalk runs along the wall, popular in the summer but deserted now in the cold and fog, except for Sal.

He's walking in the opposite direction from the Towers, the remnants of a casino that stood here in the 1880s, when the town was a thriving resort for the rich people coming up from New York.

The two towers, each with a shingled conical peak, stand on either side of Ocean Road; an arched walkway with a central cupola spans the road. On a clear night the Towers are iconic, but now Danny can barely see them through the fog.

He follows Sal, who seems oblivious.

Danny doubts it. Sal knows he has a target on his back, knows he dodged a close call with the car bomb. One hand is around the package, the other is in his jacket pocket, and Danny has to assume it's clutching a gun.

Sal keeps walking in the direction of Monahan's, a clam shack, closed for the season, that sits on the base of what used to be the Narragansett Pier.

Danny feels the pistol he has in *his* jacket pocket, closes the distance, and calls out. "Sal!"

Sal stops, turns around and peers through the fog. "Ryan?"

Danny raises his hands. "I come in peace, Sal!"

"Fuck you, peace!"

"I just want to talk!"

"Get away from me," Sal says, "before I put one in your head."

"It wasn't us, Sal," Danny says. "I swear to God we had nothing to—"

"Lying mother*fucker*!" Sal says. He takes the gun out of his pocket and points it at Danny.

Danny runs.

If this were a movie, he'd say something clever or pull his own gun and shoot it out, but it's real life—more critically, it's real death, and Danny takes off as fast as his hip will let him.

With a gun pointed at him, threatening to go off with ill intent, his legs feel like telephone poles, they're that stiff and heavy, then he hears the blast and feels the rush of air whoosh past him as the bullet misses his head.

He doesn't think the next one will miss—the killer in Sal will settle him down and he'll take the next shot into Danny's back—so Danny vaults the seawall, drops the five feet or so onto the rocks and almost topples on the seaweed-slick stones. But the sea gods are with him and have given him a low tide. He crouches down and presses himself against the wall.

Maybe it's Danny's imagination, or maybe he can really hear Sal's footsteps stalking him. Danny feels like his pounding heart is going to give him away, but his head knows that the waves hitting rock farther out are making more noise.

Still, if Sal sees him, he's a dead man, trapped between the ocean and the wall.

Like any Rhode Islander, Danny has spent many hours cursing the fog. Been lost in its soup out at sea fishing, terrified that the boat will run against the rocks. He's blessed the lighthouses at Point Judith and Beavertail for cutting through the fog and leading them home. He's been on the highway at night, or worse, on one of the small roads nearer the beach, when he had to open the window and look down to see the yellow line in order to stay on the road.

But now he blesses the damn fog pouring in from the ocean.

Crouching, hiding, he hears Sal yell, "Fuck you, Ryan! Fuck all of youse, you hear me?!"

Danny hears him. He's not tempted to answer, though, to affirm his comprehension or shout defiance.

The ocean has saved his life; he's not going to spurn that gift.

He waits a good half hour before he dares climb back over the wall. Peering up and down the seawall, he doesn't see Sal.

His shoes soaked, Danny sloshes his way back to his car and drives home.

WITH THE URN containing Tony's ashes in his hand, Sal walks down to the jetty where the old Narragansett Pier once stood. Opens the urn and tosses the ashes into the offshore wind and then follows them.

Sal Antonucci jumps off the rocks where, every other summer, some tourist drowns because he doesn't know better, into the swirling ocean because he wants to die.

Nobody is down there in winter, nobody sees him. The water is killing cold; the sea, hungry, reaches up and takes him. Sal struggles in the waves as he changes his mind and decides that he wants to live, but that's now the ocean's choice, not his.

The sea gives back only what it doesn't want.

It throws him back and he hangs on to the slick rocks until he has the strength to pull himself up.

Decides it's worth living to kill Pat Murphy.

Then Liam Murphy.

Then Danny Ryan.

YOU GOTTA GET out of town," Danny tells Pat.

But Pat won't go, even though John, his mother, even Sheila urge him to leave. Go to New Hampshire, Vermont, go down to Florida, just get out of Dogtown. But Pat, the captain of the football team, the hockey team, the basketball team—Pat the born leader—won't go.

"Then lay low," Danny tells him.

Keep your head down and on a swivel.

Tells him this even as he knows it won't do any good.

Pat has a death wish now.

It's in his blood, the Irish martyr thing. They walk to death like it's a beautiful woman.

PAM COMES TO the door.

"Where's your useless husband?" Pat asks.

"In the bedroom," she says, jutting her chin toward the back.

Fucking Liam, Pat thinks, still hiding. Well, that's going to come to a screeching halt.

"I know what you think of me," Pam says.

"Do you?"

"Same thing I think about myself," she says. "I'm a whore."

"I never said that."

"No, I did," she says. "I'm a whore, I'm the bitch that caused all of this. I wish I'd never come here. I wish I'd never met him."

That makes two of us, Pat thinks. No, that makes *all* of us.

"You want to come in?" she asks.

Liam walks out of the bedroom, notching his belt, his hair disheveled; he's barefoot and he hasn't shaved in a couple of days. Seeing his brother, he says, "To what do I owe the honor?"

"Go fuck yourself."

"These days, I pretty much have to." Liam glances at Pam and smirks. He walks over to the kitchen counter, picks up a dirty glass, pours in two fingers of scotch and holds it up to Pat. "*Sláinte.*"

Pat's in no mood. "You started all this, baby brother; it's time you got back into the game."

"That's funny," Liam says. "My dear little wifey here was just saying the same thing."

"Sal will come back into the war now," Pat says. "He'll hit back for the Morettis. We could use more boots on the ground, and it would be good for the guys to see you out front."

"You're the field commander," Liam says. "Just tell me where to go and I'll march."

"You could start by showing up at the Gloc."

"Yeah," Liam says. He finishes his drink. "Just let me get my shoes on, my gear, and I'll drive right down."

"Shave first."

"Yes, *sir.*" Liam salutes him, sets the glass down, waves behind him, and walks back into the bedroom.

"You want a drink or something?" Pam asks Pat.

"No, thanks," Pat says. "I need to go see my wife. Hurry this guy along, huh? Don't let him go back to bed."

"You want me to tell him I won't fuck him unless he goes out and pretends to be a man?" Pam asks. "Sort of Lysistrata in reverse?"

"I don't know what that means," Pat says.

"Doesn't matter," Pam says. "Hey, Pat? For whatever it's worth, I'm sorry."

"Yeah," Pat says.

We're all sorry.

So what?

Sheila isn't home when he gets there. There's a note on the kitchen table that she's gone grocery shopping and taken the baby with her. Pat goes to find her but when he gets out there, she's walking back up the street pushing a stroller.

Pat reaches down to lift up his son.

The baby *screams* so loud it's funny, and both Pat and Sheila laugh.

"He doesn't know you," Sheila says.

"I haven't been around enough," Pat says, handing the boy back to her.

Sheila doesn't argue with him. She holds the baby to her chest, makes cooing noises, and the crying stops.

"It'll be over soon," Pat says.

He sees tears well up in her eyes. Strong Sheila, tough Sheila, hard-ass Sheila, it's wearing her down, all this.

Then it comes out.

"Pat, let's leave. Get out of here."

"I can't do that, Sheel," Pat says. "I have to think about the rest of the guys."

"You think more about them than your own family?" she asks. "Your own wife? If you won't think about me, think about your son. Do you want Johnny to grow up without a father?"

"No, of course not."

"Well?"

"Nothing's going to happen to me."

"What, because you're invulnerable?" she asks. "You're the Man of Steel, leap tall buildings in a single bound—"

"Stop it."

"No, *you* stop it," she says. "Before it's too late."

"I'm trying to."

"No, you're trying to keep it going," Sheila says. "They kill one of ours, we kill one of theirs . . . I don't want to be a widow, Pat. I don't want to raise our son by myself."

"You won't."

"Let's just go," she says. "Go upstairs, throw a few things in the car, and drive away from this place."

"It's not that simple."

"It's *exactly* that simple." Tears stream down her face now.

It's hard for him to look at her. "Sheila . . . I have to go . . ."

"So go," she says. "Go to your *guys*."

"Don't be mad, okay?"

"Just go."

"I love you."

"Do you?" She rolls the stroller to the stoop, starts to take out the grocery bags.

"Let me carry those up," Pat says.

"I can do it."

"I know you can, but—"

"Just *go!*"

Pat walks away.

DANNY'S ON THE street for five goddamn minutes before Jardine drives up behind him, rolls down the window and says, "Get in."

"You crazy? I'm going to be seen with you." Danny keeps walking.

"Get in," Jardine says. "Or do you want to do this in the Federal Building?"

Danny gets in. "Drive. Far."

Jardine does, pulls out onto 95 and then across the Red Bridge toward Fox Point, where it's mostly Portuguese.

"You guys fucked up," Jardine says, "turning Tony into the Olympic torch."

Danny loves it when feds try to talk like mobsters. They think it makes them legit, when it really makes them look like assholes. He says, "I don't know nothing about it."

"One wiseguy more or less, I don't give a fuck," Jardine says. "I'm trying to tell you, you're in trouble, Aer Lingus is going down, and I'm offering you a parachute."

"Jesus, can you just talk like a person?"

"Okay," Jardine says. "Without rhetorical flourish, the Italians are really pissed now. The car bombing has brought New York fully behind them, Boston, Hartford, even Springfield. They're bringing manpower you can't hope to match. You're going to die, Danny, unless you take the hand I'm offering you. Is that plain enough English for you?"

"Yeah." Danny knows the son of a bitch is right.

"We can go right now," Jardine says. "We swing by, pick up Terri, we don't even stop for gas. You and I sit down with a tape recorder, and you get a new life."

"I won't turn on my friends."

"Pat Murphy's a dead man," Jardine says. "Liam? He's a piece of shit, which you know better than me. Jimmy Mac? Tell you what, you give me the Murphys, we'll bring Jimmy in and make him a sweetheart deal."

"You want me to flip on my wife's father and her brother," Danny says.

"Ask Terri," Jardine says. "Ask her if she'd swap her old man and her big brother for her husband and her baby."

"Fuck you."

"Scared to know what she'd say?"

As a matter of fact, I am, Danny thinks.

Sensing that, Jardine pushes. "Hey, if John Murphy could give us, for instance, Pasco Ferri, we might be able to cut him a deal."

Yeah, Danny thinks, a lot of people would like Pasco out of the way.

Peter Moretti being one of them.

"What about my father?" Danny asks.

"Whatever he did is ancient history," Jardine says. "No offense, but nobody cares."

More to himself than to Jardine, Danny says, "He'd never talk to me again if I was a rat. He'd never look at me."

"Then I'd ask you the same question," Jardine says. "Who do you owe more, your wife and kid or your old man? What your mother tells me, Marty doesn't care much about you at all."

Danny doesn't answer. What can he say? The man is right.

Like any fed, Jardine knows when to push and when to lie back. The book says he should push now, steamroll Ryan into a quick decision, keep the ball moving, swoop up his pregnant wife and close the deal.

But his gut tells him different.

Tells him to lay off a little, give Ryan a little space.

"Look, think it over," Jardine says. "But don't take too long. You don't have the time. And I'm not going to make the same offer to your widow. Where do you want me to drop you?"

Danny has him drop him on Point Street.

It's a long walk home, but he needs the time to think.

Everything Jardine said was true.

The Italians are going to kill Pat, he thinks, they're going to kill Liam and Old Man Murphy, they're going to kill Jimmy and they're going to kill me.

It's not an "if," it's a "when."

Unless I do something to change it.

Yeah, like what?

I can't go over to the Morettis; even if I wanted to they'd never trust me again and I can't blame them.

I can just take Terri and go, but she's not going to be away from her family when the baby comes. And even if she'd go, the feds will find me.

Or you can take Jardine's hand.

Become a goddamn rat.

An informer, the curse of the Irish.

A man who turns on his friends.

It doesn't get any lower than a rat.

Yeah, it does, he thinks—a man who doesn't take care of his wife and child.

PAT MURPHY SITS in the Gloc, drinking alone.

Liam never showed up, fuck him.

His boys wanted to stay but he chased them off. Mean drunk. He finishes his last shot, locks up the bar and walks out onto the street. Pat doesn't even see the car when, full of Jameson's and regrets, he shuffles out onto Eddy Street.

Sal must have been waiting.

He doesn't use a bomb or a gun, he uses the foot feed. Floors the stolen Caddy and aims it straight at Pat, who looks up at the last second, pulls the .38 from his jacket pocket but doesn't get a chance to shoot before Sal runs over him.

Then Sal puts it in reverse, then drive, reverse again, again and again, running back and forth over Pat. Then he takes off with Pat's body jammed under the oil pan and drags him for blocks before he realizes it.

Clicking out of his red rage, Sal thinks a little about self-preservation, gets out, tosses what's left of Pat Murphy into the trunk and drives away.

Leaving smears of Pat on Eddy Street.

IT TAKES THE heart out of Danny.

People are screaming for revenge and looking for Danny and his crew to deliver it. But Danny says no. Not yet, anyway, he just doesn't have the heart. You'd think that the brutal murder of his best friend would fire him up, but at some point you just say fuck it, enough is too much.

Your heart breaks, it's broken.

Liam, of course, he's all over the revenge thing, walking around the Gloc saying how's he going to get payback for his brother. He won't shut up about it until Danny says, "You can't kill Sal."

"Why not?" Liam demands.

Because you can't, Danny thinks. Because Sal is too good for you and, anyway, you're more mouth than balls. But he says, "Because if Sal is dead, he can't tell us where Pat's body is, can he?"

Sal dumped it somewhere but, of course, he ain't saying because that's tantamount to a homicide confession. Pat's mother is a mess anyway, as is to be expected, but she's especially distraught that she can't bury her son, give him a decent funeral. Until then, there can be no what-do-you-call-it, closure.

"He's not going to tell us anyway!" Liam yells.

Pam, looking pale, sits at a table staring at him and Danny can't even begin to know what's she's thinking, feeling. Cassie, she just sits at the bar, staring into the mirror, sipping a Diet Coke and fighting a battle against the booze.

"We don't know that," Danny says.

"We do know that," Liam answers. "I mean, why should he?"

The only reason, Danny thinks, the *only* reason is that Pasco Ferri might tell him to.

Not tell the cops, of course, that's not going to happen, even though the cops have already come out and said the chief suspects are two Black males apparently high on drugs. But Pasco might be willing to persuade Sal to give it up to him.

MARTY MAKES THE call to his old friend.

"How did this ever get this far?" Pasco asks.

"Pasco, can you help us out here?"

Pasco puts in the call to Sal.

At first Sal stonewalls. "I don't know what you're talking about. Don't get me wrong, I ain't sorry the cocksucker's dead, but I hear it was some moolies."

"We're not animals," Pasco says. "They just want to bury their son."

"A lot of people want a lot of things they don't get," Sal says. "I wanted a house. I wanted my friend alive. The Murphys got balls, asking me for anything."

"This is *me* asking, Sal."

Pasco Ferri isn't used to asking for anything twice. Sal doesn't want to die anymore, he knows he has to do what Pasco asks, but he wants to save face, so he slaps a condition on it. "If John Murphy comes to me personally, asks me personally, maybe I can tell him some things I heard."

FUCK THAT!" LIAM yells when he hears about Sal's demand. "I say we grab him, take him to a warehouse, hitch jumper cables to his balls, crank it up until he tells us where Pat is. Then we kill him."

Danny would like to grab Liam by the throat, take him to the floor and beat the shit out of him. This is your fault in the first place, he thinks, this is your motherfucking fault!

John says, "Is that what you think we should do, Liam? Let me ask you, how are we going to do that? How are we going to 'grab' him?"

Liam don't have an answer for that.

"In the meantime," John says, "your brother's body is rotting someplace and we can't give him a proper burial."

"After we bury Pat," Liam says, "I'm killing that motherfucker."

"You do that," John says. "To tell you the truth, son, it's about time you did *something*."

So John Murphy goes. Shows up at Sal's house and rings the bell like he's some kind of salesman. When Sal comes to the door, John says, "Thank you for seeing me."

Sal don't say nothing.

"My wife," John says, "can't sleep, she has dreams."

Sal has dreams, too. Last night he dreamed that Tony came to him and told him he should tell where Pat Murphy's body is. Says neither of them can rest until he does. Sal woke up sweating and crying, and now here's John Murphy at his door. He says, "I don't know for sure, of course, how could I, but I've heard rumors."

Sal tells him where maybe he's heard that Pat might be. Then he adds, "But this don't mean things are settled between us."

"I just want time to bury my son properly," John says.

Sal, he just nods and closes the door.

JOHN SENDS DANNY.

Danny can't help but wonder why not Liam, why not send Liam to fetch his brother's body because it was Liam's shit that was behind Pat getting killed in the first place. But he already knows the answer:

nobody is going to make baby Liam do anything hard or face up to his responsibilities. And Danny ain't going to ask John because the man is hurting bad enough already.

What can you say, Danny thinks, about John eating his pride, going personally to Sal Antonucci, hat in hand, to the man who killed his son to ask what he did with the body? What does that take? What does that do to a man? An old man who's lost his son? Danny is amazed. Awestruck. Realizes for the first time why Murphy runs the docks and his own father doesn't. It takes a strong, strong man to do what he did.

So Danny don't ask about Liam. Instead, he swings by and picks up Jimmy Mac because he knows Jimmy would want to do this for Pat.

They go at night, like John promised Sal, even though it's going to make it a hell of a lot harder to find the grave. Driving out the Plainfield Pike in an old van, Jimmy says, "You ever think we'd be making a trip like this?"

"Not in my worst nightmares."

"We gotta kill this guy, you know."

"First things first, huh?"

Get Pat in the ground. Well, first get him out of the ground, then back into the ground decently. Go through the hell that's going to be the funeral and the wake and maybe, then, think about killing Antonucci.

If he don't get us first, which he's sure as shit going to try.

The truce will last until the wake is over.

The next morning, it will be on again, and we'll be lucky to survive, never mind kill Sal.

But first things first.

Find Pat's body.

The route takes them out through the woods, then the causeway across the eastern side of the Scituate Reservoir. Sal said he'd "heard a rumor" that the body is off a fire lane before the Pike edges the water again, about a hundred yards south of the road to the right. There'll be some dead pines, then some live ones.

The body is at the base of the first live pine.

Jimmy turns onto the fire lane and drives through the dead pines. They get out of the van and shine flashlights around.

"Could he have picked anywhere creepier?" Jimmy asks.

Danny aims his flashlight on the ground in front of him and walks to the first live tree he sees. Sure enough, there's a patch of disturbed ground with pine needles kicked over it.

"Get the shovels," he calls back to Jimmy.

Jimmy brings the shovels and hands one to Danny, who digs the blade into the loose ground and steps down on it with his right foot.

He feels it hit something hard, then scoops the dirt up.

Jimmy shines the light down and Danny sees that the shovel hit Pat's head.

What's left of it, anyway.

The hair was sheared off with most of the skin on the right side of Pat's head and the eye socket is empty.

Danny drops the shovel, turns, bends over and throws up. He hears Jimmy moan, *Oh fuck oh fuck* and then the sound of Jimmy retching. Wiping his mouth with his sleeve, Danny turns back and says, "Let's get this done."

They dig as gently as they can until Pat's whole body is revealed in the shallow grave. He's in a fetal position, most of his clothes scraped off, the skin on his bare legs raw with dried blood and dirt. His right foot hangs from a single tendon, his fingers are still clutched as if trying to grab for something.

His life, maybe, Danny thinks.

They spread an old army blanket out on the ground, roll Pat into it, wrap it as tight as they can, carry the body to the van and slide it into the back.

Danny closes the doors and throws up again.

The last ride of Patdannyjimmy is them driving out of the woods back to Providence.

CASSIE IS STANDING outside Marley's when they pull up.

Danny sees her spot the car and go inside to tell people that they're there. He knows the family's waiting and part of him wants to tell Jimmy to just keep driving because it's going to be *brutal.*

"You ready for this?" he asks Jimmy.

"No."

"Me neither."

He gets out of the van and walks inside the funeral home and the whole family is there—Terri, John, Catherine, Cassie, and Sheila, who makes herself look up at him when he comes through the door.

He nods to her.

Even Pam is there, with Liam.

Who now goes into take-charge mode. He gets up out of his chair and asks, "Did you find my brother?"

"I did your job, if that's what you're asking me." Danny nudges him aside and walks up to Sheila. She stands up as he says, "You don't want to see him, Sheila, trust me on this."

"He's my husband."

"Remember him the way he was."

Then he hears Cassie gasp as Jimmy and two of Marley's guys carry Pat in.

That was bad enough, but Catherine's shriek as she sees her son's corpse wrapped in a blanket is the worst sound he's ever heard.

He'll never forget it.

They're trying to carry Pat's body to the elevator to take it down and work on it, but Catherine gets in their way, tears at the blanket, trying to rip it off to see her son. John tries to pull her away but he's not strong enough and gives up, hangs his head and pinches his fingers around his nose.

It's Cassie who manages to pry Catherine off her son's body, who holds her up and doesn't let her slide to her knees, holds her tight as she sobs and screams and pounds her fists into Cassie's shoulders.

Sheila slides past Danny, walks up and feels the blanket until she finds where Pat's head is and strokes it through the blanket.

"My husband . . ."

Then she breaks down.

Danny holds her.

THE WAKE IS a horror show.

The casket is closed, because even Marley couldn't Humpty-Dumpty the body back into a presentable condition.

Danny's secretly glad, he didn't want to sit there on and off for days looking at a waxed, made-up face that was supposed to be his best friend. The freaking casket is depressing enough, with the string of rosary beads laid on top of the polished oak.

Depressing, too, the steady stream of visitors who dutifully trickle in, spend a few quiet moments by the coffin, then flow to the seated family to say how sorry they are for their loss. Then they go to the back row of folding chairs to sit for what they consider to be a decent amount of time before they can escape.

Danny wishes he could, too.

Second day into the thing, he's coming back from the bathroom when he bumps into Liam in the hallway. Can smell the booze on his breath when Liam says, "I know what you're thinking."

"Yeah? What am I thinking?"

"You're thinking it should have been me," Liam says, like he's throwing down a glove.

Danny's in no mood for his bullshit. "It *should* have been."

"Well, we agree on *something*," Liam says, then shoulders his way past.

At the end of the hall, Jimmy has seen the exchange. "We should have done him when we had the chance."

"I wish the hell I had," Danny says.

He goes back into the room to sit down next to Terri.

"What did Liam say to you?" she asks.

"It's not important."

"What?"

"That he wished it had been him instead of Pat," Danny says.

"Don't we all."

Time doesn't pass slowly for Danny; it doesn't pass at all.

He's awash in memories.

Pat and him eating sugar sandwiches, Pat and him and Jimmy looking at Superman comics, Batman comics, building model cars. One time they were playing in a construction site and they found a rock they thought had gold in it and they thought they were going to be rich and talked for hours about the stuff they were going to buy—cars, new houses for their parents, a private jet—until they had to admit they knew it wasn't really gold, but they felt sad anyway, and slunk home brokenhearted. Or when an aunt gave Pat a butterfly net and kit for his birthday and they went hunting butterflies and Pat caught a monarch in the net but then didn't have the heart to kill it, or, a little older, sneaking upstairs to Jimmy's father's room, finding *Playboy*s under the bed. Pat behind an old screen door in the upstairs closet pretending he was a priest, hearing their confessions, making sure they made everything up or it would be sacrilege. First confession, first communion, confirmation, Pat taking it all so serious, talked about maybe becoming a priest until he started dating Sheila in high school and then that was that, Danny asked him what happened to the seminary and Pat just said, "Tits." Pat and Sheila and Jimmy and Angie and him and Terri going out together, out to Rocky Point, down to the shore, over to Newport, one time they went to jai alai and Angie won three hundred dollars and they tried to get her to blow it all at the Black Pearl but she wouldn't and put it all in the bank or the time they was playing street hockey on a hot July night on a basketball court and this guy had a stick so curved he couldn't shoot anywhere but up and he took a shot and hit Liam smack in the mouth and Pat dropped his gloves and beat everybody up and they all fought until the cops came and threw them out and then they went and got someone to buy them beer and they sat outside sipping beer and put ice on their bruised hands and laughed and talked about the fight but Pat he was still pissed about the guy's curved stick until Danny said he heard Peter Moretti had a curved stick too and Pat finally laughed or that time him and Jimmy and Pat got so drunk in high school and squeezed into a phone booth to make prank calls but then got stuck and couldn't get the door open so they called Sheila to come get them and they were laughing so hard when she came and shook her head and said she should just leave them there it's what they deserved but she opened the door and they spilled out like tin cans and lay there in the parking lot still laughing and laughing or the first time Pat took Sheila parking down at the beach and the idiot got his car stuck in the sand and had to call Danny and Jimmy to come help push it out before Sheila's dad found out, Danny remembers these things and tries not to remember Pat's flayed body in the dirt.

He dreams about it, though, the night before the funeral, the waking hours before they put Pat in the dirt again. In his dream Pat reaches up like *Help me pull me up out of here pull me up out of death* and Danny, he grabs for him but Pat's hand falls off in *his* hand and

Danny trudges brokenhearted home and lays the hand on the kitchen counter and tells Terri that's your brother and there's no gold.

The funeral is so sad.

Danny can barely make himself get out of bed in the morning, he so much don't want to face it.

But he goes down to the shore and picks up Marty and Ned, then back to the house for Terri, and they drive out to the cemetery.

And there's Liam standing there stiff with rage and guilt, Pam beside him knowing people are blaming her, maybe she's blaming herself, too. And Cassie, sober—surprising, given the situation—and she makes it through the eulogy without crying and says, "He was the best of us and the last."

Leave it to her to make poetry of it.

Leave it to her to be right.

Danny takes Marty by the elbow and starts to walk him back to the car, to the wake that's going to be as brutal as the burial. Where they'll all get drunk and tell maudlin stories about Pat, and Marty will sing old songs. As he's walking away, Danny notices that Pam is beside him. She looks at him and says, "Pat never said an unkind word to me."

Danny feels the weight come onto his shoulders, feels autumn turn to winter right there.

Because now they're without a leader.

Oh, John will still be the boss in name, or Liam might try to pick up the mantle, but that's never going to happen.

Which leaves me, Danny thinks.

Because there is nobody else.

It started with a sunny day on the beach, he thinks, and ended up with you throwing cold dirt on your best friend's coffin.

He yearns for summer and sun and dreams of a warm sea.

PART THREE

The Last Days of Dogtown

Providence, Rhode Island
March 1987

. . . oblivious, blind, insane, we stationed the monster
fraught with doom on the hallowed heights of Troy.

Virgil
The Aeneid
Book II

TWENTY-FOUR

PROVIDENCE IS A GRAY CITY.

Gray skies, gray buildings, gray streets. Gray granite as hard as the New England pilgrims who hacked it out of the quarries to build their City on the Hill. Gray as the pessimism that hangs in the air like the fog.

Gray as grief.

The unrelenting gray sorrow Danny has felt since Pat's death. Sorrow he almost wears, like clothes he puts on when he wakes up, like he's seeing the world on one of those black-and-white TVs he had when he was a kid.

Danny turns the collar of his leather jacket up as he walks to the Gloc. He isn't Danny Ryan the longshoreman, the collector, the hijack guy—he's Danny Ryan the man who has to step into Pat Murphy's big shoes.

Someone has to, and it sure as shit isn't going to be Liam.

Liam, fucking Liam, of course wants to go out and kill everyone.

Well, he wants *other* people to go out and kill everyone; he didn't want a big part of that himself, just wanted to push the buttons.

Danny talked him off the cliff. "We can't respond right now."

"They killed my fucking brother!" Liam said.

"I know that," Danny said. They killed my fucking best friend, he thinks. "What I'm telling you is we don't have the guys right now to go all D-Day."

And he's grieving, for Chrissakes, his heart is freakin' broken. His pregnant wife is grieving, too, and he has to look after her. And then there's his in-laws—Catherine is a mess and John, John is about catatonic. In no condition to run the business, never mind command a war.

So it falls on Danny.

Danny has to run the day-to-day—the docks, the union, the loan-sharking, the boosts, it all drops on his shoulders. A hundred freakin' details a day it seems, from making sure the right guys got picked on the shape-ups to seeing that collections got made, cash distributed, envelopes delivered to the cops and judges they had left. He has to assign tasks, mediate disputes, make rulings.

Bernie's been a big help with the numbers, and Jimmy takes up a lot of the slack, but it's still Danny who's in charge.

Danny who has to run the war.

Thing of it is, the fighting dies down for a while.

Part of it is exhaustion.

Both sides are just flat-out tired, worn down.

Then there's the public perception.

People would put up with a gang war—it had entertainment value—but the brutal murder of Pat Murphy was too much. A guy getting dragged down a street in the middle of the city? Parts of him scraped on the asphalt?

No.

The public is sick of it.

The word came down from the bosses of the bigger families in New York, Boston, even Chicago to cool it, dial it back, give it a rest. Don't do shit in public which should be done in private. Keep us out of the headlines for a while.

Pretty much what Pasco told Danny on the phone. "I understand you're filling in for John during his period of mourning."

"I'm helping out."

"I need you to stay your hand," Pasco said. "You know what I mean. Certain people are getting very concerned. It's not a good look, not with all this RICO shit, the trials . . ."

Danny knew what he meant. The feds were pounding organized crime with the RICO statutes and all the families were feeling the pressure. Car bombings and guys getting run over in the street weren't helping with the public image.

"I hear you," Danny said. "Does Peter?"

"He does," Pasco said. "I don't suppose you'd consider a sit-down."

"That train has left the station."

"That was his response, too," Pasco said. "I'll tell you what I told him—be smart, be discreet. If certain people have to come in on this, it won't be good for either of you. *Capisce?*"

Danny understands: If New York or Boston decide we're too much trouble, they'll come in. It will be a hostile takeover, and their first move will be to put both me and Peter in the dirt.

So there's a breather, a gasping spell of sorts.

March weather is fickle in this part of the world. It can rain or snow, sleet or drizzle or clear up. March should be the end of winter— everyone is sick to death of it and wants it to be over, but the month usually delivers what Danny thinks of as a fuck-you storm. Like *You want spring, right? Well, I've got your spring for you right here.* Then it dumps snow on your head.

Fuck you.

Right now it's just windy—a damp cold that blows up from Narragansett Bay—and Danny's glad to be out of it as he walks through the Gloc's door.

Bobby Bangs is already behind the bar and hands him a cup of coffee, a sign of Danny's new status.

Jimmy's sitting in a booth, reading the *Journal*. He sees Danny, gets up and follows him into the back room. Bernie shows up a few minutes later and they get to work going through the day-to-day.

It's almost time for lunch when they come out, and two skinny punk kids in jeans and black leather jackets are sitting in a booth looking nervous.

Danny looks at Bobby.

"I carded them," Bobby says. "They're legal. Twenty-one."

"We just wanted to see Mr. Ryan," one of them says, his voice actually cracking. They both slide out of the booth and stand up.

Jimmy pats them down, looks to Danny and shakes his head, meaning no, they aren't carrying.

"Do I know you?" Danny asks. One of the kids looks familiar, Danny's pretty sure he's seen him at a hockey game or something.

"My name is Sean South, this is Kevin Coombs."

WHAT DO YOU want with me?" Danny asks.

"We were wondering," Sean says, "if you, you know, needed anybody."

"To do what?"

"You know," Kevin says, "stuff."

Stuff.

Yeah, Danny has stuff they could do. Like hang around and wait, sort of a probationary period. Guys don't just walk in and get *in*, you gotta know them for a while. It's not you're so concerned they might be undercover cops, it's more that they might be flakes, screw-ups, cowboys who will get you in trouble.

Truth is, though, that they need fresh blood. Outgunned and outmanned by the Morettis, the Dogtown Irish could use some new guys. What surprises Danny is that they came to *him*.

They want to be on Danny Ryan's crew.

Danny has them hang for a while, run errands, go out to get coffee, doughnuts. A couple months of them making Dunkin' runs, not screwing that up, he puts them out on the street as lookouts. Then he sends them out to take some of his collections, with the warning that they better not get carried away. They don't, they use "measured violence," in Sean's words, so he sends them on a few more.

He also has them run errands for Sheila Murphy, at home with no husband and a toddler, and for Terri, who's feeling fat and miserable. Her back and legs ache and she can't wait to "pop this kid out." So Danny sends "the Altar Boys," as Sean and Kevin come to be known—to the supermarket, the drugstore, the cleaners—all the shit he'd be doing if he had the time.

Terri appreciates it but still gives him grief. "What, I married those two jamokes instead of you?"

"They're good kids."

"When this baby comes," Terri says, "if this baby ever *comes*, don't think those two knot-heads are going to be over here changing diapers, because that's going to be you, Danny Ryan. You knocked me up, not them."

"I'm glad to hear that, Terri. That's good to know."

Terri's eating increasingly weird shit.

One night Danny comes home, she's sitting at the kitchen table chucking down something he don't recognize.

"What is that?" he asks.

"An English muffin with green beans, melted cheese, and grape jelly," she says, like it's obvious.

"Wow."

"Hey, you want some, make your own. I'm off my feet."

Another night she gets on him about Madeleine. They're lying in bed watching Carson when she says out of nowhere, "I miss your mom."

"I don't."

"I do," Terri says. "I like her. And it would be nice to have her help, you know, when the baby comes."

"Yeah, because she's so good with babies."

Terri isn't letting it go. "Are you ever going to forgive her?"

"Why?"

"Why do I ask," Terri says, "or why should you forgive her?"

"I dunno. Both."

"Because I'm your wife and I get to ask questions," Terri says, "and because one day you'll be standing at her grave and you'll be sorry you didn't."

"No, I won't," Danny says. "Because I won't be at the funeral."

So Terri keeps getting bigger and weirder, and the uneasy peace between the Italians and the Irish holds up. While everyone knows it's a truce and not a peace, still everyone acts with a measure of restraint. The Irish stay pretty much in Dogtown, the Italians on Federal Hill, as guys from each side keep a distance and a wary eye but are careful to avoid any other contact, lest a careless word strike a spark.

TWENTY-FIVE

THE BABY COMES IN JUNE, one day early.

Danny would say later that Ian slid out like he was trying to beat a double play at second.

Terri, she didn't share this observation.

She's in labor for six long hours, and it's three in the morning before Ian decides to make his appearance in the world. Danny, he hangs in, he's right there with the ice chips and the encouragement and the rhythmic breathing and all that happy crap. He's seen his share of blood, although nothing like this, but Danny's a soldier and is right there when the nurses wrap up the baby and lay him on Terri's chest, saying, "Here's your son."

Ian Patrick Ryan.

Six pounds, four ounces.

All the fingers and toes.

Danny knows true happiness for maybe the first time in his life.

He don't even get that mad when, later that morning, Terri—who recovers with astonishing speed—insists on calling Madeleine. "She should know she has a grandson."

"I'm not talking to her."

"Then go down to the cafeteria and get me an omelet," Terri says.

"Didn't you already have breakfast?"

"And now I'm going to have another one," she says. "A *cheese* omelet. Cheddar."

Danny obeys.

MADELEINE ANSWERS THE phone. "Terri? Do you have news for me?"

"Ian Patrick Ryan," Terri says. "Six pounds, four ounces. Congratulations, you have a grandson."

"And how are *you*?"

"I'm great," Terri says. "I feel like I got a, I dunno, a *basketball* out of my stomach."

"I'm so happy."

"Are you going to come out and meet him?"

"I'd love to," Madeleine says. "But I don't think Danny would like that."

"I love my husband," Terri says. "But he can be kind of an asshole."

"We'll work on it," Madeleine says. "See how it goes. You never know."

"I'll send pictures."

"Please."

They chat for another minute and then hang up.

Madeleine is surprised to find that she's crying.

THE TRUCE HOLDS through summer, and it's the summer of little sleep, colic, late-night feedings, early-morning wake-ups, and Danny doesn't mind any of it. He just figures it comes with the territory, being a father, and even though Ian doesn't do a lot except spit up, poop, and sleep, Danny still loves just looking at him, holding him, feeling him get heavy as he drops off.

And Terri? She's blissful. Tired, sure, but a happy young mother with a healthy baby and a husband who loves her, which was all she ever really wanted.

There's no August beach vacation that year, of course. No Dogtown by the Sea, those days are over. Danny misses them, misses those hot lazy days when they were all still friends.

Before we started killing each other, he thinks.

Every week or so they drive to see Marty to let him see Ian, and the funny thing is Marty is a doting granddad.

He loves the baby.

Sure, *now*, Danny thinks.

Anyway, they take Marty over to Dave's Dock for his fish-and-chips but mostly Marty he just wants to hold Ian, and Danny notices his father's appetite isn't so good anymore and he's losing weight.

Sometimes on those visits Danny and Terri walk down the beach, past the house that Pasco has sold, and they each think about old times (Christ, Danny thinks, has it only been a year?) but they don't say anything to each other about it because it's too painful. Once or twice they drop by the Spindrift and have a burger out on the deck with Ian asleep in the car seat at their ankles, but it isn't as much fun being there as it used to be.

Life changes, Danny thinks, it just does.

You move on.

Or try to, anyway.

September becomes October, then Thanksgiving comes and goes and Christmas decorations start to go up.

Christmas is subdued that year.

For one thing, it's around the anniversary of Pat's death, so no one feels very festive. For another, money is tight. Even with the boosts they do, more money is going out than coming in, so there isn't a lot to spare for big parties, even if anyone felt like it.

John throws a half-assed Christmas Eve party at the Gloc—a deli spread and cookies—with Jimmy Mac playing Santa Claus, but it turns into a sodden, sullenly drunk evening, with most people, including Danny, going home early and the rest getting shitfaced, angry and bitter.

Danny, Terri, and Ian go over to the Murphys' house on Christmas Day, but it's a sad affair, with John as quiet as a stone and Catherine still half out of it on pills, a full year after Pat's death.

Sheila is there with Johnny, trying to put a brave face on it, but her presence only emphasizes Pat's absence, and Danny sees her on the edge of tears a few times. Liam and Pam went down to Greenwich to be with her family, which is a relief to Danny.

Cassie is there, stone-cold sober and clean. She went to a meeting that morning and also the night before because holidays are rough on addicts and alcoholics.

They all exchange presents, eat the ham, fall asleep in chairs in front of the television, and then Danny and Terri say their goodbyes and drive down to see Marty, who refused to leave his house to go to the Murphys'.

"It was like we weren't even there," Terri says in the car. "They barely paid any attention to Ian, except Cassie."

Christmas with Marty is a barrel of monkeys.

He and Ned had honored the occasion by cracking open two Swanson Hungry-Man turkey dinners to go with their Bushmills and then settled down in front of some bowl game they didn't give a shit about.

But Marty pretends to be pleased with the new flannel shirt

Danny gives him, while Ned is genuinely touched by the pair of leather gloves that Terri bought for him.

"How does Ian like Christmas?" Marty asks.

"He's six months old," Danny says. "He doesn't know Christmas."

"He knows," Terri says. "He's liking it."

"Was Santa good to him?" Marty asks.

"Yeah, he got him a car," Danny says.

Jesus Christ.

When they get home, Terri asks, "You don't want to call your mother, wish her a merry Christmas?"

"No, I don't."

Terri, being Terri, calls her. Stands right there in front of Danny, who's pretending to ignore her, and calls Madeleine in Las Vegas. Wishes her merry Christmas and holds Ian up to the receiver to make baby noises for her.

Then Danny hears her say, "Yeah, he's here. He wants to say hello."

She holds the phone up to Danny with a look that says if he's even thinking about getting laid sometime in the next five years he'd better take it.

Danny takes the phone. "Hello."

"Merry Christmas, Danny."

"Yeah, you too."

"Well, okay."

"Okay."

He hands the phone back to Terri, who talks for another minute and then hangs up. "Was that so bad?"

"Yes."

New Year's Eve, fuck it, they don't do anything. Danny and Terri only see the ball drop because they're up with Ian.

Then it's January, nineteen-freakin'-eighty-eight, and the war starts again.

TWENTY-SIX

IT'S NOTHING DRAMATIC, BUT THE Morettis start chipping away at the edges. Not doing any hits, not taking guys off the count, but little shit. First they muscle a Murphy loan shark off his turf, scaring him out of a bar where he did business.

Danny doesn't respond.

Then they put one of their own guys up for an office in the long-shoremen's union. He doesn't win, but it sends a message.

Danny doesn't respond.

Then Peter sends guys to intimidate bars and clubs that are under the Murphy umbrella, extorting them to pay the Italians instead.

Gang wars, like any wars, are largely economic.

They cost money to fight, and guys still have to live, pay mortgages and rent, put food on the table. Guys didn't get into this thing to join the army, they got in to make money, and if you take the money away, you take the soldiers away.

The Morettis apply more and more pressure, slowly strangling the Irish to death.

They're like those snakes, Danny thinks—what-do-you-call-'em, pythons—around our necks, squeezing and squeezing until we run out of air.

Then they'll eat us.

"They're testing you," Liam tells Danny at the Gloc. "They think you're weak. And are we ever going to hit back for Pat?"

"Not yet."

"That should be your nickname," Liam says. "'Not Yet' Danny Ryan."

For once, Danny sort of agrees with Liam. He has to do something, so he dispatches Ned Egan to become a presence at the places that have been threatened, to be a deterrent, which Ned certainly is.

That's a defensive move, but Danny knows he also has to go on the offensive.

Hit the Moretti money.

THE CAPRICORN HOTEL on Washington Street is a dump.

But it's a dump that makes money for the Moretti family. Downstairs is a nightclub that books local bands and serves watered-down drinks; upstairs is a five-bedroom whorehouse. So the johns can meet the women at the bar or just skip the prelims and go straight up the stairs.

One-stop shopping.

The Altar Boys know it well.

Danny warns them, "We only rob the johns, not the girls. Cash, watches, jewelry, no credit cards. And no violence."

This is important.

So far, the Morettis haven't hurt anyone, and Danny don't want to be the first to spill blood.

Jimmy parks in the alley out back and Danny, Kevin, and Sean go up the fire escape. Guns tucked inside their leather jackets, they kick in the rickety door and burst in yelling.

This ain't your movie brothel. No overstuffed Edwardian furniture, erotic tapestries, no madam with a voice of brass and a heart of gold, just a tired male manager behind a counter and five working girls in cheap lingerie.

While Danny holds a gun on the manager, the Altar Boys walk down the hallway, kick in doors and rob the johns of their cash and jewelry. A couple of the men think this is a raid and try to scramble into their trousers, but they all give it up without a fight.

The manager quietly says to Danny, "You know whose place this is?"

"Yeah, I know."

"And you're doing this anyway." The manager shakes his head.

"Shut up."

They're in and out in ten minutes with a haul worth maybe a couple of grand, but that's not really the point.

The point is to hit back.

They didn't even wear masks, because none of the victims are going to go to the cops.

No one's watch costs as much as alimony.

THE NEXT PLACE they hit is a Chinese restaurant downtown.

The place has been there since dinosaurs roamed the earth, and since that time everyone who knows anything knows about the carved booth.

Most booths in the restaurant have plain pillars, but one booth has one that's ornately carved with faces like Chinese opera masks. And the cognoscenti know that if you sit in that booth, you're not really interested in the moo goo gai pan or the pu pu platter. In fact, you're not interested in ordering from the menu at all.

What you want is upstairs.

So when Danny and the Altar Boys come in and sit at that booth, the hostess, a Chinese woman in her forties, comes over and asks, "Are you looking for some nice girls?"

"Not *nice* girls," Kevin says.

She's heard this one before.

She walks them upstairs.

This brothel is more elaborate, with red velvet sofas and cushioned chairs. The girls are all Chinese, dressed in Asian gowns.

If Susan Kwan is intimidated by Danny's gun, she doesn't show it as he walks her to the small office in the back. "Do you know who we're with?"

"I know," Danny says. "I just don't care. Open the safe."

She opens it, but says, "Then you are a deeply stupid man."

"I *have* heard that said." He holds his hand out for the money. "Have the girls been paid out?"

"Not yet."

Danny takes half the cash—the house share that includes the Morettis' taste. When he comes out of the office, his crew is almost done going through the rooms, robbing the johns.

Kevin is deeply amused. "One of them was a judge. He put me in juvie once."

It's a good boost. Just in, just out, this time with about six grand in cash and prizes, and no one gets hurt.

Danny knows that Kwan isn't going to go to the cops, either. She's going to go straight to Peter Moretti and ask him what the hell she's paying protection for, anyway. And she's going to describe Danny and the Altar Boys.

• • •

SO IS THE owner of a candy store when Danny and the Altar Boys go in with baseball bats and smash up the Moretti vending machines.

Likewise the night clerk of a liquor store when they go in and clean out all of the cigarettes that had come in from a Moretti truck hijack.

Ditto the manager of a clothing store when Danny and his crew force their way into the back room and take a rack of hot Italian suits.

They all say the same thing.

Danny Ryan.

YOU GONNA FUCKIN' let him get away with this shit?" Paulie asks Peter after this last boost. "Fuckin' *Danny Ryan?*"

"What do you want me to do?" Peter asks.

"Whack him."

"You remember what happened the last time we tried that?" Peter asks.

The two De Salvo brothers got dead.

But Peter looks around the office and sees his guys' faces— Frankie V, Sal Antonucci, Chris Palumbo—and none of them is taking his side. He knows his people are tired of getting hit, that they expect him to do something.

"Well, whack *some*body," Paulie says. "Hit back."

"What's New York going to say?" Peter asks. "Boston."

Sal kicks in. "Fuck New York. Fuck Boston. We laid off these donkeys a whole year, look what it got us."

Peter turns to Chris.

"If we look weak in front of the big families," Chris says, "they *will* come in and swallow us whole."

The man is right, Peter thinks. But we can't be disproportional—the Irish haven't killed anybody.

He gives his order.

But make sure, he says, don't get carried away.

ONE OF PAULIE'S crew, Dominic Marchetti, waits outside the Spindrift until Tim Carroll comes out after closing the place.

He grabs Tim before he can open his car door.

"You owe Paulie money," Dom says.

"What?" Tim asks. "No, I don't. We worked that out. I'm with the Murphys."

"You giving me mouth, you lying motherfucker?!"

Dom is a big, heavy guy; Tim isn't.

So when Dom smacks Tim across the face, his head bounces against the car with a sickening thud.

Dom is one of those guys who once he starts, he don't know how to stop. Paulie knew that and shouldn't have sent him, or maybe that's *why* he sent him, but anyway, Dom gets carried away.

He punches the semiconscious Tim three times in the face, lets him slide down the car and then stomps on his back a few times for good measure. Then he remembers what he's there for. "Tell fucking Danny Ryan to knock it the fuck off."

TIM CAN BARELY repeat the message to Danny.

Lying in the hospital bed, jaw wired shut, cheekbone broken, two cracked vertebrae, potential long-term brain damage.

"Who was it?" Danny asks. "Did you recognize him?"

"Dom," Tim mumbles. "Marchetti."

"You going to do something now?" Liam asks Danny.

•   •   •

DANNY STRIDES ACROSS the floor of the restaurant.

Il Fornaio isn't crowded late in the evening, just a few regulars lingering over coffees and cannoli, and Dom Marchetti sitting by himself on a bench seat along the wall, hunched over a plate of pasta puttanesca.

He tries to get up when he sees Danny coming with a .38 in his hand, but the table is pushed too tightly against his big stomach and he can't get to his feet—or his gun—in time.

Danny slams his pistol into the side of Dom's head, three times fast, smashing his left eye orbital and cracking his skull. Dom slumps down on the bench and throws his arms over his head to ward off the blows, but Danny knocks them aside. He shoves the pistol barrel through Dom's teeth, into his mouth, and pulls the hammer back.

Another one of Peter's guys is sitting in a booth with his girlfriend and starts to get up, but then he sees Ned Egan just inside the door and decides against it. The waiters just stand there, shocked but still. They're Providence natives, they know better than to intervene.

"You want to die, Dom?" Danny asks. "You want to die *now?*"

Dom moans something. Danny eases the hammer back down and pulls the gun out. Then he steps back and flips the table over. Plates, glasses, silverware, and pasta spill on top of Dom.

"Tell Peter," Danny announces to the restaurant, "the next message he sends, he should come himself."

He walks out.

Ned waits a second, then follows him.

The cold war between the Murphys and the Morettis is over.

The real war is back on.

TWENTY-SEVEN

I **LOST MY TEMPER AND** I shouldn't have, Danny thinks. The problem is that the Morettis have too many soldiers, the Murphys too few.

Unless we get more guys.

But there are no more Irish to get.

He has his own small crew, John has maybe a half dozen guys who will step up to the plate, Liam maybe the same. He can get a few guys off the docks but they aren't really hitters.

Sooner or later, we're going to lose the war.

But he has an idea he's been thinking about for a long time. He walks into the Gloc, little Bobby Bangs has a cup of coffee ready for him. And a bagel, toasted with butter.

Danny takes it into the back room.

"You're what, Jewish now?" Liam asks, seeing the bagel.

"Yeah, maybe."

"Jews don't toast their bagels," Liam says. "And they don't use butter, they use cream cheese."

"Can I just eat my bagel?" Danny asks. Liam goes to Miami, so he thinks he knows all about Jews. Thinks he knows all about everything.

Danny slides into the booth with John Murphy and Bernie Hughes. "We need more guys."

"Maybe we can send back to Ireland," John says.

"We've seen that movie, haven't we?" Danny asks. "We know how it ends. Last thing we need is having to babysit a bunch of strangers who don't know their way around. I'm thinking something different."

"Like what?" Liam asks.

"I'm thinking of approaching Marvin Jones."

Danny waits for the reaction he knows is coming.

They—the proverbial "they," the common-wisdom dispensers "they"—say that the day John Murphy sits down with the Blacks is the day that pigs get wings. There's no racist like an old Irish racist, Danny thinks. Danny, he don't have a lot of Black friends—okay, he don't have any—but that's not because he's prejudiced, it's just because he sticks with his own.

He played basketball against a lot of Black kids back in high school and he didn't like them much, mostly because they always kicked his ass but also because they were mouthy and always talking shit and showing off. What did the coach call it, "jungle ball"? All slam dunks and one-on-ones and shit that the Irish kids couldn't do, so Danny and his teammates took a loser's pride in playing "team basketball" like Naismith taught, which was code for "losing basketball."

"And what would you be approaching Marvin about?" John asks.

"An alliance," Danny says. "We need the manpower, we need the guns."

"We have Ned," Liam says. "We have Jimmy Mac, the Altar Boys . . ."

No, Danny thinks, *I* have Ned, Jimmy Mac, and the Altar Boys. But he says, "Marvin has about twenty guys. That would bring us up to strength against the Morettis. Maybe they'd back off."

"What, you want peace?!" Liam asks.

"You don't?"

"No!" Liam says. "I want Sal Antonucci dead. I want the Morettis dead."

"Then go out and do it, Liam," Danny says. He lets it sit for a few seconds. Then he says, "Or shut the fuck up."

Liam shuts up.

"I played ball against Marvin," Danny says. "I know him a little."

Which is sort of true, Danny thinks, if you could call Marvin slam-dunking over my head knowing him a little. And he's seen Marvin around, but who hasn't? The man pretty much runs prostitution and gambling in South Providence, so he's on the street all the time.

And the word is that Marvin wants to take the drug trade from the Italians.

"The Zulus have already taken half our neighborhood," John says.

Danny can't argue with that. The Irish who could got out to the suburbs—Cranston, Warwick, down to South County—when the Blacks started moving in.

"So you're going to offer them what, the rest?" John asks.

"I'm not going to offer them anything that belongs to us," Danny says. "I'm going to offer them what belongs to the Morettis."

"I don't know," John says. "Getting in bed with the Blacks . . ."

"Times change," Bernie says. "We have to change with them. If we don't, we're dinosaurs."

Liam asks, "What's wrong with dinosaurs?"

"Do you see any around, Liam?" Bernie asks.

Danny gets the okay to approach Marvin.

THE TOP HAT Club is mostly empty about two in the afternoon, except for Marvin and his guys sitting in a booth in the back. Danny is pretty aware that he's about the only white guy ever to walk in there, if you don't count the cops coming to get their monthly envelopes, and one of Marvin's guys gets right into his face. "What do you want?"

"I want to talk to Marvin."

"Who are you?"

"Danny Ryan."

"Wait here."

Danny watches him walk back and talk into Marvin's ear. Then Marvin slides out of the booth and walks up to Danny. Tall mother-fucker, Marvin Jones, solidly built, looking good—gray suit, red shirt, red tie. Marvin's done all right for himself, Danny thinks.

Better than me.

"Danny Ryan," Marvin says. "I heard about you."

"We played ball against each other," Danny says.

"Is that right?" Marvin answers. "I don't remember."

"No reason you should," Danny says.

"You here to play ball now?" Marvin asks.

"Sort of."

Danny lays it out. At the end of the day, they both want the same thing—the guineas out of South Providence. Marvin has been com-peting with the Morettis for years for who gets to sell heroin to his people. Marvin is of the strong opinion that it should be him. John Murphy, Danny says, is ready to share that opinion.

"Is that a fact?" Marvin asks.

"Could be," Danny says. "John wants a sit-down."

Marvin smiles. Then he says, "All right, on one condition."

"What?"

Marvin says, "Murphy has to invite us for dinner. At the Gloc."

Danny tries to remember the last time a Black ever came into the Gloc and can't. Probably because no Black has ever stepped into the Gloc, not for long, anyway. No, there was that Black woman Liam brought in one time, just to stick it in everyone's eye, but she was a model who'd been in *Vogue* so she got a pass.

Danny smiles back. "Okay."

He goes and tells John, who thinks about it for a minute, then asks, "The Blacks, what do they eat?"

"I dunno," Danny says. "Food."

"I know 'food,' but what? Soul food?"

This amuses Danny, because John has probably just taught himself to say "Blacks" and now he's catching up on "soul food"?

"I dunno what soul food is," Danny answers. "Pork chops? Collard greens?"

"What are collard greens?"

"I don't know. I just heard that."

JOHN SETTLES ON steaks and baked potatoes, which is good, because that's about as much as the cooks at the Gloc can manage. Now it's all set out at a long table—steaks, potatoes wrapped in tinfoil, green beans, a salad. Some bottles of wine, beer in buckets of ice, bottles of whiskey.

"You think I should have gotten grape soda?" John asks when Danny comes in.

"What?"

"I heard the Blacks like grape soda."

"Who told you that?"

"Kennedy that runs the movie theater," John answers. "He says when he has a movie the Blacks like, he stocks up on grape soda."

"Black *kids*, maybe," Danny says. He don't know that they even make grape soda anymore. Hasn't had a grape soda since he drank one in a single gulp in a bet with Jimmy and it came up out his nose.

A few minutes later Bobby Bangs sticks his head in and says, "They're here."

"Let them in," John says.

Pigs flying all around, Danny thinks.

Three guys come with Marvin, each of them playing the angry Black man role, scowling, each of them with a bulge under his jacket. Marvin takes one look at the spread, hands a hundred bucks in cash to one of his underlings, and says, "KFC."

Guy goes out, John fills the silence by making introductions.

Marvin's guy gets back, so now there are steaks and baked potatoes and buckets of fried chicken on the table. Danny would rather have the KFC than the overcooked beef, but he don't want to be disloyal, so he spears himself a steak.

Marvin ain't one for small talk. "So what are we doing here?"

"We want your help against the Morettis," Danny says. "Right now, they control the drug business in South Providence."

"It's neocolonialism," Marvin says. "The white man selling drugs in the Black community."

This prompts an ugly stir from the Irish side, who don't want to admit that this is now a Black community, and who have no idea what neocolonialism is, so Danny quickly says, "We want the Morettis out, too."

But one of Marvin's guys says, "But we don't want to replace them with a bunch of donkeys."

Danny don't mind Irish slurs—bogtrotter, mick, Harp, donkey— go for it. But Marvin gives his guy a shut-your-stupid-fucking-mouth glare, and the man looks down. Which means that Marvin don't think he can beat the Morettis without us, either, Danny thinks. "We don't have any interest in selling drugs."

"No," Marvin says, "you have an interest in adversely affecting the Morettis' income stream. What weakens them strengthens you."

Danny nods.

"The Italians kicking you all's ass," Marvin says.

"They're tough," Danny says.

Marvin shrugs, as if to say *Not so tough*. Like he's killed tougher guys. Maybe he has, Danny thinks. Word is that Marvin Jones has put a lot of rivals away—Blacks, Jamaicans, Puerto Ricans. "So what would you want?"

"Our unions," Danny says. "Our docks."

Marvin takes this in, and then says, "We'd want jobs on the docks."

"No," Danny says.

"*No?*"

"You get dope, women, and the numbers," Danny says. "The docks are ours."

Danny knows it's a risk that could scuttle the deal. But there's no point in just replacing Peter Moretti with Marvin Jones, and anyway, he can't get Blacks into the unions because the union guys simply wouldn't accept it, and Marvin should know that. Danny's betting that he's just testing, seeing how far he can push.

"All right, Danny Ryan," Marvin says. "You got yourself some Zulus."

Marvin laughs at his own joke and then everyone laughs. Even Bernie Hughes ventures a chuckle.

It's a win for Danny.

He don't care about a victory inside the back room, even if it raises his status. What Danny cares about is the Dogtown Irish surviving this war. This alliance changes the numbers, maybe enough to bring Peter to the peace table.

The surprising thing about the dinner is that Marvin Jones and John Murphy become buddies.

When John starts telling old war stories, Danny tries to shut him down, but Marvin waves him off—he wants to hear them. Sits there like a grandson while John goes on and on about the old days. Danny, he's just glad that Marty ain't there to chime in or start singing or something.

When John gets up to take a piss, Danny says, "Sorry about my father-in-law."

"No," Marvin says. "Respect."

John comes back in wiping his hands on his khakis. When he sits down, Marvin says, "This is how I look at it, Mr. Murphy . . ."

Danny sees that John likes the "Mr. Murphy."

"No offense," Marvin says, "but the Irish were the British niggers. My people are the Americans' niggers."

Danny is afraid John will go off, but he says, "When my grandfather got here, there were signs reading 'No dogs or Irish allowed.'"

"What I mean," Marvin says.

Bobby Bangs brings in a new round of drinks. John says, "Not the house shit. Go get the private stock."

So Danny sits there in disbelief as John and Marvin sit sipping vintage Irish whiskey and swapping stories. They're both pretty much in the bag when John says, "Can I ask you something, Marvin?"

Marvin nods.

"Grape soda," John says. "Do you like it?"

"You got any?" Marvin asks.

"No."

"Then why ask?"

NOT ALL MARVIN'S guys are behind the new alliance.

His cousin Demetrius, for instance, doesn't like it at all. "Let 'em kill each other. That's a good thing. The fewer whites, the better. Why do we want to get in the middle of that?"

"Don't we want the guineas off our blocks?" Marvin asks.

"We can do it ourselves."

"We can do it quicker with the Irish," Marvin says. "And we need their protection. They got judges, state senators, some cops. We have none of that."

"You trust Old Man Murphy?"

"He's not running things anymore," Marvin says. "Ryan is. Let me tell you about him, cousin—that motherfucker wants *out*. I can see it in his eyes. He doesn't want any part of dope, he doesn't want any part of the rackets. We get the Italians out of the way, Danny Ryan will leave us alone. Let him have his unions, his docks—chicken feed compared to dope."

"I know, I just hate honkies."

"So let's go kill us a few."

AT FIRST, PETER Moretti thinks that the alliance between Marvin Jones and the Dogtown Irish is hysterical.

It's open mic night at the American Vending office when the rumors start coming in about it, the guys are firing off so many lines about "black Irish," John Murphy growing a 'fro, the Irish finally getting some dicks worth the name.

Peter thinks it's so fucking funny he has a load of watermelons dumped outside the Gloc and a crate of potatoes delivered to Marvin's club and they all get a good laugh out of that until one of the comedians, a heroin dealer, is found dead slumped over the wheel of his Lincoln. And Marvin's witticism, "It's all fun and games until someone loses an Eye-talian," makes the rounds.

The boys at American Vending don't find that amusing.

Peter sends Sal and Frankie out to do some "coon-hunting" and they do a drive-by on one of Marvin's dealers on Cranston Street.

Marvin responds by killing one of Sal's guys outside his *gumar*'s apartment.

The papers love it.

Now they have a three-way war to write about.

Life is good.

At Danny's house, it's more like okay. With less and less money coming in, it's harder to buy diapers, formula, car seats, all the expensive shit that comes with having a kid, and Terri is feeling the pinch, plus she's getting a little stir-crazy being at home with a baby all day. And she knows that Danny has gotten a bump in his responsibilities, she doesn't understand why he hasn't gotten the bump in earnings to go with it.

"I have half a mind to talk to my father about it," she says one night when Danny comes home.

"Use the *other* half of your mind," Danny says. Last thing that would get him a move up is his wife fighting his battles for him.

"But you're the one who put this thing with Marvin Jones together," Terri says, trying to force a spoonful of some vegetable shit into Ian's unwilling mouth.

"You're not supposed to know about that."

"It's all over the neighborhood," Terri says. "Everyone's talking about it."

"Fish that don't open their mouths don't get caught."

"What does that even mean?" Terri asks, frustrated with him and her son, who dodges with his head and thinks this is some sort of really fun game. "Fish? What? All I'm saying is that with . . . Pat gone . . ."

"I don't want to talk about that."

"I don't, either," Terri says. "But someone's making that money—it isn't all going to Sheila, let me tell you, she's struggling. So who? Liam? And what's he doing for it?"

"Liam's been around."

Danny wonders why he's defending Liam, fucking Liam, to his

own sister. Yeah, Liam's been around, but all he's been doing is muttering about getting revenge for Pat, but then he doesn't *do* shit.

Terri says, "All I'm saying is, my father owes you, and he knows it."

Yeah, maybe he does and maybe he doesn't, Danny thinks. If John does, he also does a good job of feigning ignorance when Danny brings it up to him.

"And Pat not cold in his grave," John says.

"All respect," Danny answers, "Pat's been gone over a year . . . and I've been picking up a lot of the slack."

"For the family."

"I know that," Danny says. "But I have a family to think about, too."

Like your daughter, John? Your grandson? But Terri was never one of your pets, not like Cassie. Terri is that dutiful middle child, like Danny read about in the book that Terri got, who doesn't get the attention because she just does the right thing.

"You need to earn, Danny, earn," John says. "I'm not stopping you."

Yeah, but you're not helping me, either, Danny thinks. But he gets the message—John isn't going to bump him up in the union or on the docks, or give him a taste of the gambling, the protection that was Pat's. What John is saying is that Danny has a little crew of his own going now—so go ahead and earn and good luck.

Thanks for nothing, John.

TWENTY-EIGHT

SAL ANTONUCCI AND FRANKIE V go into the Mustang Club.

Normally a couple of wop wiseguys wouldn't get caught dead going into a gay bar, but the Mustang is on Sal's turf and he goes once a month to collect his envelope.

The unspoken rule about that is you always bring another guy with you. Not for protection—for appearances, so no untoward rumors get started.

Anyway, they go in and get their envelope from the bartender and it turns out tonight is Ladies' Night, which basically means lesbians get a discount on their drinks.

So in addition to the usual rough trade clad in vest and chaps, you got a lot of dykes, as Frankie V says, including a lesbian biker gang whose leathers proclaim that they're—inevitably—the Amazons, dancing to the pounding disco music.

"Unreal," Frankie says. "Let's get the fuck outta here."

"Let's have a drink."

"You fuckin' kiddin' me?"

"No, come on," Sal says. "I mean, how often you see something like this?"

"Hopefully, never again," Frankie says, disgusted.

"One drink," Sal says. "Gives us a story to tell."

He orders Seagram's straight up for each of them, and then turns on his stool to gawk at the Amazons. He knows that Amazons were, what, like giants or something, and these women come close—most of them are stocky bull dykes but a few are tall, really tall with broad shoulders, and Sal, he can't help himself thinking what it would be like to fuck one of them.

Frankie, he can't shut up, keeps up a running monologue on how disgusting the whole thing is—the fags, the lesbos—how he wants to puke, how this whole place should burn down with everyone in it . . .

One of the biker chicks makes eye contact with Sal. He doesn't look away, and a second later she walks over with one of her friends, a squat chick next to her tall buddy.

"What are you guys," the tall one asks, "lookie-loos? Because you're not gay."

"Oh, we're not gay," Frankie says.

"You want to gawk at the animals," the tall one says, "go to the zoo."

"We're just having a quiet drink," says Sal.

"Have it somewhere else," the tall one says. "You're not welcome here."

People are starting to look at them, get a little nervous. The bartender comes over, says to the tall one, "Leave it alone, Meg."

Meg arches an eyebrow, smirks, and then says, "Oh, I get it. These are the wops you have to pay off."

"Watch it," Frankie says.

"You've had a little too much to drink," Sal says. "Why don't you just walk away now?"

"Why don't *you* just walk away, cocksucker?"

"Whoa!" Frankie says. "You go down on your girlfriend with that mouth?"

"What would you know about going down?" Meg asks. Then she turns back to Sal. "This one does, though, huh? I think I was wrong about you. I think you got one of those big, gaudy guinea houses with pink flamingos on the lawn—"

"You going to let her talk to you like that?" Frankie demands.

"—and a big walk-in closet—"

Sal launches a tight, arcing overhand right to the jaw with his hips fully into it, and she goes down.

Out before she hits the floor, and she hits it hard.

"All *right!*" Frankie yelps.

Some of the other Amazons start to crowd in on them, ready to go, but Frankie pulls his pistol out. Sal stands over the woman, her head cradled in her friend's lap. She don't look so angry now, don't look so tough.

Sal thinks she looks . . . pretty.

Her friend says to him, "You a big man now? This make you a big man?"

Sal knows what she's really saying.

He feels bad. Mutters, "I don't hit women."

"That's not a fucking *woman*," Frankie says. "That's a freak, a *thing*, a—"

Sal hits him.

A straight right, and he takes a little off it at the last second, but it's to the face and Frankie's head snaps back and right away Sal knows he's made a mistake, that this isn't going to end here.

He put his hands on a made guy, and it's going to be trouble.

•   •   •

THE FUCK OUT of here," Peter says. He's sitting at a table in the Central Diner, trying to enjoy his eggs.

"I'm telling you," Frankie V says, "the guy is a *finook*."

"Sal Antonucci a fag," Paulie says. "Come on."

"You don't believe me, okay," Frankie says. "But he punched me. He punched a made guy and I want something done about it."

"He was out of line," Peter says. "No question. But we got bigger problems right now."

"Like what?"

"Like what?" Peter asks. "How about a bunch of fuckin' Mau Maus going off the plantation? I know you know about this, Frankie, I saw you at the funerals."

"So what?" Frankie says. "You're going to give Sal a pass for hitting me because you're afraid he'll go sulk again, you lose your best hitter?"

"Hey, Frankie, you want to go do Marvin Jones, be my guest," Peter says.

That shuts Frankie up.

After he leaves, Paulie asks, "What do you think? About Sal being a fag?"

"No fucking way."

"I dunno," Paulie says. "Remember how broken up he was about Tony?"

"The guy was his cellmate."

"What I'm saying."

"You know what I think about Sal being a fag?" Peter asks. "Never to be repeated? I think I don't care. After the *ditsoon* are done popping Colt forty-fives over Marvin's grave, then maybe I'll care. Until then, Sal can suck all the cock he wants."

He asks Sal to come in for a sit-down, though.

That afternoon, at American Vending, Peter says, "Fuck, every guy I know wants to smack Frankie V, that mouth of his. I can't stand the fucking guy. But you shouldn't have hit him, Sal."

"I know," Sal says. "This temper of mine. You gonna tax me for it, tax me. I'll pay."

"He's within his rights to want something."

"I know."

"Look, apologize to him," Peter says, "send his fat wife something nice—I dunno, a leg of lamb—I'm willing to forget the whole thing."

"Yeah?" Sal asks, waiting for the next Gucci to drop. Peter is an elephant, he doesn't forget shit.

"I'd like you to do something for me, though," Peter says.

There it is. "What's that, Peter?"

"This fuckin' shine, Marvin . . ."

DANNY'S SHOT CLANGS off the rim.

"You never change, Ryan," Marvin says, scooping up the rebound on the bounce. "You sucked then, you suck now."

He turns, shoots and swishes.

"There's something to be said for consistency," Danny says. He grabs the ball beneath the basket and takes an easy layup off the board. "And I thought you didn't remember me."

Even in the cold, Danny's sweating under the gray hooded sweatshirt. He passes Marvin the ball.

"I don't," Marvin says. "I'm just busting chops."

He takes a jumper.

Swish.

"I ever tell you about my mama, Ryan?" Marvin asks as Danny takes the ball. "That woman got up every damn day at dawn, went out to clean other people's houses, mop their floors, scrub their toilets. We kids didn't have a lot, but we never went hungry."

Danny tucks the ball under his arm and listens, grateful for a breather.

"You know who my daddy was?" Marvin asks. "Harold Jones."

"The singer?"

"Yeah, *that* Harold Jones," Marvin says.

He launches into a soul tune that Danny's heard on the radio a few thousand times. Hell, he and Terri used to screw to it.

"One-hit wonder," Marvin says. "You gonna stand there sucking air, or are you going to shoot?"

Danny shoots.

Clang.

"So what was he like?" Danny asks.

"Damned if I know," says Marvin. "'Papa was a rolling stone.' My point in telling you all this is that my mama doesn't clean toilets no more. She doesn't mop floors. Other people clean her toilets. In the house I bought her."

"Okay."

"What about you?" Marvin asks, chasing down Danny's rebound. "Your mama and daddy."

Marvin spins and shoots.

It goes in.

"My old man is your basic Irish stereotype," Danny says, chasing down the ball. "A bitter alcoholic. It was my mother who was the no-show."

"*That's* different."

Yeah, it was different all right, Danny thinks. He shoots and it actually goes in.

"Black rubbing off on you," Marvin says.

"You ever hear of Larry Bird?" Danny asks.

Marvin laughs. "Always the example you guys use."

"That's because we don't need another one," Danny says. He runs in, grabs his own rebound and lays it up.

"Black man would have dunked it," Marvin says.

"White man don't have to," Danny says. He flips Marvin the ball. "Word is Peter Moretti has put a hit out on you."

"I heard," Marvin says. "He gave the contract to Sal Antonucci."

"Sal's the real thing, Marvin," Danny says. "Keep your head on a swivel."

"I'm not afraid of Sal Antonucci."

But you should be, Danny thinks.

HE DRIVES DOWN to Goshen with Marty's groceries.

It would be a hell of a lot easier if the old man would move to Providence in the winter, but he's stubborn (go figure) and sticks it out in the little cottage that barely has insulation. So at least once a week Danny has to drive down there with the groceries and to see if he's still on the right side of the grass.

And it's a risk, driving down there. Driving anywhere these days, with a war on. But you can't live in fear, Danny thinks. You take reasonable precautions, you check your rearview mirror, you keep your gun close to hand and your head on a swivel and you live your life.

Dead down at the shore there in April. The vacation trailers are shut up, the hot dog stand, the ice cream shop, even the laundromat, all closed, waiting for summer to come back to life again.

Danny pulls off in the beach parking lot on the way, gets out and steps onto the sand. In the clear air, Block Island looks close, almost like he could swim to it. The water is bottle green with spindrift spraying across the tops of the waves. He watches a fishing boat, rigged for netting, make its way out of the Harbor of Refuge and wishes he was on it, wishes his life were as clean and sharp as the water, that if he jumped in, the cold and the salt and the surf would strip his skin of the film that always seems to be on it these days.

He has an impulse to walk in, duck under a wave and then swim beyond the break.

Freeze to death.

It's just a flash in the mind, not serious.

You have a wife and a kid to take care of, Danny thinks. You have Dogtown. And your old man. All relying on you.

Boo-hoo, he thinks.

Stop feeling sorry for yourself.

He turns, walks back to the car and drives the two minutes to Marty's cottage.

"You bring my Hormels?" Marty asks.

He's sitting in that chair, with the TV on loud, a steady drone. A glass of whiskey sits on an end table beside the chair.

"No, Dad," Danny says. "Every other time I come, I bring your Hormels, but this time for some reason I just decided not to."

"Smart-ass."

Danny unloads the groceries, puts some stuff in the cabinets, the perishables in the refrigerator. "You want me to make you something?"

"No."

"Have you eaten?"

"I'm not hungry."

"You gotta eat."

"I hear you're in bed with the Blacks now," Marty says.

"Just cuddling," Danny says. He opens one of the Hormel cans, finds a clean spoon in the drainer, and scoops the hash into a pan. "Why, you got a problem with it?"

Marty surprises him. "No, it's the smart move."

Danny takes a plastic spatula from the drawer. The drawer is sticky from the salt air and hard to shut. He clicks on the gas burner, then pushes the hash around the pan. "Thanks."

The hash heats up quickly. Danny spoons it onto a plate, grabs a fork and hands it to Marty.

Marty's got this sly, dirty smirk on his face.

"What?" Danny asks.

"I heard something."

Like, playing it out, making it last, Danny thinks, savoring that he knows something Danny don't for a change. "What did you hear, Dad?"

"Sal Antonucci is a homo."

A "homo"? Danny thinks. It takes him a second to remember what the word means. "Where'd you hear that?"

"Ned heard it," Marty says. "From a guy in a bar. Frankie V caught Sal in a gay joint and Sal punched him."

"What was Vecchio doing in a gay bar?"

"Collecting his envelope," Marty says.

"Yeah, I'm not buying it."

"I'm not selling it," Marty says. "You asked me to tell you what I heard, I'm telling you."

"Eat."

Jesus Christ, Danny thinks as he watches Marty shove food around his plate. Sal, gay? Doesn't even matter if it's true—if Ned heard a guy talking about it in a bar, it's as good as true. If Marty in his chair here knows about it . . .

He can just hear Frankie V spreading it around—*"I probably shouldn't be telling you this, but I think you need to know, this is just between us . . ."* Enjoying the hell out of himself. And if it's true that Sal punched him, Frankie would have gone running to Peter. Expecting what? That Peter would choose Frankie over his best hitter? That

Peter would do the right thing? "Jesus God, Dad, would you put a bite of fucking food in your mouth?"

"I told you I'm not hungry."

"We need to take you to the doctor?"

"I hate doctors."

They hate you, too, Danny thinks. You cuss them out and eye-fuck the nurses. "You bust my balls about your Hormels and then you won't eat it."

"I'll eat it later."

Which Danny knows is his cue to get out. I've brought him his groceries and his lotto cards, I've listened to his gossip, so I've served my purpose, Danny thinks. He's in a hurry to get back to being lonely and miserable.

"I'll come back down Thursday," Danny says.

"If you want."

Danny kisses him on the forehead and turns for the door.

"Danny."

"Yeah?"

"Take care of yourself."

TWENTY-NINE

THE BOY IS BEAUTIFUL.

Well, he's not a boy—that would be *too* fucked up—he's a man, but he's a young man and he's beautiful.

Sal knows this is the last place in the world he should be right now, what with the rumors running around about him, but he took the precaution of driving all the way down to Westerly, the whole drive telling himself that he wasn't going to go down there, the whole time parking telling himself that he wasn't going to go in, the whole time walking into the bar telling himself he wasn't going to stay.

The fight with Judy had been brutal.

When he got home earlier that day, she was sitting at the kitchen table with a glass of red and looked up at him like he pissed on her shoes.

"What?" Sal asked.

She was already half in the bag. "I went to get my hair done today."

"So?"

"So I'm sitting there in the chair," she said, "and these two *chiac-chieronas* next to me are talking and guess what they're talking about."

Sal was tired. "I don't know, Judy. What?"

"You."

Sal felt his stomach flip.

Judy looked at him like she wanted to kill him. "I had to sit there and listen to them laugh and giggle about my Sal Antonucci getting caught sucking cock in the men's room of a gay bar."

"That's not true."

"You know, Sal, somehow I always knew it," Judy said. "There was something about you. And then you and Tony . . ."

"He was my friend."

"He was more than your fucking friend," Judy said. "So to speak. I put up with it when you were inside, you had your needs, but—"

"Shut your fucking mouth."

"Or what?" Judy asked. "You going to hit me? Go ahead. Or do you want to fuck me in the ass, that's what you like, right? Go ahead, you can fuck me in the ass, Sal. At least that way I'd *get* fucked every once in a while."

"I gave you two kids."

"Or maybe I got it wrong, Sally. Maybe you're not the fucker, you're the fuck*ee*. Is that what you want, you want me to fuck you up the ass?"

He hit her.

Open hand across the cheek, knocked her out of the chair.

She put her hand to her cheek and glared up at him. "Get out. Go find yourself a boy, you fag."

He walked out of the house and got in the car. Pulled out onto 95 and drove south, never meaning to come here.

But here he is, two drinks in, and the boy is beautiful. Tall, lithe, dirty-blond hair, cut a little long. Silk print shirt, tight jeans, nice pair of shoes. Sal's never seen him here before. Sal's been here at least a couple of dozen times, and this boy is new.

He sees Sal looking and looks back.

Smiles.

Sal walks over. "What's your name?"

"Alex."

"Can I buy you a drink, Alex?"

"Maybe if you tell me your name."

"Chuckie."

Alex laughs. "Bullshit. You just made that up."

"Yeah, maybe."

"Well, okay, Maybe Chuckie," Alex says, "I guess you can buy me a dirty martini."

Thirty minutes later they're out in the alley, Sal with his back to the wall and his fly open, Alex on his knees, sucking him off.

Sal wraps his fingers in Alex's thick hair.

This is the last place in the world he should be, but it feels so good and the boy is beautiful.

DANNY CRADLES IAN in his arms and rocks him gently back and forth, softly singing "Mammas Don't Let Your Babies Grow Up to Be Cowboys."

They've had a hard time getting him down tonight. Terri tried everything, bundling him up tighter because maybe he was cold, loosening the blankets because maybe he was too hot, rocking him in his chair, laying him down on the floor in front of the television, but the boy kept crying and squirming and kicking.

Even the usually reliable "Mammas Don't Let Your Babies Grow Up to Be Cowboys" failed, which Ian usually falls asleep to before Willie gets through the first chorus. Not tonight, and Danny said he'd take over so the exhausted Terri could go in and take a long, hot shower.

Danny hits replay on the song for about the thirty-seventh time and starts singing again and rocking and finally feels Ian get heavy, and his breathing gets soft and rhythmic, and Danny just enjoys holding his child for a little while before he carries him into the bedroom and oh-so-gently sets him down in the crib and tiptoes out.

TERRI IS JUST out of the shower. Body and hair both wrapped in towels.

With this look on her face.

Stricken.

"What?" Danny asks.

"I felt something," she says, "in my breast."

THE WOMAN IS both buxom and statuesque. In her feathered headdress, she moves gracefully across the lawn like a beautiful, exotic bird.

Madeleine watches her.

All the models are dressed in Manny Maniscalco's most iconic creations. Madeleine made sure that the showgirls wearing Manny's greatest designs at the party following his funeral possessed the bodies to show them off at their best.

Some people in the greater Las Vegas community, the serious business types less associated with the Strip, think it vulgar and grotesque, this fete thrown on the grounds of his estate, with the scantily clad chorus girls wandering around displaying themselves. Especially so as it was the idea of a woman who, when they were married, regularly cuckolded her late ex-husband.

Madeleine doesn't care what they think.

She knew that Manny, a deeply ugly man, loved above all things to surround himself with beauty, especially of the feminine kind.

So she wanted to give him this.

Madeleine had moved back to the estate when she found out that he was terminally ill. They'd stayed in touch over the years, on the phone or for the occasional dinner, and at one of the latter she saw that he was obviously sick and pried it out of him. When, weeks later, the doctors told him there was nothing more they could do, and Manny wanted to die at home instead of in the hospital, she simply moved in to take charge of his care.

She brought in round-the-clock nurses to administer medication and to wash him, but she sat with him most of the time, kept him company through the long nights, wiped his forehead, held his hand.

They talked and laughed about the old days, the trips they took, the dinners they had, the shows they saw, the characters they knew.

When he died, it was Madeleine who closed his eyes.

She went off and cried, then pulled it together and started in on the business of planning his funeral and this elaborate send-off.

Everyone who is anyone is there, for Manny was highly regarded and deeply beloved in all of Las Vegas's interlocking circles. The mayor, the congressman, businesspeople, show people, casino types, and wiseguys stand chatting on the lawn, nibbling canapés, sipping fine wines and sharing stories about Manny.

And whispering about Madeleine, for the news about Manny's will is already grist for the Vegas rumor mill, and the gossip is that she moved in on him during his last days to charm him in his weakened state, to bring in a lawyer and, in her presence, change his will.

It isn't true.

No one was more shocked than Madeleine when the lawyer revealed that Manny had left her everything—the majority shares of Maniscalco Manufacturing, tens of millions in stocks and bonds, real estate holdings, more millions in cash. Everything is hers now—the estate, the mansion, the horses, the stables, the tennis courts, the pool.

The lawyer took her aside to assure her that Manny hadn't changed the will recently; in fact, it had read exactly this way since the day they divorced.

"He told me that you brought him beauty," the lawyer said.

So Madeleine, already rich from her own efforts, is now wealthy. She can easily afford the half million dollars she dropped on this party.

A full big band from one of the shows is playing "All the Things You Are"—one of Manny's favorites—and earlier a big recording star with her own show sang "My Funny Valentine."

One of Manny's favorite comedians, one of those "insult comics," did a roast of him—*"When Madeleine said 'I do,' the minister asked, 'You do?' No, but Manny really liked the horses, you know. Why not? He had a face like one. Hey, don't tell the horses I said that . . ."*

Madeleine had brought in the whole Las Vegas circus—musicians, singers, comics, jugglers, acrobats, musicians, and, of course, the showgirls. Now they all circulate among the guests, performing their tricks or just displaying their beauty, and it's a party that she knows Manny would have loved.

She's admiring one of the showgirls when Pasco Ferri walks up to her.

The old mob boss traveled from Florida to pay his respects and to represent other bosses who didn't think they should make an appearance in public. He was an old friend of Manny's and Madeleine has known him for years.

"A beautiful party, Maddy," Pasco says.

"I think he would have liked it," she says. "Tell me, how's my son?"

"Danny and me, we don't talk much."

"I know the feeling."

"He's a good kid, Danny," Pasco says.

"He's not a kid," Madeleine says. "He has a child of his own now."

"I heard. Every happiness."

Madeleine shrugs. "I haven't seen my grandson."

"Danny's like his old man," Pasco says. "Stubborn. You heard about Irish Alzheimer's? They forget everything but the grudges."

"I worry about him," Madeleine says. "This thing with the Morettis. Anything you can do there, Pasco, I'd appreciate it. You know I can open certain doors here. I'm not without influence with the gaming commission, for instance."

"I didn't come here to do business, Maddy," Pasco says. "Just to show respect."

"Of course." As if, she thinks, showing respect isn't part of doing business.

The party finally dies down, the guests drift off; the cleanup crew starts its work, tearing down tables, taking down tents, hauling out garbage.

LATER THAT NIGHT, Madeleine lies in bed and strokes the young man's cheek.

It's soft, almost downy.

"That was nice," she says.

Kelly smiles. Straight, white, perfect teeth. "I was hoping for something a little better than 'nice.'"

"You didn't get sufficient praise when I was moaning your name?" she asks. "You need more affirmation than that?"

He shouldn't, she thinks. He's a lovely, lovely young man and he knows it. The quarterback for the local college football team, he must have cheerleaders and coeds all over him, and yet, for some reason, he likes to come and bed me.

It's not just the gifts she gives him—the clothes, the watches—it's also something in him that likes older women.

And thank God, she thinks.

Madeleine has no illusion that she's exclusive, she doesn't want to be, and she certainly doesn't want him falling in love with her. All she wants is a regular, reliable, good fuck with a beautiful body, and Kelly is all of that.

His physique is perfection.

It's been a good thing, and she'd like it to continue, but he's starting to get a little needy.

And arrogant.

Right on cue, Kelly says, "I made you come like a rocket and all you can say is 'nice'?"

She props herself up on an elbow and looks at him. "Kelly, do you know the difference between you and a vibrator?"

He looks puzzled, and a little scared.

"The vibrator can twirl," Madeleine says, "and it costs far less to maintain."

She's about to elaborate when the phone rings.

It's Terri.

She's crying.

THIRTY

SAL KNOWS HE'S GOTTA DO something and do it quick.

Right now he has Peter's support, but that ain't gonna last forever. Peter Moretti is the original "what have you done for me lately"
boss, and with rumors swirling that Sal is gay, he wants something
done for him lately. Already guys are starting to turn their faces when
Sal comes into a room. He hears the whispers as he walks past them
at a bar, sees the smirks from the corner of his eye, knows that Frankie
V has been running his mouth.

Fucking Frankie. Sal had tried to apologize, but Frankie was having none of it. Sal sent over a beautiful basket to his house—prosciutto,
brcsaola, soppressata, abbruzze, auricchio, Cerignola olives, Biancolilla
oil, a bottle of Ruffino Chianti—but it came back unopened.

The hell does Frankie want?

The guy has some balls on him, going around saying I'm a fag.
After I do Marvin, I might decide to do Frankie.

Problem is, Marvin ain't playing by the rules. If you know a contract's been taken out on you, there are certain ways you're expected

to behave—you're supposed to go to ground, keep your head down, even leave town.

But Marvin ain't doing any of those things. Exactly the opposite: he's showboating, making himself conspicuous, going out to clubs, to dinner, hanging on the corner and in the parks, shoving it in Sal's face.

Like *You want me? I ain't hard to find, am I?*

Part of this hide-in-plain-sight bullshit is tactical, Sal knows: you stay in public because your would-be killer doesn't want to do you in front of witnesses. But still, it's showing Sal up, making him look bad.

Especially when Marvin sent a pound of fudge to Sal at American Vending with the note *Heard you liked packing this.* Sent it *there* deliberately, knowing it would humiliate Sal in front of the guys, force Peter's hand.

People are supposed to be afraid of Sal Antonucci.

He loses that fear factor, he's lost a lot.

Some wannabe might take a run at him.

So if he has to hit Marvin in front of witnesses, Sal's going to make sure they're witnesses who won't talk.

Marvin's own boys.

He could gun Jones down in plain sight in front of all of them and not one would dime him to the cops. They'll come after him themselves, because—Black or white—that's the code.

He decides to do Marvin on the ball court.

Do it the way the moolies do it.

Drive-by style.

EVERYTHING THAT SAL knows, Marvin knows.

And as bad as Sal wants to do Marvin, Marvin wants to do Sal. Because he's heard whispers, too. About himself. That he's getting soft, that as he's climbed up the ladder he's forgotten what it's like to be on the ground. Street cred is like any other commodity, you got to refresh it every once in a while or it loses its potency.

So he sets up every opportunity for Sal to come at him.

To remind his people why Marvin is Marvin.

EVEN THE MOOLIES know Sal is a fag," Paulie says, sitting at the office. "Everyone's laughing at us now."

"They don't *know* anything," Peter says, looking at the box of fudge on the table. "They only know what they've heard."

"That's what I mean," Paulie says. "Everyone hears. And how is that going to play in Peoria?"

"What?"

"It's an expression," Paulie says. "Like, what are people going to think. 'How is that going to play in Peoria?'"

"Where the fuck is Peoria?"

"I dunno," Paulie says. "The fuck difference does it make?"

"Because why the fuck would we care what people there think?" Peter asks.

"We don't."

"Then why . . ." Peter gives up.

"We care," Chris says, his head starting to throb, "about what certain people in Boston think. About what people in New York think. That we have a gay captain in our family, that we can't finish off a bunch of micks, and that now even the *ditsoon* are giving us the finger."

Maintaining a separate family in tiny Rhode Island has always been a problem, Chris knows. Stuck between Boston and New York, both of whom would like to take over and make us just a crew, the Rhode Island family has always had to be tougher, stricter, more violent. If the guys in Boston or New York think we're weak, they'll be looking to take advantage.

This war trying to take a little turf from the Irish is going to cost us our whole thing.

"So what do you want to do?" Peter asks.

"Sal has to take Marvin out—"

"On a date?" Paulie asks.

"Yeah, funny, Paulie," Chris says. "Then we'll see what we have to do about Sal."

"What do you mean?" Paulie asks. "He's a fag."

"Marvin says he is," Chris says. "If Marvin is gone, he don't say it no more. Frankie V says it, so . . ."

"So you're saying we should whack Frankie to cover up for Sal."

"I'm asking," Chris says, "who's more valuable. Who's the better soldier? Who's the bigger earner?"

"Who's the *finook*?" Paulie asks.

Jesus God, he's stupid, Chris thinks.

Peter gets it, though. He understands it's the image that matters, not the reality. "So you think we should give Sal the green light on Frankie."

Chris shrugs. "What would you do to a guy who goes around saying you're gay?"

Peter mimes squeezing a trigger.

Chris shrugs again.

"But Sal *is* a fag," Paulie says.

"So fucking what?" Chris says.

"You kidding me?" Paulie asks. "What they do is dis*gusting*. Makes me want to puke."

"You telling me you never fucked a woman in the ass?" Chris says.

"That's different."

"How?"

"It was a *woman*," Paulie says.

Peter says, "Let's wait. See if Sal handles our Marvin problem. Then we'll decide what to do."

Classic Peter, Chris thinks, kicking the can down the road. But it does make a certain kind of sense—if Marvin kills Sal, we won't have to choose between him and Frankie V.

Paulie takes a piece of the fudge.

"The fuck," Peter says.

"What?"

"You gonna eat that?"

"Why not?" Paulie says, shoving it into his mouth. "It's good."

BEHIND THE WHEEL of a boosted Caddy, Sal can see the playground from a block away.

Moolies in their hooded sweatshirts jumping up and down. Problem is picking out which one is Marvin. As he pulls up alongside the court, he remembers that Marvin is the one who doesn't suck.

Then he sees a guy in a gray PC hoodie do a cross-over dribble that about breaks his defender's ankles and go up for a slam dunk.

Marvin.

Sal rolls down his window.

MARVIN FEELS HIM.

Then hangs on the rim and sees him.

Demetrius yells, "Gun!"

Marvin lets go of the rim, as he drops pulls his pistol taped inside the kangaroo pouch on the sweaty and fires.

Then something punches him in the chest.

He's dead before he hits the ground.

SAL DRIVES THREE blocks before he realizes he's been shot.

The fuckin' monkey hit him in the arm.

The adrenaline masks the pain but he's bleeding like crazy and has to get it taken care of quick. But he can't go to the hospital that's two minutes away because if he walks into the E-room with a bullet wound, they call the cops. He drops the gun out the window and then pulls out on Route 95 and drives north. A doctor in Pawtucket is behind in his payments.

Maybe he can make it there before he bleeds out.

DANNY SITS IN the waiting room.

Doctors' waiting rooms are purgatory, he thinks. An endless wait for salvation that may or may not come. The torture of hope—you hope it's not a tumor, you hope if it is, it's benign, you hope . . .

Even the name on the door is scary.

Oncologist.

Their GP sent them there. Said this guy was good.

What's that even mean, Danny asks himself as he pages through a well-thumbed copy of *Good Housekeeping.* All the magazines in there are women's magazines. Of course they are, the people are here for breast cancer, idiot.

But what does "good" mean against cancer? The doctor can make it *not* cancer? He can change what's already there? Tell a young woman with an infant and her whole life in front of her that she's going to get to live that life?

He looks at a recipe for sloppy joes, then checks his watch again.

The time won't move. It doesn't in purgatory. What the nuns taught him about eternity. Finally the door opens and the doctor is standing there.

"Mr. Ryan?"

Danny stands up.

"Come on in, please."

Danny follows him into a small room. Terri is sitting there and she doesn't look good—her eyes are moist, red-rimmed. The doctor gestures Danny to a chair beside her and then sits down behind his desk and holds up an X-ray for Danny to see and uses his pen to point out a "mass" in Terri's left breast.

Danny flashes back to a moment on the beach, that moment Pam first arrived, bringing so much death with her.

"I like your boobs."

"Good answer."

The doctor is saying something about a "biopsy." ". . . if it's positive, we'll go back into surgery and remove the breast."

"Then what?" Terri asks. "Are we looking at chemo?"

The doctor smiles one of those "good bedside manner" smiles. "Why don't we cross that bridge if we come to it? In the meantime, we'll hope for the best."

"It's cancer," Terri says in the car.

"We don't know that," Danny says.

"*I* know it."

"Like the doctor said, let's hope for the best," Danny says.

Hope, he thinks.

Purgatory.

He just gets Terri settled in when Jimmy Mac pulls up outside. When Danny goes down, Jimmy asks, "You hear about Marvin Jones?"

•   •   •

DANNY ATTENDS MARVIN'S homegoing.

Seems like the right thing to do.

The cops wasted no time in deciding that Marvin's murder was a drive-by gang thing and said they were pursuing leads. They rounded up a bunch of rival gang members and put them through the wringer, but none of them knew anything and they all had alibis.

Marvin's own people didn't know anything either, and none of the guys at the scene saw shit.

So as far as the police are concerned, this was simply garbage taking out garbage and they waited for the inevitable retaliation with more garbage taking out more garbage.

Sal Antonucci's name was never mentioned.

And Sal's gone off the radar.

Now Danny walks up to the house on Friendship Street that Marvin bought for his mother. People are gathered on the sidewalk, the wide steps, and the broad front porch of the big Victorian that has been completely remodeled.

A few give Danny, the sole white guy, some glances.

Danny goes in.

Marvin lies in an open coffin in the living room, where rows of folding chairs, all full now, have been set up. Most of the mourners are women, who sit there in black, weeping quietly into handkerchiefs.

Danny walks over to the coffin.

Marvin took a bullet in the heart, so his face is unmarred, still handsome, still proud, almost arrogant in death. Marvin Jones believed he was invincible, Danny thinks, that nothing could touch him. Maybe we all believe that, until something does.

He steps over to Marvin's mother. "I'm sorry for your loss."

She's as handsome as her son, with the same dignity. "Thank you. I'm sorry, but who are you?"

"My name's Danny Ryan."

"How did you know Marvin?"

"We played ball together."

"Oh," she says. "But we haven't met before."

"No, ma'am."

"Well, thank you for coming."

Danny spots Demetrius standing in the kitchen doorway. He goes up to him and asks, "Can we talk?"

"Backyard," Demetrius says.

The backyard is large and leafy, with a big oak and maple trees casting most of it in shade. White wrought-iron table and chairs are set under the maple, a hooded grill up against the fence.

"I'm sorry about Marvin," Danny says.

"You're sorry you lost a field hand," Demetrius says. "I ain't no field hand."

"What does that mean?"

"Means you can fight your own battles," Demetrius says. "We're out of it."

"You don't want to pay Sal back for Marvin?" Danny asks.

"I loved Marvin," Demetrius says. "But he got us into a white man's war. I tried to tell him."

"So, what, he had it coming?"

"Something like that," Demetrius says.

"That's cold."

"Cold world, man."

"What about getting your neighborhood back?" Danny asks.

"We're going to get it," Demetrius says. "And we don't have to do nothing. Every day, fewer and fewer of y'all. Every day, more of us. All we gotta do is wait. You want to speed up the process by killing each other, be my guest, motherfucker."

"You know what Marvin wanted."

"Do I?" Demetrius asks. "Let's go back in and ask him, see what he says. You got my cousin killed, white man. I think it's better if you leave now."

Danny walks back through the house, then out to his car.

CHRIS PALUMBO KNOWS where Marvin Jones is—North Burial Ground—but he can't say the same for Sal.

It's been a week now—if Sal were dead, his body would have turned up. The man is lying low. If he'd gone to ground to hide from the cops, he would have reached out to someone in the family, to give them the word he was alive and get help. So he's hiding from the family, too.

Smart move on his part, Chris thinks, waiting it out to see which way Peter falls on the whole gay thing. I could save him the trouble and expense: Peter makes every decision based on one proposition— "What's best for Peter?"—and what's best for Peter is to keep Sal on the reservation, even if it means overlooking an occasional detour up the Hershey Highway.

So Peter will tell Frankie to shut his stupid mouth unless he wants it shut permanently, and if it comes to that, he'll give Sal the okay to whack him. Chris would gladly tell Sal that if he could find him.

He pulls up in Sal's driveway, gets out and rings the bell.

Judy comes to the door. "Sal isn't here."

"Will he be back soon?"

"Not if Saint Anthony hears my prayers," Judy says. "You want to come in, Chris, instead of standing on the doorstep like a *jadrool*?"

Chris comes in and follows her into the kitchen.

"I was having a sambuca," Judy says.

"I wouldn't say no."

She pours him a shot.

"You have any idea where Sal might be?" Chris asks, sitting down on a barstool at the kitchen counter. He sips the fiery liquor.

"I don't."

"Does he have . . . no offense, huh, Judy . . . a *gumar?*"

Judy laughs. "I only wish. I'm half-afraid he's given me the AIDS."

"So you heard about that."

"You think you know a man," Judy says. "You don't know any-thing."

Chris sets the glass down and stands up. "If he calls, will you let me know?"

"I hate him," Judy says, "but I don't want him dead."

"Judy . . ."

"I've been around this thing my whole life, Chris," she says. "I know how it is."

"Nobody wants to hurt him," Chris says.

"Bullshit."

"Truth." Chris holds his hand up.

He leaves the house convinced that Judy doesn't know where her husband is and that she won't tell him if she finds out.

DANNY SITS IN the back room of the Gloc.

"It's a shame," John says. "I liked that boy."

"Marvin wasn't a boy," Danny says.

"I didn't mean boy like 'boy,'" John says. "I mean he was young. What do we know about Sal?"

"Nothing," Danny says.

He's had the Altar Boys out beating the bushes and they've come up with shit. It's more than worrisome—with Marvin gone and the Blacks staying on the sideline, there's nothing to restrain Peter from coming hard.

He'll want Sal, though, and Sal makes a difference.

"Have you checked the pet stores?" Liam asks.

"What?"

"To see if there's been a run on gerbils," Liam says with a smirk.

"Funny," Danny says. "Funny stuff."

"I always told you Sal played for the other team," Liam says. "It's his what-do-you-call-it, his Achilles' heel."

"I gotta get home," Danny says.

"How's Terri?" John asks. "She doing okay?"

"Her surgery's tomorrow."

"I'll say a rosary."

Yeah, you do that, John. I'm sure it will help. Danny gets up. "You wanna do something, Liam? Get out there, try to find Sal."

"Don't worry about Sal," Liam says, still with that fucking smirk on his face.

"I worry," Danny says.

He worries about everything.

Mostly he worries about Terri.

They're admitting her this afternoon. Cassie's going to stay with Ian for the night. The surgery will be first thing in the morning.

It's funny about words, Danny thinks as he walks home.

Most of the time they don't mean anything. Then all of a sudden one word means everything, and I'd give anything I have to hear one word, a word that didn't used to mean anything to me.

Benign.

LIAM POURS SOME coke onto the glass coffee table. "They all treat me like dogshit."

"Who does?" Pam asks, tired of her husband's self-pitying harangues.

"Danny, for one," Liam says. "All the guys at the Gloc. Even my own father thinks I'm worthless."

I wonder why? Pam thinks, although she knows better than to say anything. Maybe it's because you started this whole thing, kept it going when you had a chance to end it? Maybe because you've sworn revenge for your brother—loudly, to whoever would listen—and haven't done a damn thing except lie around and get high. Maybe because everyone— Danny, the boys at the Gloc, and your father—knows that you're scared shitless of Sal Antonucci and won't do a damn thing except talk.

Which is what you're good at, Liam.

Talk.

"At which point, my loving wife," Liam says, "you're supposed to say something like, 'You're not worthless, Liam. They're all wrong about you. They'll see.'"

Pam snorts a line. "'You're not worthless, Liam. They're all wrong about you. They'll see.'"

"Fuck you."

"Not lately," she says. "You're usually too stoned to get it up."

"Or I'm getting it somewhere else."

"God bless her, whoever she is. Good luck to her."

"I loved you!" Liam shouts suddenly. "I gave up everything for you!"

Liam tightens the roll on the dollar bill, leans over the coffee table and snorts another line of coke.

Then another.

Then he wipes his nose. "You'll see. You'll all see. None of them could handle Sal. Not Danny, not Marvin, nobody. Nobody but Liam. You'll see. You'll all see. You just watch."

"Okay, Liam."

Are we seriously out of blow? she thinks.

Seriously?

•   •   •

SAL KNOWS HE shouldn't have done it.

Knows he shouldn't have called Alex.

But he needed a place to hide, a place to recuperate; more than anything, a place to find some comfort.

Some beauty in this fucking life.

He lies in bed looking out the window of Alex's small apartment in Westerly. It's not much of a view, the train station across the street, but it's peaceful.

His arm is okay. The bullet went straight through without breaking bone or severing an artery, and the doctor, although scared shitless, patched him up and sent him on his way.

Sal ditched the work car in Providence and got on a train to Westerly, where he called Alex.

Wasn't sure how that would be received, but Alex told him, sure, come right over. When he got there, Alex saw his arm and asked, "What happened to you?"

"Wrong place, wrong time," Sal said. "Look, I need a place to lay low for a little while . . ."

"Of course. Sure."

Alex was more than a host, he was a nurse. Put Sal to bed, brought him Tylenol, soup, took him into the shower and washed around the bandage. A few days later, when Sal felt better, Alex made gentle love to him.

Afterward, lying beside him, his finger tracing patterns on Sal's thigh, Alex asked, "So what do you do?"

"Do?"

"You know, for a living."

"I have businesses," Sal said. "I have a car dealership, a hauling business . . ."

"You're mobbed up."

"Nah."

"What do the guys think," Alex said, "about you being gay?"

"I'm not gay."

Alex laughed. "You were sure gay a few minutes ago."

"No, it's just . . . I like you."

"I like you, too."

Sal knows he's going to have to leave sooner or later, probably sooner. Go out and face whatever's in store for him.

I did what Peter wanted, he thinks, I took care of his Marvin Jones problem, so he's probably going to back me on the Frankie V thing, shut down the gay rumors. Either Frankie will have to eat shit or I'll have to kill him.

Which Peter will allow.

Because what's the worse offense, a guy being gay or a guy falsely accusing a guy of being gay?

Then again, maybe I fucked myself. With Marvin dead, Peter doesn't need me anymore and he'll throw me to the dogs.

Alex has gone out to 7-Eleven to get some shit for breakfast, so Sal gets up and uses his phone.

"Sal, what the fuck?" Chris says. "Where are you?"

"Where do I stand?"

"What do you mean?" Chris asks.

"You know what I mean."

"That shit Frankie's been saying?" Chris asks. "Nobody believes it. Come on."

"If I come back," Sal says, "I'm going to have to shut his mouth."

"You do what you have to do, Sal."

So that's it, Sal thinks when he hangs up. I get a pass on the gay thing and a green light on Frankie.

Okay.

•   •   •

ALEX USES THE phone booth outside 7-Eleven. "He's still here."

"You've earned your two grand."

"It's five now," Alex says. "The two was for picking him up. I want another three for . . . the rest."

"Greedy prick."

"I've let that pig fuck me for a week," Alex says. "I made him chicken soup. Three thousand is a bargain."

"All right. How will I know when he's coming down?"

"I'll open the shades."

LIAM GETS BACK in his car and watches the apartment.

Doesn't know if he can trust this Alex to do what he's told.

It hadn't been that hard to find the guy; there are only so many gay bars in Rhode Island, so it had taken him just a few stops to find the joint in Westerly where people recognized Sal by his description.

Then it was just a matter of finding a gay hooker who could use some extra cash and was good-looking enough to attract Sal.

That was this Alex.

I'M GOING TO take off," Sal says.

"You don't have to," Alex says.

"Yeah, I do."

"Are you going to come back?" Alex asks.

"Do you want me to?"

"That's why I asked," Alex says. "Yes."

"Then I'll come back."

Alex kisses him.

Sal goes down the stairs.

Alex opens the blinds.

•   •   •

LIAM RESTS THE rifle on the open passenger window and waits.

His hands shake.

Don't be a coward, he tells himself. Don't be what they say you are. Do this for your brother.

He sees Sal come out the door and aims at his chest.

Swallowing hard, Liam pulls the trigger.

SAL SITS DOWN and leans against the wall. He's very tired all of a sudden, like his legs don't want to carry him no more.

He feels the front of his shirt, hot and wet.

Lifts his hand and sees it's soaked with blood.

Thinks . . .

Holy Mary, Mother of God
Pray for us sinners
Now and at the hour of our—

DANNY IS BENDING over the vending machine in the hospital, trying to decide between the chocolate chip cookies and a Hershey's bar, when Jimmy Mac walks up behind him.

"Did you hear the news?" Jimmy asks.

"What news?"

"Sal Antonucci." Jimmy draws a finger across his throat.

"Jesus," Danny says. "When? Who?"

Jimmy shrugs. "Down in Westerly. He was coming out of an apartment building and someone popped him from across the street."

This could change everything, Danny thinks. Without Sal in the game, Peter might be willing to negotiate a peace. He might even just back off and settle for the status quo. Or he could go the other way with it, and hit back for Sal.

"Tell everyone to keep their heads down," Danny says. "Stay off the streets for a while."

"You too, Danny."

"They're not going to hit me in the hospital," Danny says.

"The parking lot, though," Jimmy says. "Ned will be out there. Give my love to Terri. Angie sends hers, too."

"I will."

Danny decides he's not hungry and goes up to Terri's room. They've given her a sedative, so she's pretty out of it.

"Did you get something to eat?" Terri asks.

"Yeah."

"How's Ian?"

"With Cassie, so he's great."

"I'm scared, Danny."

"I know," Danny says. "It's going to be okay."

"Promise?"

"Promise."

Because what else is he going to say?

YOU'RE THE LUCKIEST *chiacchierone* I've ever seen," Chris says to Frankie. "You know Peter was ready to punch your ticket."

"Was I right or was I right?" Frankie asks. "Let me ask you this— where was Sal when he got it? Leaving a fag's apartment. Case closed."

Alex is in the trunk of the car Chris is driving. He was smart enough to leave his place but not smart enough to leave the area. Chris and Frankie found him in the parking lot of the same gay bar where Sal had picked him up.

They're taking him to an isolated spot by an old quarry to have a conversation. Chris pulls off the highway onto a country road.

Chris is right, Frankie thinks. Whoever clipped Sal did me a big favor. Reshuffled the whole deck and now Peter is going to have to give me a new deal. I just have to play the cards right. Nice, though, that Peter was willing to have me whacked to protect a *finook*. This thing of ours isn't what it used to be.

Chris pulls off the side of the dirt road, next to the quarry. Tall reeds wave in the breeze between them and the water. They get out of the car, take Alex out of the trunk and rip the duct tape off his mouth.

"You yell, I put a bullet in you," Chris tells him, showing the gun. "No one is going to hurt you, we just want to ask a few questions."

Christ, Frankie thinks, the guy is so scared he's pissed himself.

"Who paid you to set Sal up?" Chris asks.

"Nobody," Alex says.

"What, you did it for free?"

"I didn't set him up," Alex says. "I had nothing to do with it."

"This can go one of two ways," Chris says. "One is you can tell us the truth, everything you know, we drive you back, you get on with your life. Two is we hurt you worse than you can imagine, then we leave your body in the pond. Me, I'd take door number one, but it's up to you."

Alex tells them everything.

How Liam Murphy approached him in a gay bar. Offered him two thousand dollars to seduce Sal. How he called Liam when Sal showed up at his door. Called him again when Sal was about to leave. How he opened the blinds as a signal.

"So Liam Murphy pulled the trigger," Chris says.

"I don't know."

"But he was there."

"He was definitely there," Alex says, "in a car across the street. In the train station parking lot."

"You're telling us the truth, Alex."

"I swear." He starts to cry. "Please don't kill me."

"Take it easy," Chris says. "We didn't even like the guy. Where is Liam supposed to give you the rest of the money?"

"At the bar," Alex says. "But he didn't show up."

"Figures," Frankie says.

"Next time get the money up front," Chris says. "Always get the money up front."

"I got one more question," Frankie says. "I just gotta know. Sal—pitcher or catcher?"

"Huh?"

"Did you fuck him or did he fuck you?" Chris asks.

"He fucked me."

"Well, that's something anyway," Frankie says.

"You done?" Chris asks him.

"Yeah."

"Here's the deal," Chris says to Alex. "I'd like to let you go, but you set up a made guy, and there are rules about these things."

"Please. I'll do anything. I'll suck both your cocks."

"As appealing as that sounds," Chris says, "we have a boss to answer to, so—"

"On the other hand," Frankie says.

"What other hand?"

"If we put the guy on a bus, and he promised never to come back," Frankie says, "we could just *say* we did him. Who would know?"

"Save us digging a grave," Chris says. "What do you think, Alex? Would you be willing to do that? Get on a bus, disappear?"

"I'd . . . I'd need to change my pants."

"Really?" Frankie says. "You'd be the only guy at the Greyhound station *didn't* smell like piss. But, yeah, I guess we could swing by your place."

Chris says, "But you have to ride in the trunk again. No offense, but I don't want you smelling up the interior."

"Okay."

They lift him up and put him in the trunk.

Before shutting it, Chris says, "We might stop at the McDonald's drive-through, so don't make any noise."

"You want anything?" Frankie asks. "A Quarter Pounder?"

Alex shakes his head.

They shut the trunk. Then Chris puts the car in neutral, pushes it into the water, and they watch it sink.

Twenty minutes later, another car comes by and picks them up.

"You still want to stop at McDonald's?" Frankie asks.

"I could eat," Chris says.

LIAM IS *RIPPED* when he gets home.

Totally jacked up on coke.

"I did it," he tells Pam.

"What?" She's tired, doesn't feel like listening to a coke-fueled monologue.

"What everyone said I wouldn't," Liam says. "What everyone said I couldn't. That's what."

"You want to be a little more specific, Liam?"

He sits on the couch beside her. Leans over and whispers, "I killed Sal Antonucci. Me. I did. Worthless, spineless, useless Liam."

He tells her the whole story.

Pam listens to it, and then says, "So you bribed a gay man to seduce him, then shot him from across the street. Yeah, you're a big man, Liam."

He raises his fist to her.

"Do it, you limp dick," Pam says. "I'll beat the shit out of you."

She gets up and goes in to take a shower.

FRANKIE HAS A sit-down with Peter.

"Do you know what history is?" Peter asks.

"History?"

"Yeah."

"I dunno," Frankie says, "it's things that happened."

"No," Peter says, "it's what people *say* happened. So let me tell you the history on Sal. He wasn't queer, he was a loving father and husband, the moolies killed him in revenge for Marvin Jones."

"Liam killed him."

"See, that's you not understanding history," Peter says.

"I don't get why, though."

You dumb fuck, Chris thinks. If Liam killed Sal, then Peter would be expected to respond, and the war goes on. And we don't want the war to go on, not like this, anyway. If it was some moolie, then you can spend months looking for him and no one cares. Or you whack one of them and call it a day.

"You don't need to know why, Frankie," says Chris.

"But I already told a bunch of people that Sal was a fag."

"And now you're going to tell them that he wasn't," Peter says. "And they're either going to believe you or pretend to believe you, because it's history. *Capisce?*"

"*Capisce.*"

Frankie gets up and leaves.

"You trust him?" Chris asks.

"No."

"Sooner or later we're going to have to do something about him," Chris says.

THIRTY-ONE

THE WORD "DIAGNOSED" NEVER MEANT much to Danny.

People got diagnosed with all sorts of things—sinus infections, pneumonia, mental illness. But now he learns that the word has a very specific meaning—you have cancer.

It was like creeping bad news, a wave you couldn't stop. First there was the discovery of the lump. It could have been benign. It wasn't, it was malignant. Then there was the surgery. It could have been a lumpectomy but it wasn't, it was a mastectomy. Then it could have been stage one, even stage two.

It wasn't, it was stage three.

Every crossroad took a turn toward the darker place.

Life turns into a monotonous round of chemo, vomiting, fatigue as he watches helplessly. All he can do is hold Terri's head, bring cool washcloths, watch Ian while she rests, make meals as best he can.

Meals that Terri picks at.

He watches her get thin.

She makes bad jokes about it. "Hey, look, I finally lost that baby weight."

Danny says all the things you're supposed to say. "We're going to beat this thing." "They're coming up with newer treatments all the time." Everyone says what they're supposed to, the usual clichés like "She's a fighter."

Yeah, Danny thinks. There are two fighters in any fight, and one of them loses.

He tries to "stay positive," though.

One good thing is that the war with the Morettis has come to a stop. Not officially, there's been no sit-down, no negotiation, but Peter didn't hit back for Sal and there's been no aggression of any kind from the Italians.

It seems like they've fought to a standstill.

Liam takes credit for it.

Fills the back room of the Gloc with his bragging. "Without Sal, they're done. Whoever took Sal out . . . and I'm not saying who it was, mind you . . . won the fucking war. They're finished."

Privately, especially when he's high—and he's always high—he goes around telling everyone, "in the greatest confidence," how he killed Sal Antonucci. "He comes walking across the street at me, gun in his big fucking hand, and BAM!"

"Yeah, it was *High Noon*," Pam says to Danny one night, overhearing this. "Gary Cooper over there."

"Even if it's true, he should keep his mouth shut about it," Danny says.

"How's Terri?"

"She's okay."

"She's a fighter," Pam says.

"How much coke is he doing?" Danny asks, looking over at Liam.

"Full employment act for the Colombians," Pam says.

"Why do you stay with him, Pam?"

"I don't know," she says. And that's the truth. She has options. Just the other day, she was out grocery shopping, an FBI agent approached her.

"A woman with your background," Jardine said. "From a good family. What are you doing with a piece of shit like Liam Murphy?"

She didn't answer.

"And now you're doing coke?" Jardine asked. "I can see it in your eyes. What I *can't* see is you in the joint. Pretty girl like you? Whew." He shook his head.

"I'm just trying to do my shopping," Pam said.

"Like a good little mob wife," Jardine said. "He probably has you clipping coupons by now, because, what I hear, it's not going so well for the home team here. What I'm saying is you have options."

He handed her his card. "Call me, we can work something out. You're a Connecticut girl, you don't belong in Rhode Island."

She didn't answer, but she stuck the card in the back of her purse. Now she says to Danny, "Maybe because if I leave him, all this has been about nothing."

Danny recalls the first moment he saw her, walking out of the ocean. So beautiful, so golden.

Not so much now.

He doesn't have the heart to tell her that it *has* been all about nothing.

"How much coke are *you* doing?" he asks.

"Too much."

"Maybe you should get some help."

"What?" Pam asks. "Go with Cassie to those awful meetings? No thanks. Anyway, I'm cutting down. What, Danny, you don't think I own a mirror, I don't know what I look like?"

Danny don't go down to the beach much.

He usually only goes down to bring his old man the groceries, maybe go for a quick dunk. The jaunts are guilty breaks from the pain of Terri's illness. Sometimes he stops by Dave's Dock for a quick chowder, or Aunt Betty's for clam cakes, shaking them in the brown paper bag to coat them with salt and vinegar—maybe he grabs a beer at the Blue Door.

Then he hurries home ashamed that he's had some enjoyment.

One day he asks Marty, "Why do you really think Peter pretends that the Blacks killed Sal?"

"Think about it," Marty says. "Peter and Sal hated each other—sooner or later, Sal was going to make his move. So Liam did him a favor."

"You think the war is over?"

"It's never over," Marty says. "The tide comes in, the tide goes out. You go through war, you go through peace. You enjoy the peace while it lasts, you try to survive the war. That's all you can do."

Danny figures that's about right.

He drives back to Providence and sees John at the Gloc.

The old man asks, "How's my daughter doing?"

"Come see for yourself," Danny says. Because John hasn't come over once since Terri was diagnosed. "I know she'd love to see you."

"I don't want to disturb her rest."

"She's not contagious, John."

John's eyes get watery. "It's just so hard, you know, Danny."

Harder on her, Danny thinks. And fuck you, John, you weak, selfish old prick. "Yeah, well . . . I know she'd love to see you."

Catherine, she comes over almost too much, bringing casseroles—which do help a lot, Danny has to admit—and clean laundry, but she bugs the shit out of Terri.

And Danny.

"Can't you make her eat, Danny?" she asks.

"She just throws it up, Catherine."

"But she has to eat," Catherine says. "She's wasting away, poor thing. It's those goddamn chemicals. I swear they're worse than the cancer."

Cassie comes around a lot, too, but she's pitch-perfect with her sister, hanging out watching TV, playing with Ian, just shooting the shit. She's usually there when Danny comes home, and he appreciates her.

She makes Terri laugh—"I don't know, sis, lying there with a needle in your arm full of socially sanctioned drugs? I'm kind of jealous."

As good as she is with Terri, she's that good with the baby— holding him, feeding, bathing him with a gentle humor that calms the anxious boy.

"You ever think about having one of your own?" Danny asks her one time.

Cassie shakes her head. "Not for me."

"You're so good at it."

"Not for me."

He lets it go.

Ian's first birthday arrives.

It's a big deal and Terri wants to have a party, but Danny isn't so sure. "Do you feel up to it?"

"No," Terri says. "But how many of his birthdays am I going to have?"

"Don't talk like that," Danny says.

"I want my son to have a birthday party."

"He's *one*," Danny says. "He won't know."

"I'll know," Terri says.

That settles it.

Terri wants to have it at their place, which makes no freakin' sense because it's so small and she invites the entire family. So Danny goes out and buys a Carvel's, a bunch of cold cuts, some bread, beer, wine, and soda for Cassie.

The whole crew crowds into their place: John and Catherine, Sheila and Johnny, Cassie, Jimmy Mac and Angie, Liam and Pam, and Bernie Hughes. Danny drives down in the morning and picks up Marty and Ned. The Altar Boys drop by and bring a toy truck that Ian is far too young to use, but it's a nice thought anyway.

They stick one candle into the Carvel ice cream cake and Terri blows it out for Ian, who proceeds to get more of the cake on his face than in his mouth. They sing "Happy Birthday" and open presents and it's actually a pretty nice time but Danny sees that Terri is getting tired, and Cassie picks up on it and says she has to be going as a broad hint that everyone should leave.

ONE MEMBER OF the family who isn't there is Madeleine.

Terri invited her on the sly without telling Danny, but she reluctantly declined, not wanting to cause any problems between the couple.

Instead, she holds a little party of her own, replete with a small cake, a candle, and presents that she bought for Ian. Not gifts for a one-year-old, but for a three-year old, figuring on a two-year plan that will reconcile her with her son and give her access to her grandson.

A big toy truck.

Some clothes.

And the pony that now grazes the pasture with Manny's Thoroughbreds.

So now Madeleine sits, looks at the cake and thinks about the phone calls she made to the best oncologist in Rhode Island and to the hospital.

"I want you to provide Terri Ryan with the very best treatment in existence," she told them, "regardless of cost. Send the bills to me. Just one thing—neither she or her husband are to know. Just tell them that insurance covers it or something."

"I'm not sure of the medical ethics of that," the doctor said.

"I couldn't care less about the medical ethics," Madeleine said. "What's it going to take? A contribution to the hospital? A new wing, perhaps? Do you have a favorite charity?"

Madeleine gets it done; she always does.

She only hopes that it's enough.

She sings "Happy Birthday" and blows out the candle.

THE SUMMER MOVES along into September.

Danny's favorite month. The beaches are empty, the water is still warm and the sky still blue.

And Terri is dying.

The doctors, the chemo, and the surgeries can't stop the fucking cancer.

Danny learns another word: "metastasize."

The cancer spreads to Terri's liver.

The doctors give her months.

Like that's a gift, Danny thinks, like it's theirs to give. Like they're little gods, handing out life and death.

September gives way to October and then suddenly it's Thanksgiving, and a dismal family dinner at the Murphys' with everyone trying to pretend that Terri isn't dying. John babbles on about Christmas, makes the usual lame joke about Liam eating so much he must have a hollow leg, everyone makes out like they don't hear Terri puking behind the bathroom door.

Cassie can't take it.

She corners Danny in the hallway. "I hate my fucking family."

"Nobody knows how to deal with this, Cassie."

"So we just pretend it's not happening?" She goes into the bathroom to help her sister.

It's out in the backyard—what used to be the traditional touch football game is now just Danny and Liam throwing the ball back and forth—where Liam makes his approach.

"Guess who got in touch with me?" Liam asks.

Danny ain't in the mood for Twenty Questions. "Just tell me?"

"Frankie V. He called me last night. Says he wants to sit down."

Danny's first thought is it's an ambush—Frankie is setting them up. They'll go to the sit-down and walk into bullets, and he tells Liam this.

"I don't think so," Liam says. "I think it's worth finding out."

"So go find out."

"He'll only come if you're there," Liam says. "Hey, I don't like it either, but apparently you're the man now."

"What about your father?"

"Frankie didn't ask for him," Liam says. "Maybe we leave him out of it until we know more."

Danny thinks it over.

Frankie could be an emissary from the Morettis, a preliminary peace feeler. If that's the case, it's worth the risk.

"Okay," he says. "But he comes to us. I'll pick the time and place and we'll give him forty-five minutes' notice, no more."

"I'll see if he'll agree."

"He agrees or it's a no-go," Danny says.

It gets chilly and they go back inside. Terri's sitting on the living room couch, looking pale as hell, but she smiles when they come in and says, "I finally found a weight-loss program that actually works. I should go on TV."

"You're pretty enough," her mother says.

Because nobody knows what to say. They stay for a little while longer, Danny has a piece of pumpkin pie, and then they go home, where Danny puts both his wife and his baby to bed.

NEXT DAY, DANNY sits down with his crew—Jimmy Mac, Ned Egan, and the Altar Boys.

Ned, who never says much of anything, says, "No. I'm not letting you go in there. I promised your father."

Danny has second thoughts himself.

I have an infant son and a wife with cancer, he thinks. If anything happens to me, what happens to them? But he says, "Ned, if I can make a reasonable deal, I'm going to make that deal."

"Fuck deals," Kevin says. "I say we go after them, we go after them hard, and we finish this thing."

"The man didn't ask for your opinion," Ned says. "You don't get a vote."

"The issue isn't whether I go or not," Danny says. "I've already made that call. The issue is how to make it safe."

Ned lays out his requirements—it can't be a restaurant or a bar; the Italians are too hooked in to most of them. It has to be outdoors, a place with two ways in and out, good visibility from all sides, somewhere Ned and the others can be close, with a separate getaway car. They come up with several locations, but none of them meet Ned's standards—not enough visibility, no good shooting angles, too "Italian."

Finally Danny suggests Gilead Lighthouse. "That little park above the lighthouse. Has a big parking lot, a way in and a separate way out. We don't have to worry about the ocean side—you can cover the other angles."

Ned looks to Jimmy Mac. "You and me will drive down there, check it out."

Danny says, "We've been there a thousand times."

"Then a thousand and one won't hurt," Ned says.

He gets up.

Jimmy gets up with him.

Danny goes home to check on his wife and son.

TWO O'CLOCK THE next morning, Danny sits in the front passenger seat of Jimmy's car, pulled off the side of the road that leads to the lighthouse, waiting for Liam to drive past.

Liam gave Frankie the forty-five minutes' notice to meet him along the seawall, where he'd pick him up and bring him to the meet. Ned's already in his car in the parking lot. Kevin Coombs lies in the weeds with a rifle and a night scope.

Sean is in another car. He'll give Liam a minute or so, then stay behind him to see if anyone follows.

Liam's BMW comes by.

Danny sees Vecchio in the passenger seat.

NED SEES THE yuppie car pull in.

He waits, watches, then gets out of his car, walks over and gets into the back of Liam's car.

"I'm going to pat you down," he says to Frankie.

"I'm not carrying," Frankie says.

"I gotta be sure."

"Do what you need to do," Frankie says. Then, because he's Frankie V, he has to add, "But you pat my dick more than once, you owe me dinner."

He's clean.

Jimmy waits five minutes and then drives into the parking lot.

He gets out and Liam takes his place. Ned walks Frankie to the back seat of Jimmy's car and gets in beside him, points his gun into Frankie's crotch. "You as much as blink funny, I blow your balls off."

"Relax, Ned," Liam says.

Ned don't relax.

Frankie V was always a smooth, cocky fuck, Danny thinks, but he don't look like it now. He looks scared. "You mind if I smoke?"

Ned nixes it. "No. It could be a signal."

"Can you wait?" Danny asks Frankie.

"Guess I'm going to have to," Frankie says. "I was sorry to hear about your wife's illness."

Danny don't answer.

Liam says to Vecchio, "Tell him what you told me."

Danny looks at Vecchio like *Okay, I'm listening*. What he wants to hear is that Frankie is here to set up a peace negotiation.

That's not what he hears.

"Heroin," Vecchio says.

"What about it?"

The Morettis have a big shipment coming in, is what about it. Forty kilos of heroin from the Golden Triangle, market value $150,000 per—so a cool six million. And that's before you step on it and put it out on the street, where the value could double or even triple. Biggest score ever, enough to get every junkie in New England high. The shit is coming in on a cargo ship, right into the Port of Providence, and Vecchio's crew is in charge of pickup and distribution.

"It's yours for the taking," Frankie says.

"The hell," Danny says. This guy is going to do what, drop a few mil into our hands? For what? He looks at Liam and shrugs his disbelief.

"Hear the man out," Liam says.

Danny leans over the seat toward Vecchio. Like *Okay, tell me a story, feed me the bullshit.*

"I think Peter's going to have me clipped," Frankie says. "He blames me for Sal, like I did anything wrong, like I didn't say anything that wasn't the truth."

"Get to it," Danny says.

"I need money to run with," Frankie says. "I got kids in college; if I go into the wind, who's going to pay the bills? I got rainy-day money, but we're talking rainy *years* here, if I even make it that long. I have a family, for Chrissakes. My mother is not well . . ."

He's hauling it all out, Danny thinks. The kids, the family, a sick mother . . . Now we're supposed to have what, *sympathy* for this grease-ball? Well, fuck that. Fuck Frankie V and the horse he rode in on.

Frankie keeps talking but Danny hardly listens. The deal is obvious: Frankie gives them the details on the heroin shipment, they jack it, Frankie gets his payout, they all live happily ever after.

"I'm telling you," Frankie is saying, "this puts the nail in their coffin. The war has worn them out, they're all broke, they're counting on this score to get well."

"If the Morettis don't trust you," Danny says, "why are they putting you in charge of this, it's so important?"

"You think they'd go anywhere near it?" Frankie says. "They're too chickenshit. No, it's let Frankie V take the chances, we'll take the profits, same old bullshit. Well, fuck that—good old Frankie's taking care of himself for a change."

Danny looks at Liam and says, "He's setting us up. We go to jack this shipment, we walk right into an ambush."

"On my kids' lives," Frankie says.

"I believe him," Liam says.

"Are you out of your mind?" Danny asks. "He shows you a little flash jewelry and you jump into the back seat with him?"

"We could win this war."

"They're on their last legs," Frankie says. "This will push them over. They'll have to come to you and make a deal. You'll get back the docks, everything. And the money from the dope—I only want ten keys for myself. Okay, five."

Danny don't like it.

For one thing, he don't trust Vecchio—still thinks they could be walking into an ambush. And he don't like the whole dope thing. It's evil shit, and if you get caught, it puts you away for life. And he knows that Liam ain't gonna just take the heroin and go Boston Tea Party with it, dump it in the water and cost the Morettis the millions they need to keep going. Nobody tosses millions of dollars, nobody. Liam will want to put it out on the street and get the big payday.

So Danny don't like it, he don't like it at all.

But he can tell Liam has a hard-on for it.

"I need to think about this," Danny says.

"I can't come to more meetings," Frankie says. "Shit, they knew I was here now, I'm dead."

"Go sit in the other car a minute," Danny says.

Ned takes Frankie out.

"What's there to think about?" Liam asks.

"You fucking kidding me?" Danny lays out all the things there are to think about. Then adds, "I'm not a dope dealer."

"What if it's a walkaway score?" Liam asks. "Your heart isn't in this anymore; tell you the truth, neither is mine. You have medical bills to pay, and God willing you'll have a lot more. I say we do this, cut up the money, pay my old man his share. Then I go to Florida, you take your family to California, we live our lives. Away from Dogtown."

"I dunno."

"What about Terri?" Liam asks. "This kind of money buys the best doctors in the world, the best treatment."

The nuns used to say that the devil comes disguised as an angel. That the worst things you'll do, you'll do for the best reasons. The most hateful things you'll do, you'll do for the ones you love most.

Danny tells Liam to make the deal.

BERNIE HUGHES SPEAKS out against it at the Gloc.

Cup of tea in hand, the bag still in it, he stands up, saturnine and soft-voiced, and says, "I've been in this endeavor since the beginning, when it was pretty much just John and Martin and myself, and in those fifty-odd years, we've never dirtied our hands with dope."

Liam shoots Danny a look, like *Shut the fuck up.*

"We've worked labor," Bernie says, "construction rackets, loan-sharking, gambling, we've liberated some merchandise from the docks, we've boosted trucks. But we have never stooped to selling women in prostitution or selling poison for people to shoot in their arms. Why? Because we go to confession on Saturday and communion on Sunday and we know that we will have to answer to our Lord."

He takes a long sip of the tea.

"And for pragmatic reasons as well," Bernie says. "We have good working relationships with the police, the judges, and the politicians, who are reasonable about the way the world works. But they draw the line at drugs, and we would lose those relationships."

"Don Corleone over there," Liam mutters.

"For these reasons," Bernie says, "I strongly oppose the arrangement you've made with Vecchio, and I urge you, in the strongest possible terms, to reconsider. Danny Ryan, you know better."

"This is a one-time thing," Danny says.

"Your soul is never a rental," Bernie says. "It's always a sale."

"You an accountant or a priest?" Liam asks.

"There are similarities," Bernie says. He turns to John. "What do you say?"

"I don't like drugs, either," John says. "It's a bad business we've always left to the wops and the Blacks. But we need the money, and this is the world we live in now. So I say we do it."

"And that's your decision?" Bernie asks.

"It is."

Bernie nods and sits back down.

THE NIGHT OF the hijacking, Danny sits on the bed with Terri, watching some stupid sitcom on television.

She's half out of it on the pain pills.

"I gotta go out," Danny says.

"Out where?"

"Work stuff," Danny says. "Cassie is downstairs if you need anything."

She holds up her empty glass. "Could you get me some water before you go?"

Danny takes it into the bathroom, fills it and sets it on the side table. Then he leans over and kisses her on the cheek. "I love you."

"Love you."

Danny goes to look in on Ian.

Sound asleep. Good.

Cassie's reading.

"I don't know what time I'll be back," Danny says. That's no shit. You go to jack the biggest shipment of heroin ever to come into New England, you don't know when—or if—you're coming back.

"What's going on, Danny?"

"Nothing."

She laughs. "I'm the crazy one, not the stupid one. It's in the air around here, big doings."

"How do you know about this?"

"Liam can't keep a secret in his head any more than he can keep his dick in his pants," she says. "We have souls, Danny Ryan. We have to take care of them or we lose them."

"Okay."

Cassie says, "I've got a bad feeling. I tried telling Pop, tried telling Liam. They say it's just me being crazy me, but it isn't, Danny, it isn't."

"It's going to be okay," he says.

Even though he knows it isn't. Knows that Cassie is right, Bernie is right. He knows that he's walking toward the edge of a cliff, but somehow he can't stop his feet from moving—left, right, left, right—toward the abyss. It's like something else is pushing him, something outside himself, beyond his control.

Cassie says, "I miss Pat."

"So do I," Danny says. For a lot of reasons, not the least of which is that I wish it was him making these decisions instead of me.

"Don't do it, Danny."

"I have to."

Because I'm Danny Ryan, the good soldier, he thinks as he walks out. Good old Danny, who does what has to be done.

A FEW MINUTES later, Jimmy Mac swings by, with Kevin Coombs riding shotgun. They drive over to Atwells Avenue, where Frankie V is waiting in his Caddy. Jimmy slides behind the wheel. Danny and Kevin get in back, and Kevin pokes his .45 into the back of the front passenger seat as Danny says, "Anything. Anything at all, he splatters you all over the car."

Kevin smiles and nods. Hard to escape the impression that he *wants* it to go south. Kevin likes the wet work so much he ought to wear a raincoat instead of the leather jacket.

Vecchio says, "Nothing's going to go wrong."

Nothing's going to go wrong, Danny thinks. *Something's* going to go wrong, always does, always has. This deal is wrong from the get-go. If it starts wrong it's gonna end wrong, that simple.

And he don't believe for a second that Peter Moretti is going to trust Vecchio with six million dollars in merchandise. The Morettis may not want to go near the heroin, Danny gets that, but they'll have eyes on it. And guns, too.

So it would be stupid to jack the shipment at the docks. No point. The heroin is stored in bags under false bottoms in crates of cheap tools from some Eastern European country. They'll be offloaded into a trailer. The Morettis are expecting Frankie and his crew to pick up the tractor-trailer truck and make the short drive to a truck repair place in Fox Point. To offload the shit.

Moretti people will be there waiting.

There's a vacant lot off Gano Street just after the exit road from Route 195, maybe fifty yards from the Seekonk River. That's their moment. Jimmy will force the truck off the road into the lot and then they got maybe a minute to jack it.

What could go wrong?

A lot.

The Morettis could have a car or two following the truck, full of armed guys. Or this could be a fucking ambush and an army will be waiting at the vacant lot. Or Vecchio's guys, who aren't in on it, put up a fight.

Danny asked him about that earlier in the week.

"They won't," Frankie said.

"And what if they do?"

"Their bad luck, I guess," Frankie said, miming pulling a trigger.

Which don't exactly reassure Danny, that Frankie's cold enough to get his own crew killed.

No, he don't trust Frankie at all.

Frankie's only bringing two guys—one to drive the truck, the other to sit inside the trailer with the dope. He claims they don't know what's sitting under the tools. The driver will have a .38 in a shoulder holster, the guy inside will have a twelve-gauge shotgun.

Maybe, Danny thinks. Or maybe there'll be six guys in there with automatic weapons and they let loose the second we open the door.

So Danny brought plenty of firepower. He's got himself a MAC-10 and Jimmy has a twelve-gauge of his own. Ned, he's sticking with his .38 revolver, because that's what he uses and that's what he uses.

"Okay," Danny says. "Let's get this show on the road."

DANNY SITS IN the passenger seat of the work car pulled off Gano Street just north of the vacant lot.

An '84 Dodge Charger, freshly stolen. Jimmy has a police scanner under the dash. He's at the wheel and Ned's in the back seat.

"Is this going to work?" Danny asks.

"Who's driving?" Jimmy asks.

"You are."

"Then it's going to work."

It's just another hijacking, Danny tells himself. You've done it a dozen times, nothing different, no sweat, business as usual.

No it isn't, he thinks. This isn't some truckload of eight-track cassettes or ski jackets, this is six mil in heroin. People kill for that kind of money, people die for it. This could get bloody in a hurry.

They drove past the vacant lot a couple of times, didn't see anybody, no sign of an ambush.

That don't mean it's not there, Danny thinks.

The plan is that Danny is just going to take the truck and drive away with it, but that ain't gonna work if the Morettis are following the freakin' thing. So Danny has another plan, but he didn't share that with Frankie.

The problem with the alternate plan is that it relies on Liam. Liam has to be there—on time. If Liam is drunk or coked out or just too scared to do his job—all very real possibilities—they're fucked.

Danny turns around and sees Scan's car pulled off twenty yards behind. Say what you want about the Altar Boys—and there's a lot to say—they know how to work. He has no doubts that they'll perform their assigned task.

He sits back in the seat. Now all he can do is wait.

ONE O'CLOCK. ONE fifteen, one thirty.

Where the hell is Vecchio with the truck? Danny wonders.

A thought hits him—maybe the Morettis used this pickup as a trap to hit Frankie? Maybe there was no freakin' heroin in the first place, and Frankie V is wrapped in chains at the bottom of the Providence River.

That's one possibility.

Maybe the feds are onto the shipment and busted it. The scanner hasn't picked up any unusual activity, but it wouldn't if it was just a federal op and they kept the Providence PD out of it, which would be a good idea.

Or maybe Vecchio just took the truck and hauled with it. That doesn't make sense, though. If he was going to do that, why would he bring us in in the first place?

Or maybe—

"Danny."

Jimmy nudges him, points to the headlights coming their way.

High headlights.

A truck.

"Is that it?" Danny asks. He pulls a black stocking down over his face.

"Better be," Jimmy says, doing the same. He guns the engine and pulls out. "Hold on."

No shit, hold on, Danny thinks, because Jimmy floors it, steers into the oncoming lane and points the Charger straight at the truck.

The truck's horn blasts over the roaring engine.

Game of chicken, and Jimmy ain't backing down. He's laughing like a motherfucker, going pure kamikaze here, and Danny about pisses himself as the truck gets bigger and bigger and then all Danny can see is truck and he throws his arms up over his face and—

The truck veers off, into the vacant lot.

Jimmy pulls in front of it, to block it.

Danny, Jimmy, and Ned jump out and run up to the cab, guns out, black plastic garbage bags shoved into their belts.

From the corner of his eye, he sees Sean pull in, swerve the car sideways so it's parallel to the road, and Kevin stick the barrel of his AR-15 out the window. Which is a good thing because there wasn't a follow car, there were two of them, and Kevin opens up as they start to pull into the lot.

Red muzzle flashes cut through the night.

Shots come back from the cars.

Danny imagines the shot that comes out of the dark and blows a hole in him. You get shot once, you don't forget it. Even if your head does, your body doesn't—it can still feel the shock, the pain, the life-blood pouring out. The body remembers. And now Danny's nerves and muscles are bowstring tight. He can't help it.

But the guys in the follow cars weren't ready for the automatic rifle fire and they pull out.

They won't go far, Danny thinks. They'll get out of range and keep an eye on the truck, try again when we pull out. They know they got us hemmed in here.

And the cops will be here any second.

So move.

He points the MAC-10 at the driver. "Get out! Come down!"

Frankie V is in the passenger seat. Ned walks around and points the shotgun up at him.

The driver hesitates.

"You wanna die for a bunch of tools?!" Danny yells.

He hears Frankie. "Do what he says!"

The driver climbs down. Frankie gets out the other side.

Ned pushes Frankie toward the back of the truck.

"Shout to your guy inside," Danny says to him. "Tell him to lay his gun down or we blow your freakin' brains out."

"You hear him, Teddy?" Frankie yells. "Do what he says! It's not fucking worth it!"

With Jimmy covering him, Danny opens the truck door.

Teddy stands there with his hands up, the shotgun at his feet. Danny grabs the gun and throws it to the ground, then gestures for Teddy to get out. When he does, Ned covers them while Danny and Jimmy jump into the truck.

Frankie looks surprised—this wasn't the plan.

Danny knows he has to hurry.

He and Jimmy jack the crates open, throw the tools out and start grabbing the plastic-wrapped bricks of heroin, Danny counting them out loud as he does and shoving them into the garbage bags.

"Two minutes in!" Jimmy yells.

Danny has given them three minutes, max, to do this thing. What they don't get in three they don't get, and that's just part of the discipline of this kind of work. Better to get away light than get caught heavy.

You can't spend any of it dead or in jail.

But they get all of it.

"Forty!" Danny yells.

"Two thirty-five!" Jimmy answers.

They jump down from the truck.

Danny hears the sirens coming. Providence PD responding to a "shots fired" call. They probably think it's a gang drive-by, so they're not in a big hurry. Danny drops the MAC-10 on the ground because he needs both hands to carry the garbage bags.

He doesn't get back in the car, though, but walks across the vacant lot, away from the street.

Sean speeds out.

Ned pokes Vecchio in the back with the revolver. "You're coming with us."

"What?" Vecchio says. "That wasn't part of the—"

Which is a stupid fucking thing to say.

"It is now," Ned says. "Move."

They walk across the lot, climb over a low guardrail, across a narrow stretch of grass onto some rocks that edge the river. The off-ramp of westbound 195 looms over them, providing some cover.

Danny looks back and sees flashers as two black-and-whites pull into the lot.

It's all up to Liam now, Danny thinks.

Which ain't a comforting thought.

"What the fuck are you doing?" Vecchio asks.

"Shut up."

"This wasn't—"

"I said shut up." Danny looks downriver. Come on, Liam, where are you? Then he sees the boat, an old Cobia 22-footer with a Yamaha outboard.

Liam standing at the helm.

It pulls under the off-ramp.

"Let's go," Danny says.

"I'm not getting on no boat," Frankie says.

Ned points the gun at his head.

Vecchio gets on the boat.

Danny and Jimmy toss the bags on and then hop in. Danny reaches back and pulls Ned aboard. Then he looks at Liam. "I'll take the wheel."

Liam steps aside.

Danny takes the helm, pulls out, turns the boat around and heads downriver, into Narragansett Bay, then out into the ocean.

Jimmy's cutting the bags open. He dips a finger in and tastes the powder. "It's H."

"It fucking better be," Liam says. He cranks his neck back at Danny and shouts over the engine. "Should we just do Frankie now?!"

"Leave him alone!"

"If they catch him, he'll rat us out!"

"A deal is a deal," Danny says.

It takes longer than he wanted, hacking against the wind and the chop, but he finally pulls the boat through the eastern gap of the breakwater into the Harbor of Refuge, then slows it way down and glides through the channel into a slip at Potter's Wharf, a small marina across the channel from Gilead.

They take the bags out of the boat, walk over to a panel truck and throw them in the back. Danny takes five bricks, shoves them into another bag and hands it to Vecchio.

Then he hands him a set of car keys and nods toward a Chevy

Nova at the back end of the parking lot. "It's hot, but the plates are clean. Disappear, Frankie. They'll be looking for you."

Vecchio walks to the Nova and gets in.

"We should have dumped him in the bay," Liam says.

"Get in the car." Bloodthirsty prick, Danny thinks.

It's a twenty-minute drive to Mashanuck Point.

They rented a cottage on Exit Street, a few streets over from Danny's dad's, a nondescript place no different from dozens like it there on the point. Most of them are empty in the winter—only hermits like Marty Ryan and maybe a few college students who rent them cheap.

Inside, they get to cutting up the take. Danny is going to leave his share, ten keys, here. He'll split the profits with Jimmy, Ned, and the Altar Boys, although he'll keep the lion's share. Liam takes the other twenty-five to keep in Providence and share out with his father.

They push up a ceiling panel and shove ten bags up there, then put the panel back in place.

"I'm telling you," Danny says, "let it sit. It's not going to be worth any less in a month or two."

Sell the dope off slow, Danny thinks, let the money cool out, then use it to take his family, get out of Dogtown, and start over somewhere. In some clean business. His take should be in excess of a million dollars, more than enough to buy a fresh start.

You're a hypocrite, he tells himself, using dirty dope money to get yourself clean, using other people's suffering to relieve your own, committing a mortal sin to save your soul.

But if that's what it takes, that's what it takes, because Ian is not going to grow up in this shit.

He never needs to know his dad was a dope dealer.

But you'll know, Danny thinks.

Something else bothers him.

The hijacking went too smooth.

It shouldn't have been that easy.

CHRIS PALUMBO DRIVES all the way out to Hope Valley, where there's nothing but farmers and goobers, and parks next to a little pond out in the middle of nowhere.

Which is more or less the point.

Phillip Jardine pulls up a few minutes later, and Chris gets into the FBI agent's car.

"So?" Jardine asks.

"It went smooth," Chris says. "All according to plan."

"Ryan has the drugs?"

"Him and Liam Murphy, yeah," Chris says.

"What about Vecchio, will he testify in court?"

"Frankie understands that he has limited options," Chris says. "He testifies and goes away into the program, or he just goes away. He can put H in the hands of Liam Murphy, John Murphy, Danny Ryan, the whole crew. You can ride Vecchio all the way to a desk in DC, corner office."

Chris explained this to Frankie weeks ago, when he first had the idea of setting up the Murphys. Told Frankie how he was in bad odor since the whole Sal thing, how Peter was going to put a hit on him, how there was a way out.

Go to the Murphys, sell them the heroin boost.

And the dumb donkeys walked right into the trap. Even Danny Ryan, the smartest of them, went for it.

Now the Irish are fucked.

Because Jardine used Vecchio's information to obtain wire

warrants on the Glocca Morra. He has them on tape discussing the heroin deal. Couple that with catching them in possession, open-and-shut case.

Thirty to life for all of them.

War over.

"And I got immunity, right?" Chris asks. "Across the board?"

"Just don't put any more bodies in the ground," Jardine says.

"So our arrangement is in place," Chris says. "I mean, don't forget."

"Don't *you* forget."

"Hey, you're my guy."

They both know how it works.

One hand dirties the other.

IT'S FREAKIN' QUIET the next day.

Like one of them bad old Western movies, Danny thinks, where one of the actors says "Too quiet," and a second later gets pincushioned with arrows.

The talk on the street is . . . well, there isn't a lot of talk on the street, but what there is says a truckload of tools got boosted and that's it. Even their contacts in the Providence police and state troopers don't say anything about heroin.

Danny expected at least some drumbeats from Federal Hill. After all, Peter didn't have six mil to lay out for the dope, it was probably fronted to him, so now he owes a shitload of money with no way to pay it back.

So Danny thought that Moretti soldiers would be on the streets, shaking everyone down for information, that cops on the Moretti payroll would be rattling cages, but so far, nothing.

Danny figured the police would be at his door, because it was a truck hijacking and Danny's been known to participate in such activities, and he's in a war with the Morettis to boot.

No one shows up.

It gives Liam ammunition for his argument to sell off the heroin now. "Why wait? I'll spread it around. Here, Boston, New York, DC, even Miami."

"Not now," Danny says. "Let things blow over."

They put it out too soon, everyone is going to know where it came from and who did the hijack.

"You worry too much," Liam says.

"Yeah, I worry, Liam."

"But that's you, Danny," Liam says. "You worry. Fucking Irish— always looking forward to our next defeat."

"What's the big hurry?" Danny asks.

"Because we got millions of dollars sitting down in the basement," Liam says, "and the sooner we convert it to cash, the better."

Yeah, Danny thinks, Liam likes his cash. But the last thing we need is Liam flashing a roll, going out and buying a new car, watches, jewelry for Pam. Or a freakin' house on the beach, which would be just like him. The only thing worse than Liam with coke up his nose is Liam with money in his pocket. They both burn a hole.

People would notice and start asking questions. Like, where did Liam get money all of a sudden? They'd notice the coincidence between the hijacking and Liam playing the big shot.

It wouldn't be good.

Especially when some of the people doing the wondering will be the Morettis and the feds, and he tells Liam this.

"So what if the Morettis connect us to the hijacking?" Liam asks. "What are they going to do? Kill us? They're trying to do that already."

"They'll try to get their dope back."

"Which is why we should move it now," Liam says. "Don't you want to get to California?"

"What's this?" John asks.

Danny shoots Liam a look, like *Why can't you keep your stupid mouth shut*, then he turns to John and says, "I've been meaning to tell you, the right moment never came up, but yeah, I'm going to use this money to move out to the West Coast. I'm thinking maybe San Diego."

"Does Terri know about this?"

"We've talked about it," Danny says. "I think the sunshine and the warmth would be good for her."

"What about the business?" John asks.

Danny feels himself getting pissed off. "What about it?"

"Don't you think you have responsibilities here?"

Danny looks at Liam again, like *Say something.*

"Dad," Liam says, "you've been talking about retirement for a long time. Danny wants to go to California, I've been thinking about moving down to Florida—"

"Oh, you have, have you?" John's face gets red.

"Yeah, I'm done," Liam says.

"I'm not."

"Well, maybe you should be," Liam says. "Get out, get a nice new house down by the shore, sit out on the patio, play with your grand-kids."

John points at Danny. "He's taking my only grandchild to California."

"So go with him," Liam says.

Thanks, Liam, Danny thinks.

"Spend winters out there," Liam says. "Or down in Florida. Or both. Whatever. You'll have the money to be wherever you want. Mom would love it, not worrying about slipping on the ice, breaking a hip."

"And the docks, the unions?"

"Let the Morettis have them," Liam says.

"We just fought a war—"

"For what?" Liam asks. "A dying business? Fewer ships come in here every day. The factories are all in North Carolina or somewhere. Even if we hold on to it, it's going to go away."

"Your brother gave his life protecting Dogtown."

"Dogtown doesn't exist!" Liam says. "Jesus, old man, look around you, what do you see? Irish families walking to church Sunday mornings? *Céilís*, hurley games in the park? That's in the past. It's over. And my brother is dead."

John goes into a sulk.

Liam turns back to Danny. "You do what you want with yours. I'm putting my dope out on the fucking street."

"It's a mistake, Liam," Danny says.

Bobby Bangs pokes his head through the door. "Danny—"

"The fuck you want?" Liam asks. "Can't you see we're having a meeting in here?"

"It's Cassie on the phone," Bobby says. "She's taking Terri to the hospital. She says it's bad, Danny."

THIRTY-TWO

DANNY SLOSHES THROUGH THE LONG walk from the back of the hospital lot, like he's been doing the last three weeks. Seems like the lot is always full, day or night, it's always hard to find a spot.

He's tired as hell. Only left here a few hours ago to check on Ian and try to grab a little sleep.

Ned drove him back and waited in the car.

Catherine was at the apartment, the doting grandmother. "How is she?"

"Not good," Danny said.

He looked in on Ian, sleeping peacefully, then went into his and Terri's bedroom and lay down. He mostly tossed and turned, and when he did sleep his dreams were troubled and strange. The doctors said there was nothing more they could do for her except try to make her comfortable. He thanked them in that way you always thank doctors, even when they tell you they're giving up.

Now Danny's work boots sink into the slush. Ned slogs dutifully beside him. Dirty piles of snow, topped with soot left from car exhaust, have been stacked at the corners of the parking lot.

He passes other people walking back to their cars. He can tell from their faces what news they got. Some are smiling, even laughing—maybe a baby was born or tests came back benign. Other faces are set in worry or grief, grim resignation relieved only by belief in the Virgin Mary or a special saint. Hospital parking lots are tough places—people go to their cars to cry, punch the steering wheel, just sit in stunned silence.

Like he did after he got the word.

Young mother with a son not two years old.

The old catechism question: Why did God make us? He made us to love him and share the kingdom of heaven. In short, he made us to die. We live to die, that's the whole point. Receive last rites, say a perfect Act of Contrition, go straight to heaven to live at his side for eternity.

When the nuns talked about eternity they usually meant hell. Imagine living in a fire, burning your skin, forever and ever without end. The fire never goes out and it never stops burning you, and that's for eternity. Hold a match up to your finger, boys, and feel how it hurts. Now imagine that times a thousand thousand and you have a thousandth idea of the pains of hell. They never talked about sharing the peace and glory of heaven without end. It was always about hell.

If God made us to die, he should be pretty happy with Dogtown the past few years. Forty-eight souls sent to heaven or hell since the "New England Crime War," as the newspapers like to call it, started. A body count to make God and the papers happy.

And now God wants Terri, too.

Going in through the revolving door, Danny smells that hospital smell. It's warm in there, but the air is stale and cloying. There's no way around it, a hospital smells like sickness and death.

The Christmas lights, the brightly decorated artificial tree with fake presents underneath seem almost mocking.

Jimmy Mac's waiting in the lobby. "You get some rest?"

"A little," Danny says. "You should go home. I got Ned here."

He goes upstairs.

Terri's out cold when he gets to the room. It's good, she's not in pain. Lying on her back with the sheet up to her neck, her once-pretty face thin and drawn, her skin gray. Danny pulls the plastic chair up by the bed and sits next to her. He doesn't know why. She doesn't know he's there. Off in a dream world of her own, hopefully a better one. Has to be a better one.

And now the war is over and Terri's dying.

Makes no sense.

Sure, but none of it ever did.

CASSIE SITS DRINKING a Diet Coke at the bar in the front room of the Gloc.

It's well after closing time, but she has nowhere else to go. Her dad and some of the other old men are in the back room telling lies about when they were young, and Bobby Bangs doesn't seem to be in any hurry to get out from behind the bar.

She knows Bobby has a little crush on her; it's harmless.

Another goddamn Diet Coke, she thinks. When what she really wants is a warm bourbon melting some rocks.

Be honest, she tells herself, what you really want is a shot of heroin.

Talk about warmth.

Like being wrapped in the warmest blanket there ever was.

Someone had taken a stab at decorating the joint for Christmas, some bulbs strung around the walls, a fake Christmas tree in one corner with some tinsel Bobby dug out of the basement. Trying to brighten the place up, she thinks, but the only thing that could really cheer up an Irish bar would be England sinking into the ocean.

The birth of our Savior, Cassie thinks.

Oh, but we do love our martyrs—their pictures are all over the walls: James Connolly, Padraic Pearse, and on and on. If no one else will nail them to the cross, they'll find a way to do it themselves.

And now Terri is "terminal." It's fucking awful, but Cassie can't help but feel it's karma, because they did the dope boost and this is the universe paying them back.

"Is Santa going to be good to you?" Bobby asks.

"I've been a good girl." She shrugs.

The front door shatters.

Wood splinters, hinges rip from the frame.

Cassie turns to look. Men with helmets and flak jackets stand there with a battering ram, for Chrissakes. For a second she thinks it's some weird dream, or a Monty Python movie or something, but then more men pour in behind them, guns drawn, screaming for them to get down.

Cassie slides down and grips the base of the barstool.

Hears a man yell, "John Murphy! FBI! Come out with your hands up!"

She laughs, it's such a cliché.

"What's so fucking funny?!" Jardine yells.

"You," Cassie says.

He grabs her by the hair and lifts her up.

"Hey!" Bobby Bangs says. He starts to vault the bar to defend her but one of the cops whacks him across the chest with a baton, flips him onto the bar and cuffs him.

"Cuff her, too," Jardine says, passing Cassie to one of the other cops. "You're Cassandra Murphy, aren't you? Where's your father?"

"Go fuck yourself."

"Nice mouth on you."

The cop cuffs her behind her back.

Then the door to the back room opens and John comes out. "What the hell is going on here?! Who are you?! Get out of my place!"

He strides toward Jardine like he's going to hit him.

"Daddy, *don't!*" Cassie screams.

Bernie Hughes is behind him. "John—"

"FBI, Mr. Murphy. Special Agent Jardine. You're under arrest."

"For what, being Irish?"

"For conspiracy to distribute narcotics," Jardine says.

"You should be ashamed of yourself," John says. "Bursting into a man's place of business. How much is Peter Moretti paying you, you peeler bastard?"

"John," Bernie says, "let the lawyers handle this."

"Turn around, please, Mr. Murphy," Jardine says. "Put your hands behind your back."

John does as he's told. "I hope Santa shits in your stocking."

"Is your son Liam here?" Jardine asks.

"My *surviving* son, you mean?" John says. "The one your employer didn't murder? No, thank God."

Jardine juts his chin to the back room and a squad of agents goes in. "Do you know where he is?"

"Buggering your wife, if I know my boy."

Jardine looks at Cassie. "You come by it honestly."

"Jardine," John says. "Is that French? Are you sure you don't want to surrender to *me?*"

"You won't be laughing doing thirty to life."

"I won't live another ten years," John says. "The joke's on you."

"It might be time to remain silent now, John," Bernie says.

"Are you Bernard Hughes?" Jardine asks. "There's no warrant on you. Yet."

"I'll go straight to the lawyers," Bernie tells John. "We'll have you out for midnight mass tonight. Agent Jardine, why are these other two people in cuffs? Surely you don't have warrants for them."

"Resisting arrest," Jardine says. "Obstruction of a federal agent in the performance of his duties. Whatever else I can think of."

"Pure harassment," Bernie says. "Kindly release them."

Jardine gives the nod.

The cop takes the cuffs off Bobby, then off Cassie. She shakes her hands out, her wrists already going numb. It's the heroin, she thinks, her worst premonition coming true. As if to validate it, she hears a shout from the back room. "Jackpot!"

An agent comes out holding two bricks of heroin. "There are ten more in the basement."

Jardine smiles at John. "Now we'll take your bar, too."

Cassie watches her father being walked out the door in cuffs. She follows him out. The news trucks are already out there, which means Jardine tipped them in advance. The agents push his head down as they put him in the back seat of a cruiser.

He looks collapsed, she thinks.

Like an old coat left out in the rain.

It breaks her heart.

DANNY SITS IN a chair in Terri's room. At some point during the endless night he drifts off and dreams about Pat.

"Get out of here, Danny," Pat says. "Take your family and go."

"Terri's dying."

"I know," Pat says. "I'll take care of her when she gets here, don't worry."

"Thanks, Pat."

But Pat doesn't look like he could take care of anybody. Half his face is scraped off; his skin is black and scorched from the exhaust fumes of Sal's car. He looks tired, haggard, like maybe they don't sleep in heaven. If that's where Pat is. Maybe he's in hell.

"Danny."

He wakes with a start. Jimmy Mac's hand is on his shoulder. "We gotta get out of here. They hit us."

It's part of his dream. Danny asks, "They hit us? Who hit us? Who hit what?"

"The feds hit the Gloc."

Danny's groggy.

"Danny, wake up!" Jimmy says. "The feds are all over Dogtown with warrants. I don't know how many guys they got already. You have to move, Danny. *Now*."

"I can't leave Terri."

Jimmy looks over at Terri. "There's nothing you can do for her."

"I can stay with her."

"She doesn't know who you are."

"But I know who she is."

Jimmy grabs him by the shoulders. "Danny, you have a kid. What's Ian gonna do with no mother *or* father?"

"We don't know that there's a warrant on me."

"We don't know that there's not," Jimmy says. "Christ, Danny, they could have guys waiting in the parking lot, the motherfuckers."

Jimmy tells him what happened. There are feds everywhere with their goddamn blue ball caps with all the letters on them—FBI, DEA— marshals, too. They took John, he doesn't know yet about Liam.

"Kevin?" Danny asks. "Sean?"

Jimmy hasn't seen them.

"What about Ned?"

"He's in the lobby, he won't move."

Danny gets on the phone, pulls it over to the wall so Terri can't hear, then realizes that she can't hear much of anything. Thank God, he reaches Bernie Hughes at home. "What do you know?"

"It's bad," Bernie says. "I've tried getting through to our city cops . . . detectives, narcotics squad, uniforms—no one is taking my calls. State troopers, same thing. It's a federal operation and all our usual connections are laying low."

"Get the fuck out of there, Bernie."

Because Dogtown is naked, Danny thinks. No protection out there. Our guys are either in jail or running.

A great time for the Morettis to strike.

THEY GO AFTER Liam.

Jardine hits the Murphy home in Providence, but Liam isn't there.

Jardine puts out an all-points, dispatches people to the airport, the train and bus stations.

No Liam.

The Morettis have deployed, too. Get their own people on the streets, the roads, bars, hotels, motels, hookers, pimps, and drug dealers, always with the same message: If you see Liam Murphy, you'd better drop a dime to us, because sooner or later we're going to find him, and you want to be on the right side of this thing.

Cops on the arm get the word, too—Christmas is around the corner, and there'll be a nice present under the tree for whoever brings him in.

No one is worried too much about Danny Ryan. They know exactly where he is—at Rhode Island Hospital with his dying wife—and they can pick him up any time they want.

"Wait until the wife passes," Peter tells Jardine. "Danny's a fuckup, but he's good people."

Jardine agrees to wait.

No, it's Liam Murphy they're looking for.

No one is looking harder than Paulie Moretti.

FUCK LIAM MURPHY," Peter says. "What I want to know is, where's my dope?"

"Liam has whatever wasn't in the club," Paulie says. "Trust me on this. We find Liam, we find the dope."

Peter looks over at Chris.

Chris shrugs. "He's right. But look on the bright side. The war is over; we won. The Irish are finished."

"*We're* fucking finished, we don't get that dope back," Peter says. Six million dollars in heroin, fronted to us, he thinks, by people who are not going to understand us saying it was first hijacked and then busted.

"When are you going to learn to trust me?" Chris asks. "Hasn't everything gone the way I said it would so far? We'll get the dope back."

"Minus twelve keys," Peter says.

"A small price to pay," Chris says. "We step on the rest of the shit, it will more than make up for it, you'll see."

"We have to get it first," Peter says.

"Find fucking Liam," Paulie repeats. Thinking, We get Liam, we get the dope.

And we get Pam.

DANNY CALLS BERNIE back.

The accountant's been working the phones from a cabin in New

Hampshire, talking to the few remaining connections who would take his call. A retired cop, a state legislator, a former mayor. Through them and word on the street, Bernie started to piece it together. It was even worse than they thought: The feds had a source inside the Moretti family they were trying to protect. The source—maybe it was Vecchio, maybe someone else—had set up the Murphys with the heroin treatment.

"It's bad," Bernie says. "A receptionist in the federal office says they had the Glocca Morra under audio surveillance. It was a legal wiretap under a full warrant. They have John, you, and Liam talking about both the hijacking and the heroin itself. That's how this Jardine knew to hit the Gloc."

That means the feds will have a warrant out on me, Danny thinks. Maybe on all of us.

"What about Liam?" Danny asks.

"They're trying to serve him now," Bernie says. "But he's off the radar."

"And you?"

"The feds went to my house," Bernie says. "I decided to let them interview me in absentia."

"What about Vecchio?"

"Nothing on him so far," Bernie says.

"Then he's the rat," Danny says.

"It certainly appears so," Bernie says. "But Danny, there's no indictment on you, either."

"How's that possible?" Danny asks. "If they have me on tape, Vecchio's testimony . . ."

"I don't know," Bernie says. "You need to get out of there, Danny."

"I can't," Danny says. "I mean, you heard about Terri, right?"

"Yes, and I'm sorry."

"I can't leave her."

"You have to, son," Bernie says. "If the feds don't get you now, the Morettis will. You have no soldiers on the street, everyone knows where you are, you're a sitting duck."

"I won't leave her," Danny says. "Not until . . ."

He leaves the thought unfinished.

GO," DANNY TELLS Jimmy a few minutes later, filling him in on what he's found out. "Don't even stop by your house. You can call Angie from out of state."

"No," Jimmy says. "Not without you."

"I can't go, Jimmy."

"Then I guess I stay."

Jimmy goes downstairs to take a look around, comes back up with the word that there are Moretti people in the parking lot and cars that sure look a lot like feds. "What are they waiting for?"

"For Terri to die," Danny says.

Maybe the only decent thing that Peter Moretti has ever done, Danny thinks. As for Jardine, I should have listened to him. I should have taken his deal. But I turned him down and he got Frank Vecchio instead.

Terri's out of it, morphine flowing through her.

Danny looks up at the TV.

Sure enough, there on the late-night news is a smiling Agent Jardine, standing by a stack of heroin, bragging about how the twelve kilos is the largest drug bust in the history of Rhode Island, how it's going to cripple the New England narcotics trade, about the arrest of John Murphy and the warrants out for several other "major traffickers."

"I'm sure," Jardine says, "that we'll have them in custody very soon. They can run, but they can't hide."

Danny don't know what to do.

He wishes Pat was here, Pat would know.

But he isn't here, Danny tells himself.

So *think*.

Think like a leader.

Vecchio was a rat. He came to you with the heroin deal because he needed money to go on the run from Chris Palumbo and the Morettis, so—

No, he didn't, Danny thinks.

It was a trap all the time. Vecchio set us up.

And you didn't see it, you dumb donkey. You were so worried there'd be an ambush in the truck, you didn't see that the truck *was* the ambush, that the *dope* was the weapon. The Morettis *sent* Vecchio to set you up. He was the bait and you swallowed it whole. They couldn't win the war against you, so they're letting the feds do it for them.

And now we're fucked.

The room phone rings. Danny figures it's probably Bernie with more bad news, but it ain't.

"Danny?" his mother asks.

"How did you get this number?"

"I'm so sorry about Terri," Madeleine says. "I'm very fond of her."

"What do you want?"

"I want you to get out of there," Madeleine says.

"What do you know about it?" Danny asks.

"Let's just say I follow you from afar," Madeleine says. "Remotely, as you requested. You asked me to stay out of your life and so far I've honored your wishes. But, Danny, what are you going to do?"

"I don't know."

"Not knowing is not good enough," Madeleine says. "You have a wife and a child—you don't have the luxury of indecision. You have to get out. If there isn't an indictment on you, there will be. Or the Morettis will kill you."

"Terri's dying."

"All the more reason you have to go," Madeleine says. "Your child is going to be without a mother—"

"Like me?"

She takes the punch and then says, "And if you stand there paralyzed and stay a child yourself, Ian is going to be without a father, too, because you'll be dead or in prison. Do you love your son, Danny?"

"Of course I do."

"Then you have to go," she says. "For his sake."

"I can't leave Terri."

"It's what she'd want," Madeleine says.

"How do *you* know what she'd want?"

Madeleine says, "I'm a mother."

Danny hangs up.

Then he goes down to the chapel.

JARDINE HAS RON Laframboise's balls in a vise.

Not literally, but he might as well have, the way Ronny's squirming and twisting, his brain cooking as he tries to figure a way out.

He's sitting on the old sofa in his apartment, where he got busted with two grams of coke and an unregistered handgun, a combo plate for which the bill comes to thirty years, without the tip.

"There's only one way out, Ronny," Jardine says. "I want to know where Liam has the rest of the dope."

"I don't know."

"But you do know where he is," Jardine says. "You're one of Liam's bodyguards, and to guard his body, you have to know where it is. So where is it?"

"At this very moment?" Ronny asks.

"Good, play games," Jardine says. "I can play games, too. My favorite is Send the Dumb Frog to the Worst Supermax You Can Think of and Make Sure He Gets Put In with the Spics, Where He Becomes a Pincushion."

Ronny twists and squirms.

"Let me ask it this way," Jardine says. "If Liam Murphy was looking at dying behind bars, and his out was giving you up, what do you think he'd do?"

Ronny knows the answer.

He tells Jardine about the safe house in Lincoln.

PAM SHOVES CLOTHES into her bag.

Because Liam keeps telling her to hurry. "They could be here any second."

"Who?"

"The Morettis or the feds," Liam says. "It doesn't matter which. Jesus Christ, hurry up."

Liam's been in a state since Bernie called with the news of the raid on the Gloc. He's coked up anyway, and then when he turned on the TV and saw his father being led into the car, he got all the more jacked up.

He takes the three bricks of heroin from under the bed and shoves them into his suitcase. "Thank fucking God I took these to sell, so we have *something*. Fucking Danny Ryan and his 'wait' bullshit, look what happened. Nobody listens to Liam."

He grabs her bag and zips it shut. "Enough. Let's go."

"Where are we going?"

"You know what, Pam?" Liam asks. "Why don't we sit down and

have a nice long chat about the future? We can just sit here and share our feelings until the door crashes in, how about that?"

"You said we were going to Boca," Pam says. "A nice house, out of the business . . ."

"Boca, you dumb bitch?" Liam says. "There's a federal dope indictment on me. We have to get out of the country. Mexico, maybe Venezuela, maybe farther, I don't know."

"I'm not going." Pam sits back down on the bed. "To Mexico or anywhere else. If you want to run, run. But without me. I'm not living as a fugitive."

"You think you're clean on this?" Liam says. "You're up to your tight little ass in it. You've been spending my coke money for two years. What, the feds are going to give you a pass because you're so fucking pretty? The bull dykes in the joint are going to think you're pretty, too, sweetheart."

"Liam, it hasn't been good with us for a long time," she says.

He looks pathetic. Scared, sweaty, his eyes pinned with coke. "What do you mean?"

"We fight all the time," she says. "We don't even have sex anymore. You haven't fucked me in . . . I don't think you even can."

He smacks her across the face.

It's an open hand, but it hurts, wrenches her neck. Then he's pummeling her, careful not to punch her in the face, but raining fists on her ribs, her thighs, her legs. "You think you're going to leave me, bitch? After everything I've done for you? I put my life on the line, for you, I killed for you. My brother *died* for you. I'll never let you leave. I'll kill you first. I'll fucking kill you *now*, then I'll blow my brains out. Is that what you want?"

"No. Please, Liam. I'll go with you." She's terrified.

"Tell me you love me."

"I love you."

"You're lying."

"No," she says. "I love you, Liam. With all my heart."

He gets off her. "Get in the car."

DANNY GOES DOWN to the chapel, kneels at the votary altar and lights a candle.

Then he prays. "Dear Father God, Mother Mary, Saint Anthony, and Jesus. I know I don't talk to you as much as I should and I probably shouldn't even be here but I don't know what else to do.

"Please take Terri's soul when she comes and keep her safe in heaven. She's a good person, she didn't have anything to do with all the bad things I've done. One of those innocent bystanders, and why you have to take her instead of me I'll never know. But you did, and now I have a son to take care of, and a sick old father, and a bunch of other people who need me, and to do all that I'm going to do something very wrong. A mortal sin. And I'm not asking for your forgiveness, to tell you the truth; what I'm asking for is your help to do what I have to do."

He crosses himself and gets up.

WHEN JARDINE GETS to the safe house in Lincoln, it looks like Liam left in a hurry. Clothes in the closet, food still out on the kitchen table, shit, a stove burner is still warm.

Just missed him.

LIAM DRIVES NORTH up Route 95. Doesn't say a word to her for an hour, up into Massachusetts, then says, "Why do you make me hurt you?"

Pam doesn't answer.

"We got four hundred and fifty K in heroin," Liam says. "We'll be fine. I'll sell it up in Canada, we'll get new IDs and fly down to Mexico. Right back in fucking business."

She still doesn't say anything.

"What are you, mad?" he asks. "You pouting? I said I was sorry."

"No, you didn't."

"Well, I am."

"That's great."

Up around Lowell, Liam gets tired.

He pulls off at a Motel 6 and parks the car around the back, where it can't be seen from the highway.

Pam goes to the desk to check in, gives a fake name and pays in cash. Before heading back to the car, she goes to the pay phone in the lobby.

JARDINE TAKES THE call.

Hears a woman's voice say, "Motel 6, Lowell. Room one-thirty-eight."

The woman hangs up.

He knows who it is.

Pamela Murphy.

He calls Paulie Moretti and then heads out.

DANNY WONDERS IF he's doing the right thing by going. Leaving Terri at the edge of the void, to die alone, slip away down the road to God knows.

But he knows his mother is right.

Even God is telling him to get out.

For Ian, for sure, but not only for him. I'm the leader now, I have to take care of my people.

I gotta get us all out of here.

Find a place to set our feet.

He leans over, kisses Terri's cheek.

It feels like she's already gone, like this isn't the woman he knew, the woman he loved. It's weird, he can smell the vanilla on her skin, even though it's not there; he can feel the fine little black hairs on her forearm that he used to stroke with the back of his hand when they'd lie there after making love, even though her arms are covered now in patches and tubes and needles. He can see her so clearly—not her when she was sick, but her when she was younger. Can feel her body warm asleep in bed beside him, can see her walking on the beach. Can hear her breathing softly, the way she used to when she was deep asleep, not like the mechanical rasping that comes out of the ventilator; can hear her voice—teasing, mocking, loving, tough and tender—although she's silent now, drowning under a sea of morphine, drifting out and away.

Terri's gone and he can't find the woman he knew.

Danny don't know if it's real or he imagined it, but he could swear that she opens her eyes for a second and says, "Take care of our son."

"I will."

"Promise."

"I promise," he says. "I swear."

Then he straightens up.

So what's it going to take, he asks himself.

First you gotta get out of here, out of this trap.

Say you can, then what?

Money—it's going to take a lot of money to go on the run and stay off the radar. Money for you and Ian, money for the rest of them.

Like the money ten keys of dope will bring in.

You have to get out of here and get the heroin.

• • •

WHERE ARE YOU going?" Liam asks. He's stretched out on the bed, but his hand is on his revolver.

"To take a shower," Pam says. "Is that okay with you?"

"Leave your clothes here on the bed."

"Liam—"

"Do it."

Pam sheds her clothes and goes into the bathroom. Lets the water get hot and then stands under it. The bruises have come out on her body, purple and red; her ribs hurt and she wonders if one of them is cracked. Her neck is tight from when he slapped her and she turns around to let the water hit it.

Then she slides down the shower wall.

Sits there and cries and cries.

She doesn't hear the motel room door open, but does hear a man's voice say, "Don't do it, Murphy. Let the gun drop."

Pam doesn't get up.

She hears Liam yelling, "You fucking bitch! You fucking whore! You've killed me, Pam! You've killed me! I *loved* you!"

Then she hears the door shut.

DANNY GOES OUT into the hallway, where Jimmy is waiting.

"Tell Ned to go by my place," Danny says, "pick up Ian, get down to my dad's and wait. Tell Kevin and Sean to head down there, stay in the area but don't go in. Watch for me on the road."

"What about me?"

"You're going to help me get out of here."

Jimmy goes downstairs; Danny finds the staircase to the roof and goes up. Walking to the edge, he can see all of Dogtown, the old neighborhood, the Gloc, the basketball courts, the house he grew up in, the house he lives in now.

Or used to live in, he thinks.

That's over now. It's all over.

Dogtown is gone.

He looks into the parking lot at the cars. At least one of them will be Moretti's people, another one at least will be feds. He'll know which in a minute. Then he hears the engine and sees Jimmy's Charger roar out, making as much noise as possible.

A car pulls out and goes after it.

Then another.

Good, Danny thinks. If anyone can lose them, it's Jimmy Mac, and if he can't, well, Jimmy's a good soldier. And he knows that I'll take care of Angie.

He walks to the other side of the roof and goes down the fire escape.

Five minutes later, he's on the road, headed for Mashanuck and the heroin.

Just let me get there, Danny thinks, before Jardine does.

JARDINE SHOVES LIAM into the passenger seat, then opens the trunk of his car.

A suitcase is sitting there. Jardine opens it and sees three bricks of heroin. He shuts the trunk, gets in behind the wheel. "You're fucked."

"Why are we taking my car?" Liam asks.

"Your vehicle," Jardine says, "is confiscated and is now the property of the United States government. I'm using it to take you in."

Liam figures this is his one shot. He talks fast. "You're missing ten keys. The shipment we jacked was forty kilos. There are ten still out there. I can give them to you. I can give you Danny Ryan, too.

He's the top guy now, this was his play, he's the one you want. I'll testify against him, against my father, but I want immunity. Total immunity from prosecution. I go into the program, I get a new life."

"What about Pam Davies?"

"Fuck her," Liam says. "She already cut her deal, right?"

"If I promise you'll never spend a day in prison," Jardine says, "you'll tell me where the ten keys are?"

"I can tell you where they *were*," Liam says. "I don't know if Danny's gotten to them."

"Okay. If we get the dope, you have a deal."

Liam gives him the address. Jardine drives a little farther, then pulls off into a parking lot behind a bunch of warehouses.

"What are we doing?" Liam asks, suddenly scared.

"I'm a man of my word." Jardine takes Liam's revolver and shoots him in the head, then puts the gun in his hand.

He takes the three bricks of heroin from the trunk and gets out.

A car is waiting for him.

PAM IS LYING on the bed in her towel when the door opens.

"Hello, bitch."

Paulie points the gun at her.

DANNY DRIVES.

He's made this trip a thousand times, but this time it's different. This time it's one-way. He's going to take the fucking heroin—Please, God, let it still be there—grab his father and his son, and never come back.

Sell the dope in Baltimore or Washington and then turn right.

Keep going until he hits the ocean.

California.

Use the money to put the whole crew on ice, wait a few years, and then start again, with something legitimate.

Danny drives.

Pulls off at a gas station and gets on the phone.

"What do you know?" he asks Bernie.

"They got Liam."

"Who did?" Danny asks.

"That fed, Jardine," Bernie says. "Pam called me, sobbing. Said that Jardine came to their motel room and took him away. I called our lawyers, but the feds say they can't find him in the system, the lying bastards."

Danny hangs up.

It's over, he thinks.

Liam will give the location of the heroin up to Jardine to try to strike a plea bargain. Jardine and a crew of feds are probably already there.

But he has to take the chance, has to find out for sure.

He keeps driving south, turns onto the beach road and sees a pair of headlights blink at him.

Jimmy Mac.

Danny pulls over and gets out.

"Liam's dead," Jimmy says. "I just heard it on the radio. They found him in his car up in Lowell. They say it was suicide."

"That doesn't make any sense," Danny says. He tells Jimmy what Bernie told him about Liam being arrested.

And Liam killing himself? No way.

Liam was the only person Liam ever loved.

Danny's head is freakin' reeling, trying to put it together. Jardine arrests Liam, now Liam is dead? What was it Pam told Bernie—Jardine came to their motel room . . .

That doesn't make any sense, either.

When the feds make a bust, they come in battalions, lights flashing, making a Mongolian opera of it for show.

No fed comes alone.

But Jardine came by himself, took Liam out, and . . .

Killed him.

Jesus Christ.

Think, Danny tells himself. Think like a leader.

Use your head for once.

You thought Moretti staged all this to take you out, but Peter Moretti can't afford a six-million-dollar loss, even to win the fucking war. It would cripple him. That amount of money would mean he lost the war even if he "won" it.

So why . . .

Think, Danny tells himself again. Why would Peter spend money he can't afford to lose?

Because he's expecting to get it back. Peter brings in forty kilos of heroin, he manipulates you into hijacking it, then sends Vecchio to rat you to the feds. So the heroin ends up in federal custody and . . .

Jesus Christ.

How many keys did Jardine say on television they seized?

Twelve?

You gave Vecchio five keys, you kept ten. Liam took twenty-five kilos with him to the Gloc, but then took three to sell. So there were twenty-two kilos in the Gloc when it was raided. Twenty-two, not twelve like Jardine said in the press conference.

So he took ten for himself.

He's probably got Vecchio's five, too.

Fifteen freakin' keys of dope. Say he splits it with Peter. It gets the Morettis halfway to making their investment back once they cut it up and step on it.

No, Danny thinks.

Peter isn't going to take a three-mil hit, either.

He knows there's ten more kilos out there. Jardine turned in twelve keys. If they take twenty-eight kilos for themselves, it all works for them. Even splitting with Jardine, they'll make a small profit.

Jardine and the Morettis are partners.

And one or both are coming for the other ten keys.

THE OLD MAN is asleep in his chair, a ratty old red blanket wrapped around him. The television is on, casting a dull glow on his face.

Vic Scalese, one of Peter Moretti's soldiers, looks at his partner, Dave Cousineau. "Marty fucking Ryan. Look at him."

Cousineau steps over and slaps Marty across the face.

Marty wakes up and blinks at him.

"Where's Danny?" Scalese says. "Where's your son?"

"I know who my son is."

"Where is he?" Scalese asks. He lights a cigarette.

"Fuck if I know," Marty says. "Why?"

"He has ten kilos of my boss's dope," Scalese says. "That's why."

"Ask Liam Murphy."

"Yeah, we would, except he's dead," Scalese says. "That leaves Danny and you, and Danny ain't here. So tell us where he is, or where the dope is."

"I don't know nothin' about it," Marty says. He wonders where Ned is.

"You better know something about it," Scalese says. "Or we're going to have to hurt you."

He takes the cigarette from his mouth, steps over, and jabs it at Marty's cheek.

Marty fires from under the blanket.

The bullet hits Scalese in the gut and he staggers back. The flash sets the blanket on fire. Marty tries to snuff it out and turn the gun toward Cousineau at the same time, but the fabric gets caught in the trigger guard and he can't do it.

So Marty freakin' Ryan lunges up from the chair and goes for Cousineau's throat. The bigger, younger man swats him away easily, knocking him to the floor. Then he points the gun down at Marty's face. "Last chance, you old fuck. Where's the dope?"

Cousineau's head explodes in a blossom of red.

Ned stands in the doorway and lowers his gun. Then he goes and steps on the smoldering blanket, grinding his foot to put out the last of the flames. He walks over to Scalese, who sits slumped against the wall, grabs him by the chin and the back of his head, and twists, snapping his neck.

Then he helps Marty up.

"You took your goddamn time," Marty says.

"Sorry, Mr. Ryan."

Then headlights flash across the window.

WHERE'S IAN?" DANNY asks.

"Asleep in the car," Ned says. "I didn't want to wake him up."

Danny recognizes the bodies, two of Moretti's people.

Used to be, anyway.

"They wanted to know where the dope was," Marty says.

"They what?"

"Are you deaf?" Marty says. "They wanted to know where the dope was, or where you were."

But Peter Moretti already knows where the dope is, Danny thinks, because Jardine would have told him.

Or not.

Jesus, is Jardine ripping Peter off, too? Used him to bring in forty kilos of heroin, get it stolen with the promise that he'd get it back, and then ultimately steals it himself?

Almost, Danny thinks, but not quite.

There's a piece missing.

It was Vecchio who came to you about the heroin, who set you up. But Frankie V was Chris's guy, he wouldn't blow his nose without getting the okay from Chris. So it's Chris who put this together, who's partnered up with Jardine.

This is Chris Palumbo's move to shove Peter off the throne and take it himself.

It's freakin' genius.

The Altar Boys show up a minute later. Kevin looks at the bodies and says, "Party time."

"You want us to take out the garbage, boss?" Sean asks.

"Yeah."

"Then we'll come back and clean the place up," Sean says.

"Don't bother," Danny says. "We're leaving."

They're all looking at him, waiting for orders.

Because you're the leader now, Danny thinks. Everything is fucked, everything is gone, everyone's lost, and they're looking to you to save them.

So save them.

THIRTY-THREE

DANNY SITS IN THE STASH house.

Headlights flash outside. More than one set.

Car engines stop.

He calls Bernie Hughes. "Start the clock."

Then he hangs up.

The door opens.

It's Chris.

Danny doesn't get out of his chair, just points the gun at Chris's chest and gestures for him to sit down.

Chris sits, a broad smile on his face.

"You won the war," Danny says. "I'm taking what's left of my people and leaving for good."

"You're not leaving with the dope," Chris says. "Is it still here?"

Danny gestures to the ceiling.

"I've always liked you," Chris says, "so I'm going to give you a break here. I'm going to let you walk away. Without the dope, but with your life."

Two years ago, two months ago—hell, two hours ago—Danny would have taken the deal.

But that was a different Danny.

This one has a father to take care of, a kid to raise, people to look after. And a promise he made to his wife. So he says, "No."

Chris says, "You think I came alone? I got five guys outside. You pull that trigger, you're dead. You step outside without me giving the green light, you're dead. So come on, let's be adults here, let's be men."

"Let me ask you something, Chris," Danny says. "You love your wife and kids? You love your family?"

"What the fuck, Danny?"

"Because right now," Danny says, "Sean South is in a phone booth near your brother's house in Cranston. Kevin Coombs is in one across the street from your son's apartment on Federal Hill. Ned Egan is by *your* house, where your wife and daughter are. If I don't call Bernie Hughes in fifteen minutes telling him I'm safe—using certain words you won't know—he'll call them and they will each go into those houses and kill everyone inside. The men, the women, the kids, the cats, the dogs. Hell, they'll even kill the tropical fish."

Chris goes pale. But he keeps the smile on his face and says, "You wouldn't do that. We don't touch families."

"You want to bet their lives on that?" Danny asks.

"No, not Danny Ryan," Chris says. "You're a good guy. You're too soft."

"But it won't *be* me," Danny says. "Kevin and Sean would kill their own mothers. And Ned Egan? He won't think twice."

Danny sees it in Chris's eyes. He knows it's true. But Chris, being Chris, tries another tack. "I got this fed Jardine to take care of. What am I gonna do?"

"Leave him to me," Danny says. "But you took a swing at Peter and missed. If I was you, I'd run."

Danny sees Chris thinking about it, really thinking about it. Trying to weigh up if Danny's bluffing, or if he can get guys to his family's houses in time. He needs a little nudge, so Danny says, "You'd better get going. Clock's running. And Chris? If I see you, if I see any of your people, your family's dead. Every one of them. Please don't test me on this."

Chris gets up. "I'll find you, motherfucker. One day I'll track you down and it'll be a different story."

But that's another time, Danny thinks. That's not today.

After Chris leaves, Danny gets on the phone and calls Bernie. "Tell them to stand down."

"Thank God."

Danny hangs up and calls Jardine's beeper. A few minutes later, the fed calls back.

"Meet me," Danny says.

He tells Jardine where and when.

Then he takes the heroin out from the ceiling and loads it into his car.

MARTY'S BACK IN his chair, watching the television.

Ian's asleep on the sofa with a scorched blanket thrown over him, his arm clutched around a stuffed toy puppy.

"I'll pack a few of your things," Danny tells Marty. "We're getting out of here."

"I ain't goin' nowhere."

Danny sighs. "Dad, they probably have a warrant for you, too. Even if they don't, you think the Morettis are going to leave you alive?"

"I want to die."

"Fuck, Dad."

"I do," Marty says, his voice shaking. "For years now, I've been a useless old man, no good to anybody, even myself. Peter Moretti wants to kill me? God bless him."

Yeah, Danny thinks. That's why you shot one of the guys Peter sent. "Dad, I don't have the time to argue with—"

"Go!" Marty yells. "Who's keeping you?! I'm not."

"They'll kill you."

"I don't care," Marty says.

"Do you care about your grandson?" Danny asks.

"What kind of a question . . ."

"Ian needs all the family he can get," Danny says. "He needs you, Dad. I need you."

Tears come out of Marty's eyes, roll down cheeks as dry and brittle as old paper. "Make sure you pack my other flannel shirt."

Danny lifts Ian off the sofa and the boy wakes up. He has her blue eyes and black hair, all matted from where he was asleep on the pillow. Looks scared now, and confused. "Where Mommy? Want Mommy."

"Mommy's in heaven." Danny wraps the blanket back around him, carries him out to Jimmy's car and gets him settled in the back seat.

"Wait here," Danny says, "I won't be long."

He leaves to meet Jardine.

DANNY STANDS ON the beach in front of Pasco's house and looks out at the ocean.

The wind-driven winter surf is vicious, big waves crashing on shore like bombs. It's freezing and that summer day when this all started feels like another lifetime.

The sky is slate gray now, the sun getting ready to appear on the horizon.

Danny remembers lying on the warm sand next to Terri, watching the woman come out of the water.

Knowing that she'd be trouble.

He don't see her in the water now, he sees Terri and knows, somehow, in the way that spouses feel each other, that she's slipped this world for another one. Knows also that he made her a promise—to build a life for their son.

A new life.

He's sure now that he's done the right thing.

Danny sees Jardine walk up the beach, his hands jammed into his down jacket against the cold.

Or maybe he's holding a gun.

"What are we doing here?" Jardine asks.

"Chris Palumbo isn't going to bring you your dope."

Jardine doesn't blink. "And why is that?"

"Because I have it."

"Is Palumbo alive?"

"He was the last time I saw him."

Jardine switches loyalties just like that, like he's shifting a car. "Then maybe you and *I* can make a deal."

"Here's what the deal is," Danny says. "You keep the money you've already made. I walk away. Any indictments you have on me or my people, evidence gets lost, paperwork gets screwed up . . . you're a smart guy, you know what to do."

"Or I could just bust you."

"No, if you were going to do that, you wouldn't have come alone," Danny says. "Because you know I can testify about you and Palumbo. I can testify how much heroin there was in the Glocca Morra."

"No one will believe you."

"You want to take that chance?" Danny asks.

Turns out Jardine doesn't. "Where's the dope?"

"I threw it in the ocean."

"*What?!*"

"I threw it in the ocean," Danny says.

"Why the hell did you do that?!"

"Because you would have taken it and then shot me," Danny says. "Now you got no motive to do that."

That was one reason, Danny thinks. The dope had brought them nothing but pain and sorrow. It was a mortal sin to begin with; he should never have taken it. It was cursed.

But the real reason is . . .

If you want to build a new life, a clean life, you can't do it on top of sin.

"You dumb motherfucker," Jardine says. "You stupid Irish donkey. I'll put you *under* the fucking jail, I'll—"

"Do what you're going to do," Danny says. "I'm out of this."

He turns and walks away, down the beach.

Knows he can very well catch a bullet in the back.

Fuck it, Danny thinks.

He takes two more steps and turns around. Sure enough, Jardine has his gun out, pointed.

The crashing wave masks the sound of Danny's shot.

Danny tosses his gun into the ocean and leaves Jardine's corpse on the beach.

I gave you a chance, he thinks.

You should have let me walk away.

DANNY DRIVES BACK up the beach road.

For the last time.

Ian is out cold in the back seat. His forehead is beaded with sweat, his black hair damp from the overactive car heater. A little bubble appears on the corner of his mouth and then pops.

"I didn't think it was possible," Marty says.

"Think what was possible?"

"That you were as dumb as you look," Marty says. "I have one son, and he throws two million bucks into Block Island Sound."

"You raised me."

"Your bitch of a mother told me you were mine," Marty says. "I've always had my doubts."

"Your lips to God's ears."

"What are you going to do for money now, genius?"

"I dunno."

He has no freakin' clue.

He's on the run—from the mob, from the government. He has no money, no resources, no connections, no clear idea where he's going or what he's going to find when he gets there, wherever "there" is.

But he feels clean for the first time in a long time.

Marty starts singing an old Irish song Danny's heard about a thousand times at the Gloc—

> *Farewell to Prince's Landing stage,*
> *River Mersey, fare thee well,*
> *I'm bound for California . . .*

The sun is up now and the sky is silver, tinting toward blue, one of those clear, crisp winter skies.

> *It's not the leaving of Liverpool that grieves me,*
> *But my darlin', when I think of thee . . .*

Danny Ryan drives up the beach road for the last time, his back to the cold sea, his face toward a warmer shore.

ACKNOWLEDGMENTS

In this pandemic time, it would be the act of an ingrate not to express gratitude to the health workers and essential personnel who have worked so selflessly and sacrificed so much so that people like me can sit and write books. I appreciate you more than I can express.

Speaking of appreciation, a loud shout-out to my agent, Shane Salerno, friend and co-conspirator. Without him, these books don't happen.

To all the folks at The Story Factory—Deborah Randall and Ryan Coleman—my deep gratitude for all you do.

To Liate Stehlik at William Morrow, my humble thanks for all the support and trust.

Thanks, of course, to Jennifer Brehl, for her caring editing, which vastly improved the book.

Appreciation, and sympathy, out to my copyeditor Laura Cherkas.

To Brian Murray, Chantal Restivo-Alessi, David Wolfson, Julianna Wojcik, Carolyn Bodkin, Jennifer Hart, Kaitlin Harri, Danielle Bartlett, Frank Albanese, Christine Edwards, Andy LeCount, Nate

Lanman, Andrea Molitor, Andrew DiCecco, Pam Barricklow, and Kyle O'Brien.

I also owe a debt of gratitude to the unsung heroes and heroines of the sales, marketing, and publicity staff at HarperCollins/William Morrow.

To Richard Heller, lawyer extraordinaire, great appreciation.

Likewise to Matt Snyder and Joe Cohen at CAA for the years of great representation.

To Steve Hamilton, for his support and sage counsel.

For their support and inspiration, humble appreciation to Nils Lofgren, Jon Landau, and Bruce Springsteen.

To all the booksellers and readers—without you, I don't have this job.

To the many friends and places that gave me more support than they can ever know: David Nedwidek and Katy Allen, Pete and Linda Maslowski, Jim Basker and Angela Vallot, Teressa Palozzi, Drew Goodwin, Tony and Kathy Sousa, John and Theresa Culver, Scott Svoboda and Jan Enstrom, Jim and Melinda Fuller, Stephen and Cindy Gilliland, Ted Tarbet, Thom Walla, Mark Clodfelter, Roger Barbee, Bill and Ruth McEneaney, Andrew Walsh, Jeff and Rita Parker, Bruce Riordan, Jeff Weber, Don Young, Mark Rubinsky, Cameron Pierce Hughes, Mark Rubenstein, Jon Land, Rob Jones, David and Tammy Tanner, Ty and Dani Jones, Deron and Becky Bisset, Jesse McQuery, the Flipper Eddie Crew, Drift Surf, Quecho, Java Madness, Jim's Dock, Colt's Burger Bar, Wynola Pizza, Tavern on Main, Cap'n Jack's, the Charlestown Rathskeller, and Kingston Pizza.

To my son, Thomas Winslow—for all his unfailing support.

To my wife, Jean, always, for your long-suffering, ever-patient, always enthusiastic support. ILYM.

CITY OF DREAMS,

· · ·

PROLOGUE: DAYBREAK

Anza Borrego Desert, California
1992

At last the day was breaking, the morning star on the rise . . .

Virgil
The Aeneid

DANNY SHOULD HAVE KILLED THEM all.

He knows that now.

Should have known it then—you rip forty million in cash from people in an armed robbery, you shouldn't leave them alive to come after you.

You should take their money *and* their lives.

But that ain't Danny Ryan.

It's always been his problem—he still believes in God. Heaven and hell and all that happy crap. He's pushed the button on a few guys, but it was always a him-or-them situation.

The robbery wasn't. Danny had them all zip-tied, flat on the floor or the ground, helpless, and his guys wanted to put bullets in the backs of their heads.

Execution-style, like they say.

"They'd do it to us," Kevin Coombs said to him.

Yeah, they would, Danny thought.

Popeye Abbarca was notorious for killing not only the people who rip him off, but their entire families, too. Popeye's head guy had even told Danny that. Looked up from the floor, smiled, and said, "You and all your families. *Muerte*. And not fast, either."

We came for the money, not a massacre, Danny thought. Tens of millions of dollars in cash to start new lives, not keep reliving the old ones.

The killing had to stop.

So he took their money and left them their lives.

Now he knows it was a mistake.

He's on his knees with a gun to his head. The others are tied, bound wrist and ankle, stretched on poles, looking down at him with pleading, terrified eyes.

The desert air is cold at dawn and Danny shivers as he kneels in the sand with the sun coming up and the moon a fading memory. A dream. Maybe that's all life is, Danny thinks, a dream.

Or a nightmare.

Because even in dreams, Danny thinks, you pay for your sins.

An acrid smell pierces the crisp, fresh air.

Gasoline.

Then Danny hears, "You watch while we burn them alive. Then you."

So this is how I die, he thinks.

The dream fades.

The long night is over.

The day is breaking.

PART ONE

In Some Neglected Land

> . . . exiles now, searching earth for a home
> in some neglected land . . .
>
> Virgil
> *The Aeneid*

ONE

THEY LEAVE A LITTLE AFTER dawn.

A cold northeast wind—is there any other kind? Danny thinks—blows off the ocean like it's giving them the bum's rush. He and his family—or what's left of it—his crew in cars behind him, spread out so they don't look like the refugee convoy they are.

Danny's old man, Marty, is singing—

*Farewell to Princes' landing stage, River Mersey fare thee well
I am bound for California . . .*

Danny Ryan's not sure where they're going, just that they have to get the hell out of Rhode Island.

It's not the leaving of Liverpool that grieves me . . .

It's not Liverpool they're leaving, it's freakin' Providence. They have to put a lot of miles between them and the Moretti crime family, the city cops, the state troopers, the feds . . . just about everybody.

What happens when you lose a war.

Danny's not grieving, either.

Even though his wife, Terri, died just hours ago now—the cancer took her like a slow-moving but relentless storm—Danny doesn't have the time for heartbreak, not with a two-year-old child asleep in the back seat.

but, my darling when I think of thee . . .

There'll be a mass, Danny thinks, there'll be a funeral and a wake, but I won't be there for any of it. If the cops or the feds didn't get me, the Morettis would, and then Ian would be an orphan.

The boy sleeps through his grandfather's caterwauling. I dunno, Danny thinks, maybe the old Irish song is a lullaby.

Danny's in no hurry for him to wake up.

How am I going to tell him that he isn't going to see his mommy anymore, that "she's with God"?

If you believe that stuff.

Danny's not sure he does anymore.

If there is a God, he thinks, he's a cruel, vengeful prick who made my wife and my little boy pay for the things I did. I thought Jesus died for my sins, that's what the nuns said anyway.

Maybe my sins just maxed out Christ's credit card.

You've robbed, Danny thinks, you've beaten people. You've killed three men. Left the last one dead on a frozen beach just an hour or so ago. He tried to kill you first, though. Yeah, tell yourself that. The guy is still dead. You still killed him. You have a lot to answer for.

You're a drug dealer, you were going to put ten kilos of heroin out on the street.

Danny wishes he'd never touched the shit.

I knew better, he thinks now as he drives. You can make all the excuses you want for yourself—you were doing it to survive, for your kid, for a better life, you'd make up for it somehow down the road— but the truth is that you still did it.

Danny knew it was freakin' wrong, that he was putting evil and suffering out into a world that already had too much of both. Was doing it even as he was watching his wife die of cancer with a tube of the same shit running into her arm.

The money he would have made was blood money.

So minutes before he killed the dirty cop, Danny Ryan threw two million dollars' worth of heroin into the ocean.

THE WAR HAD started over a woman.

At least that's how most people tell it: they blame Pam.

Danny was there that day when she walked out of the water onto the beach like a goddess. No one knew this WASP ice maiden was Paulie Moretti's girlfriend, no one knew he really loved her.

If Liam Murphy knew, he didn't care.

Then again, Liam never cared about anything but himself. What he thought was that she was a beautiful woman and he was a beautiful man and so they belonged together. He took her like a trophy he'd won just for being him.

And Pam?

Danny never understood what she saw in Liam, or why she stayed with him as long as she did. He'd always liked Pam; she was smart, she was funny, she seemed to care about other people.

Paulie couldn't get past it—losing Pam, getting cuckolded by some Irish charmer.

Thing of it was, the Irish and Italians had been friends before that. Allies for generations. Danny's own father, Marty—who's now thankfully dozed off, snoring instead of singing—was one of the men who put that together. The Irish had the docks, the Italians had the gambling, and they shared the unions. They ran New England together. They were all at the same beach party when Liam made his move on Pam.

Forty years of friendship came apart in one night.

The Italians beat Liam half to death.

Pam came to the hospital and left with Liam.

The war was on.

Sure, most people lay it on Pam, Danny thinks, but Peter Moretti had been wanting to make a move on the docks for years, and he used his brother's embarrassment as an excuse.

Doesn't matter now, Danny thinks.

Whatever started the war, it's over.

We lost.

The losses were more than the docks, the unions.

They were personal, too.

Danny wasn't a Murphy, he'd married into the family that ruled the Irish mob. Even then he was pretty much just a soldier. John Murphy and his two sons, Pat and Liam, ran things.

But now John's in a federal lockup awaiting heroin charges that will put him away for life.

Liam is dead, shot by the same cop that Danny killed.

And Pat, Danny's best friend—his brother-in-law but more like his brother—was killed. Run over by a car, his body dragged through the streets, flayed almost beyond recognition.

It broke Danny's heart.

And Terri . . .

She wasn't killed in the war, Danny thinks. Not directly, anyway, but the cancer started after Pat, her beloved brother, was killed, and sometimes Danny wonders if that was where it began. Like the grief grew from her heart and spread through her chest.

God, Danny loved her.

In a world where most of the guys fucked around, had mistresses or *gumars*, Danny never cheated. He was as faithful as a golden retriever, and Terri even teased him about it, although she expected nothing less.

She and Danny were there that day Pam showed up, they were lying on the beach together when she came out of the water, her skin glistening from sunshine and salt. Terri saw him looking, gave him a sharp elbow, then they went back to their cottage and made frantic love.

The sex between them—delayed so long because they were Irish Catholics and she was Pat's sister—was always good. Danny never needed to look outside the marriage, not even when Terri was sick.

Especially not when she was sick.

Her last words to him, before she slipped into the morphine-induced terminal coma—

"Take care of our son."

"I will."

"Promise."

"I promise," he said. *"I swear."*

DRIVING THROUGH NEW HAVEN on Route 95, Danny notices that buildings are decorated with giant wreaths. The lights in the windows are red and green. A giant Christmas tree pokes up from an office plaza.

Christmas, Danny thinks.

Merry freakin' Christmas.

He'd forgotten all about it, forgotten Liam's sick stupid heroin joke about dreaming of a white Christmas. It's in a few days, right? Danny thinks. The hell difference does it make? Ian's too young to know or care. Maybe next year . . . if there is a next year.

So do it now, he thinks.

No point in putting it off, it's not going to get any better with time.

He gets off the highway at Bridgeport, follows a street east until it takes him to the ocean. Or Long Island Sound, anyway. He pulls into a dirt parking lot by a little beach.

Within a few minutes, the others pull in behind him.

Danny gets out of the car. He pulls the collar of his pea coat up around his neck, but the sharp winter air feels good.

Jimmy Mac rolls down his window. His friend since they were in freakin' kindergarten, Jimmy gets a little chubbier with every year, has a body like a laundry bag, but he's the best wheelman in the business. He asks, "What's up? Why did you pull off?"

Get it over with, Danny thinks. Just say it, short and sharp. "I dumped the heroin, Jimmy."

Jimmy's shock is plain on his bland, friendly face. "The *hell*, Danny? That was our shot! We risked our lives for that dope!"

And we shouldn't have, Danny thinks.

Because it was a setup.

From the get-go.

A Moretti captain named Frankie Vecchio had come to them with the proverbial offer you can't refuse. He was in charge of a forty-kilo shipment of heroin that Peter Moretti bought from the Mexicans on the come. Frankie thought the Morettis were going to have him whacked, so he came to ask Danny to hijack the shipment.

Danny saw it as a chance to cripple the Morettis and end the war.

So I went for it, Danny thinks now.

They jacked the forty keys, it was easy.

Too freakin' easy, that was the problem.

A fed named Phillip Jardine was in bed with the Italians. The whole plan was to have the Murphys hijack the shipment, then bust them. Most of the heroin would find its way back to the Morettis.

It was all a trap to finish off the Irish.

And it worked.

We fell for it, Danny thinks, hook, line, and sinker.

The Murphys got busted and the Morettis got the dope.

Except for the ten kilos that Danny had stashed away.

It was their safety net, the getaway money, the funds that would let them go off the radar until things cooled off.

Except now Danny has given it to the ocean, to the sea god.

Jimmy is just staring at him.

Ned Egan walks up. Marty's longtime bodyguard, he's in his fifties now. Built like a fire hydrant but a hell of a lot tougher. You don't fuck with Ned Egan, you don't even joke about fucking with him, because Ned Egan has killed more guys than cholesterol.

Marty stays in the car because he isn't going to get out in the cold. Back in the day, you said the name Marty Ryan, grown men would piss their pants, but that was a lot of days ago. Now he's an old man, more often drunk than not, half-blind with cataracts.

Two other guys come over.

Sean South couldn't look more Irish if you stuck a pipe in his mouth and shoved him into a green leprechaun suit. With his bright-red hair, freckles, and clean-cut appearance, Sean looks about as dangerous as a day-old kitten, but give him a reason and he'd shoot you in the face and then go out for a burger and a beer.

Kevin Coombs has his hands jammed into the black leather jacket he's worn since Danny first met him. Long, unkempt brown hair down to his shoulders, three days' growth of beard, Kevin looks like the stereotypical East Coast punk. Add his boozing to that and you have the whole Irish Catholic–alcoholic combo plate. But if you need some serious work done, Kevin is your man.

Collectively, Sean and Kevin are known as "the Altar Boys." They like to go around saying that they serve "Last Communion."

"What are we doing, boss?" Sean asks.

"I dumped the heroin," Danny says.

Kevin blinks. He can't believe it. Then his face twists into an angry snarl. "Are you fucking kidding me?"

"Watch your mouth," Ned says. "You're talking to the boss."

"That was millions of dollars there," Kevin says.

Danny can smell the booze on his breath.

"If we could even lay it off," Danny says. "I didn't even know who to approach."

"Liam did," Kevin says.

"Liam's dead," Danny says. "That shit brought us nothing but bad. We probably have indictments chasing us, never mind the Morettis."

"That's why we needed the money, Danny," Sean says.

Jimmy says, "They'll all be coming after us. The Italians, the feds . . ."

"I know," Danny says. But not Jardine, he thinks. Maybe other feds, but not that one. He doesn't tell the others this—no point in giving them guilty knowledge, both for their protection and his. "But the heroin was evidence. I got rid of it."

"I can't believe you did us like that," Kevin says.

Danny sees Kevin's wrist move a little above his jacket pocket and knows the gun is in his hand.

If Kevin thinks he can do it, he will.

Sean, too.

They're a pair, the Altar Boys.

But Danny doesn't go for his own gun. He doesn't need to. Ned Egan already has his out.

Pointed at Kevin's head.

"Kevin," Danny says, "don't make me drop you in the ocean with the dope. Because I will."

It's right on the edge.

It can go either way.

Then Kevin laughs. Throws his head up and howls. "Throwing two mill in the water?! The feds after us?! The Italians?! The whole freakin' world?! That's wicked pisser! I *love* it! I'm with you, man! I'm with the Danny Ryan crew! Cradle to the freakin' grave!"

Ned lowers his gun.

A little.

Danny relaxes. A little. The good thing about the Altar Boys is that they're crazy. The bad thing about the Altar Boys is that they're crazy.

"Okay, we don't need a parade here," Danny says. "Spread out. We'll stay in touch through Bernie."

Bernie Hughes, the organization's old accountant, is holed up in New Hampshire, safe—for the time being, anyway—from the feds and the Morettis.

"You got it, boss," Sean says.

Kevin nods.

They all get back in their cars and head out.

We're refugees, Danny thinks as he drives.

Freakin' refugees.

Fugitives.

Exiles.

TWO

PETER MORETTI IS FREAKING THE fuck out.

Waiting for Chris Palumbo.

Sitting in the office of American Vending Machine on Atwells Avenue in Providence, Peter's tapping his right foot like a rabbit on speed. The office is decorated like a mother, because his brother Paulie goes nuts at the holidays and because this was supposed to have been a very good Christmas, what with the heroin money coming in and the Irish going out. Wreaths and shit festoon the walls and a big artificial silver tree stands in the corner with wrapped presents underneath, ready for the annual party.

Maybe I should take some of the presents back, Peter thinks, because if Palumbo doesn't show up, we're all going to be broke. Last thing he heard from his consigliere, Chris, he was headed down to the shore to get the ten kilos of horse Danny Ryan had tucked away in a stash house. That was three hours ago and there isn't anywhere in Rhode Island it takes three hours to get to and get back.

Chris hasn't come back, hasn't called.

So ten keys of horse is in the wind with him.

After you step on it like Godzilla on Bambi, ten kilos of heroin has a street value of over two million dollars.

Peter needs that money.

Because he owes that money.

Sort of.

Peter had bought forty kilos of smack from the Mexicans at a hundred thousand a key because he was desperate to get into the drug business. Guys like Gotti in New York were making money hand over clenched fist with dope, and Peter wanted in on the windfall.

But no way did Peter have four million in cash, so he and his brother went out to half the wiseguys in New England, generously letting them in on the investment opportunity. Some guys bought into it because they liked the potential, others because they were afraid to say no to the boss, but for whatever reason a lot of people had a piece of the shipment.

It would have been fine, but then Peter let Chris Palumbo talk him into doing a very risky thing.

"We send Frankie V to the Irish," Chris said, "and let him pretend that he's flipping on us. He tips them off to the heroin shipment and gets Danny Ryan to boost it."

"The fuck, Chris?" Peter asked, because what the fuck kind of idea was it to get your own dope boosted, especially by a gang you've been at war with. Christ, was Chris high himself?

Chris explained that he had a fed, Phillip Jardine, on the arm. The Irish take the heroin and Jardine busts them, effectively ending the long war between the Moretti family and the Irish.

"Four mill is too high a price tag," Peter said.

"That's the beauty part," Chris said.

He explained that Jardine would keep some of the heroin to make it look legit but the bulk of the heroin would come straight back to them. They'd have to give Jardine a taste but by the time they cut up the drugs, there'd be more than enough in street value to make up for the loss.

"Win-win," Chris said.

Peter went for it.

Yeah, and it all went according to plan.

Officially, Jardine seized twelve kilos from the Irish in a highly publicized raid. John Murphy, the Irish boss, got popped on thirty-to-life federal charges.

Good.

His son Liam got dead.

Even better.

Okay, twenty-eight keys is a fucking fortune and everybody gets paid.

Except—

Chris Palumbo and Jardine were supposed to go bust Danny and take his ten kilos.

Fine.

But—

No one's heard from either of them since. And Jardine supposedly has the other eighteen keys.

Ryan's gone, too. Left the hospital where his wife was dying, somehow got around Peter's guys, and no one's seen him since, either.

Billy Battaglia comes through the door.

He looks shaken.

"What?" Peter asks.

"Me and some other guys went with Chris to get that dope from Ryan," Billy says. "Chris goes in, comes out ten minutes later— without the dope—tells us to go home."

"What the fuck?" Peter's heart feels like it's going to jump out of his chest.

"Ryan had shooters outside Chris's house," Billy says. "Said he'd have them kill Chris's whole family if he didn't back off."

"Why isn't Chris here telling me that?"

"Chris hasn't come?"

"You think you needed to tell me this if Chris already came?" Peter asks. "Where is he now?"

"I dunno. He just drove away."

The phone rings and Peter jumps.

It's Paulie. "I just got a call from a Gilead cop. They found a body on the beach."

Peter feels like he could throw up. Is it Ryan? Chris?

"It's Jardine," Paulie says. "Two in the chest. Had his gun in his hand, one round fired."

"What about Chris?"

"Nothin'."

Peter hangs up.

The news about Jardine is devastating. The fed was supposed to deliver the rest of the heroin to them. And why did Chris take off? Shit, could he and Ryan have cooked up some deal? That red-headed guinea Chris triple-crossed everyone? It would be just like him.

Merry fuckin' Christmas, Peter thinks.

We won the war but lost our money.

All of it—the years of fighting, the killings, the funerals—all for what?

Nothing.

Unless we find Danny Ryan.